THE TOWERS

Also by David Poyer

Tales of the Modern Navy
The Crisis
The Weapon
Korea Strait
The Threat
The Command
Black Storm
China Sea
Tomahawk
The Passage
The Circle
The Gulf
The Med

Tiller Galloway
Down to a Sunless Sea
Louisiana Blue
Bahamas Blue
Hatteras Blue

The Civil War at Sea
That Anvil of Our Souls
A Country of Our Own
Fire on the Waters

Hemlock County
Thunder on the Mountain
As the Wolf Loves Winter
Winter in the Heart
The Dead of Winter

Other Novels
Ghosting
The Only Thing to Fear
Stepfather Bank
The Return of Philo T. McGiffin
Star Seed
The Shiloh Project
White Continent

THE TOWERS

A Dan Lenson Novel of 9/11

DAVID POYER

ST. MARTIN'S PRESS
New York

This is a work of fiction. All of the characters, organizations, and events portrayed in this novel are either products of the author's imagination or are used fictitiously.

THE TOWERS. Copyright © 2011 by David Poyer. All rights reserved. Printed in the United States of America. For information, address St. Martin's Press, 175 Fifth Avenue, New York, N.Y. 10010.

Grateful acknowledgment is made for permission to reprint "Uh-Oh," copyright © 2009 by George Witte, from *Deniability*, Orchises Press, Washington, DC, 2009.

www.stmartins.com

Library of Congress Cataloging-in-Publication Data

Poyer, David.
    The towers : a Dan Lenson novel of 9/11 / David Poyer. — 1st ed.
        p. cm.
    ISBN 978-0-312-61301-3
    1. Lenson, Dan (Fictitious character)—Fiction.   2. September 11 Terrorist
Attacks, 2001—Fiction.   3. United States. Navy—Officers—Fiction.   I. Title.
    PS3566.O978T69 2011
    813'.54—dc22

                                                                2011019511

First Edition: September 2011

10   9   8   7   6   5   4   3   2   1

For "Chic" Burlingame III, USNA '71,
who gave his life fighting on 9/11,

For Kevin Shaeffer, '94,

And all the others who keep on going
Day after day
No matter how rough.
They're the real heroes.

Acknowledgments

E *X nihilo nihil fit.* For this book I owe thanks to Nancy Berlage, Bobbie Berryman, Harry Black, Steve Boyer, Suzanne Brugler, Anthony Casper, Jay DeLoach, Jeanne Ellis, Richard H. Enderly, Suzanne Kettenhofen, Les Lykins, William F. Mason, Robert McFadden, Robert E. Nelson, Chuck Nygaard, Paul O'Donnell, Sarandis "Randy" Papadopoulos, Katherine Parsons, Naia Poyer, Diane Putney, Sean Riordan, Laurie Toll, David Trevino, Jennie Lew Tugend, Greg Tuorto, Curtis Utz, Judy Vann, and many others who preferred anonymity, especially those who consented to sometimes painful interviews reliving their experiences on September 11, 2001. Thanks also to Charle Ricci and Carol Vincent of the Eastern Shore Public Library, unendingly patient with my sometimes outré requests; Office of the Chief of Naval Information, both in New York and at the Pentagon; the Naval History and Heritage Command; the Office of the Historian, Office of the Secretary of Defense; the Library of Virginia; the Naval Criminal Investigative Service. My most grateful thanks to George Witte, editor of long standing; to Sally Richardson, Terra Layton, Matt Shear, and Rachel Ekstrom at St. Martin's; and to Lenore Hart, anchor on lee shores and my North Star when skies are clear.

The specifics of personalities, locations, and procedures in various locales, and the units and theaters of operations described, are employed as the settings and materials of *fiction*, not as reportage of historical events. Some details have been altered to protect classified procedures.

As always, all errors and deficiencies are my own.

No photograph records
that day's unmaking roar.

Too deep for human ears.
We wept, or cursed in fear.

Beseeched unanswered phones
Please God, alone,

. . . No explanation why;
the perfect alibi

your word, no witnesses.
You saw this coming, yes?

Our brazen structures razed,
immense collapse the praise

you craved, that roar's
descending, perfect chord.

—"Uh-Oh," by George Witte

I

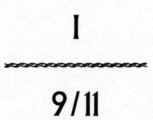

9/11

SEPTEMBER 11, 2001
5:15 A.M., ARLINGTON, VIRGINIA

IT was still dark. Yet not so long before sunrise that Dan couldn't make out the trees through the window by the breakfast table. The back of the house overlooked the creek that ran through the ravine above which the home had been built.

They lived across the river from Washington, in the suburbs that had grown up along the Metro. A brick colonial with flagstone walks and three bedrooms and a family room in the basement, though they didn't really have a family, aside from his daughter. Nan was grown up now, in grad school. Maples and elms and yellow poplars shaded the lawn. Blair had furnished it, mostly from the antique shops she made him stop at whenever they drove east to visit her parents. Other pieces were from her family's estate, things her mom and dad had let go when they'd redecorated.

A far nicer home than he'd grown up in, and it felt strange having so much room, so many things he didn't need. But when he felt this, he reminded himself of those who'd sacrificed so much so he could have this excess, this luxury, this safety. He still kept a pistol in the house, but didn't need it in arm's reach anymore.

"They really want you there this early?" he asked his wife.

Blair sipped coffee and looked at her watch. She was in a severe suit and black pumps. A light coat hung over the back of her chair. "They want me at National at six sharp. But I won't be flying commercial."

Dan grinned. She always called it National, never Ronald Reagan. "Charter?"

"Their own jet. A limo'll meet me at JFK."

"Sweet. And—when'll you be back?"

"Day after tomorrow. Maybe I'll see a show, if I can get tickets."

They drank coffee and gazed out the bay window at the backyard. The hollyhocks and peonies were long gone, the four-o'clocks wouldn't open till afternoon, but the white blooms of nicotiana seemed to glow even in the half dark.

"What are you doing today?"

"Headed in to the Building. See a classmate. Then I'm supposed to look in on Barry Niles."

She wrinkled her nose. "The one who shot you down for your promotion?"

Dan shoved eggs around on his plate. No one was guaranteed promotion, especially at the O-6 level. But he'd hoped. "*He* didn't shoot me down."

"Oh, he stacked the deck. With the other admirals on the board. He's always spoken against you, right? Kept you from getting another command, after *Horn*?"

"The proceedings are sealed."

"Dan, you're the most decorated officer in the Navy. Navy Cross. Silver Star. And the *Congressional*, for God's sake. You've pulled their chestnuts out of the fire time and again. And they pass you over for captain." She raised a finger. "Wouldn't have happened if I was still at OSD."

"That would *not* have helped. The Navy keeps outsiders out of promotion. SecNav, just maybe. SecDef, no." But he kept his tone nonargumentative.

Blair had taken the November election hard. It meant she was out in the cold; a new administration, a new party in charge. That was why she was going to New York.

"What precisely do these Cohn, Kennedy guys do, again?"

"I told you. Global financial services. Specialized equity and capital markets for institutional clients. Real estate private equity." She eyed him humorlessly. "None of which means squat to you, right?"

"It sounds like . . . it should pay."

"Oh, it will, Dan. I could cubbyhole at SAIC until the next election, but this'll build our net worth. We may not see much of each other, unless you decide to come to New York with me. But we'll come out of it with significantly enhanced personal value."

"You're sure they're hiring?"

"Good people are always hard to get," she said without a trace of modesty, false or otherwise. "How much longer do you have? Now you've been passed over?"

"June fifteenth is my punch-out date."

"Have you thought about my suggestion?"

She'd told him to call his old teacher Dr. Edward Ferenczi, the new president's national security adviser. Which would make it interesting, Dan working for one party while she was biding her time waiting to come back with the other. "I don't know. I'm still thinking about it."

"Don't wait, if you want a responsible position." Her tone was tentative, as if she didn't want to jab a tender place. "Good God, is that the time?" She grabbed her coat, kissed his cheek, gave his chest a quick raking scratch through the open bathrobe. "See you Thursday."

He was about to let her go with that, but something made him get up. A faint unease out of nowhere. "I'll go to the door with you."

The garage door groaned as it rolled up. He eyed the chains, thinking, *grease.* He caught her smile, a lifted hand as she backed down the drive, then craned around, checking her six before rolling out into the street. A pale rose glow fanned slowly out beyond the trees, like a peacock's tail.

When she was gone he stripped the plastic wrapper off the *Post,* looking at the weather first. Clear skies; she should have a nice flight. The head-lines. The new SecDef had declared war on bloat at the Pentagon. He was trimming the staff fifteen percent to start with and twenty percent more in a year. Page two, more criticism of the new missile defense program. He read this article to the end.

Judges and prosecutors were being murdered in Colombia. NATO was pulling out of Macedonia amid predictions of sectarian massacres. He shuddered, remembering a concrete shed filled with corpses, the buzz of fat flies nestling into mutilated eye sockets. When the Balkans went, they went all the way, tumbling straight through war into the abyss of savagery. More deaths in Iraq too.

He lifted his gaze, thoughts freezing behind gray eyes. Whatever he read, faces floated up. Images, smells, tastes of numb terror and desperate hope and, sometimes, incredible heroism.

He'd worn a uniform since he'd been seventeen. The Navy had been home, career, profession . . . everything. But it ate its young. Destroyed marriages. Relationships. The years had shot past one after the other at sea, or busy ashore. He'd done everything he'd set out to do. Even com-manded a destroyer, though not for long enough.

You *could* stay in for a few years, after being passed over. But what was the point? Might as well do desk work somewhere they'd actually pay. Maybe not as well as they were going to pay Blair, but better than the Navy.

The trouble was, he'd never wanted to do anything else.

3:15 A.M., PCT, LOS ANGELES, CALIFORNIA

Theodore Harlett Oberg jerked awake, knowing as he did it was going to be bad. Another shit night. He stared up into the glowing dark and blotted his slick face with the sheet.

Fuck, he thought. Fuck, fuck, fuck.

It was Sumo again. Not the only dream he had over and over, but in some ways the worst. He rolled his head to see if he was alone. Someone lay next to him. The starlet. The blonde. Laurne? Loreet? Not Loreeta. Loreena? Something that sounded like cheap cheese. He listened to her breathing. Asleep. Fuck her. Obviously he had, but what else? He'd promised himself before the party he wasn't going to drink. But by the way his mouth felt . . . actually he couldn't remember. Like a black sheet over everything. Which couldn't be good.

He inspected the hump again. No, Loreena had left weeks ago. This couldn't be her. Well, didn't matter. Long as it wasn't a guy. Then it'd be time to reach for the Mossberg under the bed. Nibble on some double ought.

He turned the satin sheets back and slid out. Padded to the window, the hand-laid tile cold against his bare soles.

His grandmother had bought land on Lookout Mountain after Clara Bow and Harry Houdini but before the cookie-cutter developments with hokey names like Dona Lisa or Zeus Drive had bookended Laurel Canyon. Somehow this little pocket from the twenties and thirties had stayed almost unchanged, a throwback to the hip, cool, funky days when his mom used to see Jim Morrison and John Holmes at the Canyon Store. Back then the guy who ran it was named Bill, and many, many deals had been made at the pay phone in front. Teddy and his friends, kids then, used to sneak into Frank Zappa's yard and light fires behind the log cabin. There were still stars and musicians around—Jennifer Aniston, Marilyn Manson—but now the Canyon was all fences and development, retaining walls gradually obliterating the chaparral-dotted gray of the slopes like concrete mold. The glow from the city was bright as dawn at midnight.

But he still had two acres of dense chaparral, and the tunnels under it he'd used to play in. A carport, down by the access road, with low-water plantings. A pool, though it was covered now. The house looked down from under huge live oaks, and standing in front of the floor-to-ceiling windows that had been the wonder of the architectural magazines back in the forties, Teddy reached behind the drapes until his fingers brushed the flash hider of the full automatic M4 he'd left leaning where glass met brick. The drapes stank of mildew. His headache throbbed. Behind him the woman grunted, rolled over, and began snoring.

His chest rose and fell. He stared down at the shimmering glitter, the scattered house lights and moving headlights of Laurel Canyon. But he wasn't seeing it.

A green spheroid. His peripheral vision made it as a grenade.

And Kaulukukui gave him that look. "War's a motherfucker, ain't it?"

Yeah, Sumo. It's a motherfucker, all right.

But us . . . we were supposed to be the meanest motherfuckers in the valley.

"You bastard," he muttered, wiping his nose on his hand. "You fat bastard."

The insurgents had pinned the SEALs in the kill zone. Four shooters, pushing muzzles over the catwalk so they could fire down without exposing themselves. He'd snap-shot back. Beside him Kaulukukui was hugging the wall, returning fire. Bullets ripped rock walls, spewing chips. Hot brass spun through the air. Dirt flew, and something hard cracked into his goggles.

"Obie! Y'in there?" The SEALs behind them, yelling past the machine gunner who'd cut them off.

"They got us stone, babe," Oberg had shouted back. "Set us up righteous. Some fucking assistance here!"

"Can't get to you, man. Got us cold."

Teddy groped for a grenade, then remembered: not even a flash-bang. Gone, used up fighting their way down from the roof to assault the hide site of the man behind this whole insurgency. Or so Higher'd said.

A shooter stuck his Kalash over the railing and emptied it like a garden hose. A bullet clipped Teddy's boot, another his harness. "Shit," he'd muttered, backing toward a corner as he kept the front sight on the balcony, waiting for the next weasel. "Pop the fuck up, fuckers." But they didn't, just kept sticking rifles over the rail and spraying lead. Sooner or later—

He'd been slamming in another mag when something flew down. It struck the ground and took a lopsided bounce. A green spheroid. His peripheral vision made it as a grenade at the same moment it struck the wall beside him.

It rolled, spinning, and rocked to a halt midway between him and his partner. The drill was to duck or roll, but there was nowhere to go. Or kick it away. But there was nowhere to kick it to. This whole end of the room was open ground.

His eyes had met Kaulukukui's across four feet of space. And the big Hawaiian said, "War's a motherfucker, ain't it?"

Before Teddy could react, he stepped over it and crouched, putting himself between Teddy and the grenade.

"No! Sumo—"

The shattering crack of high explosive. Kaulukukui had shuddered. Half-turned, a smile still curving his lips.

Then he'd toppled, exposing the raw bleeding mass that had been his back.

Shuddering, Teddy drew clawed fingers down his cheeks. Over the ridges of old scars. The cool air crawled over his skin like leeches in a Mindanao rain forest. He turned on a heel and walked naked into the next room, then down flagstone steps. A light glowed over the bar, in front of another floor-to-ceiling window. The bottle's neck rattled on the glass as he poured Grey Goose. His mouth felt stale and raw, his head slammed and his lips stung, but he got the first slug down.

He stood again before the lights, looking down. He knew this house. Had let go of that faux bamboo end table to take his first steps, or so his mother had always said. But he didn't belong here. He wasn't sure where the fuck he belonged.

"You got to catch up on your sleep," he told himself. "Important meeting this morning." He looked at the neon-circled clock over the bar. Three twenty-four.

The Movie. He'd left the SEALs to make it. A film that told the truth about combat, about men, about honor, about death. Not *Sands of Iwo Jima*, not *Apocalypse Now*, no heroes and no fools, just the sweat and blood and the kind of man it took and the kind it left once the fighting was over. He and Loki had hammered the script out over a year, endless meetings with the writers and the money people, Germans looking to move funds into the United States. He didn't understand it, but Loki said the European tax laws were such that even if you lost millions on the film, they made money anyway.

He'd said, Why do we need them? I can front this, mortgage the beach house and all that land. But Loki Dittrich had said no. Rule Number One: Never use your own money. Erase your risk. Get foreign distributors to cover half your production costs. She'd been his mother's friend. They'd gone to bed once, eons ago, "Just to get that out of the way," she'd told the then fifteen-year-old Teddy. She'd hooked him up with Breakbone Pictures. Found a million from a hedge fund. Teddy had called one of the guys who used to set fires with him—now an A-list agent—and they had Ewan McGregor and Colin Farrell attached. Russell Crowe, a firm maybe. Teddy wanted Ridley Scott, but Loki said she wanted to do the financing first, have it wrapped up before they signed a director; that would give them leverage.

That was what the meeting was about: nailing down the Germans. They'd seen the script, made suggestions, read the rewrites. Now they were flying in. They'd meet in the garden of the Polo Lounge, to lock in the memorandum of understanding.

In Hollywood, it always came down to "credit" and "money." Since he didn't need the money, he wanted "A Teddy Oberg Production" above the title. Loki said it was outrageous to ask for it on his first film. But if he produced, it'd get made the way he wanted. If he let the money people drive the train, he might as well just pick up that Mossberg and see what an ounce and a half of buckshot tasted like.

He felt a small, distant thrill; almost the way a normal person might feel when it looked as if his movie, about combat and manhood and what it did to you when a friend died, might get made.

He picked up the bottle again. Weighed the glass in his hand, one of the heavy cut-glass tumblers his grandmother had served Cary Grant and Bette Davis out of. Discipline, he thought. Duty. Above all, teamwork. All those words pounded into you at Coronado.

But what about when the team was dead? Where did a guy go then?

The first words on-screen would be the names. The dedication.

Sweat broke out over his back. He looked at the tumbler again, forced his hand to put it down. Weighed the bottle too. Throw it through the window? No. No, Obie. Set it down too. Gently. There.

The bed creaked as it took his weight. The mattress stank of mold. He needed new furniture. Tear out the seventies shag. The woman flinched when he threw the covers off. Silvery hair. Smooth shining breasts. Large, dark nipples. Oh yeah. A songwriter; just another wannabe.

"Hey there," he said, and pushed her over on her back.

"I don't want to. You're too rough. I was asleep—"

"Nobody asked if you wanted to," he grunted, twisting a fist into her hair. Get them by the hair, they didn't fight long. Pulling her head back as his hand clapped between her legs and twisted. He set his knees and followed his fingers with his prick, driving it in with his full weight. She cried out and fought, striking his back with hard little fists. She connected with a lucky blow to his ear and he started to choke her, but restrained himself just in time.

Holding her down, his other hand over her mouth, Teddy Oberg plowed toward the only personal forgetting left. Knowing even as he triggered, pale neon lancing behind his eyes, that as soon as it was over, the images would return.

6:05 A.M., EST, PORTLAND, MAINE

Two Middle Eastern men check in to their flight to Boston, with a connection to LA. One, an Egyptian architect, sets off an automated screening system as a flight risk. Security holds his bags until they confirm he's actually boarded.

In Boston, one flier takes a cell call from a traveler at Logan waiting to board another aircraft. As he and other men check in for the next flight, the security system flags more of them. Again, the security people hold their bags. But they all pass through the metal detectors and security checkpoints and quietly enplane.

At nearly the same time, five other men are boarding a flight in Washington, DC. A ticket agent finds two of them suspicious. She holds their bags until they're on the plane.

In Newark, four more young men board United Flight 93 for Los Angeles. One gets additional screening. Security inspects his bag for explosives. They find nothing suspicious. The others pass preboarding screening and all four enter the aircraft.

By 7:50, nineteen men are safely aboard four transcontinental flights.

4:15 P.M., YEMENI TIME, SANA'A, YEMEN

The armored SUV growled through empty streets, the blazing afternoon heat boiling up off uneven asphalt and ancient cobblestones. Another Suburban sped ahead, with the protective detail. In the center car, FBI SWAT members rode passenger-side front and in the back.

Special Agent Aisha Ar-Rahim was ensconced in the center seat in a bright hibiscus-patterned abaya with long sleeves, low heels, and a head-scarf, a loose shawl over her shoulders. Her round face was bent to a notebook screen. A little girl with hair in braids smiled up. A link chart occupied the rest of the screen, with boxes and arrows and phone numbers in red, green, blue. Under her abaya ar-Rahim wore a Kevlar ballistic vest. Beside her slumped a large carpetbag purse.

The heavyset guy sitting too close was Scott Doanelson. Every federal agency had a trademark, and Doanelson fit his: scuffed oxfords, Wal-Mart suit, button-down white polycotton shirt under his Kevlar. He wore the suit even when they went out—which wasn't often, since kidnapping foreigners had become the Yemeni national sport. He wore a holster, though it had been empty since the week before, when Doanelson had called the ambassador "Sweetie." But Aisha's SIG was in in her purse, along with her badge, Mace, a spare magazine of Cor-Bon +P+ hollow points, and a small red prayer rug she'd picked up on Hajj.

Doanelson had been in-country for two weeks. Aisha had been here for six months and had worked counterterror throughout the Mideast for years. Had two Civilian Service Awards, one for Bahrain, one for Ashaara, and the Julie Cross Award for Women in Federal Law Enforcement. But none of that seemed to rival the luster of an FBI badge. At least from Doan-elson's point of view.

"Think we're getting anywhere with this guy?" he grunted, pulling a Sprite out of the SUV's cold box.

"I'm establishing rapport."

"We're wasting time and dollars. Coddling fucking Islamic terrorists—"

"They're not *Islamic* terrorists," she said sharply. "Just *terrorists*. Is-lam doesn't condone what they're doing."

"I don't see them pushing back. These moderate Muslims you keep tell-ing me about."

"We recruited these people, Scott. Trained and armed them, to fight the Soviets. Sixty thousand just from Yemen."

"You saying we should've left the Russkis in Afghanistan? That would have been better?"

She didn't answer, just turned her face to the colorful façades passing by. Sana'a wasn't Somalia. Yet. The rabid fundamentalists, the Salafis, only had a toehold, backed by Saudi millions. With luck, they could save this country.

The frame of the SUV rattled; dusty wind scratched at the windows. Behind it the follow car growled, another heavy vehicle with more grim-faced, heavily armed men. The threat condition had been upped to Delta. Even here, in the heart of the capital, the desert filled the streets with sandy, tan fog. The howling wind scudded trash along the road. She yearned out at colorful shopfronts, vendors' stalls. She'd felt perfectly safe walking these streets, as long as she wore the hijab. For the first few months she'd frequented the Salt Market and worshipped with Yemeni women in the Jami al-Kabir, the Grand Mosque, and no one had said a word other than friendly salaams.

Aisha Ar-Rahim had been a Naval Criminal Investigative Service agent for twelve years. The NCIS looked into any crime involving naval personnel, grand theft to murder. It conducted criminal-investigation, contract-fraud, counternarcotics work. Being one of the few agents who spoke Arabic, she'd found herself more or less permanently assigned to force protection, espe-cially since she'd helped bring to justice the leader of a raging insurgency in a country on the Red Sea. Al-Maahdi was dead now, shot in a fracas among his bodyguards. A huge thorn in the side of US policy in the region plucked out, and all but one of the hostages safely returned. Based out of Bahrain as the Yemeni referent, Aisha had worked in-country for the last six months as part of a joint FBI/NCIS team.

At the moment, she was assisting in the interrogation of a suspect Islamic Jihad member. Abu-Hamid Al-Nashiri had been identified as a phone contact of men involved both in the USS *Cole* bombing the year before, and in a plot to attack Western-flag oil tankers. Working out of El-Hadida and Makullah, the joint team had helped the local authorities break up the bombers. They'd found an abandoned speedboat with Semtex residue, although the explosive itself had been removed.

But the perpetrators had escaped. Now phone records transferred by NSA, combined with her patient work on intelligence from local authorities, were uncovering not just a network, but a Yemeni hub to a wagon wheel of Al Qaeda in Sudan and Afghanistan. And also an as-yet-unclear effort that seemed pointed somewhere outside the Mideast, possibly even at the United States.

It was slow work. Jigsaw puzzling moved like lightning compared to building an effective case.

She leaned back and stretched, locking gazes with the little girl on-screen. Tashaara was home in Harlem. Aisha saw her every time she got back, which wasn't nearly often enough. Well, day after tomorrow, she'd be on her way. To her mother, to Tashaara—and to a wedding.

She smiled, then sighed and bent again over the keyboard, trying to boil down eighteen hours of Arabic interrogation into a one-page report in bureaucratese.

YEMEN'S president had been a close buddy of Saddam Hussein's, if anybody *was* Saddam's buddy. The president bought antitank missiles from North Korea. He'd played the Soviet Union off against the United States, back when there'd been a Soviet Union, and was now trying the same game against Saudi Arabia, his giant neighbor to the north.

Aisha had to admit the country didn't have much else going for it. In ancient times the fabled Sheba had been wealthy, exporting the frankincense and myrrh of the Bible. These days it was one of the poorest states in the Middle East, with little water, constant warfare among desert tribes, a secession movement in the south, Shiite unrest in the north, and six Kalashnikovs for every adult male. One thing she'd brought out of her experiences in Ashaara was not to expect high standards from governments only one notch above anarchy.

Her eyes went again to the picture. She'd saved one child, yes. But hundreds of thousands more . . . no one had been able to save them.

Her own experiences here had been mixed. On her second visit to his mosque the imam had invited her to chai with him and his wife and eventually asked her to hold a women's English class. The Yemenis loved guests; soon she'd had dozens of invitations, to shop at the Bab Al'Sabah, the fruit souk, the Rock Palace, to drive to Shibam to see the fortifications of Koukabanb. Dressed local, she'd shopped with a chattering throng of sisters, the darkest among a dozen. Yemenis didn't wear burka. Just black abayas, the hijab—headscarf—and sometimes (the older ones mostly) the slit-eyed *niqab*. Hundreds of women wandered among gaudily bedecked stalls and shopfronts. Colorfully costumed proprietors called, *"Shoof, shoof"*— look, look—from trays of silver jewelry, cheap gold she was warned was alloy, fabrics, spices, trinkets, shoes. And the wonderful food: peaches, apricots, walnuts, almonds, honey-filled pastries, date cookies, chocolaty *mokha*, shawarma eaten hot off a stick. She bought an embroidered head-dress for her mother, a curved, wicked-sharp jambiya for Albert, tiny silver earrings and carved animals for Tashaara.

But Yemen also hosted people its neighbors considered terrorists. The man they were going to see tonight, Abu-Hamid al-Nashiri, had been cross-ing the border back and forth even as Saudi intelligence was demanding his arrest for plotting to attack the armored limousines of their princes with North Korean antitank missiles. Not long before, the Saudis said, al-Nashiri had been drinking tea in a café here in Sana'a, and not alone, either—he'd been laughing and joking with the deputy director of the Yemeni police. Now he was in custody, but that didn't seem to mean the same thing here as it did elsewhere. The Amna Siyasi—the Political Security Organization, the main intelligence service—was riddled with Al Qaeda sympathizers.

Which led to the question, why had the president allowed American law enforcement into his country at all, after stonewalling them for years? She guessed he was hedging his bets. Angling for aid, and cooperating just enough not to become a U.S. target the way Saddam had. So far, though, the PSO had treated her with respect. Mainly, she suspected, be-cause they hadn't quite figured her out. What was a black woman, an Arabic-speaking Muslim, doing working for the Americans?

Sometimes she wondered herself.

A blare of horns, a screech of brakes. She looked up. They were at the palace.

THE usual holdup at the high iron gates while the guard asked why they were there, who they were there to see. He knew perfectly well, of course. All part of the ritual, and she kept typing while they sat there, although feeling vulnerable. The GrayWolf security men had dismounted and stood around, weapons out, scanning the upper floors of the buildings across the street. An antitank rocket would go through the Suburban's armor like a bullet through cottage cheese. "Why do we have to travel in such obvious vehicles?" she muttered.

"The air-conditioning works," Doanelson said.

"We don't need it. It's not even hot."

But finally the gate swung open.

Lieutenant Colonel Abdulaziz Al-Safani was in his usual thobe, slacks, the little white keffiyah beanie under a red-and-white-checked shemagh. His jambiya, the ceremonial dagger all male Yemenis wore, was slung over his right leg, half-covered by a gray-and-olive Harris tweed jacket that would have looked at home in Mayfair. His holstered Makharov hung reversed on the other side. He nodded to Doanelson but came right to her. Didn't take her hand, didn't hug or kiss her, the standard greeting between men. Instead he bowed. *"Salaam aleikum."*

"As-aleikum salaam, Mûqoddam. You're looking healthy today," she continued in Arabic, not bothering to interpret for Doanelson. "And what a handsome blazer. Your family, they're well?"

"Very well, praise Allah. You too look healthy, Special Agent Ar-Rahim. Your daughter, she is well?"

"Very well. Your son's eyes are better?"

"Much better, praise Allah. And your wedding—it's still on? When are you leaving?"

"Day after tomorrow, Allah willing. I'm all packed."

"He has converted, yes? Last time we spoke you were not sure he would."

She smiled. "I want Albert to say his Shahadah at the masjid where I grew up. Where my father and mother went, the girls I went to school with. Where my family still goes."

"In New York, yes? In your village of . . . Harlem?"

She wondered how Al-Safani would react on seeing the "village" of Harlem. "Yes—in my village. On 113th, between Malcolm X Boulevard and Adam Clayton Powell Jr."

"And he said yes?"

She caught Doanelson's eye. He looked irritated. Shut out of the conversation, with his hesitant, schoolbook Arabic. "Well, we had a discussion. I told him he couldn't do it just because he wants to marry me. I said that's not a worthy reason."

"He has to want it just from loving God."

"That's what I told him. And he said, 'I can love God without being a Muslim. I can stay a Baptist,' he said."

"Then he can't marry you."

"He's a man. That means he's stubborn." And, although she loved him, it was true; Albert did sometimes assume things about a woman's place.

Al-Safani looked shocked, then chuckled. A month ago he'd have just stared. She smiled at him. "But he says now he loves God enough to marry me."

The colonel threw back his head and laughed. "Let's get out of this dust! What news do you bring? I'm still hoping for the electronic package the general spoke to madame ambassador about."

Inside, Doanelson trailing, and up two flights of dusty, echoing stairs to the colonel's office. Spacious but casually dirty, furnished like a 1940s private detective's sanctum. Rusty file cabinets, scruffy metal folding chairs, tarnished brass ashtrays full of stale butts, a swaying overhead fan stirring a miasma of tobacco, coffee, sweat. A half wall with a swinging door partitioned a nook that must once have held a private secretary's desk. For the next hour they sat drinking cups of strong coffee and discussing the news. Aisha always read the *Times Online* before coming over. Al-Safani hung on anything about Mideast policy. Grist for the reports he no doubt had to submit on his dealings with the Americans, and she supplied it patiently, though Doanelson frowned and fidgeted. She'd told him before not to check his watch, it insulted your host, but he didn't seem to care.

They couldn't afford to tick off the Yemenis. Al Qaeda—"the foundation" or "the base" in Arabic—seemed to be the nickname of the loose confederation that'd attacked USS *Horn* in Bahrain, USS *Cole* in Aden, and U.S. embassies in Tanzania and Kenya. Those attacks had put Osama bin Laden and Ayman Al-Zawahiri on the Most Wanted list.

Unfortunately, Saudi intelligence had reported that the man whose office they were in, Colonel Abdulaziz Al-Safani, had been seen socializing in a café with the suspect that same Al-Safani now held in custody.

She lowered her third tiny cup of sickly sweet, molasses-thick coffee. "Have you made any progress with our friend?"

Al-Safani beckoned to the guard. Apparently he'd been waiting in the hallway, because a shuffle and a sharp order ensued.

A short, heavily-bearded man in dirty pajama bottoms and a long-sleeved yellow shirt slouched in. He wasn't shackled or manacled. He walked with a limp, and sharp dark eyes met hers for just a moment but avoided Doanelson's. He settled in the chair on the far side of the half wall. As she pulled her own seat to the partition, she caught his smell: tea and cologne and old sweat. A junior PSO officer clicked a ballpoint above a yellow notepad.

Abu-Hamid Al-Nashiri was a veteran of Afghanistan and Bosnia. He was fifty-one, his beard streaked with gray. After two months of interviewing, she knew him better than she had her father. Al-Nashiri had two wives in Yemen and one in Afghanistan. His limp came courtesy of a Russian mine. A dangerous killer, almost certainly a link between Al-Zawahiri and the Yemeni branch of ALQ. She flipped open her computer, which had been powered up and was recording everything already, and looked at the next question. The rules, negotiated between the ambassador and General Gamish, were strict. She said politely to Al-Safani, who'd perched one buttock on the partition between her and Al-Nashiri, "The prisoner was having problems with his back. Is he feeling better?"

Al-Safani bent his head to light a Pall Mall. The PSO smoked only foreign cigarettes, no doubt seized from smugglers. Without looking at the seated man he said, "Is the prisoner's back feeling better?"

"It still hurts."

"The prisoner's back still hurts."

"The surgery was probably done wrong. We could fly him to the US and have it looked at."

Al-Safani repeated this, but Al-Nashiri didn't answer. Doanelson muttered, "This isn't getting us anywhere."

"We've talked about his back before. He's worried about it. That's how this works, Scott. Find out what makes the subject tick, then exploit it."

The FBI agent rolled his eyes. The heavyset man darted a malevolent glance over the half wall at Al-Nashiri, then away. Aisha sighed and refocused. "We were speaking about the duty to oppose an apostate government. Is it the prisoner's view that the current government of Yemen is un-Islamic?"

"Is our current government an apostate government?" Al-Safani asked him.

Al-Nashiri said in a weary monotone, the same tone he'd maintained for two months, "The Quran is clear. There is no leadership other than the commander of the faithful. Power comes from God, not man's law. The only acceptable laws are those laid down by God and the Prophet. Yet this government executes those who wage jihad for God. Like Zein Al-Abidine al-Mihdar, punished for defending the faithful. Therefore it is apostate and no true Muslim can obey it."

He went on in a droning soliloquy, to which she listened closely. To every word, every intonation. Once in a while, her fingers tapped keys. She'd debrief from her notes at the video teleconference tonight, then follow up by e-mail with the text of the interrogation. The al-Mihdar he mentioned had been Islamic Jihad, executed by firing squad for killing British and Australian tourists. Interesting, though, that this time he used a different word for al-Mihdar's death. Before, he'd always said *murdered*, or *martyred*. This time, the word was softer. *Punished.* Significant? Or not?

"I'm not following this," Doanelson whispered.

"Shut up, Scott."

"What's he saying? Is this another sermon?"

"It's the standard Salafi jihadi line. Just listen."

"The prisoner says, yes," Al-Safani said, in English. Aisha stiffled a snort. Doanelson flushed. Al-Nashiri had spoken for five minutes; the official translation had been one word.

The FBI agent bolted up and paced back and forth, hard leather soles scuffing the floor. He knocked into one of the brass spittoons and only just caught it before it went over. When he circled back, he muttered, "Let's bet the house. We been here long enough. Ask him what's going down. There's something big. We know that. And we know he knows."

"This isn't some twentysomething hacker, Scott. He's gold-plated Al Qaeda. Tough as they come. The only way he's telling us anything is if I can convince him we're on God's side. If I can, we'll own him."

"Can't these PSO guys apply some persuasion? They're serving him breakfast in bed, instead. Buddies with the deputy director—"

"Excuse me?" said Al-Safani.

"Nothing. Or, yeah. Let's cut the bullshit, Colonel. Ask this asshole what Osama's got planned. Ask him—"

Doanelson stopped abruptly, cut off with a squawk as she put out one foot. He toppled, flailing, and only just caught himself on the desk. He glared, face flaming. "Whose side are you on, anyway?"

"What did the fat one say?" Al-Safani asked in Arabic.

"He was asking about the prisoner's beliefs. Whether he truly believes killing other believers is the true way of jihad."

Al-Nashiri didn't wait for the relay. For the first time, the prisoner looked across the half wall and met her gaze square on. "You say you are Muslim?"

"It is so."

"And you work for the Americans?"

"I *am* American."

He frowned and shook his head. "Americans are Christian. They worship three gods."

Boy, had she had this conversation before. "I tell you truly, I made wudhu this morning like you. Made the hajj to Mecca. I've worshipped God all my life." He held her gaze, steady brown eyes filled with hate, but also, the tiniest doubt. She forced herself to stare back. Drew a breath, then asked it. The question she'd saved up all these weeks, waiting for the moment when he might actually answer. "Many Americans are Muslim. And, yes, many more are people of the Book. But does the Quran teach us to kill them? A good Muslim treats Jews and Christians with kindness and justice. Only if they attack may we fight back."

"I'm not following this," Doanelson broke in. She waved him off, desperately holding the prisoner's gaze. Was she getting through? Would this be the payoff?

"Then that is your answer. America has attacked us. Americans must die."

"Americans helped you fight against the godless, in Afghanistan. We're trying to make peace in Palestine. We fought against the Serbs in Bosnia, to defend Muslims there. Truly, we are not far apart, you and I. Why is your belief so narrow? Is it possible, my friend, that you might be on the side of injustice?"

"I am narrow? Perhaps the woman is right. The Prophet said there would be seventy-three different factions. But only one will find favor with God. Yes, our belief is fine as a razor edge. But on that razor"—the aging man's gaze turned blazing—"our new martyrs will ascend to Paradise."

"Martyrs? What new martyrs?"

He broke into a gloating smile. "You do not yet know? The ones even now in your country. The ones—"

He halted as the colonel, rising, dropped a hand on his shoulder. "This interrogation is ended," Al-Safani said loudly.

She started to her feet. "What? No! He's about to—he started to—"

Doanelson, excited: "What did you do? What did you say to him?"

"You may not speak to the prisoner. You have broken the general's rules. Now you must leave." Al-Safani snapped to the guard, who came forward.

Al-Nashiri hoisted himself to his feet. His grizzled head hung. But instead of moving toward the door, he stepped up to the half wall, pressing his stomach against the top of the barrier. Half-turning, not looking directly at her, he beckoned.

Frowning, she took a step forward. Then another.

Without warning, he struck her backhanded across the cheek. She blinked, rocked back on her heels by the hard-knuckled blow. He brought his hand back to strike again, but she had her arm up to block. Began a chop to his throat, but by then Al-Safani and the guard were on him, shouting, pummeling, dragging him back.

At the door he grabbed the jamb. Shouted back, "The Prophet cursed traitors. We force them to the narrowest part of the road. Evil, lying woman! You are *murtadd*, you are *muharab;* you fight as a soldier against Islam. You will burn forever. But before that, believe me, we will kill you."

"Get him out of here," Colonel Al-Safani yelled. "No speaking to the prisoner! No speaking to the Americans!"

"That was terrific," Doanelson told her. "You got inside his head, all
right. Really figured out what makes him tick. We done here?"

She held her stinging cheek, blinking at the empty doorway.

7:58 A.M., BOSTON, MASSACHUSETTS

*Cabin shaking, engines bellowing, American Airlines Flight 11 climbs
off the runway bound for Los Angeles. Aboard the Boeing 767 are eleven
crew members and eighty-one passengers. Fifteen minutes later a second 767 thunders off the same strip, this one bearing the blue-and-
white logo of United Airlines. Both huge jets are fully loaded with fuel
for their nonstop transcontinental flights.*

8:14 A.M., ROSSLYN, VIRGINIA

The Metro's waffled concrete echoed with hundreds of voices, the scuff of
shoes. Dan stood behind a woman poised dancer-erect by the platform. A
dog leaned into a strap she held tightly in her left hand. Its eyes met his for
a moment, acknowledged him as human, dismissed him as no threat, and
moved on, searching the crowd that streamed by. He realized it was a Seeing Eye dog. An electronic bonging; a hiss of air; the next train glided in.
"Blue Line. Franconia-Springfield."

His gaze met the dog's again as the Metro hushed to a stop. The doors
whooshed open. He waited till those within exited, then followed the
woman aboard. What must the world feel like to her? Did she envision, re-
create it around her in her brain?

The train rushed through darkness; lights flashed and occulted. It ar-
rowed upward and emerged into blinding brilliance. Arlington Cemetery.
Green trees overhanging the right of way whipped past. A new rush of air
as the car braked. The blind woman and the quivering-alert dog sat next
to a uniformed Air Force sergeant. An aged woman maneuvered a heavy
suitcase. An Asian student slowly stroked long, black hair. Men in suits, in
T-shirts. A middle-aged woman in a sari, a vivid white birthmark glowing
on her cheek, chatted with a bored-looking girl in boots and a short leather
skirt. He stood aside as a Midwestern family, all freckles and bouncy, red-
headed children, got off.

Hurtling once again through light-filled space, Dan thought: This is

America. Not the one he'd grown up in, true. One of more varied hues, religions, customs, modes of dress, races. Not all liking one another. But somehow, each tolerating all the others. Not a melting pot. A kaleidoscope, falling into new patterns of color and beauty with each turn of the wheel.

The light vanished, became streaking darkness again. A muffled turkey-gobble from the PA system announced the Pentagon. The sergeant stirred, and Dan followed him out.

8:14 A.M., EST, ABOARD AMERICAN FLIGHT 11

The FASTEN SEAT BELTS sign has just winked out. In the back, the flight attendants are maneuvering the cart into the aisle for beverage service. The passengers are opening newspapers, books, settling in for the long hours to the West Coast.

In business class, the grim-faced, smooth-shaven little man the airline's computer flagged as a flight risk back in Portland stirs in his seat. He looks behind him, down the rows of reclined seats. Businessmen. Families. Young women in provocative clothes. Old women foolishly trying to appear young. Jews, many of them.

All unbelievers. Or, if some happen to be Muslim, they're takfir—*so deeply contaminated by the West they are no longer true followers of the Prophet, whose name he bears, peace be upon him.*

If the Plane Operation succeeds, there will be many deaths. Some innocent? Perhaps.

This does not matter.

In the thirteenth century, a scholar declared a fatwa. Anyone who aided an enemy, even if that enemy should be Muslim, anyone who bought or sold from him or even stood close to him, could be killed without infringing the Law. God would judge. If they were truly good, he would welcome them to Paradise. If evil, he would burn them in the fires of Hell. This righteous fatwa had been renewed, to bless the holy struggle against the Great Satan.

The man rises slightly and looks ahead. His two friends in the second row of seats, just behind the cockpit, turn to look back at him. They think this is a routine hijacking.

He never flew anything this large at the school. The biggest planes they had were Seminoles. Two engines, yes, but no jets. The simulator, yes. The flight-deck videos.

But it won't be the same. A chill shivers his back.

Then he chuckles at his apprehension. The end will be the same, whether he strikes the target or not. Whatever happens, martyrdom is his. God is great!

They're still looking back at him, faces pale. He smiles and puts a finger to the tip of his nose.

8:35 A.M., EST, THE PENTAGON, ARLINGTON, VIRGINIA

The escalator stretched up, up, groaning as it carried the flood tide of late-coming civil servants beneath an immense arch stained here and there with green leakage. A pregnant Marine with hair twisted in a French braid stood abreast of him, gaze lost in the distance. She slowly crept ahead as their escalators climbed.

As he reached the mall, his cell phone trilled. He started, then fumbled for it.

"Dan. Thought about my offer?"

Torgild Schrade. CEO and owner of GrayWolf Security Enterprises. A classmate from Annapolis. They'd run into each other the year before, when Dan's team had been training in close-quarters combat. "Ah—yes, I have, Tor."

"We're going to see action. A major ramp-up in our contracts. Going to need some sharp people to oversee them."

"What action's that, Tor?"

"Overseas. Look, I'll be in town soon. You still live in Arlington?"

"Yeah, but my duty station's in Norfolk. I'll probably retire from there."

"Whatever. What do you say, want to get together?"

Dan was walking now at a moderate pace past the candy stores, flower stores, bookstores of the mall. Most weren't open yet, but the drugstore already had a line at the checkout. He said politely—nobody wanted to get on the secretive multimillionaire's bad side—that he didn't want to jump without looking. "I want to take some time off, maybe get some sailing in, before I decide what to do next."

"Don't wait too long. I want you on board."

Dan reached the guards at the check-in. He held up ID card and building pass. It was the best official photo he'd ever had taken. He looked lean and distinguished. "I'll think about it, Tor. Seriously."

Schrade hung up. Dan huffed a sigh and turned off his cell, heading up the gleaming waxed tile of the ramp. He didn't need phone calls like this. Not before meeting the bane of his career. Who had—he had no doubt, though there'd never be any fingerprints—caused him to be passed over for captain.

First, though, a couple of other folks he wanted to drop in on, shipmates, classmates. A broad, polished-tile corridor stretched ahead. He searched his memory, oriented—it always took a while, when he came back to the Building—then headed for the E ring.

Dick Enders was in Naval Personnel. When Dan opened the door, Dick's face lit up. "Dan! Dan Lenson!" They shook hands. "Great to see you. Where you headed?"

"The NCC." The Naval Command Center.

"Who for?"

"Vice Admiral Niles."

Enders's eyebrows rose. "Huh. Nicky Niles. Not good news?"

"I got passed over."

"You can't be serious. What in hell do you have to do to get promoted?"

"Don't know, but I guess I haven't done it."

"Man, that sucks. Know where it is? That's Bay Four Hundred. Corridor Four." He called to the enlisted woman out front, "I'm walking Commander Lenson over to the NCC. Back in twenty."

"Sir, you have a meeting—"

"Have 'em stand by, be right back." He patted Dan's arm. "And Nicky wants to see you—why?"

"I'm not sure. To gloat?"

"Yeah, he's got that reputation."

They walked the short way, around the wide A-ring corridor, nearest to the center court. Dan looked out the windows at the sward of green, at treetops, at the bandstand gazebo they'd called Ground Zero during the Cold War. Joking that more Soviet warheads were targeted on that gazebo than on any other building on earth. Past them hurried scores of busy men and women in uniform and out, contractors in suits and ties, a polished, glossy undersecretary with his aide at heel. Dan thought of Blair. Losing her job here had upset her more than she'd let on. To be one of the most powerful women in the country, then suddenly to be no one . . . Enders kept up a running conversation as they marched. "First time they've overhauled this place since it was built. Tearing out all the windows. New HVAC, complete basement renovation. A fifth of the building at a time. Move everybody out to Crystal City, gut the wedge, rebuild it from the pillars out. Take out all the old wiring, all the asbestos. Here, you can see—this is where the rebuild starts."

A wooden construction barrier had been partially dismantled. Past it the floor turned from tile to seamless, high-tech terrazzo. Enders pointed at the new windows, explained they were blast-resistant, nearly an inch thick; the ones on the E ring were even heavier. The new walls were reinforced with steel. Faintly through the glass came the roar of a jetliner taking off from Reagan.

When they turned down Corridor 4, headed toward the outer rings, Dan forgot walls and windows and clenched his fists.

He and Niles had first met years before, when Dan had been weapons officer on USS *Barrett*, a Kidd-class DDG, with the famous spy Jay Harper. The senior officer had commanded Destroyer Squadron Six. To Dan's surprise years later Niles had remembered him, picked him off a list for the Joint Cruise Missiles Projects Office and assigned him to troubleshoot the failure-prone Tomahawk. They'd run into each other since, but the relationship, never warm, had soured further each time. What would be the opposite of having a rabbi? Whatever it was called, Niles was his. After Dan's involvement in the near-assassination at the White House, Niles had "suggested" a medical retirement. When he'd refused, Niles had exiled him to the Tactical Analysis Group. For his "protection." Dan doubted that. It was a stash billet, a place to stow him until his shelf life expired.

Which now it had. Niles was vice chief of naval operations, the first African-American four-star admiral in American history. And Dan had to make up his mind whether he wanted a retirement ceremony. What did it mean that Niles had made it to the Grail and he hadn't? He switched his mind off that self-pitying track. Retiring as an O-5 was nothing to be ashamed of. He'd survived, when a lot of the people he'd gone to sea with hadn't. Aboard *Reynolds Ryan. Barrett. Turner Van Zandt. Gaddis. Horn.* He had the rest of his life ahead.

Then why did it hurt? To be sidelined, thrown away, when it felt as if he were just learning his demanding trade?

"E ring. Here you go." Enders fitted his badge into the lock. Swung the door open, ushering Dan in. "You been here before, right?"

He had, though not in this rebuilt space. It smelled new. The walls of the cubicles were unstained, the pillars freshly painted. Only a few personal photos and notes had been taped up. Boxes of documents teetered in cubicles; people were still moving in. Otherwise it was the usual Navy office. Officers in khaki. Enlisted in blues. The desultory underhum of telephone conversations. The burnt-coffee and sweetish powdered-creamer smells of a coffee mess. The click and whisper as a printer converted GSA bond into hard copy. Four large televisions flickered at the front, the volume turned down, all on news channels. The NCC was staffed around the clock. Its thirty-plus watchstanders kept tabs on the location and readiness of naval units around the world and monitored news and the intelligence reports that came over the SIPRNET. The conference room was off to the side. A

lieutenant with an aide's aiguillette stood outside it, briefcase at his Corfams, fiddling with a Palm.

"Well, I'll leave you here," Enders said, and they shook. "Gonna be okay
with Black Teflon? The Atomic Fireball?"

Niles's nicknames. "Been there before," Dan said, but his gut was sinking away. He found his fingers checking his gig line, making sure his ribbons were in place. The gold insignia of the Surface Line. Was it really
possible he'd take this uniform off for good? A deep breath. Okay. Another.

In the background someone murmured about a hijacked aircraft. Another voice said that was exercise play, disregard anything coming over
the net from NORAD. Dan didn't think much about it. They had the watch.
Not him.

The aide came to attention. "Commander Lenson? Admiral's expecting
you." He knocked twice and swung wide the door.

8:30 A.M., NEW YORK CITY

Molly Munford, one of the Cohn, Kennedy junior executives, met Blair at the
airport. A stunningly poised young woman in Kate Spade and Gucci, Munford took her overnight bag and showed her to a black Lincoln idling behind
a chain-link fence. Blair caught her appraising glance, top to toe. Her slightly
widened eyes. Approval? Surely not envy. They made small talk on the way,
looking out the tinted windows of the limo at Queens. She checked her
makeup in a fold-down mirror.

The Brooklyn Bridge. She looked down on a three-masted schooner
moored at South Street. Dan might like visiting that, when he came to town.
If she took the job. Above it soared the incredible glittering rectangles of the
Twin Towers, lofty, inhuman. Superhuman. Glowing in the morning sun, two
enormous pillars of coruscating light.

Then they vanished, blotted out in the crowded canyons. The limo inched
through the morning traffic block by block. Park. Fulton. Streets deep with
sun and shadow. Sidewalk vendors hawked scarves, origami, watches, flow-
ers. Elbows flew at shoeshine booths outside the subway entrances. Hundreds hurried across in front of the limo's grille as the light changed, then
kept coming even as the driver nosed into the stream. He looked Pakistani.
She tried *"Khush amdeed,"* and his back-turned face lit.

"You speak Arabic?" Molly asked, looking surprised.

Blair couldn't decide if she was serious or putting her on. "That's Urdu.
I always tried to at least greet the officials I met."

"You were a secretary at defense, right?"

"Undersecretary of defense," Blair corrected her. Could she actually be this naïve? Or was this Cohn, Kennedy humor? New York and Washington were both cities, but apparently more than distance separated them.

At Church the Lincoln idled behind others waiting to discharge, adding its own exhaust to the ascending golden clouds; then inched forward again, toward cathedral arches of soaring stainless that drew the eye up into aching blue. The plaza seethed with suited pedestrians of both genders. Water cascaded beneath a golden globe that gleamed in the sun, light rippling over its gold-and-black, strangely convoluted surface, centerpiece of a flower-ringed fountain. An attendant got her door and Blair swung her legs down, taking a firm stance on what looked like recently washed tile.

Her heels clicked on cream terrazzo as she followed her escort across the lobby. Cream marble and green carpet and scores of national flags hanging from the balcony. The tall windows echoed the arches with Gothic pointed apexes. Inside, the tower was showing its age. It looked seventies, with its flat, geometric surfaces, those strange arches that were only stamped-out shapes. Yet there *was* a cathedral-like feel to it, not holy, but busy. An impersonal, immanent, all-pervading power. She'd nosed this scent at the Capitol, now and then even in the SecDef's office. The heady scent of American capitalism, the worldwide web of money and money's potency.

Molly was negotiating with guards in blazers. Blair signed in, presenting her Virginia driver's license and Department of Defense ID. She clipped a blue-green visitor's pass to the lapel of her jacket.

Her pulse sped up. The lights seemed to brighten. She felt wealth all around her, energy, like a heavy jolt of caffeine. A hundred and ten floors of it. She caught herself lagging and accelerated to match Munford's sleek, calf-flashing Manhattan stride. The girl glanced at a Rolex. "We have a few minutes. I could take you down to the shopping concourse. Or would you like to go up to the observation deck?"

Blair wavered, torn.

"It's a heck of a view," Munford added. "You can see the earth curve on a clear day. Like this morning."

Stainless-steel doors whooshed open. They stepped into a cavernous metal space, brightly lit from above. Munford's finger hovered over the button. She gazed at Blair, penciled eyebrows lifted, waiting for a decision.

8:40 A.M., THE PENTAGON

Barry Nicholas Niles's dark cheeks and forehead were freckled with darker spots, his big hands, flat on the table, freckled too. He was in blues, the uniform set off with stark white at collar and cuffs and a blaze of ribbons down his chest and broad gold stripes that would once have paralyzed Dan but didn't anymore. Niles wore the crossed swords and red-and-white-striped oval shield insignia of the Joint Chiefs. His gold-barnacled hat lay on the table. Dan wondered why they hadn't met in Niles's office, in the E ring, instead of here, out of the way. Then knew: that was exactly why. As Dan came across the room, Niles blinked heavy eyelids, then slowly rose.

"Commander Lenson," Dan said, though of course Niles knew exactly who he was.

"I'm standing for the Congressional, not for you."

"I understand that. Sir."

"Take a seat."

"I'll stand."

"Suit yourself." Niles sank back into the leather chair like a hippo back into its river. They stared at each other. Finally the admiral said, "How's the neck? You could've taken medical retirement for that."

"It's all right."

"Blair? Nan?"

"Fine."

"She'll land on her feet. By the way, heard about your promo board. Sorry about that."

"I'd think it was exactly what you wanted, sir."

A sigh. The big hands rose, suspended, spread. "This has never been personal, Lenson. It's the good of the service. Have you got plans? Vince Contardi could find something for you. Or Tom Leighty. We can find you a place on the civilian side. With Brookings, or CNA. Battelle—I offered you that a couple years ago. There's going to be a terrific up-ramp in spending, with this administration."

"I wanted another ship."

A smile. "We all want another ship, Dan. At some point we can't expect it anymore. You had *Horn*. Be content with that."

Dan leaned forward and put his knuckles on the table. "I'm *content*. But I deserved another command. You can admit it. Come on. Nobody's listening. Just admit it."

Niles blinked up into the hum of the air-conditioning. Finally he said, "Like I told you, it isn't personal. You're just not the kind we need running the peacetime Navy, Lenson. Maybe in sailing-ship days. But not now. You don't understand procedure, or loyalty, or political realities—what it takes to lead a complex organization. You're down at level four, second-guessing what's happening on level one. Second-guessing *us*. Which is why you ended up the way you have."

"I get the mission done. I always have. How about Desert Storm? Signal Mirror?"

"Maybe, though I could argue that. But you also *get people killed*. Wherever you go, bad things happen. Is it coincidence? Maybe once. Not as often as it has with you. Maybe it's not bad judgment. Maybe you're just a Jonah. But at some point, we've got to throw in our cards and say, enough's enough." Niles reared back.

"I did what I had to do." To Dan's surprise, his voice didn't shake. He felt calm. That same coolness that had always come in battle, in extremis, when he'd had to act. "I made the right decisions. They might not have been what I was expected to do. But they were right.

"I thought we had something special in the Navy. We weren't like the other services. A commander had the latitude to disobey, if that was what the situation required. And the leadership, you'd stand behind him. That was our tradition. We were proud of it. Are we like the Army now? Don't think. Just follow the decision tree."

"Fantastic," Niles said, massive face darkening. To Dan's surprise the senior officer had actually lost his composure. The admiral flicked a hand, as if shooing away a fly. "Just—fucking—fantastic. *You* made the right decisions? Then you can retire with a clear conscience. We're done here. Get out."

Dan stood bent a moment longer, searching for anything left to say; then straightened, mind abruptly empty. No point repeating himself. Niles was looking up again, evaluating him.

He came to attention, about-faced, and left. Leaving the past behind, and hoping a future lay ahead.

8:42 A.M., EST, UNITED FLIGHT 175

The pilot radios a report on a strange transmission he received from Flight 11 shortly after taking off. At the same moment, five Middle Eastern males stand from their seats, pulling out box knives and Mace. There's a struggle in the cockpit. The plane jerks and the passengers, cowed, cry out in fear.

The hijackers kill both pilots and take the controls. In less than twelve

*minutes, the aircraft is in their hands. They alter course. The new pi-
lot's nervous or inexperienced, though, and flies so unevenly some passengers throw up. Others, as well as some of the flight attendants, get
on their cell phones.*

*Some of the passengers huddle in back. They discuss storming the
cockpit.*

8:45 P.M., THE SOUTH TOWER

"The roof? Well . . . I'd better not," Blair said reluctantly. "I'd like to look
over some things before we go in. If that's all right? Maybe after we're
done?"

"Sure, sure. Actually, he might take you over to the other building for
lunch at Windows on the World. That's the top-floor restaurant."

"Cohn, Kennedy's where? Which tower?"

"This one. South, 102 through 104. This elevator's the express to 78. We
transfer at what they call the sky lobby and take the local to 102." More
people filed in, until the elevator was packed, the air thick with cologne and
perfume. Most carried briefcases and were dressed for business, though
one small, stooped man wore coveralls and carried a bucket. The car was
one of the largest she'd ever been in, with smooth stainless walls she could
see her face in, a mirrored stainless ceiling. It vibrated slightly, accelerat-
ing gently at first, then rocketing as large red numbers flickered and began
racing. The floor pressed against her soles; her ears ached. The car rocked.
But she'd flown in helicopters with military jock pilots showing off. She
worked her jaw and her ears popped.

The corridors seemed pinched, narrower, when she and Munford
stepped off. Blair leaned against cream marble as they waited for the next
elevator. "Were you here when they bombed this tower? With the truck
bomb?"

"That was a long time ago. Years. Heard about it, though."

"Don't you worry a little, working here?"

Munford frowned. "What about?"

"Well . . . does it ever sway?"

"It leans, when you have a real high wind. But you know, you get used
to it."

They stepped out of the second elevator into a dimly lit, expensively
furnished lobby. Curved sculptures floated within lighted glass, gold toned,
deep red, deep violet. These seemed to refer to no object that actually ex-
isted, but for some reason, walking past, Blair guessed the artist had had

Asian roots. Munford told a woman at a long, curved desk, "Ms. Titus, for Mr. Giory."

"You can go right in, Miz Titus. Welcome to Cohn, Kennedy." To Molly: "I'll tell Mr. Kennedy's secretary she's here."

Past the lobby was a warren of cubicles. The floor was a carpeted football field, filled with the bee-hum of many voices. It sounded like a trading floor, all right. Munford led her in a complete circuit, pointing out various departments. Blair paused at a south-facing window. the whole harbor spread below. The Statue of Liberty was a toy on its soap-cake island. Tugs and ferries drew green wave-trains across glittering slate.

Four middle-aged men in shirtsleeves were arguing around a monitor. They stopped speaking as the women neared. Blair caught one admiring glance; another heavy with resentment. Uh-*huh*. The argument started again when they were past.

Hanumant Giory's office overlooked the city, so far below Blair instinctively steered away from the window. Wasn't that the Empire State Building? Was she looking *down* on it? The streets were dark grooves milled deep into some fantastic wilderness of strangely regular stone. Massive bridges arched across a slowly eddying gray stitched here and there with dancing spangles: the East River.

The compact, dark-skinned man wrung her hand. "Ms. Titus, so glad you came to us. This will be a fruitful partnership. Do you know General Galina? He recommended you highly. Said ya were a truly sharp lady."

"I know Leon, yes. He was leaving the Building when I was arriving. Please give him my best, when you see him."

Giory maneuvered her to a couch and called for coffee. Sat regarding her, legs crossed toward her. His accent was mingled Mumbai and New York. "We don't often get the opportunity to capture someone of your rank. What we do at Cohn, Kennedy involves a great deal of risk. We *encourage* aggressiveness. Things move fast. So we need sharp, sharp people who can think on their feet. Not react ta the situation. We prefer to stay two or three steps ahead."

"I'm afraid I don't know a great deal about the bond market, Mr. Giory. And to be perfectly up-front, I haven't decided I belong in the trading arena. I've been offered a fellowship elsewhere, working on UN development policy."

"Harry, please," Giory urged, then nodded. "I understand. First of all, you would not be trading. Ya wouldn't be overseeing traders, either. If interested in speeding third-world development, you might enjoy working with our clients. We have several overseas who are very responsive to high-level contact. I won't go into names, you understand? But they're much the same as those you dealt with at Defense. In some cases, the very same individuals or families. It's as much personal diplomacy as it is finance. Are we on the same page, Blair?"

She weighed it. "Not exactly, uh, Harry. I don't want to be, or even appear to be, a front man. Or a meeter and greeter. You can find someone better suited to that."

"No, no, you misunderstand." Giory glanced at his watch. "I want'cha ta meet Mr. Kennedy. He'll be in his office soon. Understand he knew your dad?"

"That's right."

"Family's important. That's the kinda firm we are. No, you would be working at the highest levels. Reassuring new clients their issues will be in good hands."

"Really."

"Sure. Ya see, when a foreign government considers issuing bonds, the question always is, who'll buy them? To issue 'em and not have anybody buy, that'd lead to a catastrophic loss of confidence. Everything in the financial world's based on confidence. Price. Volume. Futures. Derivatives. Do ya follow?"

"Yes, but—"

Giory overrode her, throwing his hands around before the massive window. "Lemme finish, now. They need advice on the price. How the market will receive the issue. Timing. And other relevant factors. We ourselves do not issue any securities. In fact, we're barred from dealing in those we consult on, although there are certain downstream products current regulations exempt us from."

She finally got in a word. "As I understand it, you're describing the role of an investment bank."

"That is true. Very true! The bank, of course, usually acts as the intermediary between issuing agent and purchaser. And they provide expertise as well. But we're leaner, faster, and much cheaper. Some of our clients have been badly hurt by banks or, for other reasons, prefer an independent evaluation. Since we've acted for them in other capacities, we've earned their trust. We listen. Do our homework. We give good advice, especially in innovative fixed-income securities. And in fact they're asking us to provide this new service. We're hoping to grow that business and you'd head up that department. Miss Munford would be working for you, along with four others—experienced, longtime traders familiar with the ins and outs. I'd like you to meet them, get a look at your team." Giory rapped his desk. "Ya'd have to be completely objective. Not allow any other considerations to interfere with your judgments and recommendations.

Yes, yes, all this is new. We've arranged a thirty-day introduction that will allow you to become familiar with the international capital markets and relevant regulations."

He ran down at last and sat back. Blair sat back too, evaluating the feel of the place. Trying to sense if this was something she wanted to commit four to eight years to. It *was* exciting. There'd be compensation far beyond anything she could hope for in the federal executive service. Against that would be the expense of an apartment in New York, the Village or the East Side, or maybe out on the Island—she couldn't see both living and working in Manhattan. The question was, would Dan come? She suppressed annoyance. He refused even to talk about what he wanted to do. "I'd have to discuss it with my husband. He's leaving the military and hasn't quite decided what's next."

"We have several husband-and-wife teams."

That made her smile. "I don't think he'd be . . . happy working here." She glanced down again. "Though he'd love the view."

She was looking out toward the North Tower; over the immense outward spread of Manhattan, marching away under the bright, cloudless September sky, when something coalesced within that infinitely clear blue. Very small and far away, just above the most distant buildings. It glittered and she saw it had wings, but extremely thin, almost indistinguishable. She glanced back at Giory, but her eyes were drawn away again by a faint unease.

When she looked back, the speck was larger. Then it seemed to curve and disappeared behind the glass and steel corner of the North Tower. A small plane, possibly, though it was flying awfully low.

She blinked and was thinking again about the offer when a hurtling roar vibrated the windows and the back of the North Tower seemed to . . . *open up* . . . and *things* . . . strange moving things . . . began to emerge.

Her eyes still sent the raw video, but her brain seemed unable to ratify what was actually happening. The other tower was opening up, glass blowing out of the windows, a slow-mo effect, the windows and walls bulging, shattering, followed and mixed with a writhing, almost liquid *haze*, expanding toward her across less than a hundred yards of space. No, not directly at her; angled slightly to her left.

Giory must have caught her puzzled shock because he twisted in his seat just as the murky haze turned a bright white and then instantaneously into a hot, expanding orange-yellow flash.

She pitched forward, dragging him down from the window as the plate glass dented in and out like a shaken sheet of steel and the building shook. The boom came an instant later. It went on and on, trickling down into the mass of concrete and steel below them that flexed and crackled and shuddered, distributing and absorbing the transmitted energy.

Giory whispered something in a language she didn't know. She didn't reply. Just untangled from him and the chair, noticing a yellow peanut M&M lying all alone beneath his desk, and scrambled up off the carpet. They crowded side by side at the window, peering out through the narrow frame. "A bomb," he said, breathing fast. "That's Marsh and McLennan over there. I got a friend with 'em. He—"

"A bomb? No, I saw something—"

"What?"

"I don't know exactly. I'm not sure. Should we leave?"

He didn't answer, staring across to where flame was beginning to stream out of the floors opposite, pulsing, as if pushed out by some immense wounded heart.

Interpretation arrived seconds late. Some of the *things* shooting out of the building had been bodies. Human beings, still alive, if their open mouths and thrashing limbs, trying to run, to gain purchase on empty air as they curved out and down and then fell away, had been any indication.

She felt pain in her hand and realized she was biting it. She looked down. How high they were. The building her body resided in had flexed, bent, moved. How far down those tiny streets, those minuscule cars actually were. Then reassured herself: it had been the other building. Not theirs.

Something terrible had happened over there. But here, they were alive, and safe.

8:58 A.M, THE NAVY COMMAND CENTER, PENTAGON

Dan stopped outside the conference room, stretching his fingers out of the fists they formed each time he confronted the intractable face of the Navy. Like God, it had many personas. The warrior. The seaman. The comradely uncle who took care of his own. This was the one he liked least, the brazen Shiva visage of inexorable rejection. His head felt as if it were swelling, about to come off.

Someone nearby cleared his throat. Dan glanced up to see an older fellow, gray-bearded, offering a wrapped candy. Dan popped it into his mouth, bemused, as the guy wandered off, putting a candy on this desk, then on that. Butterscotch. Good quality too.

He sucked a deep breath. So the voyage was over. Annapolis, career, command. Not as long a cruise as it might have been, but one he could take pride in. He could think, now, of what came next. What he and Blair could do together, for the rest of their lives.

When he looked up again, everyone was getting up from desks and consoles, men and women, leaving keyboards and screens and papers and drifting toward the wall of televisions. He rubbed his face. Then stepped around a desk and joined them as they stood almost touching, watching. The images were chaotic, confusing: quick cuts of a city glimpsed from what seemed to be a helicopter. "What's going on?" he asked a female chief who stood hugging herself. "What happened?"

"They don't know. Airplane in New York."

"A small plane hit the World Trade Center," someone else said.

Dan blinked, still thinking about Niles, then suddenly made the connection. "Holy shit," he muttered, and pushed his way through to the front, staring up. The screen changed, became a silver obelisk, foreshortened, glittering, until three-quarters of the way up smoke seeped from a jagged rent. The announcer spoke about a light plane. "That wasn't any light plane," someone said.

"How could you hit the *World Trade Center*?"

An older officer shrugged. "A bomber hit the Empire State, back during the war. Pilot had a heart attack, that's all. Let's get back to work, people. Back to your desks."

Dan fumbled with his cell, wondering as he punched in Blair's number whether it would penetrate the concrete and reinforcing steel around them. He caught gazes directed his way; stepped into an empty cubicle. Listened to it ring.

She'd said World Trade Center, hadn't she? He glanced over his shoulder at the televisions.

The chief, at the door of what was obviously her cubicle. He tried to smile. "I think—I, uh, think my wife might be there, Chief. At the Trade Center. Could you check something on your computer for me?"

"Sure, sir. What?"

"Look up Cohn, Kennedy. An investment firm. They must have a Web site."

The address was 2 World Trade Center. He felt relieved, then worried again; was that the North Tower? The chief keyed again and said, no, 2 was the South Tower. "Thanks," he said. "She's in the other tower, then. That's great. I mean, well—thanks."

"No problem, Commander. Glad she's not there. It didn't look good, where that thing hit."

When he went out, the breaking news was that it had been an airliner. A huge jet engine lay in the street. The camera cut to upper floors bleeding a blackish gray thickness that looked solid. The tower's mast rose out of that black plume streaming across the sky. The officers had gone back to their cubicles. Some of the enlisted were still watching.

Dan was still standing with them when the camera, down at street level, suddenly slewed away, then came back and up and caught a wiping bloom of orange blossoming.

"That's a different plane," someone murmured.

"No, it's a replay."

"There's only one plane."

"There's *two*. That's the other tower it just hit."

"That's Blair's tower," Dan said half aloud.

Officers and more enlisted were pouring out now, joining him and the others. Dan stared, the eerie unreality coating his skin like a cold film of something sticky. Melted ice cream? He fumbled with the cell again. "God damn it," he muttered. Each time it tried to connect, he got a busy signal. It almost succeeded once; but there was no answer.

He stared at the tiny device in his hand, alone amid a rising tumult of raised voices and, suddenly, many ringing phones.

9:00 A.M., THE SOUTH TOWER, 2 WORLD TRADE CENTER

Blair pressed the END button. Around her, phones were ringing. Televisions were coming on. She considered calling Dan back, then tucked the cell into her purse. She needed to think about what to do next.

Giory was still staring out the window. Past him, smoke kept rising, thick and dark and somehow ashy, then thinning and turning gray.

"It was a plane," somebody shouted, not far away, audible through the thin office wall. "A jet hit the North Tower."

Giory walked to his desk, then wandered back. He smoothed his hair without looking at her. She felt ice rising from her toes. She'd been in a hotel bombing and barely gotten out. She remembered the DoD summer conference, the "hard problems" program. About the likelihood of a major terrorist strike. This didn't seem like one, but the possibility couldn't be discounted.

On the other hand, she might be overreacting. It was the other building, after all. "Should we evacuate?" she asked Giory again.

"We should stay here, I'm thinking."

"Are they still trading?"

"Well, the market just opened." He walked to the door. The noise level was much higher with it open. Phones were ringing, scores, maybe hundreds. "Is the ATS up?" he called, then turned back. "Everything's still online. CNN says it was a plane."

A distinguished-looking older gentleman walked past. He announced, "A plane hit the North Tower. Call your families; let them know you're safe. No danger to us, but if anyone wants to leave, you're free to go."

"Except for the traders," someone else yelled.

"Except for them. If you go, shut down everything properly and log out. The traders stay. If anyone else wants to leave—"

The bad feeling got worse. She picked up her purse. "I think I'll head down to the lobby. Until the situation clarifies. I'll give you a call from there."

"But—Mr. Kennedy, don't forget—"

"I don't think we'll be having lunch. Not over there." She inclined her head toward the burning tower. Noting a thin graphite-gray streaming out of the windows on the top floor, which meant smoke was flowing up through all the floors between. "You don't need to come."

"You need an escort."

A gaggle milled in the lobby. The elevator took a while to arrive, but when it did, more had joined them. By no means a lot, though. They all fit comfortably. She blinked at the back of Giory's head, wondering if her jumping ship was making a bad impression.

They stepped out into the Sky Lobby at 78 as a group of Japanese, or Japanese American, executives filed into the express elevator, which promptly closed its doors. They stood waiting in the lobby with about forty others in a subdued hum of speculation. A woman was talking on her cell. "It was a light plane," she announced to everyone. Blair tried hers again, tried her parents' number, Dan's, but didn't connect. Giory looked put out. The lobby lights shone brightly. Air sighed through the ventilators.

"They're evacuating Tower One," a man said from the far wall. He was on some sort of intercom console, she saw. "But we're okay here. No need to get excited."

The woman with the cell yelled, "People are jumping over there. My sister says it's on all the channels."

Jumping? Blair's stomach muscles hardened. Should they not be using the elevators? Were there stairwells? She remembered the way debris and then flame had blasted out of the other building. How would those above that impact point get down? Through fire and smoke? *Could* they escape? How would firemen reach them?

But she wasn't over there. She was here, where *everything was normal*. She was overreacting. Not a good signal. If she looked weak, it would get around faster than light.

Above their heads a PA system came on. *"Your attention please, ladies and gentlemen. Building Two is secure. There is no need to evacuate Building Two. If you are in the midst of evacuation, you may use the reentry doors and the elevators to return to your offices. Repeat: Building Two is secure."*

She cleared her throat. "Harry? Let's go back up."

"Ya sure? We can go down to the lobby, no problem. See what's goin' on."

"Whatever it is doesn't seem to be affecting us. If there was an emergency here, they'd announce it, wouldn't they?"

"Sure. They're always yelling on that PA, during the drills."

Another local pinged. The doors scooted back. Only two got off, though. The elevators were still running. Surely they'd shut them down if there were any problem.

She hesitated again, then forced herself back through the doors. Giory followed. Two others stepped in with them, a large African-American woman in late pregnancy and a heavyset white man in a gray suit and light blue tie with a blue-and-white lapel pin. They punched their buttons and the doors closed.

They were already at speed and she was reaching to pinch her nose to adjust her ears when the floor jolted to a huge *bang* like an electrical substation shorting out. The car rocked to one side, hesitated, canted there; then seemed to sway back, but reluctantly. The shock knocked them all to their knees. The lights flickered, went off, came on. Dust seethed in the air. The car coasted upward, then shuddered to a screeching stop. She sprawled, head lowered, waiting for whatever came next, flame or blast. When all that followed was an ominous creaking and settling, she crept to her knees, then her feet. "That sounded just like a hand grenade," the man in the gray suit said.

Giory was shaking. "That was the other building," he said, swallowing.

"What you saying?" said the black woman. "The *other* building?"

"Only thing it could be. Didn't ya feel the lean? It collapsed, fell over, hit us."

Blair shook her head. Buildings fell *down*, not sideways. But she couldn't think of anything else but a bomb. Her knees itched. They'd been burned, at the hotel. She didn't want to get burned again. Above everything, she didn't want that.

Giory was jabbing the OPEN button, without result. The man in the suit pulled at the seam in the doors with his fingernails, then jammed a pen into them and pried. Its barrel snapped off. "Won't open," he grunted.

An acridity of burnt wiring tinged the air. She found an emergency phone in the console, but there was no sound on it. Not even static.

The pregnant woman moaned, holding her stomach. When Blair followed her lowered gaze, she saw why. Smoke was bleeding up through the floor. White and thick and slow, gradually rising along the walls of the elevator car.

"It was another plane," the man said. He had a small handheld, some kind she wasn't familiar with, not a Palm but something else. "Present from my wife," he said, catching her look. "Like a two-way pager. I can get texts on it even when my cell won't work." When he held it out she read

2nd plane hit tower 2 - gt out fst as u cn

"That's what—you mean it hit *us*?" She felt sick. A second plane . . . one was an accident. Two planes . . . two were something else.

where are u   r u ok

She handed it back. He took it and started clicking, then began coughing. The smoke was getting thicker. He thrust the device back into his coat.

She examined the ceiling. Nothing resembling a way out there. But there had to be an exit. A maintenance hatch. They couldn't stay in here, they'd die of smoke inhalation. She reached past Giory and stabbed the door OPEN button five or six more times. It was dead.

The lights went out. She had a moment of sheer breathless panic, then remembered: she had a flash in her purse.

When it came on, it only carried a foot or two, the smoke was that thick. They were all coughing now. She pressed a tissue over her mouth. It didn't help. When their hotel had been bombed, she and Dan had gotten through by staying low, below the smoke. But here it was coming up from below.

From *below*. If a second plane had hit below them, they were trapped. Whether or not they could get out of this steel box. She followed the shaking beam to the console and hit the OPEN button again. Nothing, and a crackle was growing below their feet and the air was getting steadily hotter.

"There's a fire down there," the executive said, breathing hard, coughing. "We got to get out."

Giory was hammering on the door with his shoe. "We're stuck," he shouted. "Help. Help!" The clamor was deafening, but there was no response.

"We got to pry that door open," the heavy woman said. "Got to find something to pry with. Or something we can hammer in there, pry it open."

Blair bent and slipped off her shoe. Wasn't there steel in the heel? In good ones, anyway? These were Christian Louboutins. She set the spike in the seam and hammered it in with the heel of her fist. The edges where the doors met were slightly rounded and with her third blow the spike began to drive between them. The executive took over and with powerful strokes drove the heel deeper, wedging the doors apart till a thin line of darkness swallowed her flashlight's beam.

"We got to hurry," the woman said.

Blair fully agreed; the metal floor was searing her nylon-stockinged foot. The choking smoke stank of jet fuel, a smell she was more than familiar with. Giory and the executive were trying to lock their fingers in the half-inch gap her spike heel had opened, to pull in opposite directions. The door didn't give, and she bit her lip; if it had buckled, warped, it might not be possible to unseal it. "Let's all get on it," she suggested, and set her flashlight down to shine where they worked.

They bumped into each other, maneuvering, and got four hands on each door. Giory counted and they pulled for all they were worth and the doors grated and sprung. They hauled again, wheezing in the smoke. Blair's muscles were tearing but she barely registered it, and the gap widened. Four inches. Six. A foot. The car shifted and popped, the metal heating like a cheap saucepan. The woman sobbed and prayed aloud to Jesus. Smoke streamed in through the floor and sucked out through the gap. It was getting thicker, changing its smell from fuel to something darker, more laden. A barbecue stench of charred meat.

Giory slipped his shoulder into the gap and braced. They all pulled again and the doors came apart six more inches and he stepped through, hand stretched into the dark. She slipped her shoe back on and took the woman's sweat-wet hand and went through next, stepping carefully. "I'm Blair," she muttered.

"Cookie."

"You work in the building, Cookie? D'you know where we are?"

"Oh, yes, I've worked here five years now. Ninety-second floor, I think. Or close to there." She was breathing hard through a handkerchief pressed to her face. Her voice came muffled. "I don't walk so fast. Sorry. This's my second."

"That's all right, don't worry about that. Do you know where the stairwells are?"

"There's three egress stairs. A, B, and C. But there's other stairs between the floors, where they goes between offices. We shouldn't take those, unless we have to. They'll be locked, a lot of them."

"Harry," she called to the men, who were some distance ahead down the hallway. "We need to close these elevator doors. Keep the smoke contained."

"Let 'em go," Giory called back. "We just need to get out."

Yes, that was the priority. They were marooned in the sky, with a fire below them. Her skin crawled. In the dimness she pulled Cookie over heaps of what felt like ceiling tile. Doors stood open. "Is there anyone here?" the executive was yelling. They were in the central core, what had been the lobby area on the other floors, but this place was deserted, no one was answering. Around the beam of her light the darkness was impenetrable. Shouldn't there be emergency lights? "This here's a machinery floor," Cookie said behind her. "Right there, that's the stairs!" she called to the men.

At that moment a phone rang. She heard the sound, knew it had something to do with her, but for a moment couldn't remember what. Then she snatched her cell out of her purse.

It was Dan. They had just a few words, then the connection was cut off. He said it was another airliner. Which confirmed the text message. She stared at the phone, debated calling back for half a second, then thrust it back into her purse. She had to escape, not chat.

When they opened the door to the stairs, smoke poured out with a muffled roar and flickering glow. The executive pushed it closed hastily. His blue tie was smudged and awry. The air was getting hot here too, though not as bad yet as it had been in the elevator. He peeled his jacket off and lashed the sleeves around his waist. "Let's stay together," he said. "My name's Tommy."

"Hi, Tommy. Harry."

"Blair."

"Cookie."

"How far along are you, Cookie?"

"About six months."

"You were saying you knew the building?"

"Yes, well, I been here five years, but I know my office, not this floor. I never been down here. But we got to try to find a way out."

"Down's toward the fire," Tommy said. "If we go up, we go away from the fire, and away from the smoke. Then when they put the fire out, we can come back down. I'm from Chicago. That's what they tell us there, in these high-rises. You're safe as long as you're isolated from the fire."

"I don't think this fire's isolated," Blair said. "And we don't know how big it is, or how far down it goes. Harry, what can you contribute?"

"Maybe we should try the other stairwells," Giory said. "If we can go down, we probably ought to. If there's fire in all the stairwells, we'll go up, like Tommy says. Find someplace without all this smoke and wait for the fire department."

"Sounds like a plan. Is that the other stairwell?" Blair shone her light down the corridor, coughing up what felt like raw pieces of lung. The smoke was streaming up, it seemed, through the carpet. Sucking it in was like breathing powdered flame.

The executive seemed about to protest, but ducked his head, holding a handkerchief over his mouth. They tried other doors, but all were either locked or opened to smoke or roaring flame. Until at last Giory cried, "Over here. Over here."

When they forced the door open enough to crowd through, it was into a vertical concrete pipe meat-packed solid with terrified humanity. "Close the door!" many voices shouted at once. She pulled it shut behind her, both tremendously relieved and conscious of a new fear: of being crushed, or smothered, by the sheer press of frightened people intent on getting one more step lower.

The smoke was thinner here but still hot and choking. It blew steadily up the stairwell, leaded with that fuel-and-meat stink that made those in the line double and cough until they retched. The emergency lighting was barely enough to make out faces. The bare, painted concrete stair-treads were so narrow only two could stand on each; or only one, if he or she was heavy. No one seem to be making any progress. The stink of fear-sweat was as strong as the fuel smell. Faces glistened as she swung the flash, then turned it off. Better save the batteries. "Let me in?" she pleaded. Faces rigid, two women first refused to move, then crowded in even more tightly to allow her to insert herself sideways. Giory pushed in behind her; Cookie and Tommy squeezed themselves into the vertical queue.

"Don't shove. Wait your turn!"

"We'll all get out. Stay calm."

It occurred to her that this stair too might be blocked, that everyone would just stand here as the temperature increased until they roasted to death, a vertical mini-Holocaust. "What have you heard? Are we moving at all?" she asked the women into whom she was press-fitted. "Can we get out this way?"

"It was a bomb."

"No, a missile."

She told them what Dan had said, that it was another aircraft. She shuddered. Two planes . . . one could have been a suicidal pilot. But two . . . flown by remote control? Where had they come from?

The press eased below her. With a murmur and surge the crowd swayed, and everyone took a step down. But those behind kept pushing, leaning her forward until she would have toppled save for the wall of flesh below. The man in front had a briefcase slung over his shoulder, into which her chest was was painfully jammed. A hot gust eddied up and the coughing intensified, echoing in the concrete well like the barking of trapped, terrified dogs.

Over the next few minutes they advanced a few more steps. Then the press suddenly seemed to loosen, like highway traffic just past an accident. The flow speeded up. She took one step after another. But now heat was radiating off the concrete, heating the steel handrails. They must be level with the fire. Level with whatever had exploded, jolting the elevator and leaning the whole building. She got down another flight. Another.

"Blair," someone yelled behind her.

When she turned, it was Cookie, half limping, half sliding, face a mask of exhaustion. People kept pushing past, thrusting her aside. She came to a landing and halted, bulled aside by those who continued to fight their way downward, gazes intent on the next step.

"Help," she mouthed through the din. Resting her stomach against the handrail. Sweat glazed her forehead.

Blair tried to fight her way back up, but she faced a huge man whose sole ambition seemed to be to go through her. All she could do was beckon, then step to the side at the next landing. Looking up, she shouted, "Come to me. Come on, Cookie. Can't you let her in? Can't you see she's pregnant?"

"We need to keep going," said Giory.

She scowled at him. "You go on if you have to, Harry."

When she glanced back again, he was gone. So much for that . . . but some remnant of something beyond animal self-preservation must still have flickered, because two men in rumpled shirts halted, damming the crowd with their bodies, and pulled Cookie off the landing. They held her under the shoulders as she limped down. Blair got an arm around her too, and together the three helped her from step to step. She was panting; her blouse was soaked. Blair hoped she wasn't losing the baby. To her astonishment, some cursed them as they pushed by. As if their lives were infinitely more important. "Another step. Keep on going. Stay with me, Cookie. Stay with me."

Fifty-fifth story.

Fifty-four.

Fifty-three. The numbers on the landings crept by with incredible slowness. Still, the air was free of fumes now. Rank with sweat and perfume but no longer cooking with smoke. She panted, throat raw, toes masses of pain. The Christian Louboutins had always turned heads. But right now, they were turning her ankles. She envied the younger women who romped past, running shoes flashing white under skirts, purses and dress heels slung over their shoulders. She wanted to turn off and rest, the way older people were doing at the landings. But pressed on.

The stream of exiting people was moving faster now. The stairwell opened ahead. The residents of these floors must already have left. They were outside, safe; only now and then would one of the doors open and some latecomer join the exodus. Also, she figured, the other exit stairways must be open here, below the crash. Reasoning this out as she dragged her burden and her weary self down one excruciating step after another gave her an obscure pleasure.

Reasoning about things meant you maintained some tiny measure of control.

At the fortieth floor one of the men let go, no apology, just stepped away suddenly from their dragging progress and slipped into the stream. Giory and the other man they'd been trapped in the elevator with, Tommy, had long before vanished. They must be outside in the open by now. The air was cooler, though, and the lack of crowding, of frantic, hurrying, panicking humanity, was reassuring. "We'll make it," she told Cookie. Now she and the one man left supported the groaning soon-to-be mother. Their eyes met over her bent head. He winked, but his jaw was taut with effort. Or fear . . . she felt it too . . . expecting the roar of another jet. She wanted out, out, *out*. But there was no exit save this endless limbo of featureless stairs, only the painted numbers different at each landing. The same single fluorescent tube each time the steps angled left. The same putty-colored concrete.

If only she'd just kept going from the Sky Lobby. That express elevator would have had her on solid ground in three minutes. Why had she *gone back up*, after seeing the North Tower explode? For pride? A job? She'd have been halfway across town, at Penn Station waiting for the Amtrak. She'd never, *ever* go higher than four stories again.

All the other stairways had been blocked. If this one hadn't been open, they'd still be huddled up there, waiting to die.

A commotion below rose toward them as they dragged downward. Yelling, what almost sounded like cheers. Hoarse cries from raw throats.

A straining, exhausted-looking man in a heavy black coat festooned with yellow and silver reflective patches and a large, strangely contoured helmet was trudging up toward them on the left side of the stairway. Another climbed directly behind him. Both were covered with gear that swayed and clanked. They looked bulky and determined and strong, but also flushed, nearly used up. She saw why. They carried coils of heavy-looking hose, portable radios, hanks of manila line, steel pry bars, yellow flashlights, goggles, oxygen canisters. She was shaking and all she'd had to do was walk *down* stairs. She couldn't imagine carrying all that load up— her eye went to the number at the landing—twenty-eight flights. And they still weren't even halfway to the fire.

And *walking up into it*, when everyone with any sense knew to get out. Her gaze met the lead fireman's. "You managing okay?" he asked, hauling himself up on the handrail, between gasps for breath.

"We'll get her out," the guy who had Cookie's right arm said. His blue silk shirt was sweated through. "Good to see you fellas."

"Yeah, good to see you," Blair said, the words petty and inadequate. But she couldn't think of any better.

"Seen the fire, lady?"

Lady. "Yes. It's on the seventy-eighth or eightieth floor. I smelled jet fuel." He pulled himself past and she smelled sweat and rubber and smoke and char, that must be from their gear, their clothes, the fires they'd fought in the past, and a trace of garlic. "Was it another plane?" she called after him.

"Yeah. Another one."

"Be careful," she shouted. The second fireman eyed them too, tall, with a flash of blue eyes, reddened Irish cheeks, wordless. Then others, filing steadily upward, filling the stairwell with clanking and huffing and the scrape and scuff of heavy boots. They went up as her little party limped down, through what was now nearly an empty stairwell, only a few late departures scampering shamefacedly past, turning to slip by, not meeting their eyes. Not one stopped to offer a hand.

"Almost there," the guy said. *He* was sticking, anyway. She looked at her watch. They'd been in this stairwell for almost an hour. But they were almost out. The fourth floor!

But how bad was the fire, above them? Could the New York Fire Department put it out? Those men had looked as if they knew what they were doing. But all they'd had to work with was what they could carry.

Cookie said something Blair didn't catch. Then rasped, louder, "I need to rest. No. I really really need to . . . pee. Can we stop? On one of these floors?"

"We better not, honey. Let it go, if you have to. Just three more floors! We really do need to get out of here."

"Just leave me. I'll catch up. You all go on ahead. You done enough."

"No way, honey," Blair told her. "Not till we get you outside. Hey, uh, you—"

"Sean." He gave her a tousle-headed grin. Too young for her, but cute. Yeah. The chiseled look.

"Sean, let's switch sides, okay? I'm getting a cramp—"

A door slammed far above them. For a moment she thought that must be what it was. Then, that it was another plane. That distant roar. But it didn't sound like a plane.

The others had heard it too; they halted, teetering on the steps, sparrows on a swaying wire. Sean cocked his head like a border collie. The sound was like nothing she'd ever heard before. A distant slam. Slam. *Slam*. Muffled, distant, regular concussions, with a gradually building grating tumult behind them. "What the hell is that?" she muttered. "Cookie?"

"Don't know. Never heard such as that before."

"Let's go," Sean said, voice going high, but determined. "C'mon."

He was right. Whatever it was probably wasn't good. They hobbled downward. Cookie cried out. Blair lost patience with her shoes and kicked them off, then cursed as she immediately stepped on a bottle of fingernail polish fallen from someone's purse. The noise was getting closer. Louder, as if a freight train were rolling end over end down the stairway behind them. Something big, really big, Godzilla sized, had started at the top of the building and was eating its way down to them.

Slam. *Slam* . . . SLAM. Faster and faster, louder and louder. Her ears popped as if she were back in the elevator. The walls quivered. They were taking the stairs as fast as they could now, nearly running, trying to keep in step and failing, weaving, stumbling. Cookie yiped. Her hair had fallen down over her eyes and wet patches stained her blouse. Blair came down wrong and pain shot through her ankle.

She kept going. The whole stairway was shaking. The handrail quivered with each concussion. The avalanche slams came louder and louder, with that roar growing behind it until she couldn't think, as if the whole sky were falling in on them. Cookie screamed and launched herself into the air. Blair tottered under her weight.

SLAM. She jumped down a step, almost fell, her side cramp forgotten in sudden panic terror as the lights went out, plunging them into that utter blackness again.

SLAM. She sobbed and stepped down a step.

SLAM. Sean groaned, across from her in the sudden dark.

SLAM, and Cookie screaming in the midst of a noise louder than anything Blair had ever imagined could be. Needles driving into her eardrums. The taste of dust and concrete in the air, gritty on her tongue, stinging her face, her scalp, sanding the back of her neck.

The stairway reeled, then seemed to topple, and as she cowered helplessly, it all came down on her in the dark, an annihilating thunder louder than anything she'd ever heard in her life, compressing the black into something hard and incredibly heavy that all in an instant battered her bent head and crushed her upraised arms.

9:00 A.M., THE NAVY COMMAND CENTER

Dan tried the phone again. What was wrong with the thing? Just a click as if it had connected, then nothing. Or else "All lines are busy. Try your call again later."

He put it away. The images were up on the large-screen displays, dwarfing the smaller rectangles of the televisions. The watch team stared in silence. Smoke blanketed the canyons of downtown Manhattan. He tore his gaze away. The watch captain sat overlooking the room, eagles glittering on his khaki collar.

"Sir? My wife's in New York. At the Trade Center. What are we getting on this?"

"Just what's coming over the networks. CNN said some waiter saw a light plane hit and bounce off." The captain kneaded a grizzled scalp. "It's a huge complex. Lots of other buildings. Chances are she isn't in the one it hit."

"Now they're saying a two-engine jet," someone called. "Maybe a 737."

"Pilot lost control," the captain said. "Maybe a heart attack."

But wasn't that what copilots were for? Dan was turning away, pulling out the cell again, when beside him the captain stiffened. Someone gasped.

Men and women started to their feet. He turned. The screen had the ABC logo. *Live*, the caption read.

Sailing low across the city, seeming to pass behind the towering, smoking spire of the North Tower, a large, dull blue airliner, twin-engine, swept-wing, slid across the skyline of the city and merged with it. For a moment he thought, *So someone filmed it.* Then the angle changed, the network switched to another camera, on the ground, and he realized with numbed horror that the second plane had hit the tower that wasn't yet on fire. The *South* Tower.

"No," he said. If she hadn't gotten out in time . . . but surely they'd have evacuated by now. Surely.

An immense, off-center bloom of poppy-colored fire. White-hot parts shooting off like sparks. He stood frozen, appalled. He wanted to rush outside. But to go where, to do what?

Voices rose around him again. "No way *that's* an accident."

"Was it a missile?"

"No. I saw it. A fucking airliner."

Dan checked his watch, memorizing the time by some obscure re-flex. The captain said, "Listen up! Get the word out. Contact the CNO. Is the Vice CNO still back there? Get him out here ASAP. He needs to see this."

Niles emerged, arms dangling, to halt mesmerized like all the rest at the unbelievable images. Dan stared at his broad back. What they'd just dis-cussed suddenly seemed petty. A promotion board, another ship . . . now the country was under attack. By whom, they didn't yet know. But they had to act. Prevent more deaths, if they could. He took a step toward the watch captain, who was barking into a phone, then stopped. He didn't know the comm procedures here. How to run the consoles. The best thing he could do right now was stay out of their way.

He hit SEND again, despairing, and to his astonishment connected. A weird clicking, but her voice behind it. "Dan. Dan? Is that you?"

Relief flooded him. He had to put a hand to the TV support to stay on his feet. "Yeah. Yeah, it's me. You all right, hon? We're watching all this on TV."

"Not exactly," she said. Someone was shouting in the background. A crash. Screams. "What's going on? Do you know?"

Someone had turned up the audio on the displays. He could barely hear her. He pressed the phone to his skull so hard it hurt. "Where are you? Are you all right?"

"Not exactly. Dan? Dan, you still there?"

He goggled at the screen, which was replaying the plane sailing, coast-ing into the building, though it must have been hurtling, followed again by that intense yellow-red flame. "Yeah. Yeah. I just saw a plane hit—"

"What? Another one?"

"There were two. Airliners. One targeted on the North Tower, the other on the South. You're okay, God, I thought—"

"I'm not exactly . . . okay."

They were talking past each other, as if she couldn't hear, or only got him intermittently. He clamped a palm over his other ear, turned away from the televisions, from the screams and cries of horror. "Where are you? You're not still in the—"

"We're still in the tower. We were trapped in the elevator. Were you try-ing to call?"

It was so much like some special-effects-laced movie that he felt numb. Over and over on the screens flame bloomed, the deep, hot marigold laced with black of burning fuel. "Yeah. Yeah. You're in an elevator? Can you get out?"

"We already did. Right now we're on I think the ninety-second floor."
She coughed. "A lot of smoke."

He closed his eyes. She was nowhere near safe. "Stay low. Under it."

"Yeah, well, can't do that. It's under us, smoke's coming up through the
floor." She coughed and the phone rattled. "I've got to—"

"Get out of there."

"This is a strike against the homeland," Niles was bellowing behind him.
"Whoever did this, there's more on the way. The CNO's out of the building.
I'm acting in his name. All ships, all jet bases to Threatcon Delta. Pass that
direct to all fleet commands. Get me the watch commander at NMCC.
Scramble Oceana, Lemoore, and Miramar. I want fighters over Norfolk and
San Diego and a CAP over every carrier. Who's our nearest Aegis cruiser to
New York? Where's *Yorktown*?"

"Gulf of Mexico, sir."

"Who else? Where's *Normandy*? Get her under way. Get her headed up
the coast."

Dan stood back. The space, filled with horrified onlookers only seconds before, was electrified now. Every phone being spoken into. Every
keyboard in use. In minutes every Navy warship would be at general quarters, every shore base locked down. Fighters would be launching from
every airfield.

But they hadn't been the target.

He tried to take a step back. Think analytically. This enemy, whoever
they were, hadn't struck at a military base like Pearl Harbor. They'd hit the
Twin Towers. A strategic target? As far as he knew, strategy didn't get plot-
ted out of downtown Manhattan.

The only theory that made sense was Giulio Douhet's. Douhet had ad-
vocated striking sites important to a country's sense of self, to spur it into
a reaction that would let the attacker decimate the defensive forces.

But why not attack Washington, then? The White House or Congress
would make headlines, if that was what this enemy wanted. Six years before, a suicidal truck driver had stolen a Cessna and crashed it into the
White House lawn.

As a charter member of the Tomahawk community, he still weighed in
on the classified chat rooms. Talked to targeteers and operators at confer-
ences. One of the submariners he'd trained had told him about a mission
in the Sudan. A shadowy figure they'd had Tomahawks dialed in for personally. As soon as they got six hours' warning, enough to program the
inertial guidance, they'd launch. But they'd never gotten that notice, and
the missiles had stayed tubed until the end of the deployment. Later strikes
against training camps in Sudan and Afghanistan had missed him too.

48 DAVID POYER

The shadowy doctor who'd built the bomb that had destroyed *Horn* had worked for him, or had been rumored to. All directed by the same puppet master.

So if it was bin Laden, their paths had already crossed. But how could one man do this? Saddam made more sense. Humbled in the Gulf War, he must want revenge. Maybe these weren't airliners, but rented cargo jets loaded with fuel and explosives.

But again, if it was Saddam, wouldn't he be hitting Washington?

Or was it the Chinese? North Koreans? Cubans? Domestic terrorists, like McVeigh and Nichols?

Or someone they'd never imagined, didn't know about at all?

The problem wouldn't be lack of suspects. When you were the sole remaining superpower, it was King of the Hill. If you toppled, all the others would cheer. Until the next kid mounted the sandpile.

He shook himself, watching the Towers burn, and remembered: *Blair*. Tried the phone again. Fruitless. He was almost out of charge, anyway. He looked around. Everyone had something to do, except him. There—a vacant cubicle. If he could get online, log in to SIPRNET . . . he slid in. Photos of wife and kids. The guy was a Canadiens fan. Dan booted up, but the password screen stonewalled him. He tried his passwords from TAG, his old National Security Council log-in. Nothing worked. He slid the drawer out and looked inside, checked both sides of the monitor for stickies. Nada.

He spotted Niles at a table with the watch captain. "Sir?"

The admiral barely glanced up. "Make it fast, Lenson."

"I know the Sit Room captain. I can get you a line to the PEBD. In the White House basement. If I could get a password—"

"I have someone working the White House," the captain said.

Niles nodded, heavy lids drooping, then flicked his hand. "Go on, Lenson. We'll manage." The tone was dismissive: *We don't need you.* The realization burned up through Dan's gut to his face as they stared at him, Niles smiling slightly. Then they sobered, looking back at the screens.

Dan wanted to say something, but it felt useless. Picayune, in the face of disaster. He swung away for the door. Going, but unsure where. He had no duty station. No general quarters station. How ironic that when the shit finally hit the fan, he was out of the loop. He glanced at the clock: 0943.

He turned left and then left again into the shining, brightly lit corridor. Then halted, though he had no idea why.

A tremendous explosion quaked the floor and blew the overhead lights down on him in a spray of glass, plunging the corridor into instantaneous darkness. He slammed into the deck, blown down by a shock wave. His jaw struck tile.

A lacuna, a gap in consciousness. He emerged staggering, surrounded by fire alarms and shrill screams. He stood in the open between two of the Pentagon's concentric rings. The ground was asphalted, like a road. Into it, through an arched hole in the beige brick big enough to drive a pickup through, a pile of . . . debris . . . as tall as a man had been blown out on the asphalt and was burning fiercely with yellow-orange flames that gave off a dark, oily smoke. The same marigold hue he'd seen only minutes ago on the screen; the color that said instantly to anyone trained in shipboard firefighting *fuel fire*.

He had no idea how fuel had gotten here. Maybe a bomb had set off a fuel tank of some kind. Yes—a bomb. No doubt concealed by someone on the building teams during the reconstruction Enders had been talking about.

All these thoughts stopped dead as a human figure, on fire from feet to head, stepped out of the flames and walked stiffly down the pile of burning debris. It slowly collapsed as it reached the road. The sight was so bizarre he stood unable to move. Then, making himself breathe again, he pushed the door open and raced toward the fallen figure, catching the blast of radiant heat and a queerly familiar smell. One exactly like the exhaust of a turbine-powered ship, such as *Barrett* or *Horn*.

When he crouched by the body, the fat and skin were still burning. He couldn't even tell if it was male or female, though the Corfams looked small enough to be a woman's. Above him gigantic, repetitive globes of visible gas were venting from the hole in the building. As they hit open air, they flashed into flame, like fluid spouting from the mouth of a circus fire-eater. Paper and wooden debris flashed into flame. He shielded his face with one arm. From the corridor other men ran out onto the drive. Navy in khakis, Air Force in blues.

Dimly, past the gushes of incandescent gas, he made out a figure staggering aimlessly. It didn't seem to see the exit. Others moved behind it, deeper in hell. Fire was cascading down all around them. They wouldn't be alive long, as it took hold. Exactly like an engine-room conflagration. If they didn't get out now, they'd lie down, overcome by smoke, and die where they fell.

A gap showed below the gushes of flame, above the smoking debris. He took a deep breath, crouched, and ran up the pile, bricks grating and turning under his shoes. Heat blasted his skin. He buttonhooked left as soon as he was through. Faintly, from behind him, came the grating of other shoes on the rubble.

The cavelike interior was dark except for the flame and the buzzing spark of short circuits above him. Fire roared to his right, flowing down in a liquid fall. He straightened and instantly got zapped by a live wire in the sagging ceiling. Melting material plopped softly, smoking, starting small fires where it hit. One drop seared his shoulder. Maybe this wasn't a smart idea. The ceiling creaked ominously. Then he caught the elusive figure again, more distant, moving like a wayward ghost through the murk.

He started forward, stepped on something soft, and looked down. It was a face. He bent beneath a blanket of woolly, black smoke forming at chest level and began to dig. Tossing aside hot pieces of jagged metal, charred publications, dozens of pieces of red plastic and three-ring scarlet board he recognized as Top Secret snap binders. Other hands joined his and he turned streaming eyes to one of the men from the drive. "Gimme a hand," the guy said, and Dan took a step back and saw a shattered rack of electronics lying across the fallen man's thighs. Another man joined them, this one in an Air Force uniform. They got the victim free and the others dragged him off toward the hole.

Dan glanced at it, at daylight like the exit from a hellish Haunted House; then bent in a racking, phlegmy cough. He hoped somebody was doing the same for Blair, wherever she was.

The smoke reeked of burning fuel and plastic. A soldier in dark green trou and light green shirt, thirtyish, uncovered, mustached, appeared from the smoke and Dan grabbed him. "Let these guys handle the ones closest to the door."

"We stay together?"

"Stay together."

"Mick."

A distant siren was followed by *"Attention. A fire emergency has been declared in the building. Please evacuate."*

"Dan." They shook once, quick, hard, and Dan saw a piece of torn blue-gray cloth from some sort of curtain and picked it up. He tore it in half and handed part to the sergeant and wrapped the rest over his own mouth.

The plopping spatter from above was growing, as was a strong stink of burning . . . horsehair? Looking up, he saw more fire up there. Swell. The wiring was melting. Probably whatever rebar was holding up the sagging concrete too. This wasn't unfamiliar territory. Every Navy man put in thousands of hours in fire parties, fire drills. With a three-inch hose and a fire party behind him he could fog down this space, cool it below flash point, and start pushing that fire back. Fog and foam.

But he didn't have a hose. He hesitated, then went on, stepping carefully over shattered electronics, smashed, smoking computer monitors, a shining hydraulic strut, a bent, jagged cage of steel bars. Mick followed. This had to be a SCIF, a radio-shielded space for classified comms. That made sense of the red plastic too.

He came to a blasted-apart concrete wall and climbed through. A piece of rebar came off in his hand. He started to throw it away, then kept it.

Past the twisted bars lay a zone of shattered, burning plywood. It was covered with fuel, not all ignited yet. He stepped over an instrument panel that looked as if it had come from an aircraft. Something pink and gray had been forced through it as if by enormous pressure. It glittered with particles of glass. The soft drops plopped and sizzled down. The smoke was getting thicker. He came across scorched cans of ginger ale and soda and cracked one and poured it over the cloth. That helped, but his eyes were tearing so badly he couldn't see where to step. They should have full-face masks and OBAs. Helmets, firefighting boots, gloves, flash gear. Not Certified Navy Twill uniforms whose woven polyester was beginning to melt-laminate itself to his shoulders. Another body, facedown; he turned the head over; past help, blasted to white bone from the chest up.

He left it and staggered on, turning back only once to make sure of the exit. The round light glowed smaller now, vague through the smoke. Couldn't lose sight of that. That panel had been off a plane, a big one. So was the shattered aluminum that glittered and steamed all around. He stepped on something and lifted his shoe. A purse. A hand with a ring still on it gripped it.

Two planes on the Towers. Another here. Where else? The CIA? The Capitol? The Statue of Liberty?

Another ten yards and he'd turn back. While he could still get out, though his khakis were torn and his hands burned and his shoes were smoking.

By now he and the air force guy weren't walking, but clambering on blistering hands and torn knees over toppled cubicles, piles of smoking paper, smashed computers, cables and wires tangled with pieces of concrete and partition walls and blasted-off chunks of the pillars. Not all that different though than when he'd had to crawl through *Horn*'s shattered hull. A moan diverted him and he groped in the obscurity, pulling up toppled dividers, but couldn't find anyone. The moan didn't come again. He found another body, a piece of jagged aluminum driven through its chest.

Another groan, this time from above. He glanced up to see a woman in an Army uniform hanging from a hole in the second-story floor. Her open eyes blinked beseechingly at him. The fire was crackling above her. The ceiling was sagging. As she stretched out an arm, it collapsed. More pillars followed with a hollow roar, and she disappeared.

Chairs, copiers, file cabinets, wrapped with wire and smoldering. Everything in here was going to burst into flame, perhaps in seconds. In those seconds, anyone who was going to be saved, would be saved.

A human shape in the smoke, reclining in a chair that had been pushed back against the buckled wall by the blast. Dan climbed over a smoking, shredded desk until he could look down into its face. Only there wasn't any. Blast or flying metal had scooped it away from the forehead down: eyes, face, jaw, leaving Dan looking into a running mass of blood pulsing from bared bone and sinuses. The hair was burned to ash and the neck was charred. Bubbles worked deep in the mass. The chest rose and fell. The head slowly rolled back and forth. Dan hesitated, unable to look away. He started to reach for a shoulder, then stopped. Looked toward the now distant glow of daylight. Up, at the sagging ceiling directly above, dimly visible through the gathering smoke.

He gripped the smoking uniform at the shoulder, once, hard. The faceless one winced. But otherwise didn't respond. Dan backed away, over the desk, down the pile again. And crawled on.

Past another huge pile of toppled masonry and brick and smashed equipment. He figured he was back in the command center, but in the dark and smoke it was impossible to be sure. The space was dotted with support columns, except where some terrific force had swept them away, or left meshlike ghosts of bent rebar with all their concrete blown away. Body parts everywhere, flesh ripped from bones, smoldering torsos, heads, legs, feet, torn apart and shredded and plastered against those partition walls that still stood amid the smoldering heaps of desks, chairs, copiers, file cabinets. Some parts looked flash-charred, while an arm's length away a checkbook fluttered untouched on a desk. Soon it would all be engulfed, that was clear. Twenty feet away a stream of pure fire arced down onto a file cabinet, which burst into flame. The smoke hurt. It was freighted with burning plastic, off-gassing insulation, burning fuel. Tears and snot streamed down his face. A red-hot band was tightening around his heart. His feet were strapped with lead, like an old-fashioned helmet diver's.

"We better get out of here," the airman yelled. Dan coughed, nodded, started to pull back. Then heard the groan again.

The whiteboard was pinned under a huge chunk of jagged concrete. They pulled that off, then the board, to find two bodies in Navy khaki. The watch captain's back was charred black, as if he'd taken the full force of the wave of fire. The other body was unmarked, but they were both dead.

No; the one on the bottom stirred. They got him up between them and hauled him back over the pile to where the others hustled him off.

Dan was backing away when he saw a shape moving deep in the murk. No, two shapes, stumbling along, hands groping out. Wandering blindly in the smoke. One fell. The other helped him up. One of the shadows was huge, distorted, inhuman, humpbacked. They were headed across his front, away from the exit. He screamed after them, but a wall collapsed and more fire poured down, blotting out his puny cry. The smoke ate them.

"Let's go," his partner yelled.

Dan pulled out of his grip and slid back down the pile, feeling sharp edges X-Acto hands and legs but without pain. "Over here!" he screamed again, crawling across smashed tables, body parts. The smoke was blanketing right down to them, black, thick, solid as tar. He caught sight of one of the figures again and lifted the bar in his hand and pitched it as hard as he could. He couldn't see where it went. It disappeared into the murk. But it must have struck one of the shadows because the next thing he knew, the big figure blundered out of the smoke and into him. Dan seized it and yelled into its ear, "Follow us. We know the way out."

"Lenson?" the shadow rumbled.

Niles had looked humpbacked because he was carrying a sailor. The admiral turned and shouted, "Over here. All of you, come to me." To Dan's astonishment, more figures emerged, creeping over the wreckage, crippled, smoking, burned, but still moving. One even dragged a briefcase.

They were all crawling toward the distant daylight when with a muffled *whoomph* the ceiling collapsed. A ball of flame ignited, kicking Dan into a wall as if he'd been pitched into it by two linemen. He almost blacked out, then felt a big fist clutch his shirt. The fabric tore and the fist shifted to his web belt, lifted, then threw him toward the light.

He crawled out hacking, drooling black snot, collapsing against the outer wall and vomiting into a black puddle of oil-coruscating water. Others stood aside until he straightened, then led him back toward the corridor.

He collapsed there for some minutes, trembling so hard it was close to convulsing, examining the blood dripping off his palms, which were black with soot and ash and fuel. He ought to feel something. Rage? Sorrow? But it wasn't here yet. A headache pounded like barbarians slamming a ram into a castle gate. Someone held out a bottle of water and he poured it over his head, sluicing off soot, and drank the rest. It almost came back up, but he breathed slow and closed his eyes and kept it down.

He kept coughing up black phlegm and spitting it onto the muddy tile. A smoky haze lay over the drive, above the heads of men bringing out more bodies. Now and then one would move or cry out. Medics bent over these and got them onto backboards, and others carried them off down the corridor. Two men were talking. They said the Twin Towers had collapsed. Dan thought that unlikely. Blair was there. But there was something odd about that because he wasn't really sure who this "Blair" was. His brain seemed to be calling in long distance. The men said the Sears Tower in Chicago had been hit too. They said a truck full of explosives had gone off outside the State Department.

Someone blocked in his light. Army, a light colonel. "We okay, Commander?"

"Just getting my breath."

"Were you in there?" Pointing to the blown-out hole.

"Just came out."

"Any more in there?"

"If there are, we're not going to get to them."

"How about this corridor? Is it clear?"

Dan tried to concentrate. "Four. This is four. It's clear a little ways. Up till the C ring, I think."

"Can you get into the spaces that are on fire?"

"I don't think so. Either the walls are blown out or the doors are buckled."

"How about on the second floor? That's Army Personnel. Did they get out? Do you know?"

That explained the bodies in army uniforms, and the woman who'd fallen through the hole in the ceiling. He said he didn't, but they could go look. Where was the emergency response? But when he looked at his watch, only fifteen minutes had passed. It seemed like much longer. Still, there should be firemen. Police. When he stood, the corridor reeled. He steadied himself against the wall. Made himself take a step. Then a couple more.

He and the colonel found a stairway and went up.

On the second floor the smoke was even worse than it had been down below. The heat scorched Dan's cheeks and forehead and he pulled his undershirt up over his mouth. They went down the corridor trying to get doors open, but all were either locked or jammed. The colonel pounded on the doors but no one responded. Dan took a knee, then went to all fours, gagging. His throat was closing up. His hands and legs kept cramping and a red thread was lacing itself across his visual field. He rubbed his face, but that only scrubbed in some kind of grit that was all over him.

"You don't look so good," the colonel said. "Can you walk?"

"Can't breathe. May have to . . . have to pack it in." He gagged again on something deep in his throat that didn't belong there. He struggled to get air, then coughed until the red thread got larger, much larger, and somehow sucked him down into it.

He must have passed out again. When he came to, he was still in the corridor, looking up at the ceiling tiles, being carried between two men. A smoky pall drifted between him and the ceiling. His skull was being compressed in a hydraulic vise, but much worse was the thing blocking his airway. He could only get a breath now and then and, in between, had to cough out thick, sticky mucus. He got out, ". . . going?"

"Got to evacuate," one of his bearers said without stopping. They were really humping along; the doors were flying past. He caught the number on one; they were almost to the A ring. "Another plane on the way."

". . . 'nother?"

"Four minutes out. Got to get you out of here."

The thought barely registered, as if there were so much horror in the day already any addition was high on an asymptotic curve. He marveled vaguely at how well someone must have planned, to strike the most powerful country on earth such savage and unexpected blows. He turned his head and gagged, then concentrated on getting the next breath. It didn't come, that thing in his throat was blocking it, and he twisted and threw his arms out, panicking, as a black, rotating tunnel opened and sucked him down.

THEY must have carried him all the way out to the courtyard because the next time he came to, a brilliant blue sky lay looking flat just above his eyes, and dappled shadows of trees with smoke rising behind them. People were running and shouting all around. Another plane had hit Camp David, a woman called. Sirens ululated. Firemen jogged by. He stared up at the smoke. Terrified. Like trying to breathe through a pipe straw. The harder he tried, the tighter his throat closed.

What he'd been trying to feel in the corridor came through just for a moment then. *Find out who did this, and kill them all.* But then his airway closed again, and he had to put everything into the battle for one more lungful. The thing in his throat was growing. Choking off his last bit of air.

He passed out again, and when he came up this time, not only couldn't he breathe, someone had forced the spigot of a gas pump into his mouth. It was rigid and sharp-edged, and they were jamming it down his throat, talking urgently in some foreign language. He fought them with his last strength, sobbing. The black came in again, sweeping him around the toilet bowl in tightening circles. Then a wasp stung his arm, and he tipped up on end, like a torpedoed ship sliding under, and went down for good.

10:00 A.M., EST, ABOARD UNITED AIRLINES FLIGHT 93

After taking control the four hijackers warn the passengers to stay in their seats. The young, clean–shaven men inform them there's a bomb aboard. They're returning to Newark, where they'll present their demands. This feels so familiar from a hundred movies the passengers obey. In all their lives, most have never been physically threatened. They've been told over and over that if they are, they should not resist. "If confronted by a criminal, a weapon, a threat, do as you're told; cooperate; do not anger them." The police, the courts, the government, the military, detectives, fire crews, SWAT teams will rescue them. This too they've seen on a million television screens.

Do what you're told. Don't resist.

Comply.

Their new pilot climbs to forty thousand feet and heads toward Washington.

The FAA and the Command Center are trying to get jets in the air, but the air defense system, unalerted and geared to intercept threats approaching the Atlantic coast, is slow to reorient.

Meanwhile the passengers are on their cell phones. The news filters from seat to seat. Two airliners have crashed into the Twin Towers. A third has hit the Pentagon.

Someone isn't just hijacking airliners. They're crashing them into buildings. Turning them, and their occupants, into flying bombs.

A new understanding filters through these average citizens.

Within ten minutes, something within them shifts, changes. Doing nothing will end in their deaths, and those of others. They may die. But first, as Americans were once used to doing, they will fight.

A little before ten o'clock, led by a few men, they mass in the rear of the plane, getting ready to rush the cockpit.

A passing National Guard transport reports the aircraft waggling its wings. Shortly thereafter, it crashes south of Johnstown, near a little town called Shanksville.

Everyone aboard dies. But whatever the intended target—the White House, the Capitol, a second blow at the Pentagon—by the passengers' sacrificial bravery, no one else is killed.

7:25 P.M., YEMENI TIME, SANA'A, YEMEN

The embassy cafeteria was packed with staff Aisha had never met; she hadn't known there were this many Americans in Sana'a. Strangely, not one Yemeni, though dozens were attached to the embassy—drivers, maintenance people, translators. As if they knew this wasn't where they wanted to be. Not today.

The televisions were tuned to different channels, CNN, the BBC World Service, but for some reason the one with the biggest crowd was Al-Jazeera. Maybe the picture was better. Though by now the images were burned into her mind. Smoke pouring from the towers; a vast holocaust staining the sky. She watched each time the airborne cameras panned, relieved each time to see that as best she could tell, the pall was drifting southeast, across to Brooklyn. Not that she didn't care about people who lived in Brooklyn, or the thousands who must have died when the towers collapsed; but Tashaara and her mother lived to the north, three blocks above Central Park.

The flower-flame logo of the Arabic satellite channel flashed, and a modestly clothed, dark-haired commentator began speaking excitedly. Beside Aisha, Doanelson, the FBI agent, was breathing hoarsely. Sweat darkened the armpits of his gray suit. He nudged her. Muttered, when she frowned at him, "What's she saying?"

"What is she . . . ? The same thing every other channel is."

"I can't follow when they talk that fast. She looks happy. Are they gloating?"

"Scott . . . she's reporting the deaths. She's saying airliners hit the buildings. There's no gloating. Believe me. An accident this huge—"

"Whoa! This is no accident." Scott's cheeks were flushed; he mopped his face with one sleeve. "This's the same guys who hit the *Cole*, who hit the embassies. Same as your little dance buddy, Al-Nashiri. *'Allahu Akbar.'* You know who I mean."

She studied him, heart sinking. He couldn't be right. Not this great evil. "You believe that?"

"Nobody else has this kind of organization. We're going to have to refocus the whole investigation. Find out how it all links up." He seemed to remember something then and blinked and put a hand on her shoulder. "We're really gonna need you."

She examined him quickly; looked around. Noticing only then that she sat in the center of a cleared space, that the cafeteria chairs around her were empty. Doanelson was still holding her shoulder, but to the others it might have looked like the sort of grip one used to apprehend a criminal. They stared at her abaya and headscarf with loathing in their eyes.

She looked back at the screen. A street full of chanting demonstrators— dear God, no, of celebrating Palestinians—were screaming joyfully and waving signs. She understood suddenly that everything had changed and would never again be the same.

II

An Altered World

1

Los Angeles, California

TEDDY slumped in his Camaro outside the restaurant, sucking on a Coke, trying to get his head clear. He'd punched the alarm and almost missed getting up. But then had remembered the Germans—the *investors*—and pushed the sheets off by sheer strength of will.

And discovered long, smooth legs that led to a Brazil-waxed, pouting heaven. The silvery blonde's thighs had parted, and for a moment he'd been tempted again. Until the headache sledgehammered him like a bolted steer and he staggered into the 1940s-gorgeous bathroom that was now seedy, mirror speckled, tiles missing, and gagged over the sink.

Fifteen minutes later, showered, dressed, unshaven—but that was okay—he pulled out of the driveway headed for Beverly Hills. The traffic on Laurel was horrendous. He pounded the wheel and cursed. Flicked the radio on, then off again. Loki would kill him. Hanneline Muruzawa, from Breakbone Pictures, would be there too. A year's work on the script. Dozens of meetings. Now the Germans wanted to look into his eyes before they wrote the check. He wasn't sure what they expected to see, but Loki had been clear. Without them, there'd be no film.

Another red light. He rooted his notes out of the glove compartment, from behind the holstered HK, and tried to focus.

Credit and money. Everything came down to that. Credit and money, and money was credit and credit was money, so it was really only about one thing in the end.

Which meant he had to go in acting as if he had it, even if he didn't.

A honk from behind. He flipped up a finger. Imagined for a savage moment taking the HK out and shutting the asshole up for good. But just then the light went to green, and he swore and stomped on the gas.

THE Polo Lounge was off the main lobby of the Beverly Hills Hotel. Loki had wanted the Germans to feel as if they were being treated right. Teddy didn't mind. The McCarthy salad was good. They made the steak tartare at the table. The hostess walked him through the dining room into the garden area. Private booths lined what he couldn't help thinking of as the perimeter, the booths deep green under peach walls, screened by hanging plants and dangling ivy. You saw famous faces here, stars, producers, executives, deal makers. This morning, though, the urbane waiters in white jackets and black bow ties stood amid empty tables set with heavy silver and fine china and good linen.

A hell of a contrast with MREs salted with powdered camel dung, the way it blew up off the desert in Ashaara.

He found Loki Dittrich at a table on the sunny patio, where they could almost see the pool, could smell the chlorine on the morning air. He bent to kiss the shadowed, lovely cheekbones of the legendary beauty she still was, even after all these years. Dressed western, a checked shirt, fitted Levi's, boots gleaming with silver and turquoise. Loki introduced a slight woman with shoulder-length hair, Asian features, and no makeup as Hanneline Muruzawa, producer of *Market Basket* and *Leave Her to Me* and *Mean Eddie*, plus plus. Teddy got a handshake that surprised him with its strength.

Loki introduced the two middle-aged banker types in suits as Hirsch Gerlach and Werner Neustadt. Teddy gave them both hearty handshakes, watching them react to his six foot two and the scars radiating out from his nose like a Maori warrior's. He could've had those lasered, but why look like everybody else? He took a seat beside Muruzawa. A little past his age bracket, but a seriously sexy lady. A waiter who introduced himself as Dominic leaned to pour coffee.

"Good flight in?" Teddy asked the Germans.

"We sleep very late, I am afraid," said Neustadt. "Jet lag. It is very nice to meet you at last."

"Very interesting, Mr. Oberg, this script. About where it is, Ashaara," Gerlach said. "*The Brotherhood*. You have been there, I think? In that unhappy country?"

"From the start of the insurgency. Lost a good friend there."

"Our friend's a BTF," Neustadt put in. Teddy glanced at him; where'd he get that? BTF—Big Tough Frogman—was a SEAL putdown.

"This is . . . the Aleko character? He is Japanese?"

"Hawaiian," Teddy said. There were no Japanese SEALs. No Jewish ones, either, at least that he'd ever run into. Had this guy even read the script?

"I would like to hear why you want so much to make this film," the younger German, Neustadt, said. "Why it will resonate with the American market."

By now Teddy had pitched it so often he didn't have to think. "It was because of Sumo—I mean, Aleko. I want to do a film that finally tells the truth about fighting, about honor, and about death. Not *Sands of Iwo Jima*, but not *Apocalypse Now*, either. No heroes and no fools—just the reality of combat and the kind of man it takes, and the kind it leaves once the fighting's over. Why will it resonate? Every man wonders how he'd act if it really came down to it. That's what Chief Strange comes face-to-face with, in the insertion and raid scene."

"Have you seen *Stalingrad*?" Gerlach said. "German, but it sounds like what you are describing. A very antiwar film."

Teddy said antiwar wasn't exactly the message he had in mind. He caught Loki's glance; *Never say the word "message,"* she'd told him often enough. Then Dominic was back and he looked at the menu, starting to get hungry. Loki got oatmeal. Muruzawa ordered Alpine muesli. The Germans ordered big breakfasts, heavy on the meat. So did Teddy, to mirror them. And a big Coke for his head.

"Werner was saying, his investors like the script," Muruzawa said. "And Breakbone likes the concept. I've talked to distributors. Loki tells me you have Ewan McGregor and Colin Farrell. Those are very hot names right now."

"Crowe," Loki put in. "Ridley Scott."

"Russell's a maybe. I have a call in, but let's leave that to one side. We need the financials firmed up before we go any farther."

Werner cleared his throat and put the menu aside. "We can do it, but we can not do it all." Though Neustadt was younger than Gerlach, Teddy thought he held rank. "Our goal, you appreciate, is not exactly the same as yours. Of course we want to make a good picture. If we can, a great picture. And your dead friends, heroes, yes. We Germans know something about dead heroes.

"But our goal is to protect the money. That is our prime directive, you might say. *Star Trek*, eh? We must cap the budget. Ten million dollars, US."

Teddy glanced at Loki. She'd estimated fifteen. On-location shooting in Morocco. Special effects from Industrial Light & Magic. Muruzawa smiled but didn't give him any clues. He diced his corned-beef hash, letting it perk in his head.

Money and power. He didn't have money in this picture. Not yet. So he decided to bust their balls. Outrageous to ask for it, for his first movie. But it would stick it to them. They'd have to say no, then compromise somewhere else. So at the end, he'd still end up with more than if he hadn't been a selfish prick.

"A Teddy Oberg Production" above the title still wouldn't give him complete control; a lot depended on the director. But clout . . . that it would give him.

But it would be stupid to say this. That would put his nuts in their vise, let them whipsaw him.

"I can make it for twelve," he said. "If I get dollar one gross profit."

Muruzawa looked dismayed. The Germans traded glances. Neustadt chewed a whole sausage before he said, "Actually, we were thinking along those lines too. To close the gap. Here is what we do. We defer your *entire* fee. Push it *all* to the back end. You'd come out with better numbers, in the finish. If that is okay with Breakbone—"

"That part's your deal," Muruzawa said, making a quick hands-off gesture. "We just do what we do best. Package the film with hot talent and a good director, and keep the show on budget."

Teddy looked through the glass from the sunny patio into the bar. Someone had turned on the television. People were standing in front of it. Others were walking toward it in bikinis and trunks from the direction of the pool, where his grandmother had watched Johnny Weissmuller perform his famous rescue. It didn't sound like a fantastic deal. "Loki? How you feel?"

"Your decision. This is going to say, 'A Teddy Oberg Production,' after all."

Sneaky Loki, slipping it in. But the Germans didn't react, which surprised him again. He didn't let it show, just ate more hash. He washed it down with the rest of the Coke and lifted the glass as Dominic went by.

"Okay, your fee goes to the back end," Werner said, as if everyone had agreed, but Teddy didn't object. Neustadt went on, "We cap the budget at twelve. That is an absolute; we cannot put in more later; if you seek additional financing, it cannot dilute our percentage. Now, our next suggestion. We have a tremendous new actress. Very talented. Very beautiful. The Loki Dittrich of our time." He smiled at Loki. "She even started as a skier, like you, *Liebchen*."

"We saw it more as a buddy movie," Muruzawa put in.

"The numbers are down on buddy movies. The problem with this script is that there is no love interest. Her name is—"

"I don't need to know her name," Teddy said. "Which of you's banging her? This is a gritty war movie, for Christ's sake. There's no room for a bimbo."

Neustadt's eyes turned hard; both men sat back in the booth. "She is not a bimbo," Gerlach said.

Loki put her age-spotted, bony, elegant hand over Teddy's. "Teddy's got his thinking cap on," she said. "The pilot. There's a helicopter pilot, right? She could be a woman."

"And she grabs a gun," Neustadt said. "And comes up behind the insurgents and—"

"There are no fucking female helo pilots in the special forces," Teddy stated. "And even if there were, she sure as fuck wouldn't 'grab a gun' and insert herself into a firefight." He wadded up his napkin and threw it on his plate.

"I understand. But we really want this girl in the picture," Gerlach said. "Not us personally. But the principal. You know how this is. Loki certainly does."

"It's not the first time it's happened in pictures," Dittrich chuckled.

"You can jam your fucking cunt up your Nazi ass," Teddy said. "With her skis on."

Or rather, he wanted to, but kept his teeth clenched by sheer will. His headache was back. He signaled to Dominic. "Got any champagne?" He needed something with alcohol in it.

"Same for me," said Loki. "Let's make a fucking movie, as Teddy would say."

"A mimosa," said Muruzawa.

The Germans curtly shook their heads.

Dittrich got up and frowned at Teddy as she passed. He got up and followed her. Through the window he saw more people gathered around the TV in the bar. A disaster movie, it looked like.

"You'd better get yourself under control, boy," she told him. "They gave you a point of gross. I couldn't believe it. Halfway decent box, that's a *lot* of money. You are so close to making this project. But you can't put their girl in for a bit part? When that's all they're asking?"

He massaged his temples, not meeting her gaze. The headache was blinding.

A green spheroid.

"War's a motherfucker, ain't it?"

Yeah, Sumo. Yeah. It's a motherfucker, all right.

"I know you go way back, Loki. Seen a million deals. But there was no woman for a kilometer in any direction when we took down Assad's compound."

"That was what *happened*. But this is a *movie*, Teddy. Nothing about it is real. Nothing! And they're right about buddy pictures. You can't do a prowar film, with all guy actors. Not in this town. Not in this century."

"I keep telling you, it's not prowar—"

"It'll *look* prowar. That's why I went to the Germans. Everybody else turned me down." She bored in, holding his eyes, his shirt collar between her fingers. His gaze followed her bony, flat chest down into her man's western shirt. "And I haven't told you this before, but the scene where Aleko dies in Strange's arms, and Strange—this tough, macho SEAL—he starts bawling on the way to the medevac, it looks, you aren't going to like this, but it looks *gay*. Not that I have anything against, I've played for that team now and then. But I'm telling you, it's going to film gay or, even worse, hokey. Having a woman's only going to help. Then *she* can die in his arms, like Rachel Weisz in *Enemy at the Gates*."

"This is exactly what I hate about this town. What I don't understand is, why did I come back?"

She shook his arm. "Don't be a child! Of course it'll be your movie. Your name'll be on it. Now come back to the table, protest, give in, then ask for something *you* want. You can't have everything your way. You know that. You grew up here."

Teddy ground his teeth, looking away from her. "Fuck it. Make her the pilot," he grated, in a strange, low voice. Dominic came past with champagne and Teddy grabbed a flute off the tray, spilling some, chugging it as he pushed out of the sunlight, off the patio, into the bar. Shaking her head, Dittrich went back to the table.

He stood watching the television, the air cold on his sweaty arms after the hot glare on the patio. No one around him said anything. They just stared at the screen.

After a while Muruzawa came in. Then Loki. Last, the Germans. They all stood together watching.

Werner's cell went off. He flinched and walked back outside to answer. When he came back, he said, "We are sorry. There will be no financing. Not now. Not with this. The plug is pulled. It is no one's fault. I am very sorry."

Teddy set the empty glass on the bar. The footage kept running, over and over, the immense towers collapsing on themselves, thousands of tons of concrete and flesh turned to pillars of ochre smoke that flowed slowly as a thick toxic syrup into the streets.

"Where are you going?" Loki said, snagging Teddy's sleeve. "We can salvage this. Let me massage the financials. Forget Morocco. We'll shoot in Arizona. Give 'em a couple of days. They'll come back. Teddy!"

Teddy Oberg half turned on his way out. He said, eyes not really on her, "Sorry, Loki. Hanneline."

"Teddy. I've put my time in on this too. *Where do you think you're going?*"

"Thanks for everything." He waved vaguely, as if all this were already ten thousand miles away. "I got a war to go to."

2

Alexandria Hospital, Alexandria, Virginia

SOMETHING in his throat. He was breathing, somehow, but something was wedged there. Choking. Trying to get it out. Can't move hands. Tied up.

The Black.

Coming to again, indeterminable millennia later, floating up. So they had him in the tank. The aliens were so cunning. Convincing him he was human, when he was anything but. They'd try again, though, he was sure. Try to convince him he was from Earth.

Forcing something down his throat. Sucking his brain out of his skull. The humming began, then the horrible sucking and gurgling as the machine began eating him. He didn't want to. He *didn't want to—*

He opened his eyes to brilliant light and snouted alien faces. He couldn't move. They'd paralyzed him with their stingers. Implanted their horrible eggs.

"Is he responsive?"

"Mr. Lenson. Are you awake? Don't try to talk. Blink up at me. There's a trachea tube in your throat."

He blinked. They discussed him as he drifted floating, helpless, a stellar-grade agony in his lungs. Was he still in the saucer?

One of the faces said, "This might hurt."

When the tube came out, it was as if his whole trachea were coming out with it. A terrifying suspicion dawned: He *was* human.

"He felt *that*," a female voice said.

The male voice. "Don't try to talk. You're in Alexandria Hospital. We'll give you something for the pain."

The sting of an injection. He fell through centuries of silver sea, then slowly surfaced again. This time the face over him looked familiar. Dark-haired. Gray eyes like his own.

"Nan," he croaked. Her hand was warm on his arm. He flinched.

Something was biting his finger. He lifted it to see a cord trailing off out of his vision.

"Don't talk, Dad. You breathed so much smoke your larynx swelled up and your airway collapsed. The doctor said you'll be all right. He took the restraints off. But you have to lie very still and drink some of this when you can."

She was lifting his head like a child's. The way he'd used to lift hers when she was sick. Tears blurred. He was human. He was alive. She was his daughter.

Then it all rushed back, the impact, the explosions, the fire—

He grunted and she had to hold him down. When he gave up thrashing and concentrated on keeping the air coming, she sat back, folding her arms just the way her mother used to.

"You're going to rest now," she said. "And when you wake up, I'll be right here."

On that note, he thought of telling her he loved her. Tried, perhaps, to say so; but finished neither the thought nor the utterance before he slid back down. A fish in a warm, thick sea . . .

"MR. Lenson. Are you listening? You had a close call with smoke inhalation, at the Pentagon. You remember the attack?"

"Yes . . . when?" He was horribly hoarse and thirsty. He seemed to remember something, but it kept teasing away when he got close. "Nan! Where—"

She leaned into view over him and he relaxed. The doctor went on, "That was yesterday. You came here in critical condition, but you seem to be pulling through. Some military people were here asking about you. Including a very large, very impressive African-American man. You weren't conscious, so we didn't access him. He said to tell you, 'I pay my debts.'"

"'I pay my debts,'" Dan echoed. But didn't understand. The only very large, impressive-looking black man he could readily think of was Nick Niles. But somehow, he couldn't see the guy taking time out to visit. Much less admit to owing him anything.

"I'd say you're out of immediate danger, but we want you to stay for observation. You're getting medication for your pain and also to reduce the swelling. You may notice shortness of breath with exertion. It'll take time for your lungs to fully heal. Do you smoke?"

". . . No."

"Then don't start. You may have residual scarring and shortness of breath. You may have persistent hoarseness. I want to keep you here at least another day."

". . . Others."

"We have plenty of beds, if that's your question. Everyone's being treated." The doctor rose, glancing toward the door. "I have other patients, but I'll be back. Press the button on the side of your bed if you need attention."

"I'll take care of him," Nan said. She groped across the sheet, and he felt her hand again.

SOMETIME later he suddenly remembered and tried to get up again. ". . . Blair."

But he could read in her face his daughter didn't want to answer. He waited for the bad news. To help, he muttered, "I was on the phone with her. Just for a few seconds. After the South Tower got hit. She was with some others. Trying to find a way out. Something about an elevator. We didn't get to talk long."

"We don't know," Nan said. "I called Grandma. She hasn't heard anything either. Grandpa's getting packed to drive to New York and look for her."

She took a breath and looked away. "But . . . the towers collapsed. The whole World Trade Center. Some people got out. She might be all right. But I won't lie to you, Dad. You always said, people you love deserve the truth. And the truth is, a lot didn't make it out. Thousands."

He closed his eyes. Didn't want to believe it. That didn't mean it hadn't happened. But it was like Schrödinger's cat. As long as he didn't know she was dead, she might still be alive. Some people said they could feel if the other was dead or alive. He doubted he was that intuitive.

"Mom called. She wanted to know if you were all right. I told her you were here. I hope that was okay."

"Sure, sure." He and his ex didn't get along, and now that Nan was grown, they didn't bother with the appearances. He tried to tug himself upright and succeeded. The room was smaller than he'd guessed.

He saw what he wanted. But just getting his upper body vertical had exhausted him. His throat felt as if somebody had thrust a hot poker down it. Nan plumped the pillows and he sank back. "Television," he muttered. She hesitated, then handed him the remote.

He watched all that afternoon. There was nothing else on. The cameras kept replaying the collapse, then cutting to the wreckage. Hundreds of police and firefighters had been inside. Teams were cutting their way in, searching for survivors. So far, though, there didn't seem to be much hope. If Blair had gotten out, where would she go? He remembered his cell and sent Nan into the closet. His clothes were there, but the phone wasn't.

Fallen out of his pocket, most likely. He asked her to call Blair's cell, but didn't even get voice mail.

He wasn't the sharpest knife in the drawer. The drugs. Probably his blood still wasn't carrying all the oxygen it usually could, either. But as he watched the screen hour after hour, several conclusions sank in.

Someone smart and determined had studied America for a long time. He, or they, had used suicidal fanatics to turn fuel-laden airliners into deadly weapons. Most astonishing, the plan had worked to perfection, except for one aircraft, whose passengers had apparently revolted. Given their lives, but saved what the commentators seemed to think was either the Capitol or the White House.

The president had seemed first bewildered, then confused. Then he'd simply . . . disappeared. To an "undisclosed location"—a strange and somehow ominous locution. Dan figured it meant Air Force One, dropping from the sky at remote bases to refuel. The military's airborne command posts would be aloft too, the ones that screamed out of Langley and Colorado at a moment's notice. The vice president seemed to be making all the decisions. The networks occasionally showed the Pentagon, which was still burning.

At first he was numb. Then angry. Thousands of innocents. A darker day than Pearl Harbor. Civilians had died there too, yes, but they hadn't been the primary targets.

Then anger itself soothed beneath the silver singing of the drug, and he saw more deeply.

Whatever had designed this was no unlettered barbarian. He understood the language of symbols, and the oceans of molten hate on which the tectonic plates of culture floated. Bin Laden, if he was indeed responsible—and he seemed to be the primary suspect, according to the networks—had attacked the towers once before. He'd attacked Washington before too, a strike Dan, and others, had aborted at the last moment, delivery aircraft already in flight, a deadly cargo swelling their aluminum bellies.

This time he'd succeeded, and burned his message into eyes and memories around the world. Now every American thought of Islam as the enemy. Already the most ignorant and violent were attacking women who covered their heads, shooting out the windows of mosques, harassing anyone who even looked Middle Eastern to them. Every Muslim now carried that image too, but subtly altered to a two-horned syllogism: *America is my enemy*, and *America is weak*.

The United States would strike back. Its leaders would counter *America is weak* by setting in concrete *America is my enemy*. Go to war, and create millions of united enemies where there'd been scattered hundreds.

But not striking back would only confirm the charge of weakness, of softness, of a rotten empire ready to be brought down.

An irresolvable dilemma.

Exactly as bin Laden had planned. No doubt he was celebrating today, wherever he was.

All this the drug showed Dan with unbending clarity. He lay staring at the screen, his daughter beside him, overcooked spaghetti, limp lettuce, and lime Jell-O untouched on the tray. And felt the world change.

What would his role be? First, they had to locate the men behind this. Then, destroy them. Inevitably, the initial response would be largely Navy. The sea service owned the forces on station around the world. There'd be carrier air strikes, missile strikes. Later, perhaps, the Marines and SEALS would go in.

And there was Blair. Playing into bin Laden's plans or not, he'd avenge her. And the thousands of others who'd died in those obscene columns of ocher smoke. That scorched-black, still-smoking patch of Pennsylvania hillside. The still-flaming roof of the Pentagon.

He watched, listening to the panic, the uncertainty, the bewildered rage. Watched again panicked thousands streaming through ash-shrouded streets. Then turned down the sound and reached for the plate. He wasn't hungry. His throat flamed. But he forced himself to chew, then swallow, hauling the plastic fork up trembling again and again.

Soon he would need all his strength.

3

Sana'a, Republic of Yemen

DEAD air yielded to a ringtone. Aisha's hand tightened on the phone. The office had belonged to the regional security officer, but the task force had taken it over. A small room on the third deck, windowless, with a secure phone, whiteboards, a SIPRNET terminal cadged from the defense attaché, a folding table. She visualized the telephone beside his bed, in Wilkes-Barre. Beside the Chinese-style furniture his ex-wife had picked out. Checked her watch again; he should be home from work by now. If he'd gone in today; from what they were saying on CNN, a lot of people hadn't.

A click. Then silence. "Albert?" she said. "Bertie, is that you?"

"Aisha?"

She closed her eyes, visualizing his kind brown eyes, his hound-dog face. They'd met aboard USS *John C. Stennis*, during the battle group's deployment to the Arabian Gulf. Albert had been a Programs Afloat College Education instructor, teaching algebra and beginning calculus. As the only civilians aboard, it had seemed natural to sit together in the wardroom, or carry their trays to the same table on the mess decks. Over the weeks between ports, a friendship had grown. They'd kept in touch afterward by e-mail and made a date to meet again when they were back in the States.

She knew the statistics. Not many brothers wanted to commit. But Albert had been worth waiting for. "It's me. You sound so far away. I can hardly hear you."

"Oh. Where . . . where are you? Are you all right?"

"Yes. Yes, I'm still in Yemen." She checked her watch again; the team was going to meet in seventeen minutes, discuss what to do. The world had gone upside down. The images were appalling. The tremendous towers disintegrating, turning to dust before their eyes. Thousands killed, the *Early Bird* and *Times Online* said. She rubbed her forehead, eyes squeezed shut.

Even though intel had predicted it for years—nonstate actors, weapons of mass destruction, nerve-gas attacks, dirty bombs—it still felt unreal.

And it seemed that Muslims, or rather, fanatics who called themselves Muslims, were responsible. "Are you still there?" she asked, though she could hear him breathing, and a tinny, excited voice behind him. Was his television on?

"Yeah. Still here."

"The news? Is that what I hear?"

"Yeah." Patterson seemed to shake himself. "Did you talk to your mom? She's worried about you. And worried you might think she was hurt, or Tashaara. They're both safe at home. Tashaara's not going to school today."

"I talked to them. Got through half an hour ago. We didn't talk long, though. Did they say anything about the mosque?"

"Maryam said there were cops there. Protecting it, I guess."

Aisha seized the nettle, but gently. "I might have to stay out here, Albert. We might have to put the wedding on hold."

"Your mom's already done that. Called the cake people, and the caterer, and the, uh . . . the imam."

Aisha closed her eyes. Forced a resignation she didn't feel into her voice. "Well, that's probably the best decision. For right now."

A hand on her shoulder. Tim Benefiel, embassy security. She resisted the impulse to shove the hand off. "Meeting, Aisha. Ambassador's office."

"Be right there."

"What's that?"

"Just talking to somebody here. We're going to an increased level of . . . never mind."

"Higher security? Are you on alert there?"

"Forget I said that."

"You're not in danger, are you?"

She remembered the hatred in Al-Nashiri's eyes, his threat. She rubbed her cheek; it still ached where he'd slapped her. "No, we're safe here. You can tell Maryam that. But even if we have to postpone, that doesn't mean you can't do your Shahadah, Albert. You and Imam Sala'am can do that without me."

"Yeah, I know. But if you're not here—"

"It's very low-key, Albert. You just say the vows in front of witnesses. Accept God, and they'll all help. They'll be your family. You said you missed having a family." She checked her watch again. Five minutes. "And you'll have me, and Tashaara, and we'll all be together. And maybe someday—we're not too old yet—"

"Aisha. You don't get it."

The sinking feeling intensified, as if she were in an elevator, dropping fast. "What's wrong, Bert?"

"I'm not converting."

"But you were going to—we agreed—"

"That was *before*. I talked to a preacher here. He strongly recommends I not do this. Not now. Not ever."

"Meeting, Aisha." Doanelson, the FBI man pushing past.

She pressed the phone to her ear. "I don't understand, Bert. If you don't convert—"

The distant voice hardened. "Why does it have to be me? Get baptized. There's Baptists in Harlem, aren't there? You said your people in Carolina were Baptist. And your grandmother in Detroit. You'd only be coming home."

She inhaled, but there didn't seem to be any oxygen. "So you mean—you're not marrying me?"

"We can get married. But *you* have to convert. Not me. I'm not going to join a bunch of religious murderers. Those people who hijacked those planes, Aisha. They didn't just kill white folks. My cousin knows a woman who died in the South Tower. I'm not joining any religion like that."

"We're not all—"

"Aisha, meeting! *Right now!*"

"I'll call you back, I have to go," she said rapidly, and hung up. Pushed her fingers into her eyelids, took a deep breath. Searched blindly for her purse, before she realized it was under her chair, right where she'd put it.

THE ambassador wasn't in residence. Mrs. Bodine had left, Mr. Hole wasn't yet in-country, so Fontanelle, the DCM, deputy chief of mission, chaired. She barely heard his first few sentences, but forced herself to tune in, to forget her shaking hands. She *wasn't* going to weep. Not about her own little concerns, when so many had just died.

It might not even be the attack, or the religious issue. Asking anyone to be part of your life, as a law enforcement professional, was asking a lot. From what she heard from the other women, it was even chancier for a female agent, with a signed mobility agreement underlining that "home" was where the NCIS sent you. Finding a man willing to put his own career second . . . but she'd thought Albert, with his footloose, ship-following lifestyle, might be able to cope.

Now, it seemed, he wasn't even going to try.

When the meeting ended, she cupped her elbows in her palms and walked slowly back through the embassy. Through a disturbed buzz of voices, the electronic emoting of television; every set was on. Staffers were cleaning out desks and packing briefcases and taking pictures of each other in front of the windows. Every screen was replaying the same footage. The silver-black blur of an approaching aircraft. The towers, subsiding like melting sand castles. Screaming people running, pursued by a formless, light-sucking void. A blizzard of paper and ash.

And falling bodies.

Today, for the first time, photographs of young men; swarthy, clean-shaven, or with mustaches, scowling into passport cameras. She went into the women's room and locked herself into a stall. Stood, then knelt. The tile hurt her knees. She waited, staring at her face in the water.

When she was done throwing up, she cleaned herself up and went back out. Stood in the door of an office, making herself watch the coverage. Trying for professional objectivity. This was a crime. Perhaps the greatest in American history. She was a trained investigator. Sworn to serve.

The DCM had said they had twelve hours before the evacuation. All dependents had been sent out of Yemen after the car bomb at the British embassy. Now the rest of the staff was pulling out. Except, of course, for the joint team.

We'll stay, she thought. But what will we do? Yemen's a long way from Manhattan.

But not that far from Saudi. "At least two of the suspected hijackers held Saudi passports," the screen was saying.

The Saudis. After the bloody occupation of the Holy Places in 1979, they'd bought off the Islamicists with cash and jobs. Promoted their fundamentalist, intolerant Wahhabism with billions of petrodollars for new mosques, madrassas, institutes of Islamic jurisprudence from Morocco to Indonesia. They preached against women's rights, democracy, and secular law. Not all fundamentalists were terrorists. But when they rubbed up against the modern world, a certain minority, already primed with paranoia, would detonate.

Now the chickens were coming home to roost. Bin Laden was the shadowy heir to construction millions. His family was Yemeni, his father a Saudi confidant. The son had fought in Afghanistan, befriended dictators in Sudan, then gone back to Afghanistan to finance and support the one-eyed Mullah Omar and his rabid Taliban.

This wasn't the Islam she knew. But it was the face the world was seeing now.

The man in the office, a passport control officer, turned from his screen and saw her. They were acquaintances. Had drunk coffee together in the little cafeteria with its shelves of plastic pastries and pots of hot soup and glass-fronted soft-drink machine. She smiled. But now his face closed. He didn't greet her. Just looked away and began packing his briefcase. Ignoring the dark-skinned, too heavy woman in the generous abaya and the headscarf that might well be taken for a hijab, out in the streets of Sana'a.

She clenched her fists, nausea rising again at the back of her throat. And turned away.

BENEFIEL and Doanelson were in the task force office, for a wonder not on the phone. She went for it immediately and got to it a second before the FBI man. "I'm calling Washington," he growled.

"So am I." She punched in numbers and waited for the hiss and beep of the sync.

"Executive assistant director for CT. Special Agent Coates."

"Jeremy? This is Yemen Joint Task Force, Special Agent Ar-Rahim. Aisha—we met at the Arabic seminar. I guess I shouldn't ask how it's going today."

This conversation went better than the one with Albert, but not much. Did they want her back in Washington, to help with the investigative effort? The answer came after a hesitation: not just now, they were reorienting, calling back recently retired agents. She should stay where she was; the task force might even be beefed up. She offered to help translate. If they e-mailed documents, she'd turn them around overnight. The service was short of Arabic speakers, she knew that. Again, the hesitation. No, the FBI would take the lead on that. Force protection, that was what they needed from the Yemeni Resident. Keep the channels open to local law enforcement and intelligence agencies.

Doanelson was striding back and forth. Glaring at the phone. She frowned at him. Mouthed, *Find another one.*

"I'm seeing on TV, they're saying the attackers were Saudi and Egyptian Muslims. Is that the official word?"

"Still an open question, Ar-Rahim. I understand your concern. But that's all I can say right now. The Pentagon's still on fire. We can see the smoke in the sky from out front by the cannons. I'll keep you in mind if we need you. Otherwise, just sit tight."

The other phone rang, the local outside line. Doanelson eyed her. He didn't like to answer it because usually whoever was calling didn't speak English. She waved to him to pick it up. He folded his arms and looked at Benefiel. The junior NCIS agent got it. He listened. Held it out. "Aisha. For you."

Doanelson sighed and left the office. "Have them call back," Aisha told Benefiel.

"It's General Garmish's office. Colonel Al-Safani."

Thoughts leapt through her brain, driving out disappointment and resentment. Al-Safani. Whose office she'd been slapped in. Whom Saudi counterintelligence had reported deep in discussion, at a café, with the man the PSO now held in their dreaded cells deep below the headquarters. Who almost certainly had links with ALQ.

She wrapped up the call to DC and accepted the other phone. *"Saheeda, Mûqoddam Al-Safani."*

"Mahabtain."

"Khayf halick, sadiki?"

"Quayssa, shukran. Your Yemeni accent improves each time we speak, Special Agent."

"I will say the same for your English."

"You are too nice," he said and giggled. Then sobered. Went back to Yemeni. "We are shocked at this news from New York. These are the same criminals we are fighting here. These dangerous killer elements of bin Ladenism. Will your president remember we offered aid against them? When the time comes?"

What aid? she thought, but said only, "We will remember our friends. And also those who sheltered the ones who drew the sword against us."

"General Gamish wishes to personally offer our openhearted assistance. This is on the order of our president."

"Shloon." Please tell me more.

"Gladly. May I invite you to headquarters, and discuss what concrete form our cooperation will take?"

"When?"

He said as soon as possible, even that night. She took him at his word and said they'd be there shortly. *"Mumtaaz. Fee aman Allah. Ma'a salama."*

"Fee amman Allah. Ma'a salaama."

Doanelson came back in as she hung up. She squinted at him, wondering what was in the mind of the shifty, cunning man who sat in the hot seat of Yemen's presidency, to make him suddenly declare his allegiance. Or had he? Playing it straight had never been Ali Abdullah Saleh's style. Why such a sudden change?

She told the FBI man, "The general wants to see us. Right away."

AS it turned out, Gamish had called the DCM first, who'd handed him to the regional security officer. Who was scheduled for a video-teleconference and said he'd send his people and come as soon as he could. Meanwhile Gamish's second-in-command, Al-Safani, had called Aisha.

Which left her in charge of the three agents who careered out of the embassy in armored Suburbans, lights flashing, sirens wailing, rifles at the ready in the lead vehicle and even, this time, one of the Yemeni army's jeeps out in front. The time for discretion was past. Now anyone who neared the convoy or attempted to block it would be fired on. She didn't like it. It would just make everyone hate the American intruders the more. But it couldn't be argued with now. She'd just have to do things the embassy's way.

At least, when she was on official business.

Sana'a street life wound down after midafternoon, but though it was nearly dusk, the streets seemed even emptier than usual. As if everybody were inside. Both Al-Jazeera and the state channel were playing footage of the collapse nonstop. As the cars howled down the ancient streets, jolting and rattling on cobbles, Doanelson told her he'd reached FBI headquarters. "And?" she said, watching men watch them from the shadowy doorways of closed storefronts. The rifles and heads of their escorts moved restlessly, scanning the rooftops as the call to prayer sounded. She ignored Doanelson's and Benefiel's glances. Said a short *du'a*, for missing prayer, but kept her eyes straight ahead.

"That was what I wanted the damn phone for. Good thing I got through. We got new orders. Whatever's necessary."

"Beg your pardon?"

"The interrogation. Al-Nashiri. They said, use whatever means necessary. Find out what he knows about the hijackers. Their plans. Any other operations. He's the highest recently active ALQ in custody. At least, that we have access to—the Paks and Russians might have some, but so far they're not sharing. Vacuum it out of him and send it back."

She rocked as the speeding SUV took corners. "Whatever means necessary." She'd never heard the phrase used before. Not in federal service. What did it mean?

The gates of the castle were open. The barrier was up. The guards were ranged along a newly sandbagged emplacement from which the flared barrel of one of their big Russian machine guns poked out. The lead jeep turned into the courtyard. A slim figure silhouetted against floodlights— the colonel—waved the white cars through. "Putting on the dog, this time," Doanelson murmured.

Gamish's office was large, with a queerly-carved gold and veined marble fireplace in the old Ottoman style. Another of so many offices she'd sat in across the Mideast, playing chess with so many spymasters and police chiefs. Or maybe poker was the better analogy. Accepting another of how many thousands of cups of bitter coffee. Plowing through the chitchat that had to be endured before anything substantive could be addressed, however tangentially.

This time, though, the formalities were brief. Gamish was in full uniform. He took her hand, surprising from an Arab male. Bowed over it. "This is an evil day for your country. And, I fear, for ours."

"Thank you, General."

He waved a hand. "Another call from the prime minister. People think he is powerless, in our system, but believe me, that is not so. We are prepared to cooperate in your investigations. Completely. We will also extend refueling facilities for your navy once again."

"Thank you, General. And for these very helpful arrangements . . . ?"

"There will be no price. No haggling." His narrow face sharpened. "We too are beginning to realize there are no limits to which these people will not go. We accepted Saudi money. Saudi religion. But you should not swallow honey without inspecting it for ants. Al-Nashiri is yours."

She glanced at Doanelson. He took a step forward, and she hastily turned back to Gamish. "Ours? How do you mean that, General?"

"Direct interrogation. With all the assistance at our command."

"About time," Doanelson muttered. "Let's take the gloves off."

"The gloves indeed, Special Agent Doanelson, are about to come off. I hope you will like what you see and hear, when they do." Gamish looked grave; Benefiel apprehensive; Al-Safani grim. Understandable, if he'd backed or helped these people. It had to have been with Gamish's consent, or even President Saleh's; but backblast always seemed to take out the level just beneath the higher-ups.

She caught a glimpse of her own face in an age-freckled, marble-and-gilt mirror. She looked neither frightened nor vengeful. Only determined.

"Shall we get to it?"

She nodded reluctantly, and followed Al-Safani to the marble steps leading down.

AFTER Al-Nashiri's interrogation, no one said anything in the SUV on the way back through the dark streets. It was 4:00 a.m. Close to dawn. Her ears were still ringing, knees still shaking. She gripped her purse. Across from her Doanelson and Benefiel did not meet her eyes. Each seemed sunk within himself.

They'd split the interrogation. First, her and the FBI. The implication being that they were the good guys, or at least the ones who wouldn't get their hands dirty. But this time, when Al-Nashiri stayed defiant, the PSO had taken over. Doanelson had wanted to go down to the basement with them; she'd had to read the riot act to keep him from sitting in. And seen the unspoken question in his eyes: Why are *you* so concerned?

But sometimes that was what counterintelligence was like in the Mideast. At least Gamish hadn't insisted they watch.

Whatever's necessary.

At any rate, the PSO could no longer be accused of not cooperating. She cleared her throat, remembering Al-Nashiri's battered mouth when they'd brought him back. His hands had trembled uncontrollably; he'd looked shriveled, decades older. "We'll have to write this one together," she muttered.

"Ma'am?" said Benefiel, jerking. He wiped his face with his sleeve. Losing one's innocence was always traumatic.

"The interrogation report. We write it together. Only what we observed. Only what he told us. About the breaching attack."

They'd gotten a lot, though not all of it was usable. She'd have to evaluate it dispassionately, which she certainly couldn't just now. Yes, Al-Nashiri had been ALQ. The link between the locals who'd planned the ship bombings from El-Hadedah, Makullah, and Ashahr. Al-Safani had been involved, all right. He'd stood with downcast gaze as the prisoner accused him through his shattered mouth. The colonel had murmured about keeping contacts open. Aisha hadn't probed it. Allegiances were shifting. Better to keep that process moving, than point fingers.

They hadn't learned much about New York. The old man didn't seem to have been privy to that operation. But now they knew who had the Saggers, the antitank missiles. Where they were headed. And they had names: Yemeni, Saudi, Afghani, British. More suspects to pick up, more grist for the databases. Bin Laden's reach was daunting. The organization was far bigger than she'd thought. Worldwide.

They also knew something more immediately important.

A foreign ALQ cell was going to attack the embassy. A breaching attack. Blast through the walls, push in a suicide squad, kill everyone. Al-Nashiri didn't know who, only that they were foreign and would be based here in Sana'a. She had to tell the deputy chief. Get security beefed up. She and Doanelson would send a joint report, write it together. Now, before dawn.

She'd gotten no sleep at all, and there probably wouldn't be any tomorrow either. She stretched and hid a yawn. Her mouth tasted of vomit. She put her head back against the cushions, trying to forget what the old man had called her, over and over, through the bubbles of blood.

4

New York

B LAIR didn't so much emerge or swim up as simply open her eyes and there the world was again. A shape hovered in the striped light from a venetian-blinded window. It had a name. Names were attached to objects. But the names themselves wouldn't come.

Other, less geometric shapes came and went. After a time she recognized them as people, but nothing more.

Later she put a name to a transparent bag of fluid hanging by what must be her bed. Then, suddenly, to a voice. She rolled her head and opened an eye. "Dad?"

"Honey." Her father smiled, familiar reddened cheeks and big, broken-veined nose, looking older than she remembered. His skin coarser, silver hair thinner, with sun blotches she didn't remember being there before. As if she was actually seeing him, rather than the picture she carried in her mind from long ago. But his hand on hers felt the same, big and rough and warm. "Back with us?"

"Think so."

"Don't talk. You need to rest."

"The Trade Center."

"Let's talk about that later."

"Dan . . . where's Dan?"

He didn't answer. Maybe she hadn't actually said it aloud. She got her left hand up after a struggle with something soft and touched her face. A hardness guarded it. Had she grown a shell? "I can't see out of this side."

"That's a bandage. The doctors had to fix your eye. But you'll get it back. You'll get everything back, honey. Now just go back to sleep, okay? I'll be right here. Right here with you."

She closed her eyes and lay resting. Holding his hand.

. . .

"MS. Titus. Ms. Titus."

She felt stronger, but her whole right side hurt. She couldn't move her right arm or leg. She slowly realized they hurt like fucking sin. Was she paralyzed? Where was her dad? A nurse came and turned her over. Did she need to go to the bathroom? She did but it was a long and humiliating task, and when it was over, everything really, really ached and burned.

She lay and tried to remember, and little by little it came back. Except she couldn't remember getting out. She recalled the firefighters, trudging up the stairwell as if scaling a mountain. Calling after them to be careful. The scrape and rasp of heavy boots and heavy breathing. Then she and Cookie and Sean going on down the empty stairwell. Cookie so heavy. Sean flashing Blair a grin. And then the slamming. A noise she'd never forget, as if the sky itself were falling in on them.

Maybe there at the end a hot hard fist of wind, a flash of scorching air. Burning her as she screamed.

Then . . . then . . .

She fought her breathing until she got it back under control and lay there flaming in pain.

A male face over hers. Murmured questions. Then the head of the bed powered upward. The rest of the room rolled up into view. A man in a white coat, and across from him, her dad. Silent. Looking worried.

"Blair, I'm Dr. Doen. Your surgeon." Stocky and serious-looking, about forty. Two young women standing behind him, holding clipboards. Jotting notes. "Do you know where you are? Has your father told you?"

"A hospital, I assume."

"Do you know what year it is?"

"Two thousand and one."

"Good. You were brought here four days ago from the South Tower. To what point do you remember things, Blair?"

"I was with two others. In the stairwell. We were almost to the ground floor. Then we heard a noise. A huge noise. I woke up here."

"That noise was the South Tower collapsing. You're a lucky woman. *Very* lucky; always remember that. Okay? You were pinned under hundreds of tons of burning wreckage. A rescue team from Ohio found you buried in a stairwell, covered with concrete. They had to put a fire out to get to you, which explains your burns. But you must have been close enough to a wall or some support structure to have some shelter when the building came down." Doen glanced at something in his lap.

"What about the others?"

"I'm sorry. What others?"

"Sean and Cookie. They were with me."

"I don't believe they made it," Doen said, looking at his lap again. "At least, you were the only one brought out alive from that section of the collapse."

"How badly am I hurt?" she whispered.

He cleared his throat. "We have hundreds of other injured to take care of, so I'm going to be brief and factual. All right? You sound as if you can handle it. They tell me you're a federal official?"

"I—I was."

"That explains the senators and generals who keep leaving messages. Well, you're seriously injured. You have fractures to the right hip, right arm, and crush and burn injuries to the right face and eye. It took us seven hours to put you back together. The fractures were simple breaks. I think you'll be happy with the way the arm heals; the hip may be a little rougher.

"The facial injuries are more complex. We saved the eye, but the face will be a challenge. When the skin goes, reconstruction's difficult and not always satisfactory. Hard to say, but I'd guess you'll get a lot back, but not everything. Do you want to hear more? Or is that enough for now?"

". . . More." She groped with her left hand, encountered her father's. Gripped it.

Doen told her about crush and burn injuries and what happened with full-thickness skin loss and cartilage. She'd lost her right eyebrow and ear and eyelid and other skin on her face. Some of the facial bones were broken, but she forgot the names as soon as he said them.

"Is there . . . brain damage?" she muttered. Her father looked away.

"Don't think so. Crushing's not as bad that way as high-velocity impact. You're getting a pretty heavy titration of painkillers. Once we taper that off, you'll have more pain, but your acuity should return. At that point, we'll get some of these bandages off. Then we can discuss follow-up surgery. Reconstruction." He looked at one of the women, then back at her. "We have specialists to help you cope with this. A shock. I know. But remember, like I said—you were lucky to survive. Thousands didn't. Any questions?"

She asked if he meant plastic surgery, and he said yes, but he didn't want to get into the details; surgeons would give better advice once they saw what kind of damage they were dealing with. He stood and her dad stood too. They shook hands and Doen patted her shoulder. Then he was gone.

She lay and looked into the light. Her dad came back. Then she remembered; how could she have forgotten? "Dan. Did you hear from . . . where is . . ."

"His daughter called. He's in hospital too. Smoke inhalation, but not critical now. There was an attack on the Pentagon as well."

The Pentagon too? She tried to struggle up. What else didn't she know about? But her father's hand pressed her down again. "Just lie quiet, I'll tell you."

He told her things she both couldn't believe and yet recognized as what the secret estimates had long predicted. Nonstate actors, spreading terror in the name of religion. The president declaring a crusade. She squeezed her eyes closed, feeling something crawling inside the right one, the hidden eye, as she did so. A queer, nauseating tickle. She wanted to go to the office. Her old office, in the Pentagon. Maybe it was wrecked by now. What about her aide? Her staff? The civil service civilians? Would it be a breach of protocol for her to call and find out? Well, she didn't give a damn if it was.

"Dad? I want to use your phone."

HE wouldn't let her. Kept telling her to sleep. But it hurt too much to sleep. Finally she told him she had to pee again, to get the nurse. As soon as he was gone, she began worming her way to the side of the bed.

It was incredibly painful, and she was sobbing by the time she could stretch out for the phone, where he'd left it on his chair. She almost slid off the bed, but finally snagged it. Concentrated, and pushed in numbers.

By the time he came back, she'd talked to one of her old staff buddies at House Armed Services, to her former military aide, and to Bankey Talmadge, the oldest warhorse in the Senate. She hid the phone under the pillow and sent her father out for a *Post.* As soon as the nurse was done, she was back on the phone again. Dan's cell didn't answer and all she got at home in Arlington was their answering machine. She tried Nan's number, but there seemed to be a lot of traffic and some of her calls weren't going through. She called two generals and caught one, then talked at length to a political appointee in the West Wing. She was from the other party, but they'd both been DAR State Regents and always gotten along and sometimes even traded favors. Under the table, of course. Girl to girl.

When she was done, she checked the battery. Not much juice left. She tried Dan again. Again, no luck.

She called a three-star woman admiral and then a congressman from Maryland. She called Hanumant Giory's number at Cohn, Kennedy, thinking the call might be forwarded, but got only the "number has been disconnected and is no longer in service" message.

She hid the phone as the door opened again. Her dad, with the paper. She felt nauseated and weak, and it was much harder to read small print with one eye than she'd expected. He offered to read to her. She accepted gratefully and lay back with eyes closed, sipping a glass of water, while he went down the front page and then the international news. Just as she'd gleaned over the phone, the administration was beating its chest about all-out war. Ridiculing the previous administration as weak on terror. She remembered the mountains of Uzbekistan, and those were just the foot-hills of the Hindu Kush. Pushing a U.S. force into those mountains . . . the last time the Army had done anything like that was in Korea.

Slowly, through the pain and weakness and confusion, anger rose. This administration would push their own agenda. Channel billions to their pa-trons. What else was new? Her own family had done the same thing during the Civil War. It was the nature of politics, and of war. But it didn't mean whoever had done this wouldn't have to pay. They *had* to. For all these dead.

The only remaining question was, what role would she play in it?

NOT until late that afternoon was her dad able to get him on the phone. When her father held the cell to her ear, she almost couldn't speak. Finally murmured, "Is that you?"

"Blair. Been trying to get through. . . . How are you? Your dad said you were pretty badly injured."

His voice was so hoarse it sounded like a bad Louis Armstrong imita-tion. But it was him. He was alive. They traded war stories and commiser-ated about whatever evil star had put them both at their respective ground zeros. He said he'd gotten out of hospital two days before, stopped by the house for a uniform change, and was now in Virginia Beach.

"So you're back at TAG?"

"For the moment."

"What's that mean?"

"It means, JCS didn't have any con plan ready for something like this. We're waiting for Higher to come up with one. Once we get that . . . I can tell you then."

She couldn't get any more than that, and he probably didn't know any more. She knew the military planning system would be grindingly slow. The administration was making warlike noises, but it would take months to get a sizable force anywhere. Like the buildup to Desert Storm. "But, Dan, you're Navy. Isn't this going to be a land-forces job?"

"Come on, Blair. That's TAG's job, to address emergent threats."

"Emergent *naval* threats, Dan. Does bin Laden have a submarine?" Her dad was gesturing, looking angry; and she was getting tired; her head was sagging back into the pillow. Abruptly she was exhausted, as if she'd just hiked up Everest. "I've got to get off. . . . Don't push it too hard, Dan. You always do. And don't *volunteer*, okay? You're not twenty anymore."

"Look who's talking. I'll try to get up to see you, if they let me. Say hi to Checkie."

She sank back, resentful. He had a job. She had no task, no position, and with the other side in charge, the war would not go well; they were such fucking amateurs. The pain had been gathering force. Now it was a fire glowing deep in shattered bones, a torch scorching her shattered face. She put a hand up, felt the hard shell of the bandages, forced her fingers away.

"We'll take you home," her father was saying, gathering up the paper where she'd discarded the sports section, the classifieds. "As soon as you're well enough to travel."

"Dan and I have a house in Arlington, Dad. Remember?"

"He won't be there. He'll be overseas. And you need to get away, Blair. You're not in government now. You heard Dr. Doen. You'll need more surgery. Need pampering. You can't just plunge right back in."

She turned her face away. "Into what, Dad? What can I plunge back into? Anyway, you're right—I *am* tired."

A tap at the door. The nurse, with an injection. She breathed slowly, and little by little the pain retreated. Leaving only the tremendous weakness, the incredible fatigue.

"Can you get the blinds, please? I'm going to just rest for a little."

They rattled, and the room darkened. She closed her eyes and started to slide into sleep.

A slam echoed through the building. Or maybe she'd imagined it, but she still flinched and tensed, gasping as muscles contracted around broken bones. Just a stairwell door. Or someone knocking over a chair.

A cold sweat broke out all over her back. What floor was she on? How high? She wrung the bedrail, wondering if she could lever herself out if she had to. But then what? She wanted to be on the ground floor. She wasn't going to be trapped again. No more tall buildings. Not ever.

She kept herself from asking her father the floor number. But not by much.

5

Sana'a, Yemen

NESTLED in the comforting folds of a dark blue burka, in the cigarette-smelling, too-soft backseat of the battered, rusting Nissan taxi, Aisha watched the buildings go by. They were in every tone of tan and cream and white, with such intricate, abstract carving the stone sunscreens resembled lace. A string of beads she'd bought in Mecca worked through her fingers. She sighed.

Everything had come apart since 9/11. In the world, and in her personal life. Albert didn't even want to talk on the phone, keeping his answers brief, always in a hurry to get off. Her stomach had been bothering her ever since that first long night in the cellars of the PSO. God knew plenty of bugs were going around Sana'a that tore through an American digestive system; but she suspected that wasn't all that was going on. She hadn't actually seen serious interrogation—oh, call it by its real name, Aisha—before. Maybe other federal agencies had, the notorious Other Government Agency, but not hers.

She'd heard the stories, of course. Few security forces in the Mideast had scruples about "enhanced interrogation," as the messages from Washington were terming it. The same techniques the Yemenis had employed with the old man and, since then, others the political security service had rounded up, based on his confessions.

She didn't believe she was acting against her faith. These monsters were not fighting for Islam. But that didn't mean that the names the old Salafi had called her didn't tinkle down inside her like shattered glass and lodge there, grinding and bleeding. And how could you trust what someone said when his only motivation was to stop the pain? Beating people to a pulp, then expecting what came out to be the truth—why did you even need a trained investigator?

She shook her head and blinked out the window. No interrogations were scheduled for tonight. The madness of the first week had died down, but the threat remained of an attack against the embassy. Yes, Aisha, she reminded herself, *that* had come out of the interrogations. The DCM had called them in. Find out who's behind it, he'd said. Help the host country target them.

She'd been through one embassy attack, in Ashaara, and had no desire to see another. Whatever it took to stop it, that she would do.

No huge Suburbans or army escorts, either. Not this time.

She was going to investigate this her way.

CROSSING the street in black embroidered *sharshaf*, the traditional women's outer garment, only her eyes showing. Veiling wasn't law in Yemen, as it was in Saudi or Afghanistan these days, but most conservative women veiled, and it had its advantages. Such as going into the city without sirens and flashing lights and an armed escort. She was armed—the SIG was tucked into a shoulder holster, not her purse, in case the latter was snatched—but other than that, she looked like any of the dozens of veiled shadows shopping, visiting, towing a crying child to a clinic. Not all were in black; the older women wore cover-ups in bright reds and blues. Spindly, dark Yemeni men in white robes and suit jackets strolled by in couples, talking, hand in hand, each with a dagger stuck into his belt. She went down an alley, hooked back to cross her own trail. No one looked at her twice. She walked two blocks at random, making sure she hadn't been trailed, before turning onto the street she wanted.

Like most residential lanes in the old city, this was extremely narrow. No car could make its way back here, so a medieval quiet reigned. The filigreed windows towered up and up, so close on either side someone could reach out from one side and touch the fingertips of one leaning from the other. It would have been picturesque except for the universal habit of pissing in the street, which made her hold her breath whenever the wind died.

She'd met Hiyat through the mosque. She lived in the Old Town and had invited Aisha to come by one afternoon. Yemeni women did chores and shopping in the morning, then got together in the afternoons to drink cardamom tea and eat honey pastries and talk. A *tafrutas* was the same as what her grandmother in Detroit had called a hen party, and the gossip was the same: whose husband was doing what, where to get the best cut of meat, whose son or daughter had gotten in trouble or was about to. The language changed when the women were alone together; got earthier, more colloquial. But she could nearly always follow it, and when they got too deep into dialect, Hiyat had interpreted. Aisha had shown them pictures of Tashaara and her mother and aunts, and of course they had to see Albert's picture too. It had been fun, a break from investigative routine. She'd looked forward to coming again.

This time when Hiyat opened the door, though, she looked surprised. It only lasted for a second. "Aisha, my American friend. Come in, you are welcome here, peace, peace."

"Peace to you, girlfriend. Hiyat, you look so lovely!"

It was true. Slim as Aisha could only remember being as a teenager, her long, dark hair pulled up to reveal a startlingly pale, long, graceful neck. Hiyat was only in her thirties but already had two boys nearly full grown. Four other women were sitting on the carpets in the diwan—a living room, sort of—the TV blasting music, toddlers fighting in the corner. Aisha said, *"Salaam tahiyah,"* and they nodded back; but they too looked taken aback. She recognized Gaida and Jalilah, who dropped their gazes to cups of tea and plates of cookies balanced in hennaed fingers. Here no one covered up; they were in colorful dresses, some quite stylish. Aisha pulled her own *sharshaf* off and took the low stool Hiyat showed her to.

The shyness didn't last. Soon they were offering her perfume and dates, and asking whether America was going to make war on Muslims. For sheltered women in a backward country, they seemed well informed. They knew the hijackers were Saudi, for one thing. "Salafis," Gaida said darkly. "They come here and make trouble. We were good believers long before they came, spreading new ideas. They're as bad as the Jews."

"As the Christians," one of the other women said, one Aisha didn't know. Hiyat introduced her.

Aisha didn't ask any questions. She just wanted to hear what they thought. She politely declined to have her hands hennaed and, after an hour, decided it was time to move on. It would be a long walk to the mosque. She rose and gathered her skirts, said her good-byes.

Hiyat went to the door with her. Gave her a hug. "You are the only American I know. Tell the others we're not all terrorists."

"They know that." Aisha hugged her back, but wasn't sure her words were entirely true.

Her stomach cramped as soon as she was out in the street, making her sorry she hadn't visited the toilet in Hiyat's. She looked left and right, but didn't see anyone who showed any interest in her.

The narrow, twisting lanes of a bread souk reminded her less of Arabia than Central Asia. Vendors' cries filled the dusty air. Men on buzzing, smoking Suzukis bumped past, threading between pedestrians. She walked on ancient cobblestones worn level by centuries of sandals and cart wheels. Pastries and flatbreads lay gathering flies and dust, only cursorily protected by sheets of thin plastic that flapped and crackled in the wind. Cheek bulging with qat, the methamphetamine-like leaf some Yemenis chewed all day long, a vendor bent to serve a man in a red ball cap from a coconut-juice dispenser. The gloomy, mustached president scowled down from billboards, from dusty banners. Schoolboys ran past shouting, play-ing tag; a tortoiseshell cat with a stumpy tail stalked something under one of the barrows.

Again she circled back, eyeing the alley she'd emerged from. No one she recognized, no one following her.

She decided against another taxi and walked for nearly a mile through the fading afternoon, striding along, heavy purse bumping against her hip. Men's gazes slid off. She kept glancing at her watch. Hardly anybody ever arrived on time, but as the teacher, she owed it to her students to be there at the dot of six.

When she went into the cool shadows of the room in back of the mosque, they were waiting. Not as many as usual, but the best students were there. All women, of course. And as always, they'd set a chilled lemon drink on the table to thank her. She adjusted her headwrap to uncover her face and unrolled the lesson plan stuffed in her purse.

AN hour later she stood outside the heavy wooden doors, feeling better. A visit to the women's room had helped. Maybe she could even accept Albert's decision. If his love had been that shallow, she was better off knowing now, rather than five years down the road.

Then her heart stilled.

Someone across the street had on a bright red ball cap.

She examined him in microsecond flicks, never looking in his direc-tion. The twentyish man looked, for a moment, American. His fair skin was ruddy with sunburn, and he had the same close-cropped hair as the embassy guards. Blond hair gleamed on sinewy forearms above an over-sized, aviator-style watch like the ones the marines wore on liberty. The same aviator-style sunglasses, too. But no marine would sport that ragged beard running down chin and throat, nor the gold earring. He stood with thumbs in belt loops, one leg hitched up behind as he leaned against the wall of a tailor's shop. A cigarette smoldered in his mouth. A black sports bag with a Nike swoosh, the kind you carried a baseball bat or racquet in, sagged at his feet.

She fussed with her purse as if she hadn't seen him, then turned and started walking. She went two blocks without looking behind her and re-sisted the temptation to look into windows, even the mirror in front of a jewelry shop. Turned right again. One block; another right turn.

When she passed the mosque again and glanced toward the shop, he wasn't there.

She shook her head and turned on one heel as if she'd forgotten some-thing. Went back up the street she'd just come down. Ice touched the back of her neck when halfway down the block she saw him coming down the same alley she'd just exited. His jeans were skintight, but the athletic bag sagged with something heavy. He didn't look at her, but she caught the slightest hitch in his step.

Stuffing a sudden acceleration of the heart, glancing away, she kept walking, strides even, unhurried, even as one hand, hidden under abaya and heavy, all-cloaking *sharshaf,* unsnapped the thumb tab and loosened the automatic in its black nylon sheath. Nine rounds of Cor-Bon +P+, and another magazine in reserve. It should be enough, although she wished suddenly she'd worn her Kevlar. No one would've noticed, under all the cloth.

Unless others were with him.

He turned and followed her, fifteen, twenty yards back. By now she had the click of his boots down—cowboy boots?—and stayed to the left of the street, an arm's reach from the shopfronts, so that if he came up behind her, he'd be on her right and would have to turn all the way around to identify her and fire.

They walked that way for five blocks, due east toward the embassy. Youths passed on sputtering motorbikes, and she almost pulled the SIG. It was a common assassination tactic, a handgun to the head from a passing motorbike. But these passed harmlessly between her and Red Hat, weaving and shouting, eyes bulging yellow, drunk on qat.

She kept looking for a taxi. She could step in, tell him to move out fast, and maybe escape in a scorch of rubber before her pursuer could unzip the sports bag and pull out whatever he had in there. Or she could hail one of the blue-and-white sedans the city police drove. But just as in Harlem, when you really needed a cab, or a cop, they were somewhere else.

The street widened. Dangling lights glowed ahead. She noticed with a start that it was already dusk. The rugged mountains behind the lacy buildings, the tall minarets with strange, rounded domes she'd never seen anywhere else, glowed a pink-and-rose fire.

She came out into the spice souk and breathed easier. Not that he couldn't overtake her here. But she guessed he'd want more privacy than was available with throngs picking over squash and tomatoes, drinking chai at open-air tables. Many were in the same black *sharshaf* she wore, and she suddenly saw how she'd outfox the man drifting along behind her. All she had to do was join that crowd around the tangerine barrow. Six, maybe seven women, some large as she. She'd thrust herself in among them, hunch to their height, pull the burka over her face, and drift out the other side. Leaving him to choose among six undistinguishable silhouettes in black.

She started that way, then slowed. Was that all she wanted? To escape? Her fingers brushed the weapon again. She was a law officer. No powers of arrest, not in a foreign country, but she could take him into custody. Hold him at gunpoint until the police arrived.

No. She was in a public marketplace. If she pulled a gun, he'd pull his. And some of these unsuspecting shoppers and vendors, or the kids running and shrieking underfoot, would die. If that was an automatic weapon in the bag . . .

She couldn't arrest him here.

But she couldn't just let him go, either. Yes, "officer safety." What they'd drilled into the new agents at FLETC from their first day in basic. Don't walk into a situation they're going to have to carry you out of feetfirst. Seek cover. Call for backup. Avoid tunnel vision. No heroics. Just good procedure.

But one of the enemy had stepped into sight. From that, she *could not* walk away.

What day was it? Thursday?

She turned on her heel and crossed the square, not toward the tangerine barrow, but toward a side street. Twenty steps up it was an old marble entrance, grand in its way, but stained with smoke and time. She reached into her purse, but not for Mace or even her badge.

Instead she handed five hundred riyals, a couple of dollars, to the old man at the little glassed-in cage, almost like the peepshow booths she'd goggled at as a child in Harlem and always been sharply pulled away from by her mother.

The heat hit her first, then the smells. The steamy warmth and the rich perfumes of expensive soaps. Almond. Coconut. The minty reek of wintergreen. The hall was lined with booths. Gray-haired women in white nurse uniforms or voluminous, colorful abaya sat vending towels, soaps, pumice pads, the latest rejuvenating lotions from Paris and Switzerland. Ahead, dimly glimpsed through a wavering humidity, a lofty space echoed with screams and laughter. Sunbeams solid as opal glass slanted from skylights in a barrel vault through a pall of steam that undulated above an immense bathing tank. Each doorway framed a tableau from centuries past. Hefty odalisques reclined on benches, draped with towels and thick terry bathrobes, or breast-stroked slowly across the pool. From an alcove came the meaty slapping of fists into solid womanflesh as a masseuse plied her trade. Aisha passed nude women chatting on stone benches as sweat gleamed on thighs and shoulders. A tearoom, samovar bubbling, where matrons sampled dishes of almond cookies. A shy girl giggled in pink-cheeked splendor as teenaged friends rubbed perfumed oil into her breasts, pumiced the soles of her feet, braided her hair in an elaborate coif.

Hiyat and Gaida had told her about the *hamam*s. For five days they were reserved for men; but on Thursdays, they were sacrosanct to women. No man would dare follow her in here. He'd be torn apart, by the bathers themselves or by any Islamic male who witnessed such a sacrilege.

She paid a crone with boils on her nose another hundred riyals for a private changing room. The door latched, she had a moment of doubt as she took her cell from her purse. Would it penetrate these ancient stones? But the signal was there and soon she was talking to a sleepy-sounding Colonel Al-Safani. The sleepiness vanished as she told him where she was and what she wanted him to do.

A few hours later she walked down into the courtyard of the security palace toward the white Suburban. Usually Doanelson opened car doors for her, but today he didn't stir. He looked ticked off. Beside him Tim Benefiel cowered. The junior NCIS agent took her hand as soon as she got in. "Sure you're all right?"

"Perfectly."

"You shouldn't have gone out. The deputy chief's furious. He says—"

"Who is he?" the FBI agent interrupted. "They got any idea?"

He meant the man in the red hat, whom the PSO had nailed precisely where Aisha had told them to look: in the lane outside the *hamam*, waiting for her to emerge. The object in the Nike bag had turned out to be a Czech Skorpion submachine gun.

"His passport's Bosnian. In the name Mujagic. He's European, all right."

"That could be ugly."

"He's ALQ. No doubt about that. The question is, what's he doing here?"

"Going after you?"

"Not likely. Not originally, anyway. They wouldn't send him all the way to Yemen just for that." She rubbed her sweaty forehead. "Gamish thinks he's an enforcer. The guy from out of town they send in to do the dirty work. But if he was a pro, the first thing I'd have felt was a bullet in the spine. More likely, he's a recent recruit. I might have been his first assignment."

Her voice started to waver, and she shut up and reached for a bottle of water. She'd been in danger before, in takedowns and hostage swaps. Still, her body seemed to react more violently, the older she got. Or maybe being a mother had something to do with it. She coughed and spoke on roughly, pretending more control than she felt. "The colonel's there. The general's taking a personal interest. We'll have some answers soon. Might even get lucky."

Benefiel: "A direct link to bin Laden?"

"Not a Bosnian. I can't see them trusting anyone other than an ethnic Saudi. But he might point the way," she told him.

Doanelson seemed displeased. No doubt his report would dwell on the risk she'd run, the safeguards violated. But the enemy stepped out into view so seldom, she'd had to take him down. If she was right, the Bosnian was just a foot soldier, one of the once-nearly-assimilated European Muslims radicalized in the crucible of Srebrenica. But it was the only way to learn more; to target those shadowy higher-ups who'd turned airliners into missiles.

She was just glad she didn't have to be in the basement of the palace when the man who'd been assigned to kill her met the police who were supposedly, now, on the side of the Americans.

"I don't like it," Doanelson said. To her surprise, his hand covered hers. "That they went for you. Next time you might not be so lucky."

Her eyebrows almost crawled off her face. Before she could say anything, their cell phones rang, all three simultaneously. Doanelson got to his first. "Yeah?" He listened. "Step on it," he told the driver, but they were already turning into the embassy gates, past the marines, the emplaced machine guns. The steel gates clanged shut behind them, and the moment they did, forklifts snorted forward, lifting concrete barriers like offerings to the gods of war.

THE helicopters arrived an hour later. She had that long to pack, but she didn't need an hour. Everything she owned in Yemen fit in a duffel, her purse, and her notebook computer case. Benefiel helped carry her gear out to the open field that was the makeshift landing pad. No one seemed to know what had triggered it; only that they were evacuating, everyone except a marine security team, who'd stay to prevent looting. She didn't know if it had anything to do with whatever her stalker had been persuaded to say. Or whether the NSA had simply heard the breaching operation being discussed somewhere around the world.

But word was it was imminent, and the Yemeni government had advised the Americans to leave. So she bent under the rotorwash, head clamped between the Mickey Mouse ears the flight crew pressed on them, and followed the junior agent up the steps to settle in the familiar canvas seats.

They pendulumed out of the dusking sky to match speed with a gray behemoth: USS *Duluth*, LPD-6, thirty miles off Aden. The sea was an ominous cobalt. Far off on the horizon stood *Tarawa*, the helicopter carrier that centerpieced the ready group, and the smaller, more jagged silhouette of a destroyer, a Burke- or Spruance-class, she couldn't quite make out.

She'd worked aboard them all. That was what they'd trained her for, as a fresh greenie. Resident agent aboard a carrier. Or ashore, at a naval or marine base, chasing down felonies, running death scenes. She'd had no idea then how many of her classmates, including herself, would be thrown into the world of counterterrorism. Chasing deadly, elusive, globally connected criminals, motivated not by greed or momentary passion but by cold ideology and deep calculation. She'd had to learn to develop relationships with people of other cultures, respond to their concerns while keeping her own mission in the background. Jurisdictional understanding, religious sensitivity, political awareness—minefields for all agents, but for a Muslim doubly so, or maybe cubed. She wished she'd studied more psychology, social psychology, group dynamics. Economics, sociology, international relations, religion.

Sometimes she wondered if she still belonged in the field. At some point, she was going to fail the physical. Her hips hurt, and looking in the mirror was more depressing every year. Maybe she should think about going back to school.

Or maybe, she told herself sternly, think about taking your dragon-slaying to a higher level. All over the world, an aging, baby-boomer, bureaucratic machine was being shoved into combat against an asymmetric, cunning, more agile enemy than the Soviets had ever been. The NCIS needed cultural awareness, languages, mind-set change. They needed *her*.

But would Washington realize that? Or see her as just another raghead?

The chopper flared. The flight deck grew until it passed from sight in the side window, and she reached up and gripped the handhold, bracing for an overshoot or an accident, gaze flicking to the red-and-white-striped EXIT decals she'd have to swim for underwater, upside down. Her fingers tightened. Sweat broke under her earmuffs.

No. She belonged here. If for no other reason than to prove not all Muslims were terrorists. In the United States, influential voices were claiming otherwise. Saying war was inevitable. That Islam itself was the enemy and killing Muslims the only answer. They wanted bombing, invasions, a new Crusade.

Which was exactly what the tall, cunning Saudi hoped for. If he could persuade Islam the West was its foe, that Americans were enemies and crusaders, he'd already won. And more would die than had perished in the towers.

Far more.

6

Tampa, Florida

T HE end of September, and the air was like a slap with a hot, wet towel under a glaring sun that broke waves of heat up off the parking lot. Dan coughed into his fist, throat spasming as Monty Henrickson looked for something he'd dropped that had rolled under the rented compact. The airlines were flying again, but with excruciating slowness; searches and patdowns at every boarding, even the domestic ones. Silent, skittish passengers; a sense of pervasive fear. The Pakistani at the Hertz counter smiled too hard, acted too eager to serve. Another delay at the base gate, their identifications and orders scrutinized, mirrors wanded under the car. A second ID check at an inner perimeter of razor wire and sandbagged fire points. More concrete barriers, sandbagged emplacements. Air Police in sky-blue turtlenecks, shorty M4s assault-slung over Kevlar.

Dan snapped his briefcase shut, the old one with the JPM-3 logo he'd pulled out of the closet in Arlington with his reference materials. Coughing into a tissue, he looked up at three windowless stories of faceless brick.

He remembered showdowning the GS-14 in charge of a facility much like this over whether Tomahawk could even be used for a conventional land-attack mission. In those days it had been a nuclear bird, a slow but certain retaliation long after the unthinkable had already happened. Either that, or a ship-to-ship counterpunch to the Soviet navy's heavyweight Styxes. The aviators had seen it as a threat; the Air Force had tried their best to kill it. Only Nick Niles's ruthless bulldozing, and maybe in some small way Dan's own contribution, had pulled it out of development limbo and made it a functioning weapon. Now, you wouldn't think of carrying out a strike package without clearing the way with TLAMs.

He massaged his throat, missing the woman he'd lost back then. Not that he had any regrets. He loved Blair. As he'd loved Susan too.

One had left. Another had died. But he'd never *stopped loving* them. And he figured now he never would.

"Still works," said Henrickson, looking up from his handheld. "Not even cracked. Hit pretty hard, too."

"That's great, Monty."

"Micklin Gradzny. That's who I talked to. Who we check in with."

"Let's do it," Dan said. The door hissed open; a tough-looking sergeant in Army greens bore-sighted them. Dan and the shrimpy little guy who outthought and outworked just about everyone else he knew, who'd been his right hand before, fished out their IDs and orders again.

While they were exchanging those for a CENTCOM access arranged during the flight down, Gradzny came out. He was a civilian, in short sleeves and a tie.

The Central Command compound was much newer than the headquarters complexes in Norfolk and Washington. CENTCOM—US Central Command, based here in Tampa since the mideighties—was in charge of US forces in the Mideast and Central Asia. Dan had been attached to the command before, going into Iraq as an on-the-ground targeter under Schwartzkopf during Desert Storm. The current incumbent was another Army four-star, Steven Prospero Leache. Leache had been troubled over the last year by allegations of sexual harassment, but had kept his job so far. Any pushback in Afghanistan would belong to him.

Dan didn't know where Leache himself was, but doubted it was Florida. He'd probably be in Oman, the new overseas headquarters, or on the road drumming up host-nation support. The face Dan was dreading was Lemuel Bedford Forrest Wood, Leache's J-3, director of ops and plans. The officer responsible for planning the upcoming war.

The last time Dan had seen Wood, the latter'd been a lowly one-star, commanding a joint task force in Eritrea, and Dan had been walking behind the president, carrying a briefcase of nuclear flip charts and a secure radio. Dan rubbed his mouth; neither of their previous interactions had been positive.

But TAG worked for SURFLANT, which worked for LANTFLT, a component commander under JFCOM, which served as a force provider for the other CINCs, or theater commanders, around the world. A lot of acronyms, and who knew where Dan's orders had originated, but there wasn't any way to say no.

Not that he wanted to. From what Monty had gleaned, the crisis action team here—operational planners, intelligence targeters, strike experts from all four services—were cutting and pasting a short list of standing contingency plans to match the taskings coming down from the national command authority. It sounded like exactly where Dan wanted to be. If he had to put up with resistance, it wouldn't be the first time.

Gradzny took them down a rubber-tiled corridor Dan didn't remember—
the building had been rebuilt since the last time he'd been here—and out
into a briefing room glassed in above a much larger theater area. They
were the first ones there; Gradzny put them in seats against the wall. Dan
got his hard-copy slides and notes out and went over his brief again.

The room filled up over the next twenty minutes. One-stars and O-6s,
Air Force, Army, Navy, Marines; not just from CENTCOM; he saw breast
badges from JFCOM, DIA, JCS. Two midgrade officers introduced themselves, once they put his name tag together with the light blue ribbon
danced with stars. He tried to be gracious, or at least not to growl at them.
But true to what they'd said at the hospital, it took a while to shake off
the effects of smoke inhalation. He was still coughing up stuff, and his
voice didn't sound like his own even to himself. But maybe it was good to
have the name recognition. Even if he didn't have a career anymore, he
could still turn it to advantage sometimes. Speak up and be listened to.

"Attention on deck," someone said. Everyone stood, looking toward the
door.

Wood was gray-haired, rail-thin, spectacled, in battle dress with his
trademark ivory-handled Beretta 9mm in a thigh rig. He looked much as
he had in a blowing sandstorm in Eritrea. Dan remembered the clatter
and whine of gunships; the griping of dusty, tired troops; the hard, tanned
faces of the legionaries of the Border. Wood's grimace of distaste as he'd
offered his commander in chief a bottle of water.

Just as Dan thought this, an Army captain carrying a case of shrink-
wrapped bottles handed him one. "Everybody got water?" Wood said,
looking around. "Let's get started." He took a seat at the head of the table
and put his hands flat on it.

A navy captain kicked off. "This is a first briefing to get started on Crescent Wind, the strike package for Operation Infinite Justice, the punchback
for the attacks of 9/11. You all have the commander's intent in front of you
in the briefing package.

"Unfortunately, we don't have an op plan in the can for Afghanistan. We
do have an intel package pulled together. Colonel Bullard, from JCS J-3,
will present the overview."

The Air Force colonel put up PowerPoint slides that looked as if they'd
hastily been generated from news photos. Blurry, and the color was off,
but the images were familiar. The Towers. The Pentagon. A field of debris in
Pennsylvania. And a familiar turbaned visage, smiling through his beard.
The room was silent. Then a new logo, followed by a photograph of an immense explosion somewhere in a desert. This had obviously been canni-
balized from an earlier brief, since it still read NORTHERN WATCH.

"Operation Infinite Justice will be the response to the attacks on New York and Washington. Bin Laden has claimed credit and the president intends to take him at his word. This time, there will be no photo-opportunity attacks. We suspect he currently resides in Afghanistan. This safe haven must be destroyed as the first step in the War on Terror."

Bullard explained that OGA—Other Government Agencies, milspeak for the CIA or its associates—was already in that country to link up with the enemies of the Taliban, the Northern Alliance. At the same time, pressure was being brought to bear on the Kabul regime by both the United States and the Saudis to close Al Qaeda's training facilities and extradite the leaders. "We're giving them a last chance to cooperate, but so far, Mullah Omar's sticking by his friends. State is finalizing agreements with other nations in the Gulf and Central Asia to let special forces operate from bases closer to Afghanistan than our current locations in Bahrain, Diego Garcia, Oman, Kuwait, and Turkey.

"If Omar doesn't give bin Laden up, the next stage will be a bombing campaign against Taliban and ALQ facilities in Afghanistan. JCS is still considering follow-on options. One is to commit twenty thousand troops, with additional supporting forces. The other option being considered is special-operations-heavy."

Wood's light blue eyes were fixed on the briefer. Now he said, "Special ops is dependent on heavy intelligence support."

"Correct, General. We could put in small teams, supported from the air, but the effort would be high risk and low probability of success unless we could guarantee high-quality intel on a near real-time basis—such that we could actually target the individuals and groups we needed to hit. That's our biggest problem, all around—lack of actionable intelligence. After the Russians pulled out, we forgot Afghanistan. We're paying for that now."

Wood nodded, and the colonel put up a new slide. "Whether for the conventional or specfor-heavy option, the first mission-essential task will be to degrade air defenses and communications so we can command the battle space. The Taliban have significant assets, primarily MiGs and SAM-7s, based here, here, and here . . . Kabul, Jalalabad, Kandahar. Other primary targets will be training sites and command, control, and communications sites. Operation Crescent Wind will be a replay of Desert Fox, the attacks on Iraq with cruise missiles and smart bombs to knock down air defenses so we can see our way forward."

The last slide was blank except for a date. "That's what we're here to plan. The bombing will begin no later than October sixth."

A low whistle from Henrickson. Dan blinked. Another round-the-clock exercise. No; this time, not an exercise. He coughed phlegm into his hand-kerchief. It was still coming out black. Soot from burnt fuel and burnt bodies.

Strike back? Sounded good to him.

Wood sat back, gazing at the overhead. "Well, I'll make a couple of re-marks.

"General Leach is working with State to consolidate an international diplomatic and military alliance. We have the UN resolution. And the NATO Article 5 resolution. We're moving, and the pace will accelerate. Plan on this basis: CSAR and logistics out of Uzbekistan. Tajikistan's closer, but the Soviets lost a lot of planes going over the mountains. We have a liaison team there setting things up.

"To the south, we can run B-52s and B-1s out of Saudi, CSAR out of Oman, with forward refueling over Pakistan. That's a long way, I know. We're still looking at that problem. *Kitty Hawk*'s in Japan. We took her air wing off, and we'll get her under way with helicopters and Special Forces. Get her on station off the Pak coast."

Wood's eye lit on Dan. "That'll take about two weeks," Dan said. "From Japan."

"Commander . . . Lenson."

"Yes, sir."

"That's right, at full speed, eleven days. So we'll have some more options in a week or two."

An Air Force general started asking questions. He wanted DIA to con-firm the target data he was being given. How they knew a SAM-7 was on Hill 3337, how they knew four Hinds were based at Bagram, whether the MiGs were still operational. He seemed equally doubtful about refueling.

Wood said the bombers would have to operate out of Diego Garcia. He turned back to Dan. "You're working Tomahawk, Lenson?"

"Just got here, sir, but it looks that way."

"Can the Navy take out these EW radars? SAM sites?"

"We can do a laydown, but there are friction points."

Wood nodded and Dan got up and clicked his laser pointer on. He had only a few slides, most of which he'd picked up in a one-day firehose at Fleet Combat Training Center, Dam Neck. FCTC trained the operators and had the latest information on the TLAM Planning System upgrades. The first slide showed flight parameters for the improved missile. The next showed flight radii from the Arabian Sea, the closest body of salt water.

"We have fifty missiles moving toward launch points aboard *John Paul Jones*, *Philippine Sea*, *Key West*, and HMS *Triumph*. Most are Block III birds with the GPS capability. Reliability, eighty-five percent; CEP, twenty feet. Unfortunately, we can only cover the southern-tier targets."

"What's the range?"

"About 870 miles."

Wood studied the slide. "That doesn't look like 870 miles. How far out are you shooting from?"

"That's because it's not a straight line. The flight path zags between GPS points to avoid terrain features and AA. Then, at the target, we switch to a high-accuracy terminal guidance system.

"But the problem's only partially range. We originally designed TLAM to fly at sea level, and even in the overland mission, it flies nap of the earth. The engine, control surfaces, and radar altimeter algorithms are all optimized for low attitude flight." Dan put up a slide he'd done himself the night before. "Let's say it's going up a series of mountain ranges. Like we see as we go north, into Arghandab. Thirteen, fourteen thousand feet high. We can probably make it over those. But TERCOM will have you dipping down after each peak. With the relief we're seeing farther north on the computerized topography, we won't make it up out of the valleys. The bird will impact on the next rise in terrain."

"Is that in software?" someone asked.

Dan looked at him for a second, remembering the smoky stink of burning RJ-4 fuel, the thunder of a chute in a Canadian blizzard. When he'd almost frozen to death, following up why the birds kept crashing. His mind following that back into the guts and innards of the hydraulics, the tail surfaces . . . "Yeah, but also in the rear elevator dynamic throw response. I have a message in to General Dynamics to see if they can patch some of the code, gain us more maneuverability. I'm just saying, right now we're limited in our penetration of extremely high-attitude, high-relief mountain areas. This makes the Kush a pretty effective barrier."

Wood didn't look pleased. "We'll need ordnance on these C4I targets. I was depending on the Navy. Like we depended on you, Mr. Lenson, when my guys got ambushed at Kerkerbit. When you called off my strike package."

Dan took a deep breath. It had been too much to expect that Wood would forget that. "Not my call, General. I was just the guy sitting in the chair at the Sit Room. For the record, I still think we should have supported you."

Wood looked away. "Okay, go on."

"We can commit for Kandahar, Dolangi Airfield, and points twenty miles north of a line from Band-E Kojok to Kabul. To some extent we can angle in from the southwest and fly up the valleys. That uses more fuel, but we just can't hop over these washboard ridges the way manned aircraft can. It'll be touch and go. We'll be able to cover most of the south, though."

One of the officers said, "We have some indicators bin Laden's in Kandahar. That's the Talibs' spiritual capital."

"Give me actionable targeting, and we'll nail him," Dan said. "Even if it's a bunker. I can put in a detonation delay."

"You've already said manned aircraft have the advantage—"

"That's enough," Wood said quietly, but they all went silent. "We can blame intel for not seeing this coming. Or the Navy for weapons that don't work in the mountains. Or we can give a cunning enemy credit. He picked the one place on this planet we'd have the most difficulty getting forces to, and the hardest place to sustain them once they arrived. The Afghans didn't beat the British. Or the Soviets. The terrain did.

"But we will prevail and we will achieve vengeance. I'll expect more answers, and probably a hell of a lot more questions, twenty-four hours into this.

"Thank you, gentlemen." Wood shoved back his chair, and everyone rose, at taut attention, the Army guys most of all, until the door closed behind him.

7

Coronado, California

ARCHED space echoed with the muted stutter of suppressed gunfire. The huge new range was custom designed. A vast, smooth concrete floor you could set up with barriers, mazes, all the IPSC stuff the competition guys liked. Teddy stood back, weapon slung, observing. Every SEAL was a safety officer during live-fire practice. Today it was room clearing, taking down a mix of bad guys and innocents. Something they all knew cold, but only unending drill kept the reactions sharp. A tenth of a second could make the difference between taking down a bad guy and getting taken down yourself. Especially if the bad guys had any training, Russian-style Spetsnaz or some homegrown version. So they drilled for hours on end, until no one had to think. They were in work clothes: some in jeans, civilian gear, the rest in BDUs or the black tacticals for night missions. Every day someone new walked in, called back from leave or training or less essential duty somewhere else. They were even pulling some of the already-deployed platoons in off the amphibious ready groups, the ones that wouldn't, presumably, be sent into action.

The Teams were going to war.

He'd tried his best to get back into what he considered his homie unit, but there weren't any open billets. They'd offered him the DEVGRU, where he'd get his hands on the latest tech toys before everybody else. That had been tempting. But he figured experienced bodies would be at a premium. There were only about two thousand SEALs. Eight teams, six platoons each, plus the guys in the head shed. You couldn't just issue any sailor the Budweiser. They had to qualify in diving, parachuting, close-quarters battle, hand-to-hand, demolitions, sub lockouts, HALO ops.

So he'd asked for a day to think it over and called Master Chief "Doctor Dick" Skilley. Skilley had barely survived the train-wreck insertion in Grenada and done countersniper in Desert Storm and Bosnia. He'd taken out fifteen snipers in Mogadishu with the bolt-action M24. Teddy knew him from sniper school at Camp Atterbury. "Hell, Obie," Skilley had grunted. "Sharp young dude with your trigger skills should be able to write his own ticket. After that great shot you made last year. Why the hell they jerking you around? Oh . . . heard you lost your—that big guy you were always hanging out with. The Indian."

"Hawaiian. Sumo. Yeah."

"If I was you—"

"Go on."

"I was you, I'd stay on the West Coast. If you want in on this here War on Terror they're talking about."

The Doctor had called a warrant officer he knew at SPECWARGRU, and somehow some guy who wanted to go East went East, and suddenly there was an open billet and Teddy had thrown his duffel into the Camaro and locked the house and not looked back.

Echo Platoon. A new team, new guys. But the Teams were a small force; you ran into the same faces again and again, at HALO school, at the ranges, lockout training, SDS, demolitions, the breaching course at Quantico, language training. If you didn't know a guy, you usually found you had at least one friend in common. He scratched a bristly chin. Most everyone had beards, goatees, mustaches. Going shaggy, they called it. Getting ready for booger-eating country. Gear packed, four-hour standby. They didn't know when. Or where. But it'd be soon, the CO said. Any day.

Teddy had walked the tiled hallways feeling like he was back where he belonged. The other guys were taking the piss out of him, as the Brits said. Ribbing him about Hollywood. About not being able to make it on the outside. He gave as good as he got. Familiar territory. The competition, every minute, whether you were doing rope drills or turning over spareribs on the grill at the Friday-afternoon cookout. Guys who were loud, guys who were soft-spoken, but everybody in it together and all of you knowing you could count on each other.

He pulled his weapon off his shoulder. The stubby black SOPMOD M4 was an M16 chopped and customized for room clearance and urban combat. Naval Surface Warfare Center, Crane, Indiana, had taken the design a step further, with a flattop receiver mounted with a reflex sight, flip-down iron sights, a thirty-decibel sound suppressor that looked like a perforated cigar container, and a rail interface that let you bolt on various handgrips, lasers, lights, and IR illuminators.

One of the junior guys, Swager, came over and said, "Yeah, we got to get something better."

"Better than this?" Teddy patted the weapon.

"Five-five-six is too much of a mouse gun for me. *Guns and Ammo*, last month—"

"I read that article too," Teddy said. "What those civilian writers don't understand is, this isn't a one-round weapon. 'A 5.56 doesn't punch as hard as a .308'—true. But you put this thing on auto, it's a different animal. No recoil, so you stay on target. No pistons, so there's no off-centerline thrust. Hose that lead out and blow the whole room away."

He and Swager traded jabs in an argument they'd had going all day. On most missions, SEALs could carry what they wanted. You could go with a SIG or a Glock as your sidearm, or some supermodified .45 like a Kimber or a Les Baer. Teddy never carried the GI-issue Beretta; one had blown up in his hand, firing Italian steel back into his face. For a submachine gun, he liked the MP5, from his days spidering up containers on board-and-searches, taking down oil rigs in the Gulf. They always worked, to the extent he'd started to leave his sidearm behind and just take extra mags—until one day on the deck of a qat-smuggler his main weapon had stopped a bullet and he'd had to go to his knife to eviscerate a raghead trying to bayonet him. By unanimous acclamation, he'd gotten the Bonehead Award that day. Since then he'd carried a SIG. Some guys liked a 249. Even a shotgun; he'd seen good work done with scatterguns, though he didn't care for the slow reloading—that could put you in a world of hurt. When you were going in covert, they used foreign weapons. AK-47s were a popular choice with the more badass guys, though Teddy considered the things inaccurate and avoided them when he could.

But after ten years of it, on floats in the Med and Red Sea, antiterror missions out of Stuttgart, snatching insurgents in Ashaara, taking down Iranian submarines and Saudi dhows and Chinese merchant ships, he knew it wasn't the weapon that made the warrior. It was what was inside. Sand. Guts. The Right Stuff.

The kind of stuff Sumo Kaulukukui had had.

Never leave your buddy. Dead, wounded, or alive. He had that to fight the regret: He'd never left Sumo. Been with him to the end, facing the family in dress whites as the honor squad had fired the traditional three blanks into the air. They'd flown Teddy back for the funeral. All the way to Hawaii, with a twenty-four-hour turnaround. The SEALs took care of their own.

He looked at Swager. Did this kid have it, that to-the-end courage? That tall, that pale, he'd be hard to disguise on a FAR mission. Most SEALs were from the heavier trades, machinist's mate or boiler tech or hull technician. A lot of boatswain's mates, just because the test was easier—you only needed like a 52 raw score. But Swager was a knob turner, some kind of electronics tech. Inevitably, given the Teams, that had become his nickname, Knobby. And Teddy had never heard of a SEAL from Rhode Island. The kid tried to talk like some kind of gun aficionado, but just came off sounding like a gear queer.

The stutter of suppressed full-auto fire echoed again. Men ran bent over, firing on the move. A hostage-rescue scenario. Which could be adapted into a target snatch, taking down bodyguards, sparing the HVT—the High Value Target.

Or not. The head shed was still developing the mission. The scuttlebutt was they were assigned to roll up OBL himself. Teddy doubted that. Something that big, they'd assign to Delta, or the CIA's supersecret Activity. The SEALs wouldn't politick to get a mission, like some segments of the community. But at least they were going, and about time. Late September, and the country was starting to ask: What are we doing about 9/11?

"Second relay, to the line. Chamber empty, bolt forward, magazine inserted."

He checked his weapon and joined the huddle to the side of the door. Number Two this time. A silent tap on the shoulder of the guy ahead; a clap on his own, from his backup.

The breaching round went off with a dull slam, the breacher stepped back, and Teddy followed Number One in tight on his ass and sidestepped and swept his corner. SEALs didn't go in yelling at each other, the way SWAT teams did. With a suppressed weapon, you wanted to keep surprise from room to room. The clearance team had to trust each other. If Teddy glimpsed a bad guy in a corner that wasn't his, he had to leave him to somebody else. Not too fast, not too slow. *Pop pop pop.* Two to the chest, one to the head, and he swept the rest of the room, then they took a half wall set up out of plywood and the second room and the third, rounds clattering. There was the hostage, don't shoot. More bad-guy dummies trolleyed out from a side alcove on rails, and he fired till he ran dry and reloaded, mind empty, a craftsman absorbed in his work. Noting only with a corner of consciousness that the lanky form next to him was just a little slow. As if Swager were taking that last extra tenth of a second to make sure he wasn't shooting the wrong dummy.

BUT then something happened Teddy didn't expect. "CO wants you," one of the staff element petty officers said, and pulled him off the drill. Still in his gear, sweating, he jogged down the passageway to the head shed.

"Obie," Commander Vann said, "close the door."

Teddy closed it.

"I'll make this short. You got a lot of experience. More than the rest of my incomers, reserves, retreads. Doctor Dick vouched for you, I understand. And I just learned I have a problem. A big problem."

When an officer had a problem, it was usually you. But Teddy couldn't think of anything he'd done, or not done. Actually, he'd only been back a couple weeks. "What's that, sir?"

"One of my chiefs just failed his pre-dep physical."

Teddy didn't like where this was going.

"I tried for a waiver, but the medical side's not cutting us any slack. They waivered him before; they won't release him overseas again. I know you're new to this team, but based on your record, you should be carrying some command responsibility. I want you to take over Echo. I can fleet you up to E-7, with the GRU's concurrence."

Teddy wanted to say, "I'm not sure I'm up to that, sir," but he didn't. He'd been a squad leader, after all. "Give it my best shot, sir. Uh, are we really gonna get in on this? Some of the guys are saying they're going to hold us in reserve, let Delta and the Rangers—"

"You'll get all the action you want, Obie."

"That's good, sir. Where you figure we're headed? Just so I can make sure we have the right gear?"

"Need to know, Obie."

"Yes, sir. Just figured I'd try."

"The chief will introduce you tomorrow at quarters. I'll be there. And he'll keep handling all the predeployment paperwork and evals and so on rather than putting it all on you. But once we deploy, you'll be the man. Don't let us down."

"WHAT'D he want?" Knobby wanted to know.

"Nothing," Teddy said, still trying to wrap his head around it. Maybe he should've told Vann no. Maybe it wasn't too late. They couldn't *make* him take it. He could refuse, like Montgomery Clift in *From Here to Eternity*. Anyway, a lot of shit was involved in sewing on a chief's crow. Carrying the book around, the initiation. He just didn't want to. Maybe he'd tell him that.

Tomorrow.

LIEUTENANT Dollhard told them to make it an early night. He wanted them all available on sixty minutes' notice. Dollhard was a mustang, an ex-enlisted, older and much harder than you expected of lieutenants, few of whom had tattooed biceps, either. He took no shit from anyone, including Vann, and nobody made any cracks about his name. Teddy had looked reluctantly over at Swager when they were toweling off after the showers. "Want to, uh, go out in town? We pump on out to boogerville, not gonna be any Jameson's there."

"Sure, Obie. But we're not drinking hard, are we? Like they say, you can't soar with the eagles if you hunt with the owls."

"Absolutely," Teddy said, heart sinking. *Not drinking hard, are we?* But maybe the kid was right. If he was going to take over the platoon tomorrow, he'd better be sharp. Not screw up first shot out of the mag.

MULVANEY'S Gingernut was a fake-looking Irish pub across from the Del Coronado. A sign out front said WHY DO THEY CALL IT TOURIST SEASON IF WE CAN'T SHOOT THEM? Nothing to show it was a Team hangout, unless you counted the Harleys and sports cars and jacked Jeeps and even a full-size Hummer.

The interior smelled like beer and hot grease. The bar was full, guys Teddy recognized from training over the past week, plus old farts that must be the local retirees, Viet vets, and gawkers who just came in to tour the zoo. Teddy ordered the Reuben. A lot of women, sitting in twos. Frog hogs showed up around every base that had a SEAL team. In a way it was annoying. On the other, wasn't it what every man wanted? He got another Harp and drifted out onto the back patio. Make this the last, then he'd get back. The late-afternoon sun fell through the trees, warmed his face as he lifted it, eyes closed, seeing only red, red, bloodred.

"Fresh meat," a woman said.

Teddy opened his eyes. He took in chunky thighs, slim waist, the obvious core muscle of her torso. Dark hair. Jeans-clad legs wrapped around the stool. A bulge under her left armpit that wasn't her tit. "A cop?"

"Busted." She stuck out her hand. "Salena Frank. Sheriff's Department, up in Vista. You?"

"Teddy Oberg. What brings you to Mulvaney's, uh, Detective?"

"Came with my girlfriend." She looked into the bar, where an overweight blonde was slamming down schnapps, then beer. At that rate, Teddy thought, they'd have to pour her into bed.

"So what're you? Designated driver?"

"Got it in one."

"You're shitting me," he said, then noted the Pepsi. "You're *not* shitting me."

"She wanted to come, and I admit, I was curious. This place has a rep. Like a cop bar, only you're not cops." She looked at his hands. Then at the scars on his face. "You're a SEAL, right?"

He shrugged. "Something like that."

"Ooh. 'Something like that.'" She grinned like a little girl in braids. "What, you can't tell me? It's all secrety-secret?"

"It's not a secret. Just, it's safer for the ones who have families. Like undercover cops, okay?"

"It sounds so macho."

"That gets blown out of proportion. We just have jobs, that's all. 'I stand on the wall providing that blanket of freedom you sleep under.'"

"A Few Good Men," she said.

"Yeah." Then he remembered Sumo and scowled. Tossed back the drink. "And, yeah, there's some danger."

"I lost a partner last year," Frank said. "Domestic dispute. Woman came out of the basement with a hammer. He never saw her coming."

"Is that right." Teddy looked her over again.

"That rogue SEAL guy, what's his name—do you know him?"

"That was Team Six. I never met him."

"But what are you doing here, anyway? In the States, I mean? Aren't we supposed to be at war? Do you believe this stuff? About the CIA and the Israelis being behind it?"

"Why would the Israelis bomb the World Trade Center? It was full of Jews, wasn't it?"

"Then why are you still here? Why aren't you out kicking ass?"

"Maybe next week."

"Next week. A lot could happen by then."

He gave her the eye back. "Yeah. I guess it could."

"Want to arm wrestle?"

What the fuck? "Uh, sure."

She got him in a wrist lock and stared into his eyes. He was looking into them when her free hand slid between his legs.

Then she nailed him. All the way over, a clean takedown that knocked the beer right off the table onto the floor. She guffawed and jumped up as he rubbed his wrist. "Come on. I'm over at the Del Coronado."

"What about your friend?"

"She's got a key too."

IT was different, he had to admit. Usually they didn't like it rough. Halfway through, her friend came in, staggering drunk, and spread out on the bed next to them and starting bringing herself off as she watched.

When they were done, he looked down at a little plastic toy rabbit Frank handed him. "What's this?"

"Congratulations. You're now an official San Diego Sheriff's Department badge bunny."

He was resting up, getting ready for a rematch and wondering which it should be—Salena again, or Bridget this time—when his cell went off. He rolled to his pants and rooted through the pockets while Salena coughed and lit up and Bridget started rubbing herself again.

It was the head shed. The recall.

He hadn't intended to spend a lot of time saying good-bye. But somehow Salena got her cuffs on him, and both women took turns doing nearly professional things they'd obviously done together before, until he absolutely couldn't even pretend to get it up anymore.

"See if you get anything that good where you're going," the blonde said as Salena tucked her San Diego County Sheriff's Department card into his undershorts.

AND everything just kept going faster and faster. The usual deployment routine, only speeded up about sixteen times, like rocketing down a greased chute with nobody knew what at the bottom. By 0300 they were at the Military Air Command terminal, the floodlights out so no one could see them, kicking their duffels onto Praetorian Airways 106. Destination: unclear, but anywhere in the Mideast; you went either the northern route, Bahrain, or the southern, Oman. He figured this for a southerly.

The chief he was relieving, the one whose blood pressure was too high to deploy, handed him a drab computer case jammed not just with the computer but with a thick mass of folders. "Real sorry about this, Oberg. I wanted to do a complete turnover, but you're just going to have to ask the master chief to help you out."

Great, Teddy thought. He wasn't feeling so hot. The whiskey. The girls, sucking what felt like life itself out of him. The Zippo-stink of jet exhaust blew over them, hot and smoky.

One man's evil had created a whirlpool, a hurricane, a black hole, and the world was gradually starting to circle it, everything and everybody getting drained down. Like with Hitler. Or Lenin. Now, bin Laden. Thousands of people, then millions, spinning faster and faster.

Knobby Swager stood motionless, pale, shaking. Teddy was about to look away, then remembered: He was in charge now. He grabbed the kid by the back of the neck. Talked for a couple of seconds, got him squared away. Word came to board. "Let's move, troopers," he shouted. Like some sergeant from a John Wayne. Yeah, well, life was like the movies sometimes. Yo, Oberg, he told himself, slapping each man as he went by. This is where you wanted to be.

You wanted it real?

This was the real thing.

III

The Gates of the Citadel

8

Prince Georges County, Maryland

THE house had been in her mother's family since before the Civil War. Its hand-baked primrose brick looked soft enough to eat. It dominated thousands of acres of rolling fields and woodland. The Blairs had been landowners, slaveholders, politicians, statesmen. One had sat in Lincoln's cabinet. The Tituses were more recent, but Checkie's father had done well in banking, a career his son had followed too. Her parents' match had not been seen as unequal.

Dan didn't feel as confident that he belonged here. Who the hell was he, anyway? A working-class family. An alcoholic ex-cop for a dad. How lucky he'd been to find her. And how astonished when she'd accepted him. Welcomed him into a bigger, wealthier, more influential world than he'd ever before moved in.

A tobacco-brown Crown Vic was parked kitty-corner across the stone gates. As Dan eased to a halt, uniformed men glanced into his car. "Why the guards?" he said, automatically getting his ID out. There'd never before been security here.

"Mr. Titus hired us," one said. "You the son-in-law? Lenson? Go on up, sir."

Her mother opened the front door. Queekie Titus was still beautiful, and even more imperious than her daughter. Her hand was kitten-soft, and the cheek she pressed ever so briefly to his smelled of lavender. "Dan. We were so glad to hear you were coming."

"I can't stay long, Queekie."

"The Navy. I know. My father was in during the war, did I tell you that? I believe I did. But I can make up a room for you, shall I?"

"I can stay for one night."

"How wonderful. Blair's in the sunroom. We had to bring her home. You can't actually rest in those hospitals. Always waking you up to take a sleeping pill." She led him through, held the door for him. "Blair, sweetie. Dan's here."

. . .

SHE'D been drowsing, drifting in and out in front of the television, a book on her lap and the polished platinum croon of the drugs lulling her. She didn't like what they did to her thought processes. But without them her bones ached, and her face hurt as if locked in an iron mask. When she managed to make sense of the news, it was frightening. Death counts from the attacks had reached three thousand. Something called the High Office of Homeland Defense was being created. It sounded like one of Orwell's ministries from *1984*. Someone had mailed anthrax spores to ABC, NBC, CBS, and Tom Daschle's office in Washington. The whole postal system was shut down. It had to be Al Qaeda. Who else would attack the mail system, Congress, Peter Jennings, Tom Brokaw, and Microsoft? No American would do such a thing.

Or would he? Americans turned guns on their presidents. They shook their children to death. Tempted young men into their apartments, killed and dismembered them, and boiled their heads. But what was the answer? A police state, like some of the commentators seemed to want? Tyrannies were more murderous than individuals. She stared unblinking at the unblinking screen. Every few minutes the bewildered, simian visage of the nation's chief executive returned, feigning resolution, feigning understanding, swaggering, blustering. She couldn't believe he'd actually used the word "crusade." Bin Laden himself could not have chosen a better rallying cry, to roil the Muslims they'd have to depend on to prosecute any punitive action.

When her mother called, she groped for the mute button, then struggled to sit up. To hold her arms, or one, at least, up to the weary-looking man in khakis. He smelled of sweat and the outdoors when she hugged his neck. Suddenly, desperately, she wanted him close. She made a muffled noise into his shirtfront she herself couldn't interpret.

When he gently untangled himself and pulled up a chair, she lay back and tried to catch her breath. His hair was even shorter than usual. Was it grayer too? It seemed like months since they'd seen each other. Just a quick trip to the city for an interview. "You're here."

"Got lucky. Talked them out of a long weekend."

"You drove?"

"Straight through. Except for a stop at the house, to pick up some things."

She searched his face. "How long can you stay?"

"Not very long. Overnight."

"Where to this time?"

"Points east."

She squeezed his hand. "You look like you need some rest. But your voice—it sounds better."

"Still raw. But it's getting better, yeah." His fingers traced her cast. Was his gaze sliding away, off her face? The damage was still concealed, still covered, but it flamed steadily beneath the dressings: *Remember me.*

Dan had been studying her since he came in. The light had haloed her at first, too bright in this glass-walled, quarry-tiled room looking out over a paddock, miles of hills, woods a riotous mosaic of fall color. Then out of it she'd emerged: strangely foreshortened, irregular beneath the flat facets of taut blanket. The air seemed too cold for a sickroom. No. She wasn't sick. Only gravely hurt.

"All right, tell me," he said.

"They say I was in surgery for seven hours. Three ribs. Two breaks in the right arm. One in the upper thigh. Those are all knitting.

"They saved my eye, but it—I lost the eyelid, and a lot of skin. That's a big deal for reconstruction, apparently. I'll have scars—they say that's how healing occurs—but later on a plastic surgeon can cut them out. The ear—well, there's going to be trouble with that. Cartilage, apparently, doesn't heal the same way bones do."

He squeezed her hand. Wanting to kiss her again, but afraid of hurting her. When she'd sat up to hug him, he'd caught the tug of pain on what was visible of her face. What he could see was wan and haggard; what he could not, he tried not to imagine. "Don't take this the wrong way. But I want you to know, no matter what, you're still beautiful. To me."

"I know, Dan. That's not one of my worries."

"Good. Long as you know. How's the pain?"

"Stiff-upper-lippable. Except at night, sometimes—then I can't always play the martyr."

Her mother came in with a tray. Set it down, then looked, just for a moment, nonplussed. "Oh—Dan. I forgot. Sorry. I'll get some Coke." She carried the whiskey decanter out like an acolyte bearing away the sacred wine.

Blair clamped a hand over a laugh. Suddenly it seemed funny. Then it didn't. Past Dan she caught the secretary of defense, then the prime minister. A bearded man in a headdress stood beside them. Oh, God, bin Laden? She rubbed her exposed cheek, confused, wishing she could scratch the terrible itch that crawled and bit beneath the inaccessible, dark side of her face. When she looked again, the three men were gone.

"We're going to start bombing soon," he was saying. Dan, not the men on the television.

"Are you going after him?"

They both knew who *he* was. Dan said, "I'm not sure exactly where yet. I got TAD'd to CENTCOM and they're forward-basing a targeting and intel group. I suspect pretty much everybody's going to get thrown into this."

"A massive response. Like Desert Storm."

"That's one of the options being considered."

"Where?"

"Afghanistan. I don't think that's subject to classification. Since the SecDef's spreading it all over the networks."

She blinked. "Uzbekistan will probably let us base there. The Tajiks—they'll be wary. Can we supply through Pakistan? That'll be the key. I met with Musharraf last year. He has his own jihadists in the Tribal Territories; his security services funded the Taliban in the first place. The way I'd approach him—"

Checkie cleared his throat from the doorway. When they looked his way, he wandered in. Shook Dan's hand. "Good to see you." He rubbed Blair's head awkwardly. "She's been asking for you."

Looking at them side by side, it was hard to remember Checkie wasn't her biological father. He was Queekie's second husband. Not a bad guy, Dan guessed, but not easy to feel comfortable with. Or maybe that was his own problem. "Well, I'll leave you two alone," her stepfather said. Then wandered out, the door slamming with a little puff of dust and flaking paint behind him.

Blair kept drifting from apathy to something akin to sharpness. "You know what's hard? Suddenly having nothing to do. No impact on events. No . . . calendar."

"You could call Margaret. Have her make you one up."

"Not funny. How would you like it if you suddenly became . . . no one?"

"You're not 'no one,' Blair. Just on the sidelines after taking a bad hit."

"I loathe football metaphors."

"You'll be back on the field in no time. Carrying the ball again. For a touchdown."

"Oh, my God. Do all military people have to talk in clichés? Hey, will you turn me over? Not that way . . . this way."

He worked his hands under her, and although the burned patches were still tender, got her over on one side. Then took a second to wheeze. They looked at each other and burst out laughing. "This is how it'll be when we're eighty," she murmured, shaking her head.

"That won't be so bad. If we're together."

She captured his hand again. Glanced toward the door. Then pulled it down, under the blanket.

Dan felt the rough edge of the leg cast, the binding around her ribs. In between was warm flesh. Below was a land he remembered. Eyes closed, she lay back. "A little lower . . . that's right . . . oh. What if Mom came in . . ."

It built, hovered, but then seemed to slip away. Submerge, back into the numbness. Numbness or pain. Her only choices these days. She reached down and stopped him. "Never mind. It's not working. Almost did. Maybe later."

AFTER she went to sleep, he sat with her parents watching cable news. A clip showing a demonstration in Iran came on. They were burning effigies of Uncle Sam and the president. SUPPORT ISLAMIC RESISTANCE one sign read. "We need to teach these people a hard lesson," Checkie said. He looked at Dan. "You saw the guards, at the gate? The whole country's going to be like that, if they have their way. We're supposed to microwave our mail now. I hope you'll tell me we're going to straighten them out. I mean, body-count-wise."

"I guess we'll see, Checkie."

"Are you going over there, Dan?" Queekie looked worried.

"That's what my orders say."

Her soft hand warmed his. "God be with you, Dan. And don't worry about Blair. We'll take good care of her."

"Yeah, we'll take care," Checkie said. "She's going to need a lot more surgery, you know."

"On her face?"

"Her face, her ear, her eye. Then they've got to take those scars away." Her mother looked at the television. "She'll have to go through physical therapy. That will be very painful."

Blair's father gripped the arms of his chair. Said between gritted teeth, "Take the fight to them, damn it. Wish I was young enough to. No more of this pat-a-cake, like the last guy in the White House. We need to wipe these animals off the face of the earth."

AT three Dan's portable alarm went off. He dressed quietly, stripping the dry-cleaning bag off a set of khakis. Pinned on tarnished silver oak leaves; rows of ribbons; a gold Command at Sea pin. His old "water wings," the surface warfare insignia, a destroyer, bow wave rolling out from her stem. His TAG tag with the unit shield and LENSON in block letters. His battle dress uniforms and desert boots were rolled in the duffel. That, an AWOL bag, and his computer case held his life now. It felt high schoolish, leaving Blair with her parents, but she needed care. And her face . . . what could you say to her about that? He'd watched her use her beauty on men many times. It had both attracted and repelled him, until he'd realized what lay under that cold perfection, that intellectual detachment. Not frigidity. Quite the opposite.

A real double whammy: first she had to leave Defense, then this. How she'd deal, he couldn't guess. And he'd be in the same situation soon. Retiring as an O-5 was respectable. Maybe not that great for an Academy guy. But respectable.

Bullshit, he told himself. With his record, it was a slap in the face. But all he could do was do the best he could. Just as he'd done since stepping aboard USS *Reynolds Ryan* as an ensign, so many years before. He combed his hair in the dark, remembering humping his luggage up that brow, her rusty, dinged-in plates materializing out of a shroud of steam. And before that, lifting his right hand on the sun-baked brick of Tecumseh Court on a blazing day in June. *I do solemnly swear that I will support and defend the Constitution of the United States against all enemies, foreign and domestic . . .*

All over America men and women were loading up. Across the Mideast, the Pacific. Shaving. Pulling on uniforms, flight suits. Boarding transport aircraft and ships.

Going to war, against the most shadowy enemy America had ever faced. A man and a movement of suicidal zeal, bubbling up from pious but up till now largely peaceful millions. The Arabs he'd met, he'd liked. He didn't think violence was typical of Muslims. If anything, they seemed more tolerant than a lot of Christians he knew.

But maybe that was changing. If it was, the struggle would be horrific. And September the Eleventh would not be the only date etched in blood.

The makeshift hospital room was dark. A motionless form snored in an armchair; the private-duty nurse. Dan took his wife's hand. Tears stung his eyes. He blinked and coughed.

She came awake, rushing upward from blackness into the warmth of his lips on hers. Disoriented. Then she struggled to sit up. "Oh—you're going?"

"I have to." He sounded hoarse again.

"Be careful, Dan. No more Signal Mirror missions. Have them check that throat."

"I will. And you, get well. Don't worry. About anything." He kissed her again, smelling her hair and the damp-earth scent of perspiration beneath dressings. Forced a smile. "You're going to be back on your feet a bigger knockout than ever. And we'll have a lot of years together."

"I love you."

"I love you."

Fingers trailing apart. Parting.

The scrape of a closing door. Then the murmur of a starter, the crackle of gravel under tires.

She lay watching the shadows cast by his headlights slide across the ceiling.

He glanced into the rearview as the house shrank behind him, then vanished; and a dark and lonely road opened ahead.

9

Sana'a

H EY, A-*ee*-sha. Lookin' good there, girl."
       "Dream about it, Lance Corporal."
   "I do, I do. Ever' night. Goin' out? Hot date out in town?"

She grinned at the young marine manning the gate. *Far* too young for her. They'd heard about her fighting side by side with Gunny Kaszyk and the rest of the security det at the embassy in Ashaara City. That seemed to make her part of the Corps. "Thinking about it," she told him.

"We locked down solid here. Nobody supposed to leave." A quick glance inside the gate shack. "Ain't nobody lookin' but me, though. You slip on out, girl, I ain't seen nothin'."

She hesitated, peering through the rotating bars of the pedestrian entrance, like some slaughterhouse machine designed to slice human bodies into horizontal sections. She was in burka and *sharshuf* again. Armed, and with a fully charged cell phone. Already sweating and finding it hard to draw a full breath in the bulky Kevlar ballistic vest. Feeling as if she needed to go back and use the toilet one last time, although she just had.

Should she venture out yet again? The last time, they'd put the Bosnian on her trail. Taking her hostage was the least-threatening construction she could put on it. Kidnapping was becoming a cottage industry here, although the main targets were Brit oil executives. But the Bosnian in the red cap was off the game board. For good, according to Colonel Al-Safani.

She and the rest of the embassy staff had spent a week aboard *Duluth*. The interlude had taken her back to her days as special agent afloat aboard *George Washington*. The time with Commander Candy. These memories filled her with mingled shame and pleasure. Looseness outside marriage was not pleasing to God. But, oh, how sweet it had been. She'd never given Albert what she'd given Wilkes. Maybe she should have. Her fiancé didn't answer her e-mails now at all, and when she called, he was short with her. He'd said nothing more about converting. Not that there'd been long to

talk. Connectivity was tight, and the ship's company seemed to resent anyone else using their broadband.

From *Duluth* she'd flown to Bahrain, where she'd checked in with the
Middle East Field Office, then strolled past the pool and the Dome for
much needed visits to the ship's store, the beauty shop, and the commis-
sary. She still had some kind of respiratory bug from Ashaara, but when
she'd gone to the branch clinic, who was there but the same clown of a
doctor who'd been drunk out of his mind at the Diplomat Hotel brunch,
singing onstage with the Filipino cover band. He wouldn't see her because
she was a civilian, and arguing with the office girl hadn't done any good. She
had more luck at the Bahraini pharmacies, which carried everything and
required no prescriptions. They'd given her German antibiotics for her
lungs and something Turkish for her bowels, and she'd come back with a
decent supply of tampons, underwear, deodorant, and other necessities
neither the Yemeni souks nor the embassy store could supply.

The embassy hadn't been attacked. The PSO had gone in with a full-scale
raid based on information from Mujagic's interrogation. To her surprise—
it didn't usually happen—she'd been routed an info copy of the CIA's after-
action report. Four men had been picked up and subjected to preliminary
interrogation. One, a Yemeni national, had been released; the three foreigners were being held for further interrogation. She'd requested access,
but that hadn't come through. Al-Safani said it appeared that based on the
quantity of food in the apartment, and testimony by a woman who'd cooked
for them, not everyone in the cell had been captured. He suspected the
others had left the country, tipped off, somehow, in advance of the raid.
The prisoners seemed to be the foot-solider type, Yemenis and Egyptians,
although it was possible they could be persuaded to reveal more than they
themselves thought they knew.

She'd shivered, and asked no more questions.

They had a new on-scene commander. Roderigo Caraño was an FBI SSA,
supervisory special agent, with a crim background but no CI or CT experience. He'd flown in from Washington with two New York Police Department
agents to augment the investigative element. Insisted on full briefings from
her and Doanelson, then started issuing orders. Order One: No agent was
to leave the compound without full security. An understandable precaution
if you wanted to keep your butt papered, but not the way to get the job
done. In her humble opinion.

And now it was Thursday again. A workshop day, and she'd missed
quite a few. Her students thirsted after English as if the language itself
meant a better life. Their existences in Sana'a—even that of the relatively
wealthy women—were so limited. How could she leave them without one

of the few windows they'd ever had? But Doanelson had warned her not to go out alone. Tim Benefiel had asked her not to, when she told him where she was going. He'd offered to go along. To a mosque? She didn't think so. Better to walk inconspicuously than travel in a convoy. The only way, under Force Protection Condition Delta, she could officially venture into the city.

She stood looking at the gate. Go? Or stay?

She whispered a *du'a*, and nodded at her admirer to unlock the gate.

THE sun had declined above the earth-and-cream teeth of the city, the truncated, narrow, rammed-earth buildings like skyscrapers sketched by a child. She walked quickly, hidden in the crowd, along the embankment on the west side of town. Below shone the dark asphalt of a road laid at the bottom of what had once been a wadi, a dry streambed. Cars hissed by, the small European and Japanese types the Yemenis imported, each with windows open and radio on. She crossed by a footbridge, her leather slippers clapping, the cars murmuring beneath, motorbikes buzzing, the warm wind breathing in her face. At each corner of the stairs leading down the ammonia musk of urine welled up. The shaft of the minaret rose, bright orange light outlining each stage like a rocket being groomed for ascent. Behind it lifted the dark, jagged outline of the mountains.

At the bottom of the stair she stepped to the side and stood concealed in shadow. Waited, fingers brushing the butt of her SIG. She needed a toilet, badly, *badly*. Oh, dear. The prescription did not seem to be working. Men stood motionless in brightly-lit arched doorways. Were they watching her? They did not seem to be looking her way. Others sat with legs crossed, smoking and sipping coffee beneath rippling plastic awnings. A boy careened past on a bike, shouting to playmates strung behind.

She stepped from the alcove and hiked with cloth swishing toward the mosque. A truck with a defective muffler crackled past, trailing choking exhaust. Men sauntered in pairs, holding hands. Music welled from open-air storefronts beneath a massive billboard displaying, once again, the opaque and cunning features of President Ali Abdullah Saleh Al-batel. She stopped to check out Indian and Pakistani tapes and videocassettes. Many seemed to be religious, but vacancies on these shelves suggested certain offerings had hastily been removed. She moved on and fingered a colorful scarf. Turned her head; but the street behind was empty, save for two women lingering at a display of plastic shoes. One's face was covered, the other not, a fresh teenage girl with heavy, dark eyebrows.

"They are from Iran. Very fine fabric, very low price."

"How much?" she said, but her accent must not have been quite right because his gaze came up from the scarf to her face. A fluent gesture: *Make me an offer.* She replaced it and strode on, coughing in the dust and exhaust.

At the mosque a squatting old man waved her in. She stepped out of her slippers and set them in one of the wooden boxes. Washed her feet in a tiled trough. But the carpets were covered with sitting men listening to the imam; a funeral was in progress. She turned aside and went downstairs to the restroom. Feeling a bit better, face washed, she padded down the corridor to the bare, undecorated room where she held her class. Five women glanced up as she let herself in, and she relaxed, smiling. Unwrapping her covering, she seated herself cross-legged before them.

AN hour later she stood from Isha devotion, the funeral party having left. Feeling the peace of prayer but also a little creaky in the knees as she straightened, with some effort, from the *sujud* prostration. Apparently women prayed at home in the Old Town, because she was the only female in the mosque.

She stretched discreetly and wandered toward the exit, unwilling to leave the transcendent, empty quiet. The class had gone well. Making progress, but they were *so* fucking shy. "Good morning, Miss Ar-Rahim." "Is this seat taken?" "I am very pleased to meet you." "Where are you from? Are you from Saudi Arabia?" Next time, she had to bring something printed, so they could review at home. Or tapes; surely the Public Affairs Section had something she could check out.

She found her braided-leather slippers in the box and leaned one-legged against a wall to slip them on. Her students departed, holding hands, chattering until they hit the gate, then falling silent as black-shrouded ghosts. The street was brightly lit with hot-yellow sodium-vapor lamps. Compared to most of the Mideast, Sana'a sparkled. Not like Egypt, Ashaara, Djibouti. She shivered, remembering that last hellhole: the warped, diseased beggars, jaws grinding, their poverty and ignorance drugged with qat; the endless, choking dust. Here the souks were still busy. The farms produced. People worked. The schools weren't great but they were still open. People trusted each other. Gradually, almost imperceptibly, Yemen was dragging itself upward.

Women in black were out sweeping the streets. Children wove and shrieked among them, playing tag. She pushed herself briskly out the gate. Turned right, striding along. Remembering to stay alert, despite this sense of peace. Down the street a truck idled, the exhaust rising in blue clouds.

She'd almost reached it when she remembered her purse. Her nice carpetbag purse. Left in the classroom. At least her sidearm wasn't in it, but everything else was: official passport, badge, Mace. Better get your mind back on the job, Aisha-girl. She wheeled and turned back, puffing at her absentmindedness.

The blast enveloped her in orange fire, a soundless impetus that launched her like the thrust of a carrier's catapult. Time slowed as she tumbled, impelled in dreamlike flight.

She got her hands up to cushion her crash into the steel grille of a shop, then crumpled to the cobbles, ears ringing. She couldn't hear a thing over the bells in her head. Heat penetrated the cloth and Kevlar on her back. She pushed up to her knees facing the street. The SIG, safety off, pointed trembling in both hands.

Over the sights: a smoking crater, ruined storefronts, scattered, burning bundles of rolled cloth. The smashed wall of a house. A twisted, burning mass of steel and springs that must be the remains of the truck. The metal shell of its tank was bent outward like the hull of a popped kernel of corn.

Then flames roared, sound at last penetrating the ringing in her skull. Above that, screams. A blackened figure danced past, beating at fire that fed on shriveling skin. The light standard above where the truck had been parked still vibrated like a plucked string, bent upward from the blast. A column of expiring flame and greasy, brownish, petroleum-smelling smoke filled the street and blew hotly into her face. Burning fuel, burning cloth, burning flesh. Cold horror crawled her skin.

She lurched up and forced herself to trot awkwardly, encumbered by vest and clothing, pistol still extended, toward the carcass of the truck. Pools of lambent fluid drained over the cobblestones, flickering, then bursting into full flame in leaping orange glares. She shied between them as they grew into great leaping pyres and emerged at last from the flame-swept area in a combat crouch, sweeping the street beyond with the muzzle of the SIG.

A metallic-green, four-door sedan was pulling out farther down the street, heading toward the sunken road. Faces in the backseat turned to stare. A short black tube withdrew into the car even as she took a stance and aimed. Fifty yards. Center of mass hold. But civilians beyond were running in both directions, some toward the flames, others away. She started to take up on the trigger.

Then released it. She couldn't clearly say she knew what the black tube had been. Or if they were connected to the bomb. But what *did* she have? "Some Robbers Are Happy When Caught"—S-R-A-H-W-C. Sex, race, age, height, weight, hair, eye color? She photographed the car in her mind. Light green, squarish, left rear bumper crumpled as if rear-ended. A dark smear on the right-side passenger door. Three twentyish, dark-haired men in the backseat. She squinted, trying to make out the plates. There *were* no plates.

The sedan vanished. She lowered the pistol as horns honked, as a distant siren brayed against the stars. Put it away and bent to beat with her hands at one of the sweeping women, who was moaning as flames devoured black wool. Neighbors were running out, alarm and fear stamped into shocked eyes above stubbled beards. The same anguished horror she'd seen in so many faces, in many different countries. That she'd seen on television too: the expressions of Americans fleeing an ocher cloud speeding to consume them in the streets of their greatest city.

The face, not of terror, but of its victims.

THE general's, much later that night. After the calls, the meetings, the dressing of her knees where she'd cut them. The silence of the ornate office. On one side of the table herself, Caraño—the new SSA, swarthy, black-mustached, and bulky in the vest he wore even indoors—and Doanelson, now junior in the FBI stovepipe. The embassy security officer should've been there, but wasn't. On the other side: Al-Safani, Gamish, and a quiet, dark-skinned man in civilian clothes and rep tie, introduced as "Mr. Abdu-lilah, who is very close to the president."

Aisha sat too shaken to say much as Al-Safani went over what they knew in a colorless voice. The tally was eleven dead; twenty-three injured; seven shops damaged; windows blown out all along the street. "Some of the dead were children," he said. "There would not have been nearly as many save for the funeral passing by, and a children's group from the mosque. There is speculation the attack was aimed at the funeral. The deceased was a politician of a former regime."

"Do you really think that?" Doanelson spluttered. The FBI man was in his trademark scuffed black oxfords, gray polyester, and white, button-down shirt, but now his holster hung heavy with a big stainless automatic. "They attacked a funeral with an antitank rocket—a Chinese Type 69, based on the pistol grip. That's the official theory? Some dead politician?"

"Not necessarily," Gamish said after a long moment, during which Al-Safani glanced his way.

Caraño cleared his throat. As far as she'd seen, he had even less Arabic than Doanelson. The mustache was okay, but his bullying scowl wasn't going to work with Arabs. Nor the way he tapped a finger on the table like an irritated headmaster. "Your president bought Type 69s from North Korea. Some went to your organization. Then they disappeared. The man you took into custody—Abu-Hamid Al-Nashiri—made threats against foreign leaders."

"If you mean the House of Saud, we have close ties with Saudi intelligence." Gamish did not look intimidated. "This is an Arab concern. No reason for American involvement."

"The king travels in an armored limousine. The Saudis asked for Al-Nashiri's arrest. Where is Al-Nashiri now?"

The old man who'd slapped her, accused her of being a traitor to Islam. The one who'd been seen before his arrest drinking tea in a café in Sana'a with the same PSO colonel sitting across from them. Gamish seemed to weigh his answer. Finally he said, "He was released. After cooperating, and undertaking not to resume his activities."

Caraño slammed his palm on the table. "Released?" He let the word hang. *"Released?"*

"He is still under surveillance," Al-Safani offered, but without much conviction.

"I see. And now those same rockets blow up a gas truck just as our agent's passing." The SSA glowered at her. "True, she shouldn't have been exposing herself. But *she* was the target."

"That's not certain," Benefiel put in. She looked at him; who'd suddenly appointed the junior agent her protector? She narrowed her eyes but he avoided her gaze.

The security officer came in, excusing himself, greeted everyone, and took a chair at the foot of the table, between the two delegations. After the usual preliminaries he said with marked respect to the so-far-silent Mr. Abdulilah, whose coal-black eyes had flickered like dark fires as he followed the exchanges, "We would be very grateful, sir, if you would share your view of the situation. And your intentions; how you plan to bring those responsible to justice. "

The civilian looked at his fingernails. He said distantly, "There is no claim of responsibility."

"Actually, sir, there is." Al-Safani cleared his throat. "It came up half an hour ago on their Web site."

"On their Web site?" said Gamish in Arabic. "And it says what?"

"A new organization calling itself Al Qaeda in Yemen. Retaliation for the arrest of their Yemeni and Egyptian brothers. It hails the brothers who carried out the heroic attack."

"What's he saying?" Caraño broke in.

Aisha winced; you didn't interrupt a government minister. "Pardon me, sir," she said to Abdulilah. Then, to the senior agent: "He's describing something that just appeared on the Web."

When they returned to English, both the general and the civilian minister looked somber. The embassy official took over. "With all respect,

Minister. Your president wants the electronic package. Weapons. Transportation aid. And all those the United States will be happy to provide. But you must understand the situation has changed. Our own president has said, 'Those who are not with us are against us.' You can't continue to protect these people and also expect our help. In fact, I will be frank. There has been discussion about classifying your government as a supporter and harborer of terror."

"This would not be accurate, or fair," Abdulilah said. For the first time he looked concerned.

"It might help if you could be more transparent with us."

She cleared her throat and sat forward. The security officer looked expectant. "Yes—Agent Ar-Rahim?"

"May I shift to Arabic? Thank you." She got the minister to at least flick his eyes to hers for a fraction of a second. A woman, a black woman, and an American, lecturing him. Of course he'd hate it. But he had to get this message. The security officer had phrased it as a threat. Politely put, but a threat nonetheless. Fall in line, or take your place with our enemies.

It would be better if he understood it a different way.

"*Sa'adatuka*, we understand the difficulty your president faces. That aiding us may seem to be acting against Islam. But let me ask this. The men who detonated this explosion in your streets? Killing children returning from school, old people returning from a funeral. Were they acting justly, according to the Book?"

Neither answered. So she did, for them. "Anyone who kills innocents in the name of God is an oppressor. Not *jihadi* but *irhabi*. Not martyrs but *mufsidun*. Murderers and evildoers, who corrupt the body of the Faithful. Servants of Shaitan, not of God.

"Minister. General." She shifted to the plural form, both to denote respect and to increase the formality of the warning. "Please do not make the mistake of thinking these are the enemies only of America, or of Israel, or of the house of Saud. They are your enemies too. Remember how Al-Nashiri argued. 'No leadership other than the commander of the faithful—power comes from God, not law—the government is apostate and no true Muslim can obey it.' If they prevail, there will be more bombings. Many more; and they will turn against those in power, as they have in Afghanistan, Saudi Arabia, Sudan. They seek your power for themselves, to remake the land in their unholy image. Those who want to teach and build will depart. There will be no employment for your young men, so they too will join those who preach violence.

"In the end will remain only dust, and madmen, and killing without end. Yemen will become another Somalia. That is the vision they have for you."

Abdulilah, whoever he was, played with his pencil, standing it up on the eraser, then letting it topple. Glancing at the security officer, she saw he, at least, had followed what she'd said, although the non-Arabic-speaking Americans looked baffled.

The minister said in English, in a soft, flat, almost dead voice, "And what is it you would have our president do?"

Caraño said angrily, "Get serious. Commit the PSO to rooting out Al Qaeda. You know who its members are."

The security officer said more gently, "Treat them as enemies of the state, instead of allies against the Saudis."

Abdulilah turned palms upward. "You argue well. Especially you . . . woman. I will take your words to the president. But I say this. You think we know everything. In truth, we may know less than you think. If we could lay hands on these people, we would certainly do so. But it's not that simple."

"Make the effort," she said, and this time both Caraño and the embassy official backed her up, nodding. "Or face the consequences. Not just from us. From them too."

DOANELSON sulked the whole ride back. Aisha stared out at the passing streets. No one was out. The terror was starting here too. She kept rubbing her arms. She felt cold. Remembering again and again how close she'd been to the swelling hull of the tanker truck. How easily she might have been right beside it when the rocket had pierced it and detonated.

As she trudged up the stairs to the office, her cell went off. She fumbled the phone out of her bag and ducked into the women's room, hoping it was Albert.

But the voice was that of Hiyat, her friend from the women's circle. Aisha recalled date pastries, a long, graceful neck under glossy black hair. But the words were nearly unrecognizable. "Aisha, Aisha, he is dead. He is dead!"

"Who? Hiyat, calm down. I can barely understand you. What's wrong?"

"Husayn, Husayn. He is lying dead in the street. They say you were there. They say—"

Aisha got the story by broken words, sentence fragments. One of the children at the mosque had been her friend's eldest. Only fifteen. Aisha couldn't think of anything to say as the woman wept and cursed. Aisha couldn't think of why she'd called, either. But she said what she could think of to say, and Hiyat at last came to why she'd called. "I know where they are."

"Where who is? Who are we talking about, Hiyat?"

"The *irhabi*s who killed him. Here, in our neighborhood. Foreigners. They leased four apartments. Paid for the whole year, all at once. They bought cars, and a truck. Not Yemeni, they did not belong here. But no one wanted to speak out, and our husbands don't . . . they don't want to say anything, even now. And so we pay . . . *Husayn!*" Hiyat screamed again, the anguish of bereaved mothers for a million years lacing her cracked voice like barbed wire. Aisha closed her eyes and prayed.

"Where are they?" she said. And the woman told her, between curses and prayers. Aisha cradled the phone and tore off a paper towel. On its dry, pebbly surface she scratched notes, directions. "How many? And where are they from? Do you know that?"

"I'll call you in a day or two," the distant, fading voice said. "And we, the women, will give you what you seek."

10

Base "X," Gulf of Oman

H OOYAH, hooyah, hooyah, hey! Today's another easy day!"
Teddy sweated furiously, slogging through the sand. The heat was overwhelming, bad as he'd ever felt it. An abrasive paste of sand and sweat gritted between his thighs. His boots thudded remorselessly into the ground. He had to stay in front.

Now, he was the Chief.

Above his head the cloudless sky blazed beneath an unfeeling sun. In Masirah, nearly directly beneath the equator, it was high summer all year round.

The team had deployed to a place few even among the well-traveled senior petty officers had ever heard of. The island was forty miles long and barren as the backyard of hell. It lay fifteen miles off the coast of Oman, itself only a vague idea in most people's minds. It had been a British base since before time began, but after Desert Storm the United States had poured money and concrete, and now the airfield's immense silver-black-streaked runways shimmered in the heated air as if seen through a beaker of boiling water. Four-engined cargo planes thundered in and out, and helicopters clattered in from seaward to load slings of palletized bombs and dangling howitzers and black, droopy bladders of fuel. Diego Garcia lay over the horizon, where the logistics for any major Navy or Marine effort would funnel through. Closer in through the blue haze lay the *Theodore Roosevelt* Battle Group, shortly to be augmented by *Kitty Hawk*, en route from Japan.

The base was dedicated to cargo handling, supporting the battle group with the fabled "beans, bullets, and black oil." Which explained why the SEALs were living in hastily erected tents in a compound a quarter mile inland of the runways instead of in permanent buildings. They were used to tents and razor wire and the distant barking of guard dogs, but the dust, humidity, and heat were remarkable even for the Middle East. Outside the wire dozers had scraped out berms and firing lines. They'd been here a week, acclimating and training. The bombing campaign had begun, but they still had no word as to their destination. Guesses, yes; scuttlebutt aplenty. But nothing concrete.

Teddy's calves were cramping. He turned and ran backward through the warm, stinging surf, looking back.

He had sixteen men in Echo Platoon, though only three trailed him today along the shining strand. The two officers, Dollhard and Verstegen, were back at the HQ tent. Two men were in sick bay: Foss, with a scorpion-fish spine in his foot from the day they took a Zodiac out to the reef for scallops; Catron, with an eye infection exacerbated by getting elbowed during a spirited game of wadi ball. (On Masirah everything was *wadi*. Wadi ball, a vicious combination of volleyball and lacrosse that included hand-to-hand combat at the net. Wadi lizards, ugly beasts with huge heads, suspicious eyes, and tongues as fast as an Old West gunfighter's draw. Wadi foot, wadi ass, wadi eyes, and wadi hair for bed-head. Even wadi water, which meant no water at all.) The others were into their own morning workouts. Lifting or grappling or unarmed combat; some out swimming; others doing a full-up pyramid in a hangar converted to a gym; overhead squats, push-ups, Supermans, working on glutes and hams. They did pull-ups on bars they'd welded up and staked into the sand with the help of the same Seabee construction crew that had helped them refurbish their tents. SEALs weren't into mass PT.

Teddy figured what he needed was basic endurance. Combat wasn't a sumo match; it demanded endurance and core strength, not muscle mass. They claimed whatever bug or worm he'd picked up in Ashaara was cured, but he still didn't seem to have all his drive back. Right now he was at the end of his rope. Still up front, but a glance back told him the others didn't look near as stove up as he was feeling. They were fit but not huge, few bulky guys or classically ripped bodybuilder types. He wished he could see Sumo's silhouette back there. His teammate had towered over everyone else, but always kept up. That was the secret. You can if you think you can. Mind over body. So Teddy was still out front, even if it took five hundred milligrams of Motrin twice a day.

Fortunately, he had a couple tricks up his sleeve. He swerved toward the surf, gentle today, cool-looking but warm as soup, green and white stretching out toward coral reefs tickling the horizon. He jogged out knee-deep, a gentle gradient on this beach, until each step dragged at his legs and salt burned his abraded thighs. Then turned and faced them.

"Buddy on your back," he yelled, and to grunts and wheezes each grabbed another and swung him to his shoulders. "To that pointy rock," he yelled, and slapped each burden-bearer on the ass as he staggered past, wet, sandy, dripping, sunburned, with a buddy's weight sagging across his shoulders. "Speed! Speed! Pick it up, operators! Helo ahead, medevac, your buddy's bleeding out!" They'd be carrying this and more if they had to pull back under fire, eighty or ninety pounds of gear apiece, a wounded buddy, and gear for two. Only knowing they could do it would get them through.

No enemy trained this hard, or fired a Marine division's annual ammo allowance every week. These were the fittest, finest fighters on the planet, with only a few other outfits even worthy to be mentioned in the same breath. If you knocked them down, they got back up. Shoot them, and they kept shooting back. This was where he belonged, not talking bogus deals in la-la land.

He ran after them. When the last man buckled and fell full length into the water, Teddy picked up the guy's buddy and carried him on himself.

THE whine of turbines not far off, the trundle of huge silver fuselages. Teddy remembered this from years back, from Desert Storm, when he'd been a wet-behind-the-ears sugar cookie fresh out of BUD/S. As the plane taxied in to the apron, maintenance vehicles and pallet handlers rolled to meet it. Men and women in USAF coveralls trotted on interception courses. They converged like ants tackling a big silver grubworm, and the hatch came down and everyone swarmed aboard. A smoky mirage of tea-stained air heated the already sizzling afternoon. The turbines whined down out of supersonic to a basement subsonic that quaked in his gut.

The command tent was clustered with others in the SOF compound, inside a separate ring of wire. One small Korean-made air conditioner was laboring manfully but not making much headway. Its louvers were aimed at the computers, so none of the head shedders could be accused of bagging it. Though of course they still were. The Echo leader, Lieutenant Dollhard, ran a hand down a scrubby goatee, mesmerized by a screen. "Settling in okay, Chief?" he murmured. "How about Ozzie's kid?" The four-year-old had swallowed a needle.

"Got that resolved, L-T. Reached back and got it taken care of. Kid's okay." Teddy gave Dollhard stats on the sick list, how soon they'd be tits up again. Added that Alonzo was catching up on his pistolcraft, and that the Air Force security detachment had agreed, when asked politely, not to idle their trucks upwind of the SEAL hootches anymore. Dollhard massaged his beard again, still fascinated by the screen. He was a bit older and considerably stockier than the usual SEAL. Teddy didn't make the mistake of thinking this meant softness. Some of the meanest mothers in the Teams had gathered a slight pudge around the midriff. Both that and the air of absolute calm came with years of hanging it out over the edge. Their OIC, Officer in Charge, was ex-enlisted too, a Team guy from way back.

"Any orders yet, Commander?"

"Yeah. Our downtime's over."

"We good to go?"

"Warning order for embark tomorrow. Don't leave anything; we won't be back. Pass that to the shooters." Dollhard went over the embark schedule and what gear they'd need. Teddy listened hard. If they needed a piece of gear where they were going, and they didn't have it, it would be more than a ding on his eval. The lieutenant handed him the clipboard and gave him the nod that meant he could go about his business.

ON the way out, Teddy passed the nod on to Master Chief Stroud, a leathery little asshole who essentially ran the headquarters element. "Hey there, Turd Man," Stroud said sotto voce, a slow smile stretching his weathered cheeks. Teddy took a grip and just smiled back.

Even now, he only remembered flashes of his chief's initiation.

They'd held it in the Kill House, probably because it would be easier to clean up. And the House was the most soundproofed, secure area on base. They'd modified an old ghillie suit and painted it shit brown. So that when Teddy had had to go before the High Judge with his green Charge Book to plead his case, the Judge—this same Stroud—just had to ask what he was. And Teddy, the hapless selectee, had had to say, "I'm a piece of shit, Your Honor."

And Stroud had cleared his throat and said, "Yeah, I guess something always has to slip through the marine strainer."

It hadn't gotten any more pleasant, or less insulting, after that. But *Easy Day* wasn't just a catch phrase. After Hell Week at BUD/S, every day was an easy day.

Teddy had heard all the stories about initiations, but he'd thought they'd been toned down after Tailhook. If this was toned down, he wondered what they'd been like in the old days. Three strippers from out in town had stood at the door collecting cover charges. For a extra few bucks, a chief could get a finger diddle. Unfortunately, there'd only been two selectees, Teddy and another guy from the tech side who didn't have his Budweiser but who'd gotten dragged in since they had so few other Slugs. And since everyone was getting ready to deploy, Stroud had said, why not?

Anyway, everyone had arrived already loaded, in some cases so drunk several of the already-frocked chiefs had to be locked in the ammo room to sober up so they could even make it to the swearing-in stage. After a sleepless night in the "coffin" wondering what the horrible smell was, drinking the "Truth Serum," reciting every response to the numbers he could remember and taking the bombs when he didn't, and dancing the cancan in the Talent Show, Teddy had barely been able to read the CPO creed. But maybe things *had* been toned down because there was no stripping down, no lit tampons up the ass, no canoe paddles, duct tape, or dog food, and the strippers had left after taking the entrance fees. (Or maybe just gone elsewhere with some of the older Genuines; Teddy had been otherwise occupied. And in any case, not interested; the strippers had been worn, bloated women, old amigas of the master chief's, apparently.)

Anyway, "Hey there, Turd Man," Stroud now said. Wagging a finger.

Teddy just smiled. "Hey, Master Chief."

"Water and ammo and comms, Chief Oberg. Water and ammo and comms."

"Right, Master Chief. On it." Obie held up the load list, but Stroud snatched it out of his hands and started to cross things off, sneering. Teddy wavered—Dollhard had just told him this was final—but didn't protest. Stroud handed it back with slashes through a third of the items. "Snivel gear. Pogey bait! Tell your LPOs, drop the crap and take more ammo. Never have too much ammo."

Obie considered this bullshit, like a good deal else of what Stroud said, but didn't voice the opinion. Stroud was the last guy in the unit to sport the yellow-and-red Vietnam service ribbon. He'd served with names that were legends in the Teams. His sneering *pronunciamientos* might not be current doctrine, but they were worth considering. In his mind, Teddy restored several of the items the command master chief had deleted, but added four more cases of Mk 262 and 7.62. "Got it, Master Chief."

"Think this is *amusing*, Oberg?"

"No, Master Chief."

"You got the attitude. I'll give you that. But let me tell you something. A chief don't need attitude. He needs to *manage*. You don't pay attention to your gear, your logistics, and your chow, attitude don't mean shit. Let the officers display the fucking leadership. You just make goddamned sure everything's there when your troops need it, and it all *works*. Be goddamned sure your LPOs take what you need, and *only* what you need."

"Okay, Master Chief, and this embark—"

"Oh, yeah. We're goin' back to Fleet Navy for this ride. Complete fucking uniforms, got that? They can keep their beards, but no Willie Nelsons. Keep the cameras out of sight, and tell 'em to leave their flippers in their gear boxes. Now get the fuck about your business."

Walking through the HQ tent, Teddy saw notebooks being unplugged, desks folding up, files going into boxes, comm gear into form-fitted foam cutouts in hard-shell cases, cables being rapidly zip-tied into bundles ready to unroll again in some other makeshift location, some other sand-gritty tent or bunker or commandeered mud-brick madrassa. SEAL teams went intel heavy. The usual sources took too long in a tactical situation, so the Teams brought theirs along. They got chaffed as "intel pukes," but no smart SEAL looked down on his intel guys.

Outside a Humvee honked, and men shouted in the distance. Teddy staggered as the heat hit him again. Afghanistan couldn't be any worse. Then he corrected himself. No. It could always get hotter. And it could always get worse.

Or better, the way a SEAL looked at it.

There was much to be done, and Chief Oberg set about it.

2000 hours in the staging area. The lights burned images bright as day. Across the field leaping figures testified wadi ball did not cease with the going down of the sun. Heavily laden SEALs bent beneath packs, duffels, and weapons cases as they scuffed through the still-roasting air. They wore desert BDUs with unbloused trouser cuffs and floppy bush hats and Oakleys and Camel Baks. They carried Steiner binoculars and LST-5B line-of-sight radios and ruggedized Motorola MX-300R bone phones and ear mikes and UHF/sat comms. And short-barreled special ops modded M4s spray-painted in camo patterns and SIG 226 pistols and M240 light machine guns and AT4 antitank rockets. They clanked and creaked as they trudged past. But hardly anyone spoke.

2210. with a roar and a tilt backward, the COD—Carrier Onboard Delivery—flight left the runway to climb into hazy darkness. The plane was smaller inside than it looked sitting on the strip. The SEALs rode four abreast, belted into backward-facing seats, gear slung into the webbing above them, under their seats, carried on their laps. There might have been more gear in the plane than air. As it climbed, the temperature dropped. Cold air blasted from overhead, bringing a welcome coolness to heavily burdened men.

They could debark from this aircraft, jog across a flight deck, and load into a helicopter for insertion. Teddy, nodding out to the thrum of the propellers, didn't think that'd happen, but it could. He remembered going out on QRF patrols with Sumo and Bitch Dog and what was his name— Whacker. Two, sometimes three, insertions a day. Too noisy in the stripped-down, metal-walled SH-60 cabins to talk, even to think. Everybody covered in a thick, greasy film of sweat. Pitch-dark aside from an orientation strip down by their boots. So gear heavy, their jaws were all they could move. Teddy could almost taste the pineapple gum Sumo's mom used to send him from Hawaii.

Don't think about that. He touched the hilt of his thin-bladed Glock knife. It'd been with him for so many missions it was almost like a good-luck piece, though he didn't like the idea of good-luck pieces. Solid planning, extra ammo—those were his good luck charms.

The familiar tension of the hours before action. Alone, unspeaking, Teddy thought: This is what I missed, back in LA. This amped-up sense of absolute reality. He searched downturned, inward faces, remembering histories and nicknames. Vaseline. Harley. Steff. Two Scoops. Oz. A story behind each name. Some read. Others slept, heads vibrating to the engine drone. Some just stared into space, maybe rehearsing how to blow a steel door or defuse the antihandling device on the electronic version of the Chinese Model 1989 antipersonnel mine.

But this time there was a difference. He frowned, groping for it.

Before, he had one guy to worry about: himself. No, two: him and Sumo. Now he had thirteen enlisted and two officers to take care of. It was a heavier load than he'd expected.

He smiled sardonically in the roaring dimness, imagining what Master Chief "Poochin'" Stroud would have to say about that.

0200, aboard USS *Kitty Hawk*, CV-63. A cavernous, dimly lit compartment deep within the carrier. The deck was scuffed charcoal nonskid with red and white stripes, lights glaring high above, the air hot with paint and lubricant fumes. The whole enormous carrier had been turned into a floating special forces base. With her fighter and attack wings off-loaded, the hangar bay was packed with black-painted insectile forms, antenna-spiked and heavily armed. Teddy recognized Blackhawks, Chinooks, Pave Lows. Clunks and the rattle of chains bled through the overhead. He found it comforting to be wrapped in eighty-six thousand tons of American steel, American fuel, American explosives. And six thousand Americans, at least half of whom had given the heavily burdened SEALs fist-bumps, high fives, and V-for-victories in the passageways on the way down from the flight deck.

"Take a knee," Dollhard said. The men shifted, heads up, blinking off lack of sleep. Teddy stood behind his platoon, arms folded. Beside him stood the assistant OIC, Verstegen. His battle dress uniform was already rumpled, starting to smell. "All present? Chief?" Teddy raised a hand, nodded to confirm the muster. "Everybody ready to double your racks?"

"Hoo-yah!"

"Afghanistan," Dollhard said, putting the first PowerPoint slide on the bulkhead-turned-screen. Five sets of black arrows showed various forces' movement to contact. Rebel yells echoed. Suddenly everyone was noisy, pumped up. Sailors clumping past in turtlenecks and denims and heavy black flight-deck boots glanced at them.

"We're doing something that's never been done before. Instead of a conventional force-heavy operation, Infinite Justice will be a spec-ops show. They gave it to us. They expect us to deliver."

"Hooyah," shouted several men again. The others followed, half a beat behind.

The OIC grinned. "As such, we'll be linking up with and lending support to indigenous forces that have been opposing the Taliban for years. Now, with our help, they will prevail."

Slide two. Hard to see in the overhead glare, so Teddy tapped a petty officer's shoulder and sent him to get them dimmed. "Areas currently held by the Northern Alliance, as of October fifteenth," Dollhard said. They were unimpressive; an oval dead centering the country; a dent from the northwest; another patch of crosshatch to the northeast. Most of the slide was pure green, apparently meaning enemy. "Next slide." It came up as the lights dimmed.

"Overall concept of operations. Following up on the suppression of air defenses, Special Forces ODAs comprising Task Force Dagger were inserted in the north on nineteen and twenty October. They linked up with a warlord called Fahim Khan to assist his Northern Alliance forces in an attack toward Mazar-e Sharif, the regional capital and key city in the north.

"A second team linked up in the Daria-el-Souf with ethnic militia led by General Abdul Rashid Dostum. Dostum commands the Uzbeks, the largest faction of the Northern Alliance. He's slippery. Fought for the Soviets, when they were the occupying power. But right now he's on our side.

"The intent in the north is to assist local forces to take Mazar-e Sharif, the Dariá-el-Souf valley, the old Soviet airfield at Bagram, north of Kabul, then Kabul itself. Other operations may take place at the Shahi Kot"—a laser-scarlet dot speared and wandered—"and closer to the Pakistani border.

"The southern portion of the country has de facto been assigned to us. The Navy and Marine Corps."

Another hooyah, muttered this time. The men shifted, focusing in.

"Kandahar. Second-largest city in Afghanistan. Population, half a million. Regional capital. Founded by Alexander the Great. Elevation, one thousand meters, thirty-three hundred feet above sea level. Bounded on the west by the Arghandab River. Surrounded by fruit orchards, cotton fields, and sheep-grazing lands. Kandahar Airport has two runways capable of taking C-130s and C-17s. The city links by road to Farah and Herat to the west, to the northeast Ghazni and Kabul, to the north Tarin Kowt, to the south Quetta, in Pakistan."

Dollhard took a breath. "Kandahar's the Taliban's home turf, where the attacks on the World Trade Center and the Pentagon were planned. Mullah Omar made it the capital of the Islamic Emirate five years ago, and there are strong indicators both OBL and Omar are still there. Forces loyal to them will naturally concentrate either in Kandahar or the mountainous regions to the east of the city. So, who do they give the toughest job to?"

"To us," the men roared.

"Correct. We started hitting targets in the city with cruise missiles fired from the Gulf. Initial targets were the airport, command and control, and air defense. Navy air will begin flying strikes tonight. Bomb damage assessment's available on the intel side, and I strongly recommend you leaders check that against your maps before insertion.

"Here's what we have on our plate to start. Echo Platoon's assigned to a mixed SBS/SEAL task unit to be known as Task Force Cutlass. Our taskings are still under discussion, but may include one or more reconnaissance insertions before establishment of a Marine forward operating base. Right now we're on four-hour standby. I recommend you find your racks, get a shower, and get your heads down, because we could launch anytime." Dollhard glanced at his watch. "All right, everybody, let's—"

"Attention on deck!"

The call came from the hatchway. A middle-aged officer in flight-deck coveralls and a khaki combination cap stepped over the knee-knocker. Silver eagles glittered at his collar. Teddy came to attention as his men jumped to their feet.

"Carry on," the captain said. Teddy assumed he was the carrier's skipper, but he could've been the air boss. He didn't say, but maybe it didn't matter.

"Just a brief welcome to the Battle Cat. USS *Kitty Hawk*. Your quarters may be cramped, but we'll have hot food and showers whenever you want them. Right now, you folks are our main battery.

"We have Navy, Marines, Air Force, and Army aboard. Total, over a thousand spec-ops folks. The dust hasn't settled on the Trade Center and the Pentagon. We're going to bring some of what they visited on us back to the Taliban and to Osama bin Laden. Before we're done, they'll regret they ever took on the United States of America."

This time when he finished, no one cheered, no one spoke. Only a grim silence rested on their thoughtfully bent heads.

11

Sana'a, Yemen

S HE sat in the SUV, sweating. The engine was off, and that meant air-conditioning too. It wasn't that hot outside, under an arch of stars. But she'd always perspired on a raid; in Bahrain, in Ashaara, even back in the States. General Gamish had promised a roll-up of the leaders. Maybe the mother cache of Saggers, like the one that had almost gotten her and had killed so many innocent Yemenis. Including Hiyat's eldest. Her friend hadn't called back, though Aisha had paid careful attention to her cell and tried to reach her several times. No answer; leaving her to wonder what had gone wrong.

A double rap; Colonel Al-Safani's elongated visage at her window. She pressed the unlock button. He wasn't in his usual thobe and keffiyeh and jambiya but in full Russian-style battle dress, even a helmet in place of the red-and-white-checked shemagh he wore in the office. His flak jacket was hung with perfectly spherical green grenades, like unripe pomegranates. Instead of the holstered Makarov, a brightly polished AK that looked as if it belonged to the Yemeni equivalent of the guards at Arlington Cemetery was slung over his chest. "We're ready to go in," he muttered.

Doanelson had already gotten out, was pissing against a wall; he shook off, zipped, and turned. Caraño had been on the guest list, but hadn't seemed interested. Behind her Benefiel jerked out of a doze. She put a hand on her junior agent's wrist; then a finger against her lips.

They got out on a cobbled street so steep she had to grab the car door to stop herself from sliding. Half the sky was eclipsed by one of the cliffs that walled the city. The lights from the apartment building towering behind them illuminated ropes, truss work, some sort of structure leading up the cliff. She had no idea what it was for.

"Which building?" she muttered. Al-Safani pointed. She looked aside in the dimness and made out men standing in rough lines to either side of the door. The back of the building faced the cliff. She whispered, "Back door?"

"Already blocked."

"Neighbors? Did you warn them?"

"No. It's best to go in cold. As little notice as possible." The PSO officer spoke in a low voice to a shorter man who came up, and Aisha caught the superior-to-subordinate tone. She glanced up at the windows, some lit, others dark, and edged away, loosening the SIG in its holster.

"This way," the colonel murmured.

Doanelson, doubly bulky in Kevlar, followed. Aisha too was wearing the ballistic vest, but in the night, in her dark abaya, she didn't see how anyone could see to target her. Unless they had infrared scopes, which, considering the money behind their organization, was possible. "We didn't get much of a briefing," the FBI agent said to the colonel. "What's the plan? Assaulting force? Backup? What do you expect inside?"

Al-Safani kept glancing away. His explanation sounded hasty and somehow misleading. The ten-member team of the PSO's Rapid Reaction Force would infiltrate up the stairs as quickly as possible and once in position assault into the apartment. Three snipers overlooked the back, which, like most Yemeni buildings, didn't have fire escapes—how could mud brick catch fire?—but did have wooden back porches or verandas where families took the air after dark. From there, it was possible suspects could drop with ropes from the third floor, where the intelligence said they were located. If they did, the snipers would take them out.

Aisha glanced up at the cliff, its black mass poised over them as if to fall. Unless they had some way up, it would act as a perfect barrier; even if someone managed to exit the apartment, she couldn't see how they could escape the others—"catchment" teams, Al-Safani called them—huddled with weapons ready behind cars at either end of the block. Her gaze met Doanelson's. The FBI man raised his eyebrows; she nodded.

"Sounds good," Doanelson said. "Where you want us?"

"Back here's best. Out of the line of fire." Al-Safani winked at Aisha. "The last thing we want is for our American guests to catch a stray bullet."

Benefiel didn't seem to care for this. Her assistant asked if he could get closer. The colonel said jovially that he understood, young men wanted in on the action; to follow him. They vanished in the direction of the apartment entrance. Aisha checked her weapon again, adjusted her Kevlar, and settled in. From somewhere up the cliff came an unearthly chuckle. "What the hell was that," Doanelson said uneasily.

"Hyena?"

"They have hyenas here?"

"Didn't you ever go to the zoo?"

"What zoo?"

"The Sana'a zoo," she said patiently. They'd had leopards, baboons, a cute little caracal—a sort of bobcat. Small cages, but with what they had to work with, it had been neatly kept. She'd taken pictures of each animal and e-mailed them to Tashaara.

The FBI man squatted in the dark. She fell silent too, remembering this preraid combination of boredom, sleeplessness, and jitters. Her first, in San Diego, on a broken-down cabin cruiser in the base marina reputed to be used by a dealer who targeted the local marines. How her pulse had pounded, crouching under the pier! The dealer, a retiree, hadn't been there, but they'd found weapons and drugs, enough to pass a warrant to local law enforcement. The gate guards had arrested him a week later. So run-of-the-mill, yet, at the time, so exciting.

Twelve years later, was the thrill still there? Enough to give up relationships, and time with her daughter?

A stir ran through the shadowed forms. Then, on some unheard signal, they streamed in. The radio crackled with orders. Doanelson frowned, a sure indication he couldn't follow the conversation.

Several minutes later, flashes came from an upper window, the distinctive blue-white glares of the British flash-bangs the Yemenis used. Their explosions reached street level as distant cracks. She cupped her ears for return fire, but heard none. No other lights came on. No one came out onto his balcony.

Al-Safani, on the radio: "Aisha? Scott? You can come up now. I believe we have the situation well in hand."

BUT when they got up there, the colonel was nowhere in sight. She and Doanelson lingered in the haze-shrouded hallway. Her eyes and nasal membranes stung. Tear gas; she squatted to get below it. Someone was screaming inside. She noted that unlike in the United States, the other apartment doors stayed firmly sealed. She called ahead, "*Isma'!* Assault team? We're coming in."

She stepped cautiously through the haze, flashlight and weapon extended. The acrid fumes mixed with the bitterer, just-as-choking gases from the flash-bangs. The screams sounded as if they were from children. Her fingers tightened on the pistol. In the States, you tried to get kids out of the way by some pretext before you went in. She couldn't believe they'd used gas, either. Usually, in a raid, gas handicapped the entry team as much as or more than the people they were taking into custody. It also increased the chances of civilian casualties, due to the difficulty of identifying targets through vision-restricting masks.

But this isn't the States, Aisha, so stop expecting it to be. She followed her gun's muzzle around a corner and found herself covering a woman. Three children huddled against her, eyes blown wide as they stared up. The PSO troops were pulling clothes out of closets, pushing trunks over to dump the contents, rifling suitcases. "Where are they?" she asked the woman, snapping it out in peremptory Arabic between coughs. Glass shattered as the troops flung windows open and leaned out to yell down to buddies in the street. Cool air flooded in, but the gas lingered, roiling, clinging to every surface, reluctant to depart.

"I don't know—I don't know who you're talking about," the woman mumbled through a fold of cloth held to her face.

"You take her. I'm going on," Doanelson said, behind her.

Aisha said to the Yemeni woman, "Yes, you do. The men who live here. Where are they?"

"No men here," the woman said. "My husband only. He is a trucker. He is often away."

"Where is he now?"

"I don't know . . . maybe Saudi. Yes, he must be in Saudi." The woman clutched her weeping children. "Hush, the woman won't let them hurt you. She will keep us safe."

A Saudi connection; and a trucker would have a great cover for smuggling. But as she went from room to room Aisha saw no weapons, no bomb-making materials, no radios or computers. In one small room a motionless bundle lay in a makeshift crib against the wall. She approached, pistol pointed, but it didn't move. The girl seemed asleep.

She went back to the woman. "Where are they? We'll find them, you know. When did they leave?"

The woman began wailing, pulling at her hair. "I told you! Only my husband! That is his picture, on the wall. My daughter is disabled . . . she can't move . . . I told them come in, search, do whatever you have to do, but they started shooting, and then she couldn't breathe."

Aisha felt cold. Daughter? Disabled? She went back into the other room, found a trooper pawing at the bundle of blanket. He pulled back the cover to reveal a motionless face, a gaping mouth, eyes that did not open. A wheelchair with a bedpan stood in the corner. Brownish foam stained the mouth. Aisha bent and put a gentle hand on the girl's forehead. It was still warm, but the bubbles at the corners of her lips did not move at all.

SHE caught up to Al-Safani as he was climbing into the truck with his men. Lifted her hand, almost timidly; she didn't want to appear to be ordering him around in front of his troops. He still looked displeased, but tossed his helmet in, turned back, dropped off the truck. Confronted her as it gunned its engine, the roar echoing from the tenements.

"Where will the hot washup be?" she asked him. "I'd like to come. If I may."

She got a blank look. "The what?"

"The . . . meeting, after the raid. To discuss what went wrong."

"Nothing went wrong," Al-Safani said, regarding her as if she weren't making sense. "A very successful operation. As your deputy chief of mission will report, I believe."

She wiped her nose; the gas seemed to be digging into her sinuses. "Maybe I didn't understand. Wasn't this a raid to nab—I mean, apprehend—I mean, catch some of the ALQ members you gained intelligence on from Al-Nasiri? Wasn't that the mission?"

"This was a successful raid."

"Well, I don't see anyone who looked like ALQ. Just women, and kids. And what about the dead girl?"

"Dead girl?"

"The one in the back room, Colonel. The quadriplegic!"

"That one was dead long before the raid. Her condition had nothing to do with us."

Get a grip, Aisha. You gain nothing by confrontation. She forced calm into her voice. "Was this a wrong-door raid, Colonel? We do those too. It happens."

"A what?" He wasn't looking at her again. Not a good sign, with a Yemeni male.

"When a raid hits the wrong address. The wrong apartment."

"No, this was the correct address." Again, that feeling he knew something different from the version she was getting.

"But there was a family there. Children. Couldn't you have waited until they left?"

"There are often children where we raid," he said, frowning as if it were a stupid question. "How not? Even the Salafi evildoers have families. I tell you, this was the right address. It is simply unfortunate that the men we sought seem to have departed, just before we arrived."

Yes, she was tempted to say, how very unfortunate. Hurling his words back into his face. That would not be wise. Not wise at all.

But, oh, how she wished she could do it.

THAT evening, back at her stolen office, sitting with fingers poised over the keyboard. Studying the screen.

Results of the raid: Only women and children were encountered, and a handicapped female 16 years of age died, apparently from tear gas. This agent's impressions were that none of those taken into custody (all female or below the age of 15) were ALQ, local Salafi, or even sympathizers or family members. The entire operation appeared to be aimed solely at paying lip service to US demands for action, while the actual subjects of interest are either carefully avoided or warned in enough time to depart and sanitize the premises.

This conclusion, in conjunction with the release of Al-Nashiri (suspect D546576), causes this agent to conclude that either:

1) the information D546576 and/or others gave PSO was a false lead, due perhaps to application of torture, resulting in misleading information given simply to feign compliance; or

2) the PSO is still shielding the real (read: foreign Arab) bad guys in hopes of their carrying out a planned strike against the Saudi royal family or government figures.

She sat back, stretching her neck. It was all so speculative. Of course most investigative work was, but counterterrorism was even murkier than pursuing qat smuggling or stateside rings that stole ammunition or weapons.

The NCIS had little training for the intelligence function. Now she was being drawn into another world, chasing deadly, elusive criminals with close ties with host governments; so cunningly woven into the fabric of their societies that just trying to identify them was like wandering through a wilderness of mirrors.

She'd worked a Mafia case out of the naval air station in Sigonella that reminded her of this in some ways. But Yemen was Sicily squared. Was it feasible that senior officers in the PSO, or maybe even above that—the slippery Minister Abdulilah—were still facilitating the people they were now pretending to pursue? Had supplied the weapons that had nearly killed her?

Benefiel came in, looked as if he were about to say something; then just sat and logged in. They both had terminals now, one good thing the augmented investigative element had brought along with Caraño: a container of computers, chairs, file cabinets, stationery supplies. They no longer had to beg ink-jet cartridges from the attachés.

Okay, she thought, tapping her nose. Let's look at it from their angle. The Honorable Abdulilah and General Gamish and Colonel Al-Safani.

They want to push back against Saudi activity on their borders. So the PSO facilitates a plot against the Saudis. Or maybe it's not the whole organization that's helping Al Qaeda, but some key member of the regime. Let's call him X. So, X hears the president's public denunciations of ALQ, or AQ, as the FBI called it; but he's a clandestine supporter. Or maybe not, but still wants to use it as a cover, a smoke screen, his actual intent being to foment an attack on the Saudis and blame it on AQ, with the always slippery Yemeni president holding tight to plausible deniability.

Okay, *why* attack the Saudis? To send some sort of message, to warn them off? Or, an alternate explanation, to trigger more friction; generate enough internal fear and coercion that the president reverted to a fundamentalist foreign policy, as opposed to the semicollaborative relationship with the United States he seemed to be developing at the moment?

Benefiel cleared his throat. "Want to, uh, get a sandwich?"

She ignored him. So who was X? And if indeed there was an X, and she was anywhere close to his rationale, then, investigatively speaking, how would she get any traction on him? They needed access to the day-to-day relations of Yemeni officials with the local Salafis. Which they'd never get if they depended on the PSO itself, and if X was within the PSO. Or above it—if X was someone like Abdulilah, at the ministerial or even presidential level.

Okay, how else? Usually, when you had an idea who your perp was, you started with those close to the suspect. In Sicily, she'd turned the driver who took Signore Salvatore Lo Tocco to work every day. Worked from him to the dry cleaner who got the drugs onto the base, and passed the package to the Italian "Catturando" organized crime unit that had picked up Lo Tocco and his consigliere in Palermo. The big guys seldom thought twice about the little people around them. The secretary, the clerk, the guy who gave him his haircut. But the help saw the comings and goings, overheard conversations. They understood what they witnessed and sometimes were willing, given a promise of protection, to testify.

But whom could she recruit? She massaged her eyes. Round and round, but the bottom line always was, she was stuck in here, unable to operate, unable to interview or act. They had to operate through the local agency; and odds were the PSO was at the root of the problem.

After a little more reflection, she filed the report. Then went downstairs to the cafeteria. And there he was, sitting morosely in front of a tray of beef Stroganoff. Caraño himself, with Doanelson. One of the NYPD detectives stood a few yards away, watching television and jingling change in his pockets. The two FBI agents winced as she plunked her tray down. "Agent Ar-Rahim," Caraño noted, glancing up.

"Rod. Scott. A word?"

"Scotty was telling me how the raid went. Sounded pretty effective, eh?"

"Sorry to be negative, but I'm afraid I don't agree." She gave him what she felt were the results, contrasted with what the PSO was claiming had happened. Doanelson frowned; pushed salad around, but didn't interrupt. "Those are my conclusions," she finished. "Either they got bad info, or they're dirty. To put it in words of one syllable. And we've got a dead bystander."

The SSA shook his head. "Sorry about the girl. If it *was* a reaction to the tear gas. But now you're telling me we can't trust the general That's tough to believe. Gamish has assured me they're in full cooperation mode."

"I don't trust *anyone* in this country, Rod. I tried, when I first got here. But the more I learn and the more I overhear, the less I trust." He looked doubtful, the way she'd figured he would; not being able to depend on the host government would make their job much tougher. But she pushed ahead. "I have to be able to do fieldwork. Very limited, and I'll be very careful, but I need to be able to get out of the embassy. At least for atmospherics. I need you to clear me to do that."

The senior agent was already shaking his head. "No, Aisha. It's too risky."

"But then we're totally isolated. How can we accomplish the mission from in here? Inside this glass jar?"

"We depend on our allies," Doanelson said around a mouthful. "Like we're supposed to. Not go charging off running some kind of secret superspy operation on our own."

"Atmospherics are nice," Caraño said, "And I agree, you'd be just the person to put out there. But I can't risk an agent to gather them. Not after you've already been threatened. I can't, Ar-Rahim; you're too valuable."

"Too valuable to put to work?"

"No, to lose, in what may be a very long war. We *have* thought about this. But over and above that, we can't risk our relationship with the PSO and President Saleh. That would send very bad messages to some very highly placed people. Far above our pay grades."

"They're not being straight with us, Rod. They're playing both sides."

"But isn't that better than playing just one? They're saying the right things. Maybe as time goes on, they'll realign actions to rhetoric. Their position's fragile, too. They have to balance helping us with appearing not to. A lot of their political support comes from the fundamentalists."

"Who are—"

"Just let me finish, okay? They're walking a knife edge. The whole society could go either way. And last—no, don't interrupt me—I have direct orders from the DCM not to let you out the door again." Caraño took her wrist; she had to keep herself from jerking away. "They tried to kill you twice. You're not to leave the compound again unaccompanied. Understand? No English lessons. No visits to the mosque. You will not leave here except with the rest of us, in convoy. They've targeted you and it's our responsibility to protect you."

"I'm *restricted*?" she said, not believing what she was hearing. "How in the hell am I supposed to—look, Rod, I speak the language. The only one on this team who does. You're saying, we're going to depend on the very people who funded these killers in the first place to tell us about them? And this furthers our mission how?"

"You heard the man," Doanelson began, but she rounded on him so furiously he dropped his fork onto the tray with a clatter.

"Scott, I swear, keep out of this, or I'm going to shove that FBI badge where there's no Kevlar, do you understand me? I'm protesting this, Rod. We have troops going into combat. They still don't know how many thousand dead in New York and DC. Our orders are to do what's necessary. You're saying that includes torture, but not fieldwork?"

She waited, but neither responded. Just looked at their trays. Finally Caraño sighed. "Protest it if you want, Aisha. You're a good agent. Just a little too involved with the local situation, if you know what I mean."

She didn't have a response to that, or, at least, any that didn't seem childish or unprofessional. After that, she couldn't stay and eat with them. Pretend they were all still on the same team. So she slapped the table, hard, rattling the metalware, got up, and walked out.

The least she could do, though, was to leave her tray for them to clear.

12

Night Raid

A hundred feet off the waves, the helicopter was completely blacked out. Teddy sat with boots planted wide and forty pounds of C4 explosive strapped to his chest, letting the vibration lull him. Almost not believing it was actually coming off. Across from him Oz, Scooper, and Smeg stared sleepily back or avoided his eyes. They'd had to leave Foss behind; the scorpion-fish sting was infected; he might lose the foot. Catron was still in pain, but had fought off the doctors, insisting he could see well enough to fight.

But what lay at the end of this flight . . . the thought crawled like a rash itch up inside Teddy's backbone, ran like startled ants out along his upper arms.

No one knew what they were flying into. They were supposed to be in and out before the Taliban command, whatever was left of it, knew they were there. But that was how a lot of operations had started, and not how all of them had worked out.

The helicopter throbbing around him was Air Force, a nonreflective, dead-black Pave Low bird that seemed like the biggest aircraft Teddy had ever been aboard. Certainly it was bigger than any other rotor-winged aircraft he'd ever seen. In the muted lighting the thing had loomed over *Kitty Hawk*'s flight deck, wide as a tractor trailer, the turbines way up there screaming in a hushed thunder that quivered in his belly, the strange-looking half-tail strobing red light so that the rotor looked motionless. A refueling probe jutted like a cannon. Pylons like flying buttresses grasped pontoons and sponsons, flare dispensers, electronic-warfare pods, antennas. The blades stretched nearly across the flight deck, and three other birds were spinning up at the same time spaced along it.

Intimidating. He was used to the stripped down SH-60s the Navy used for insertion, a cramped box of a fuselage, stripped metal, bare hydraulics, open doors. Yelling at the pilots to communicate. Climbing up into these

things had been like climbing into some future century. The 160th Special
Operation Aviation Regiment had led raids into Iraq during Desert Storm
and Panama, done the Liberian evacuation, the Iraqi no-fly zone, and other
operations that hadn't made the media. They did infiltration and extract
of special forces and CSAR, combat search and rescue; they could navi-
gate where no other aircraft could and spoof or distract most radars. This
was what war looked like with unlimited funding, time, and technology.
The Air Force way. This single bird could have lifted the entire platoon,
plus a Zodiac rigged to drop. He almost felt lonely in here with only thirteen guys.

Thirteen of his own guys, that is. In black, padded flight suits, the six
air crewmen moved agilely as chimps from handhold to handhold, writhing
among the motionless SEALs. One was strapping himself into a minigun
mount on the back ramp. That was encouraging, if they had to dismount
into hostile fire.

Teddy knew the plan. But he wasn't sure he had faith in it. Maybe it had
started out like a SEAL mission, at least a little.

But then, it had started to grow.

HARDLY any country in the world was farther from the sea than Afghanistan. None of their combat swimming or SDV training was going to do any
good there. It was desert and mountain, and the only ways in led over
countries that were either totally hostile, such as Iran, or at best dubiously
neutral, such as Pakistan. But the planners had laminated together Air
Force and Navy capabilities and come out with a plan that for sheer audac-
ity rivaled the Honey Badger mission to rescue the hostages from Teheran.

Their tasking was to launch from the sea, overfly Pakistan, and achieve
tactical surprise against an enemy who had to know they were coming.
Their target was the main Taliban radio station north of Kandahar, which
intel suspected also housed an operations center. Also, not far off, was a
compound said to be used by Mullah Omar. They'd roll in, take down his
personal security detail, and either kill him on the spot or scarf him back
for trial. This sounded challenging, and they'd planned and rehearsed it in
the ninety-six-hour mission request, planning, and execution cycle cus-
tomary for the Teams. Now, they were lifting off. Into a dark, windy, rainy
night—ideal for undetected transit. He'd spent most of the hours in between shuttling between intel and flight ops, but still no one seemed sure
what would happen if a bird went down.

Their goal was five hundred miles inland, but map miles weren't helicopter miles. Their twisting course—threading international boundar-
ies, fretted by mountain ranges and deserts—snaked around population

centers, antiaircraft radars, and commercial air routes. The round-trip was over thirteen hundred miles. It would take seven hours to fly in, and the helo crews would have to endure another seven out.

Then suddenly the whole thing had ballooned. The old saying—"Peace before war, but if there's a war, we want a piece." Rangers were hitting the airstrip in a separate Army mission, and the supersecret Deltas were to assault a compound inside the city also used by the same high-value target the SBS and the SEALS were after. Rangers would be providing security for that part of the operation too.

Meanwhile, Charlie Platoon was doing a recon on an abandoned Russian airstrip to the southwest. The Fifteenth MEU was tasked with establishing a forward operating base there, but the Marines weren't ready to launch. Until then, someone had to make sure no one occupied the strip. So Charlie, aboard another Pave Low, would split off shortly after they crossed the Pak border. They'd infiltrate via a desert LZ and lay up in an overwatch position until the Marine helicopter-borne assault.

His own team's objective, "Tantalum," was the original core of the mission. But all these inserts were taking place nearly simultaneously. In other words, not only was deconflicting the freqs a motherfucker, the possibility loomed of a massive clusterfuck. So in the end SOCOM had split the Navy's piece of the operational headquarters raid, Objective Cottonmouth, into two elements, one landing north of the objective, the other southwest. Echo and Bravo got the north end, all the US operators together, which made sense—even if the SBS was good, you didn't want them operating too close; that was how you got blue-on-blue casualties.

The whole plan made him feel hinky. Generally when you took a unit behind enemy lines, success and even survival depended on two things: how well you planned a totally "clandestine" operation; then, on how well your platoon actually executed your plan. For a small unit to do almost any other type of behind the lines operation was called "going Hollywood" and tended to get everyone killed. SEALs preferred to slip in and out without anyone knowing they'd been there. "Leave no footprints in the sand." The success of future ops depended on your ability to remain an unknown to your enemy.

Not that the Teams hadn't participated in classic compound assaults. They had, but whether they succeeded depended on initial surprise, speed, close coordination between all units from beginning to end, and bringing overwhelming force quickly to bear on the objective.

In those frenzied hours there'd been a lot of discussion about how large a force to commit. The thing had started out as a multiplatoon operation. But bigger wasn't always better. SEALs had almost always operated in small groups, six or eight men. Others were better trained for large-scale sweep-and-destroy ops, which this seemed to be turning into—Marines, Army Rangers, "conventional" rather than "special" forces. Teddy had made the point they could get too numerous to achieve surprise, yet at the same time not be heavy enough to prevail if they sucked in a sizable opposing force. But intel had said in the Enemy Sit brief there shouldn't be much opposition. Few Afghanis were committed enough to the Taliban to die for them.

The team had done a walk-through and talk-through at half speed, then a briefback, then done it again at full speed with full gear. Teddy had spent most of the previous night poring over photos, memorizing possible bunker locations and fields of fire. Remembering what Stroud had said. Attitude. Leadership. Management. Yeah, and at the end of it, killing the enemy.

But this time he had to try to tone it down a little. Concentrate on his guys. Not be so much the killer who came out covered in blood, flourishing his knife.

The droning of the rotors was his own pulse. The droning of the turbines was the *om* in his head. He breathed deep, let the stress out. Breathe deep, let it out.

Craning past the gunner he caught something dim outside, glowing in the dark. The gunner was leaning into the slipstream, looking ahead. The aircraft rocked, nudged him in his seat. Went nose-down, then nose-up. The airframe jolted. He flicked the night-vision goggles on just for a moment, conscious he had to conserve batteries, and picked up the other 53 making its approach to a jellyfish shape floating in the night.

Refueling. No clue how they'd picked up the tanker in these black skies. The helicopter floated weightless, motionless except for the drone and pulse that was now part of his bones. He remembered suddenly, with a quirk of the lips, how he'd put a mission not much different from this in his screenplay. If he'd brought a camera, he could have gotten some stock footage.

ONE of the gunners shook him awake. A helmet clunked against his cranial. "Fifteen out," the airman yelled. Teddy blinked and straightened his spine. He clicked the little switch on the goggles and pulled them down.

The night went green and black, granular and disorienting with one eye split into two. The night vision picked up heat so that past the gunner the other 53 orbited with comets of aventurine light that were the tips of the main rotors, and above them the top cover, swift, small blurs of radiance, fast movers. He was glad they were there. He unbuckled, struggled to his feet, and felt his way toward the gunner's station as the man charged the weapon. Looked over his shoulder as the starlit sky gave way to the darkness of the ground. Only not absolutely dark. Here and there queer patches of phosphorescence glowed, speckled by pinpricks of light. Heat sources? He couldn't make sense out of it. It wasn't anything you'd see on night ops in Southern California.

He straight-armed the last SEAL in line and the wake-up call went on down the line and across the aisle. Men stretched and shook out muscles. Gloves crawled around gear like starfish disassembling a cadaver. He returned a thumbs-up from Oz and nodded to Lieutenant Dollhard. A lot of people. He hoped it didn't turn ugly, on the ground.

Five minutes, the crewman's spread fingers signaled. Then he laid a belt of 7.62 into the minigun.

The helo banked and Obie grabbed a handhold as they plunged, executing some sort of sudden evasive maneuver. Up out of the darkness swam a cluster of the small, hot lights. The huddled village not far from Omar's compound, he guessed,

From the lead 53 a wire-straight intermittent ray reached out. It searched the ground, and where it touched, dust boiled and iridescent light rippled and flashed. A second stream licked out from the gunner on his side. To a hellish burst of noise the rotating barrels of the minigun glowed bright emerald, spinning around their axis as bright hot bars of light darted down and burst into fragments of hot green fluorescence that bounced high into the air. At the same instant more hot bright points, fluctuating rapidly, burst from the sides of the lead bird and shot at incredible velocity out and up and then down into the night. They ricocheted off the hillside, suddenly revealing buildings and vehicles below.

The helicopter was banking hard, corkscrewing out of the air. IR flares burst from either side, trailing billows of glowing green smoke that twisted in the rotorwash. Beams of intermittent light traced down. Explosions flicker-lit the hillsides like strobes at a rock concert. The two escort Pave Lows, empty of operators but ammo-heavy, were lending a hand with suppression, along with a much heavier series of detonations from the AC-130 gunship farther off. Teddy kept an eye on Swager. He figured Knobby as the problem child, the dude who'd be shaking in his shit if anybody was. The kid was hunched over his butt-grounded weapon. What little Teddy could see of his camo'd face was blank. They all looked inhuman, with the goggles, the green and black paint, bulky and overloaded with weapons, magazines, grenades, explosives, trauma kits.

The air crewman pointed. Teddy levered himself up against sudden g's and lurched toward the ramp, bracing himself on the line of shoulders along the way.

The ramp jerked and began coming down on an immense panorama, like some National Geographic giant-screen special in full 3-D. *Forces of War*, or *Apocalypse in Afghanistan*. Across the blackness tracers searched like the finger of God. Answering balls of flame leapt skyward, burning so brilliantly they haloed in his goggles, then slowed, declined, fell away into guttering death. The mountains pulled forward and back as they illuminated, went dark, illuminated, as if they were stage sets. A mile away something exploded, leaping skyward and tumbling end over end with terrific force and blinding light. He had to admire the production values even as his gut writhed and he kicked the heavy coils of fast rope down the ramp into the blackness below. Jesus God, the wind was *freezing*. The blackness seethed as the chopper settled, and the dust he'd feared boiled up and rolled out in a curtain that rose all around as they dropped into it. Just before they did, he caught the wink of muzzle flashes to the left. Bigger than AKs, and his guts compressed again.

Yeah. Way better than surfing.

"Let's go! Go, go!" he shouted, though he knew they couldn't hear him through the combined roar of straining turbines and both miniguns. Bullets bit the fuselage with a pa-*clunk*, pa-*clunk* like sheet aluminum being hit with a rivet gun combined with the whiplash crack that meant whoever was shooting at them was so close the bullets were still supersonic. Dollhard was first down the rope, grabbing it and swinging out like a kid at a swimming hole before vanishing into the murk. He was followed at one-second intervals by Tatie, Oz, Smeg, Bucky, Scooper, Steff, Vaseline, Harley, Moogie, Tore, Dipper, Mud Cat, and the Air Force air combat controller. Hospitalmen, enginemen, boatswains, gunner's mates, quartermasters, IC men, torpedomen. Flung out into the chill air that whistled through the holes. More bullets clattered around the interior. With total relief Teddy clamped his gloves on the rope and dropped after them.

HE hit in total blackness unrelieved even by the goggles. The cold air gritted his teeth like chewing on sandpaper. It smelled like shit and kerosene and burned-out firecrackers. Buffeted by rotorwash, crouching as he jogged, he blundered into another bulky shadow and caromed off; looked up to catch the elongated blackness of the helo roaring like an enraged father above them, already shrinking; he oriented and jogged forward again. They'd walked through the actions on the objective in rock drills in the bomb bay, then run it live on the flight deck, so everybody knew where to go and what to do when he got there. He glanced at his diving compass as a fresh gust of sand and dust surfed over them. Mountains, left. Something angular ahead, sparkling green in his electronic vision. The Air Force had vetoed going in covert; the Taliban had heavy machine guns around the compound and station, and these had to be suppressed. Which the AC-130s were still doing, reaching down from the darkness all around the horizon but most particularly directly ahead. And the tracers weren't all going one way.

"Bound forward! Go, go, go!"

He pushed through the dust and caught up to Dollhard, who was signaling a bounding advance in three-man wedges. They leapfrogged over a sloping field corrugated with dry furrows. The dirt felt loose and crumbly beneath his boots when he leapt up and ran, and his balls drew up inside his groin. A minefield? But it didn't seem to be. At least, none went off. Thirty yards away rubble walls stretched across his field of vision. Just high enough he couldn't see over. Past them a stand of stunted trees marked what he guessed was the wadi. Past it was Objective Cottonmouth. *Cross the stream, move rapidly uphill toward the compound.* He'd have preferred to land right in the compound, just plaster it with the minigun, then fast-rope down inside the walls. But again, the 160th had veto power; too much danger of a rocket grenade up the kilt. So they had 150, 200 yards over more or less open ground.

Up again, a dash forward, then sinking to a knee. M4 aimed, but not firing yet. The tracers were still flying down ahead of them into the compound beneath the buzz-saw drone of the Spectre, but no one seemed to be firing back. Up and forward, a fast jog, lengthening the pace, concentrating on getting across that open field. A man tripped and went down, arm shooting out before he hit in a puff of dust. Teddy couldn't make out who, but yanked him to his feet and slapped his back. "Sporty, eh?" he yelled through a steel-wooled throat.

Suddenly he felt like Superman. Invulnerable. The C4 was heavy as sin, but he liked having it there. The stuff absorbed bullets like wet clay. With it and Kevlar he felt as if he were in a tank. He coughed sticky dust into his glove, snorted it out a running nose, and flicked it off. "Let's get in there and kick some . . . kick some Tali ass."

"You got it, Chief."

The lead wedge hit the wall and went over, clumsily but fast, two men throwing the first over, then being hauled up themselves. Down, then up, then forward. The walls clattered apart as they vaulted them; just rough, irregular stones the size of shoeboxes stacked between concrete-block pillars. Nothing on top, no wire or glass. So far he hadn't seen any wire at all, which seemed odd for a headquarters compound. Could they have the wrong one? The whole floor of the valley had been covered with the rectangular outlines of walled fields, walled homes. The GPS readings checked, but intel had been known to finger the wrong buildings before.

Another stone fence, then a short road no one had briefed and he hadn't noticed from the imagery. "Set up here," Tatie, the Echo One squad leader, yelled to the 240 gunner, slapping the top of the wall. "Fire 'em up. Put a belt over our heads, then overwatch."

Mud Cat yelled, "Copy." Teddy looked both ways, observed the field of fire, approved. He slid down a slick short chute into the wadi. At the bottom mud, but no water. Bushes looming black in the green of the heated earth. He floundered ankle deep, stepped in a discarded tire and nearly went down, but recovered and careened on as the 240 began ripping out rounds, the projectiles hissing overhead and whacking into what sounded like mud on the far side of the wadi.

The covering fire cut off as they reached a wall twice as high as a man at the top of the other side of the depression. As drilled, the demo men peeled off and the others faced outboard and upward, covering the top of the wall, as they went to work. The first iteration of the plan had had them going through the front gate. Teddy had pointed out everyone always went through the front gate. This time, why not go in the back? Even if the enemy was alerted by the helos and Spectre, no one would expect them from that direction.

He crouched as the two smaller charges went in at an arm's stretch either side of him. DEVGRU had a manual on how to blow practically anything, including mud-brick walls. The shaped charges would drill in to break it up milliseconds before the main charge blew it in. On the other hand, since the explosions would startle out a world of bad guys, who'd rush to the area as quickly as possible, there was no room for hanging around after they went off. The rest of the op had to go like clockwork; neither the SEALs nor their extraction helos wanted to be around when said bad guys arrived.

He pushed up his goggles and turned them off. There was enough light now from the tracers and flares to see by. He placed the haversack carefully, screwing in a steel hook and hanging the heavy sack of C4 from it at chest height. Then pushed the detonators into the depressions he'd already rammed into the malleable explosive and handed the det cord off to either side. Just as he did this, someone from inside shoved a barrel over the wall and fired off a magazine of 7.62, spraying and praying, right over their heads.

"Fire in the hole!" All three peeled off and pelted for everything they were worth. When Teddy counted ten he threw himself full length and covered his ears.

The detonations came so close together they were one, like a lightning bolt hitting an oak forty feet away, shaking every filling he had and coating the air with a fresh layer of grit and dust mixed with the ammoniacal tang of nitrates. He was on his feet as soon as the shock wave passed, yelling, "Go! Go!" and sprinting back toward the wall. Without the forty-pound burden of the haversack, he felt as light on his feet as a high school running back.

From the darkness above, those pencil-thin beams searched again. The drone of the Spectre underlay the growing crackle of small-arms fire, the deeper booms of the 105 shells going off. It all echoed off the mountains, deepened and lengthened to a thunderstorm. The flutter-pulse of the orbiting helos throbbed like the heartbeats of malevolent dragons. Teddy laughed, trotting toward the dusty breach, air sawing in and out of a scratchy throat. He crouched, M4 to his shoulder, holo sight on, left hand tight on the vertical grip, not firing yet but ready to. The entry team formed up, then charged through, Dollhard yelling at them, Verstegen's too-tall form jumping up and charging ahead as the 240 gunner behind them cut loose a burst at something down the wadi. The tracers flew down there but nothing came back. That was okay. No ammo resupply, but he'd rather the Louisianan put out a few unnecessary rounds than let someone up that excellent avenue of approach. Come to think of it, he should have put out claymores to secure the flanks.

The second team hit the gap and Teddy took a last look back—left, right—scrutinizing the night. Hit the bone mike. "Mud Cat, Tore, you on this? Got our backs?"

"Got it" and "Secure on your right" came back. He clicked off and followed the second team though the blown wall.

Cored with rock, apparently, but still fiftysome pounds of explosive had flattened and blown it inward and across the courtyard that hearted most residences in this part of the world. No sight of the shooter who'd fired at him; either under the rubble or somewhere on the roof, whole or in parts. Along with the tac lights some of the guys had lasers on, and the dust in the air swirled through the needle-thin beams as they darted from door to door. He counted six doors, some open, others closed. The clearance teams were going through them. A flash-bang jerked glaring light into existence for a microsecond within badly fitted rock walls, and someone screamed. A woman's cry, or a child's.

Teddy caught Dollhard in the center of the courtyard. He was moving up to the lieutenant when two doors slammed open and muzzle flashes chattered. He wheeled and returned fire, but the twist threw his aim off, and for a moment he was left standing in the open returning fire from whoever was invisible inside, not a good setup. Dollhard was firing too, both of them on full auto, pouring it in the way you did to convince whoever was in there to quit. The tracers came up at the bottom of their mags, and they both hit the releases and swapped out at the same moment. The second 240 gunner was firing too, a ripping burst that chewed smoke and dust up, but when he stopped whoever was in there fired again. "We're not making an impression on these guys," Dollhard grunted.

Teddy was already sprinting left, though, and snap-aimed and fired the grenade from his 203 through the door. It clanged into something not only solid but metallic, a strangely artificial sound in this world of rock and mud, and instead of going off bounced back out into the courtyard and hopped a couple of times in the dust and rolled to a halt. Dudded.

Dollhard was yelling in what Teddy guessed was Pashtun. Telling them to surrender, probably. All he was getting from inside was what sounded like catcalls, jeers. *"Allahu Akbar"*—he knew that one. "Jesus fuck," he snarled, reloading on his belly behind some kind of low wooden . . . water trough? Hadn't seen any animals, though the shit stink was overpowering where he was lying. If it *was* animal shit. He was shivering, even geared up and layered. Nobody'd told him it would be like the fucking Arctic. He fired another grenade. This one went off in there but didn't reduce the volume of return fire. He kept seeing hints of something each time a muzzle flashed. Angular and fairly big, by its shadow. A renewed stutter from a 240, behind them. Distant thuds of the howitzer shells coming down from the Spectre. Breaking up any attempt at reinforcement, he hoped.

"Covering," the lieutenant yelled, and Teddy stuck his barrel over the trough and let go. Dollhard leapt up, took four strides, and overhanded a pitch through the double doors. A burst flickered at the same moment, and the stubby OIC staggered and went down.

The incendiary blasted fire all through the interior of what immediately became evident was a garage. Screams burst out, but two men kept firing even as they burned, hunched over the treads of what Teddy, yelling for someone to help him get the lieutenant out of there, realized was a bulldozer. No wonder their bullets had ricocheted. As he dragged an unresponsive Dollhard into cover, secondary explosions shot renewed showers of sparks up through a ruptured roofline. Where did these sheep-fuckers get a fucking bulldozer? Then the roof fell in, illuminating a peeling red star on the machine's flank just before flaming beams and debris covered it.

The corpsman took over, propping Dollhard's head up and getting his gear off. Teddy left them and followed Echo One, which had plunged into the warren on the left, continuing to take rooms down. When he left the now fully firelit courtyard, coughing and spitting into the chickenshitty dust, he found them mustering prisoners in a hallway. The Talibs sat with legs crossed and heads bent, custody bags over their heads, hands zip-tied behind them. The SEALs threw weapons clattering onto a pile in a front room. "Any of these fuckers Omar?" Teddy asked the squad leader over the bone mike.

"Nah. They all got two eyes, Chief."

"Fuck. How many more rooms?"

"Two more, Chief. Then we're up to the front gate."

"Get it done. Make sure that gate's locked and barred. We don't want anybody at this rodeo we didn't invite." He switched back to Echo Two, which had followed Lieutenant (jg) Verstegen around the burning garage toward the antenna. Petty Officer Wasiakowski said he was setting demo on it and the transmitter, plus they had a lot more ordnance. Teddy told them they could thermite the weapons in place, but he wanted the ammo carried out into the wadi before they nuked it. "Tell Verstegen we want all male EPWs back in the courtyard for extract. Get some fire in your ass! There's always gonna be more weapons. We can't stick around here fingering each other's buttholes."

The roar-whine of a 53 going over, as if reminding them to enplane and get the hell out of here. Already in the distance AKs crackled and a higher-pitched rattle might be an RPK. Intel had doubted the locals would back up Johnny Taliban if foreign infidels fell out of the sky. Teddy wasn't so sure. He shoved the hooded captives along, ignoring the wailing of the women. Little kids sobbed, clutching their fathers. This left him unmoved. He didn't mind hate-filled looks. A lot of kids in New York City would never see their parents again. "Wait a minute! Where you think you're going with that?"

"Souvenir, Chief."

"Fuck that. Find a pistol, you can keep that. But no AKs. On the pile."

"Roger that, Chief."

He figured one or two would go back anyway, but if they were smart, they'd keep them out of his sight. He didn't think much of the Kalashnikov. It was for people who had to be told not to shit where they drank.

In the courtyard again as thermite M14s went off, trickling molten iron down into piles of weapons with hissing flares. Guys were carrying crates of ammo out and pitching it down into the wadi. Past the breach a Pave Low was settling, kicking up the same huge dust cloud as it had dropping them off. A burst rattled from Mud Cat's 240. What the fuck was he shooting at? The wind gusted, booming a hanging sheet of tin on the burning garage and whipping great gouts of sparks away to whirl amid the stars. He got on the channel, got Echo One out the breach to set up security. Teddy frisked each prisoner as he filed past. They were small men, but, God, they stank. He found a knife under a droopy shirt and whacked the SEAL escorting the prisoner with it. "Good thing I found this, dickhead, or you'd be pulling it out of your kidneys. Quit cheese-dickin' around and *search* these sand monkeys."

"Aye, Chief."

"Okay, hold 'em up there. Gangway. Chief coming through."

He was climbing the rubble at the blown hole at the back of the compound, boots slipping and grating, when he heard a cough. The whine of some kind of starter. Then, a clatter, and then, as it caught, the full-throated roar of a big diesel. He scrambled through the gap and oriented on the sound.

From another wall, down the wadi, smoke was rising. It was down there, throbbing steadily in the night. Another bulldozer? A truck? That's what it sounded like. A *big-ass* truck.

A heavy crunching. The rattle of stones.

With a bellow, something very large indeed crashed out through, or maybe over, a wall. He glimpsed it for a second, blackness in motion, then lost it. He ran to the edge of the wadi, pushing down his NVGs. Caught it shambling left to right, figures loping after it shimmering in the heat-detecting lenses. At the second glimpse, a chill passed through him like a low-voltage shock.

The intel briefing had told them everything known about the enemy order of battle. Type, number, location, weapons, satellite photos, and written analysis. Not one had mentioned this. But he'd seen that black parallelo-gram, glowing heat-white from its rear deck, before. Not exactly state-of-the-art. But still not what any SEAL wanted to see on a battlefield.

It was a Soviet-era BMP, the armored personnel carrier the Russians had left scattered across Africa and Eastern Europe as indiscriminately, though not in the numbers, as the ubiquitous AK-47. Hidden, like the bull-dozer. So the satellites never saw it.

For a moment he thought the wadi would trap it, that they could fire down at the weaker top armor. But the engine snorted as it pitched up and climbed at a forty-five-degree angle, then slammed down and rumbled out onto the field. Half armored personnel carrier, half light amphibious tank, the thing was all danger. Thirteen tons. Off-road speed, thirty miles an hour. Even as he thought this, a stream of burning light darted across the field at it from the helicopter, which was already slamming its rotors into positive pitch to take off. The 20mm shells hit square, but when the dust cleared the monster was still snarling, tossing its head as it took the undulations of the furrowed field like an angered bull, the long barrel of the 73mm smooth-bore coming around to search for prey. From somewhere in his memory, some drowsy briefing hall, came *Later variants uparmored for service in Afghanistan.*

"Armor, left flank. Crossing left to right" came over the tac net.

Ahead Dollhard was being carried between two men. His eyes were open, staring upward, but the way his head lolled, he was dead. Teddy looked left and right, finally caught Verstegen's too-tall, stringy outline against the still-burning garage. These people must have captured and then hidden all sorts of equipment from the retreating Russians. Including the heavy MGs that now barked all around the valley, making it more and more dangerous for the helicopters. Shit, he hoped they didn't have any old Stingers. The immediate problem, though, was still turning its turret, searching them out. It traversed past the now ascending Pave Low, then belched flame. The shell went wide and exploded somewhere in the distance. The chopper banked away, pouring on the power and firing a whole new series of flares, more or less in reflex, Teddy guessed.

A renewed crackle of small arms began behind them, from the compound they'd just left. The M240 ripped, ripped again. The fire slackened. But as soon as Mud Cat stopped, it picked up again. A flash flickered, and something bulky and glowing flew slowly overhead, wobbling as it went.

He caught up to Verstegen as the jaygee signaled the men into line from behind a stone fence slumped into rubble. They gazed up from where they lay, weapons pointed to the flank. One man was unlimbering an AT4, the only thing they carried that might make a dent. The warhead was warranted for 420 millimeters of steel, but any uparmoring had no doubt included a standoff plate, to set off and disrupt the shaped-charge jet.

Verstegen must have recalled this too because he beckoned the man with the antitank rocket toward him. Another echoing blast of dust and flame, and a second shell screamed over their heads. Teddy jumped to his feet, sprinted over, and dropped behind the rubble. Where was the air combat controller? He put out a call on the tac circuit . . . no joy. A possibility chilled him: Could the Air Force controller have made it to the helo? Was he even now on his way out, leaving them behind? They were all trained to call in air support, but the ACC had the codes, the freqs, and the radios.

"Could be a shit sandwich, Obie."

"Yes, sir, concur. What's the plan?"

"It's an ambush. We assault into it. Covered by the AT4s."

True, this was one of their immediate action drills, but he didn't think assaulting a BMP with small arms and AT4s was smart. "Maybe not a good idea, sir. And if they've got any more of them hidden away around here—"

"What do you recommend, Chief?"

"Be better to pull back. Into the compound, if we have to. Call the Spectre, let them handle it. We can't use the primary extraction LZ. They can just follow us and knock the helos down when they come in."

"It's too late to call off the extraction."

"No, sir, it isn't. Tell them to abort and prep for an alternate LZ. Have the platoon fall back through the rally point and through the alternates until we find a position they can extract us."

Verstegen looked undecided. Which was not a good expression to see, at the moment.

The BMP let off another round. This too sailed over their heads, but not as high. Why was it just sitting there? Maybe going down into that ditch had busted something? But as he watched it rocked, then rolled forward again. Uncertainly, slewing side to side. Whoever was driving must be learning on the job. Obviously he didn't know how to aim the main gun. Making it slightly less dangerous, but if it just wheeled around and came in on them, they weren't all going to make it. And he had the feeling that was exactly what it was about to do.

"Stand by. Blast area clear—"

"Clear—"

A lance of flame and a cloud of dust and bitter-smelling smoke erupted behind the prone SEAL to Teddy's right. The rocket motor flared as it left the tube, then winked to a glowing ember that shrank rapidly. It missed the still-turning vehicle, not by much, but enough, and exploded in a mud building beyond, blowing a hole an arm's width across. The clods banged on steel but that wasn't going to hurt anybody. Teddy had a momentary urge to grab an AT himself, but steadied down to concentrate on talking in the Spectre. Unfortunately it was at the north of the valley, dueling one of the antiaircraft sites; balls of fire were flying down from the Bofors and lighting up the hills. An incredible bleedover was on the frequency. It sounded like three, four people talking at once. He shook the handset, cursing.

He was still trying to talk them back to Tantalum when with a deafening roar the Pave Low swept over the compound. Its minigun chattered and more dust and smoke leapt up.

The long barrel trembled, cranked upward a bit more, and fired.

The shell ripped through the helicopter like a flare off the surface of the sun. The aircraft staggered away, sagging to port, and nutated down into another compound. Hot pieces came up glowing and tumbled back to earth again. A hollow, metallic *crump.*

When he switched his attention back to the tank, the wedgy, slanted-forward snout was coming out of the dust and smoke at them. Whoever was driving had finally mastered the steering and the accelerator. Smaller figures shifted and blurred behind it, trotting forward.

Verstegen rose up and yelled to advance, throwing a leg over the stone wall.

Teddy took three swift strides, caught the leg as it swung down on the far side of the wall, and set his Bates Ultra-Lite inside the assistant pla-toon commander's boot. He rolled Verstegen over his hip and slammed him into the ground. Pinned him there, on the far side of the wall from the others, and spoke into his ear. "You tripped. *Sir.* That's a good thing. Be-cause nobody's going to follow you out there. Get that installed in your brain housing group, okay? Now, order me to handle this. Or I'll hook your fuckin' ass up, here and now."

"You . . . you'd better take charge. Chief." The jaygee was gasping, his tone mingled relief and resentment. Teddy knew he'd pay for this. But right now he wasn't going to waste worry on it. He rolled back over the wall, scuttled on hands and knees along as someone in the oncoming ar-mor figured out how to fire the machine gun. Slugs whacked around him, cracked past, but no one seemed to be hit. Yet.

"Stand by . . . blast area clear . . ." The last two antitank rockets fired with a sound between a thud and a hiss, with a cloud of blasted-up dust that sparkled in the greenlit darkness. An explosion; another cloud; but no evident effect on the target.

That was it. Nothing was left to stop the oncoming monster. It turned for the point the antitank weapon had fired from and rolled forward a few yards before hesitating again. Teddy turned his back to it and fired out a mag into the flashes from the compounds to either side. They all seemed to be aiming high. The bullets hummed and sighed above them. Firing blind, into the night. He was about to order fall back and cover, each man firing out his magazine in turn to cover the retreat of his buddy, but sud-denly realized something. That was why the BMP was proceeding so hesi-tantly. The driver couldn't see them.

"Cease fire. Cease fire!" The order leaped from mouth to mouth along the ragged wall. Teddy followed it with the word to pull back toward the ditch. "Covering fire, but only on the compounds," he told the 240 gunners. "Fall back through the compound, head for the alternate LZ. Everybody look for the ACC. We got to find the ACC."

"He's back here" came an unfamiliar voice. Teddy rolled into the ditch, popped up, oriented, and hit the bone mike again. "Send him to the ditch, goddamnit! Where the fuck's he been?"

"Had a close shave. Roof fell in, knocked him cold. "

"Well, get his ass up here! Now!"

The controller was hustled up. A bandage patched his temple, but he seemed to have his shit together. The distant drone of the big aircraft changed pitch and grew louder. The BMP roared and slewed anew. Its gun boomed again.

A bolt darted from the heavens and exploded. When the boiling murk settled, the tank lay like a stepped-on toy, burning fiercely. Teddy kept his reticle on it, but no one emerged. The flames grew. There were no more infantry out there, just shapes fading back toward the fields and compounds beyond.

He remembered the shot-down helicopter. "Ski, take four guys and the corpsman over and secure the crash site. Survivors out, bodies out, rig for demo. I'll be over in a couple'a minutes."

The drone of the Spectre retreated, floating out over the valley, echoing from the hills. The battle of titans had ended. The crackles and booms from below were waning too, as if taking down the armor had climaxed the action. Another 53 was lining up on the field. Abort? Go to the alternate? Teddy decided for the primary. He straightened, keeping a stone wall between him and the field in case someone out there had a sniper rifle. He sent Scooper out to pop a strobe for pickup. Then pulled out a PowerBar and wolfed it, going over the mission objectives. Get Dollhard on the first bird out, with the prisoners. Sanitize. Retro everybody else. He and Verstegen would be last off the ground.

A last bullet whined disconsolately overhead. Fired at long range as the enemy pulled out. He rubbed his face, sagging, realizing only now how exhausted he was.

Light armor. Heavy machine guns. Probably a hundred enemy, all told. A helo shot down. If the guy in the BMP had known how to drive it, the Talibs could have rolled up the platoon. Not one guy in the garage had surrendered. They'd fought to the end. It didn't make him feel good about what would happen once they got these dudes cornered, where they couldn't retreat. It would be bloody. Grunt-side work, for the Green Monster. Marine shit, not SEAL duty. Next time: claymores, AT4s, antitank mines, and have a heart-to-heart with Verstegen about who actually called the plays when they were in contact.

The ACC, slumping past, burdened with gear. "You okay, Chief?"

Teddy gave him the big grin, bent over, still sucking the dusty, freezing, smoky air. From the wadi came the wailing of the prisoners as they were herded up toward the chopper and captivity. "Just another easy day, buddy. Just another . . . easy day."

13

Sana'a

TO Aisha, the moonless night seemed twice as dark without a counter-surveillance element supporting her, without contractor escorts, with no one in the car with her except for Hiyat and the other Yemeni women.

Her friend from the mosque did not look nearly as youthful or beautiful as she had at the *tafruta*. Her dark eyes were shadowed; her swan neck sagged her head against the window. Gaida was driving. Jalilah sprawled in the passenger seat. Aisha wasn't sure whose Mercedes this was. Probably Hiyat's husband's. He built houses overlooking the city, on steep slopes no one had thought could be built on. When Aisha had gotten in, they'd clung to each other. Hiyat had wept, but without passion. As if tears held no relief anymore.

"He was such an obedient boy," she kept muttering. "So . . . good."

Aisha sat itching beneath full Kevlar, pistol holstered under a dark burka, Doanelson's personal number already predialed in her cell. Tim Benefiel was trailing them some blocks back, but just now she was seriously doubting if this meeting was wise. Going out against orders . . . tonight could be the end of her career.

The women were vying to bombard her with opinions. "Hiyat's right," Gaida spat. "These Salafis, they're not Yemeni. We knew God before foreigners came along to tell us how to pray. And now they blow us up? It's got to stop, that's all. My husband went to their meeting. He told me. About how we had to restore the caliphate, how the Jews and the Americans had to be stopped. I told him, I don't know any Jews, but I know an American, and she's just like us."

Jalilah said, "Still, I don't know if this is smart. Taking her to them? What if they decide we are *murtadd* and kill us? Such things have happened in other lands."

"If you allow it, they'll happen here too," Aisha told them. "You're brave to do this. Many more must know about them. But they keep silent, I guess."

Gaida said, "Oh, we all know them, yes. They leased those apartments. They paid with riyals, Saudi money. The whole year, one payment. They bought air conditioners. Trucks. They have women in. And a guard in the hallway, with a gun. It's in a bag, but we all know it's a gun."

Which meant the PSO had to know too, Aisha thought. Did that make what she was doing tonight more or less dangerous? But if she'd gone through channels, gotten host-nation clearance, the people they were going to see would have disappeared. Warned, by the very officials who were professing their cooperation. She had no diplomatic immunity. If the PSO apprehended her, she'd be subject to arrest, a nasty spy trial, or PNG'd— declared persona non grata. None of that anything to look forward to, career-wise.

But what should she have done? Huddled behind the embassy walls, as Caraño wanted? Let Yemen go down the same drain as Sudan and Somalia?

"What kind of bag?" Aisha asked, trying to ignore a little voice insisting, Homegirl, you are way out of your depth. "A black gym bag?"

"That's right. How did you know?" The older woman frowned, and Aisha reminded herself, Shut up. Let them tell you. Don't tell them.

"We knew," Hiyat moaned. "But our husbands told us not to make trouble. So now Husayn is dead."

What Aisha found most astonishing was not that she was out here, but that they were. Most Yemeni women were illiterate. They had no health care, not even midwives. These three were wealthy—they had doctors, no doubt; their husbands were rich. But even so, driving was forbidden, and the way Gaida was swerving from lane to lane showed she hadn't had much practice on an actual street. Even being out at night, with other women—this had to take a courage Aisha could only dimly grasp.

"No more mothers should cry," she told them. "We'll end this. Where exactly are we going?"

"You will see, you will see," Gaida said, chewing on a fold of black cloth as she slewed around a corner, tires shrieking. Aisha was glad traffic was sparse. If anything had been coming in the other lane, they would have just front-ended it.

THE car eased to a stop behind one of the gingerbread high-rises in a thickly populated quarter. She took a quick look around as they got out, but couldn't see the mosque dome; couldn't make out, from the dim cutouts of the mountains, exactly where they were. Somewhere west of the Old Town, but inside the 60 Meters Road that ran like a beltway around the southwest. She counted five stories of lit windows. Craning back, she made out lights at the top too, archways, the writhe of palm leaves in a light breeze. A sun-cheating rooftop garden.

Two women stood waiting near overflowing trash cans, muffled to the gills in black and strangely faceless in the dark. Gaida exchanged hushed words with them. Then one waddled forward and without a word took Aisha's hand. Thick, powerful fingers padded with calluses explored hers. Dark eyes flashed from a featureless shadow.

"She comes with us?" An accent Aisha didn't recognize, the voice roughened, careless.

"Yes."

"*They* do not know?"

"No. To them she will be one of yours."

The heavyset woman harrumphed, looking Aisha up and down like a poor cut of meat. Then turned and waddled away. A square of light appeared as a door opened, revealing dimly lit steps.

Heading up.

She turned to see all three of her friends standing beside the car. Making no move to follow. "You're not coming?" she muttered.

"*We* can't come, Aisha. They'd notice us."

"And our husbands—"

"They are all men, you see. These Salafis."

She saw; oh, yes. But what about her? "They won't notice *me*?" she whispered.

No response from the shadowy figures beside the chromium sparkle of the Mercedes. At last, a barely audible mutter. "You will see. But be careful."

The heavyset woman called angrily. Aisha flinched; hesitated. And at last turned and followed her to the stairs.

THE kitchen was extremely small, hot, and, with four women working furiously, crowded. A single overhead bulb flashed off boiling pots, gleaming trays, plates of hummus, chef's knives dicing tiny chilis. A fan with a bent blade went *clack-clack-clack* but didn't cool the air. Aisha smelled mint and chives and coriander, garlic and cardamom, coffee and cumin. And the women themselves, powerfully unwashed under many layers of unlaundered black cloth. Small bowls crowded the sideboard. A teapot whistled on an electric plate. The women hardly spoke, bustling about as if each knew in advance where the other was going to step. But whenever Aisha made a move, she bumped into someone. Eyes studied her from within basketlike masks. Their hands were African black, much darker than her own. Prespiration ran down under her dress. She panted in the steamy heat. The women explained nothing, said nothing, just worked. They were making *salta*, a heavily seasoned meat stew, and *shafout* with *lahuh* bread, like pita bread soaked in a spicy buttermilk sauce. A tray held dates, honey pastries, Turkish-style cakes, walnut and chocolate cookies, sweet egg breads. A refrigerator chugged. If not for the fear in her belly, she might have felt hungry.

She finally guessed who these women must be. The Al-Akhdam were black Yemenis, descendants of Ethiopian slaves. More like the untouchables of India than anything else. Their very name meant "servant" or "slave," and they were confined to tumbledown ghettos, restricted to trash collection, sewer work, when they could get work at all.

And cooking, of course. Just like her grandmother's mother, back in Carolina. Their flat, quick gazes cut her like honed knives. The largest and oldest seemed to be in charge, but the youngest looked no more than twelve. Whom did they belong to? She didn't even want to ask, to upset whatever arrangement Hiyat had made to slip her in among them. She seized a rag and began wiping countertops, sinks, stovetops. The worn cloth snagged on congealed grease. She blinked sweat from her eyes. She couldn't catch her breath. What the hell was she doing?

A bead curtain clacked and swayed, cutting the room beyond into strips of color. Still scrubbing, she eased between the women, toward it. Peered through.

This room was brightly lit. Eight or nine men sat on a figured carpet, listening with rapt attention to something being read aloud. The air was thick with some unfamiliar perfume. Some wore Saudi-style robes. Others, slacks and Western-style shirts. Not all were bearded, but all had a focused, humorless look. Most were in their twenties. Only one, sitting in an easy chair, was older, the back of his head tinted with gray. He faced away from her, so she couldn't see his face. He was the one reading, in a droning singsong.

Her vision shifted, narrowed. Weapons lay beside each man or leaned in the corners. AKs, mostly, and a few pistols. Curved magazines lay about, and gray-green boxes of Chinese-made cartridges.

She wondered if there were antitank missiles somewhere too. In a closet, in a crawl space. Under a carelessly thrown rug.

A heavy hand on her shoulder, pulling her back. "Do not look at them," the older woman grated.

"I'm sorry." Aisha dropped her eyes. Stepped back.

A clap of the hands. "Bring us coffee," a male voice called peremptorily. "And tea."

The big woman held her gaze. The hand tightened on her shoulder. "You take tea," she said slowly, in that unfamiliar dialect. Spacing her words, so Aisha understood. "Follow her." She jerked her head, and Aisha found herself looking down at the twelve-year-old.

Who with perfect sangfroid lifted a carafe and slipped through the beads into the diwan.

Aisha hung back, starting to shake. She couldn't. Then she reminded herself sternly, This is the chance you wanted.

The beads rattled more loudly as she lurched through, tottering on weak knees. Trying to balance a tray that suddenly weighed a ton. On it shifted and rattled sugar, Nescafé, chocolate-coated French mints.

The men did not look up. They were silent, listening to a tape that spun through a cassette player. The older man leaned over it. From it squawked a thin, high voice she didn't recognize.

"Hundreds of people used to doubt you and few only would follow you until this huge event happened. Now hundreds are coming to join you. The only ones who stay behind will be the mentally impotent and the hypocrites. Hundreds of people will go out to Afghanistan."

Then came another voice, and the hair stood up on the back of her neck.

She knew this one: deliberate, educated, dignified. The man who inspired his disciples to suicide for his lost caliphate. Who'd murdered thousands and intended to kill many thousands more.

"We calculated in advance the number of casualties," bin Laden mused. *"Who would be killed, based on the position of the tower. We calculated that three or four floors would be hit. I was the most optimistic of all. Due to my experience in this field, I thought the fire from the fuel in the plane might melt the steel frame and collapse not only the area where the plane hit, but all the floors above it. This was all we had hoped for."*

"Allah be praised," said the first voice.

Unable to feel her hands as they gripped the tray, Aisha moved from guest to guest following the girl, whose sure little feet stepped between outstretched legs and rifles, careful to touch no one. The listeners did not look up as they passed, save to take a teacup from the girl and hold it as she poured, or to help themselves to sugar or mints on Aisha's extended tray. Each man took only one mint. They were riveted to the voices, one thready and deferential, the other carefully enunciated, as if to remain audible through many copyings of the tape.

"I listened to the news and I was sitting. We were not thinking about anything, and all of a sudden, God willing, the news came and everyone was overjoyed. Everyone until the morning was talking about what was happening and we stayed until four o'clock, listening to the news, every time a little different. Everyone was joyous and saying, 'God is great,' 'God is great,' 'We are thankful to God,' 'Praise God.' And I was happy for the joy of my brothers. That day the congratulations were coming on the phone nonstop. 'God is great, praise be to God.'"

She approached the older man, who was still hunched over the player, face lowered so she couldn't see it. He waved her away impatiently, not looking up.

Get a grip, Aisha. Start acting like a federal agent. She pushed the tray forward, to force him to glance up. Age fifty to fifty-five, large nose, dark complexion, Arabic extraction. Was that a wen on the right cheek? An old scar to the left temple?

Looking annoyed, he glanced up from the player, and she stared full into the face of Abu-Hamid Al-Nashiri.

Her blood froze and her breath stopped. Remembering a basement, and this man's curses, and his blow. His very smell was familiar. She waited an endless time for him to shout, to draw the ornate dagger at his belt.

Instead he dropped his gaze and gestured her away. She took a shaky breath, sucking damp cloth into her mouth, and remembered, All he can see is my eyes. She took a step back. Then another, easing her weight away on numb legs.

She turned her back as soon as she could and moved from man to man, bending to serve, scrutinizing each face, noting each distinctive mark, estimating ages. Her heart hammered so hard, sparkling flakes drifted up from the corners of her vision. One younger man glanced up, and her heart froze again; but his gaze slid off as if her face were black ice.

Their fingerprints. She had to sequester the teacups. If only she could get a photograph. Her camera was in her bag. But the thought of poking a lens through the bead curtain chilled her marrow. Those ornately hafted knives would so easily slide out of those belts.

"He told me a year ago: He saw in a dream, we were playing a soccer game against the Americans. When our team showed up in the field, they were all pilots! He said, 'So I wondered if that was a soccer game or a pilot game?' Our players were pilots. He didn't know anything about the operation until he heard it on the radio. He said the game went on and we defeated them. That was a good omen for us."

She stepped over a rifle and approached the last one in the room, a sullen-looking youth who sat cross-legged a few feet from the others. Listening, but with a faint sneer. At what, she couldn't tell. Eighteen to twenty, short hair, no beard or mustache, no visible scars or marks, a black TRANS-FORMERS T-shirt and ragged jeans the color of dusty skies. The girl offered him hot water, but he refused with an irritated gesture, as if brushing away a fly. The girl stepped away and Aisha almost followed, but turned back and offered the tray one last time.

The boy glanced up, then away. He reached for a mint, fumbled among them, came up with four. He was popping them when a frown creased his brow. His eyes came back to the tray. Followed it to her hand. Up her wrist.

To her watch, which had slid down as she bent to serve. He examined it, then lifted his eyes to her face.

She realized too late what she'd done wrong.

She'd looked back, met him gaze to gaze.

He seized her wrist. "Uncle! Come look at this. Look what the slave is wearing!"

She stood rooted, unable to move. Tried to tug her hand free. But the boy held on. She groped for the pistol with her other hand, under the abaya. She'd never shot well weak-handed, but she'd take out Al-Nashiri first. Then the boy, since he was closest. By then the others would have their rifles up, and she wouldn't have to worry about who to shoot next.

Instead a resounding slap to the nape of her neck jerked her whole body, and the tray catapulted out of her hands. The boy screamed as hot water flew into his face, followed by a hail of thin mints. The next moment Aisha was cowering under a stream of mingled abuse and apologies by the large woman, who was hauling her bodily out of the diwan by one ear. It hurt like hell. Aisha moaned, and then, when the woman shook her and pinched harder, even louder. She was hauled through the bead curtain, the men shouting, the boy's keen rising above the rest. Then slaps cracked. "Shut up, stupid boy! Silence!" the older man roared. "The sheikh speaks from the Place of Kings, and there will be silence when he speaks!"

When Al-Nashiri came through the bead curtain, livid and scowling, Aisha was already on the floor, being beaten with soup ladles. As he entered, the woman handed him a stick. "This clumsy Sudanese is new. Hardly even speaks the language. Here, I am not strong enough to beat her as she deserves."

Aisha rolled over just in time as the stick whistled down. Pulled arms and legs to her stomach, presenting her back, both instinctively and to protect the pistol; striking something that hard under her clothing would instantly give her away. The Kevlar absorbed most of the blows, but they still hurt. One on the head made her ears ring, and stars danced before her eyes. She clutched her face, holding the cloth in place. Above all else, he must not recognize her.

The Saudi straightened, breathing hard. "No meal for her tonight," he ordered. The woman followed him to the curtain, wringing her hands, apologizing again and again, asking him to beat her too, ducking her head and striking her breast. Aisha thought she might be overdoing it, but maybe not.

When he was gone, the beads swayed and clacked. No one spoke in the kitchen for a long moment. Aisha took her hand off the pistol under the abaya. Then dropped it to another pocket.

She made absolutely sure the flash was off as she aimed the little camera between the still-swaying beads. They were gathered around the player again; the soft, cultured voice spoke on and on. Pressing the camera to the jamb so it would not pick up the shaking from her hands, she took a photograph. Then another, zooming in on faces.

Another.

A hand on her back, murmured pleas to stop, to leave.

One more. Hands shaking, she plunged the camera back into the folds of her abaya. Turned to the sink and found a net bag she stuffed teacups and mugs into, one after the other.

The back stairs, dimly lit and tilted as in a dream. The cups jangling in the bag.

The Mercedes idling, dark shapes taking her arms, ushering her in. Her pulse hammering in a splitting headache. Lifting her hand to the second car that came rolling out of the night: the SUV that had trailed them from the compound, Benefiel's young, anxious face peering out through the windshield as he rolled up.

"Hello? Scott?" she said into her cell.

Doanelson's voice, a little slurred. Into the bourbon, no doubt. "Uh—yeah. Who's this? Aisha?"

"Get on the line to Al-Safani," she told him. "I know exactly where these guys are."

THE next morning, in the deputy chief's office. With that eminence himself, thunder-browed, leaning back as he pondered the charges Caraño had just brought. Benefiel was sitting mouse-reticent to the side, out of the line of fire. But not, Aisha thought, out of the blast zone. She sat with hands folded, waiting for the guillotine.

She'd gone back up the service stairs alone, while the assault team assembled. Led the four serving women back down, gently, quietly, until they were out of the way and safe. Then nodded to the colonel, who stood in full gear by a line of fidgeting, nervous-looking interior security troops. Just as in the first assault, when the girl had died, they carried AKs and tear gas grenades and flash-bangs and resembled goggled monsters in their Czech masks. Al-Safani's expression had been a mixture of inscrutability and irony as he listened to her describe how many terrorists there were, which floor they were on, how they were armed, how many accesses to the apartment there were.

The DCM swiveled lazily. Time stretched out. She surreptitiously checked her cell for any texts from Washington. Nothing yet.

Finally he said, "Tell me again what they said about bin Laden."

She focused, trying to recall each word and even the way it had been uttered. "It was Al-Nashiri. He said, 'The sheikh speaks from the Place of Kings.'"

"The Place of Kings." The DCM rolled that around on his palate; the FBI supervisory special agent frowned. "Where is the Place of Kings?"

"I have no idea. But *he* must."

"As a matter of fact, he did." The DCM picked up a sheaf of faxed paper, let it fall. "This time they were expeditious. I think the gloves really are off, now."

"As long as the president thinks it benefits him more than it handicaps him, to be seen working with us."

The diplomat sighed. Tilted his head this way and that. Brought his chair down and swung to face her. "I'm not pleased, Agent Ar-Rahim. I expect my orders to be obeyed. State can't host other agencies if they're off on their own."

"I understand that, sir."

"On the other hand, an intel coup . . . Can't gainsay that. Especially if what NSA expects to be in their cell phones is actually there."

"Thank you, sir."

The intercom. "Sir, Mr. Abdulilah on line one."

"Thanks, Cheryl. Be right with him. . . . I'm going to defer further comment. There's a president-to-president call scheduled early this afternoon. What happened last night may get brought up. Anyway, I'm going to defer forming an opinion until then."

She kept her expression neutral, even let Caraño hold the door for her. He gave her a sour look but didn't say anything until they were outside. At which time he muttered, "This isn't personal."

"I never thought it was, sir."

"I think it was ballsy. Uh, gutsy. Just not well advised. Not well advised at all. I'm the supervisor on scene. You take tasking and direction from me. Not go off on your own special mission, risking the lives of two agents. I can't overlook that, no matter what the DCM decides."

"You've made that clear, Special Agent. Just one thing. A favor."

"What?"

"Leave the kid out of it."

"Tim?" The FBI agent considered. "Leave him out of my report? Sorry, can't do that, Agent Ar-Rahim. He was off reservation too."

She briefly considered how to answer him and could think of nothing that really suited. So she just turned away. She had a message back to MEFO to draft, after all.

THEY met again late that day, out front of the embassy, where three shining black automobiles were drawn up idling. A smooth, placid face turned toward her in the rosy light of the dying sun. "Agent Ar-Rahim," he said, bowing slightly. "Peace be upon you."

"And upon you, brother."

The DCM nodded soberly. "Mr. Abdulilah has news for us."

"It is good news, I believe," the little minister with the coal-black eyes said. "Passed to your president by mine. The men we took into custody last night have confessed. They have given much information about their activities in this country, and their plots against the persons of our brothers across the border in the Kingdom of Saudi Arabia. We have information about the current location of Osama bin Laden, which we will pass to you immediately. We have also recovered significant quantities of armaments, stolen from our army stocks by sympathizers."

"I'm very glad to hear that," she said. "Working together, we can do wonders."

The DCM said, "An NSA team's on its way. I've requested access to the recovered computers and cell phones." He looked past Abdulilah to where Gamish sat stone-faced in the lead limo. "The general expects to work with us—following these electronic records, and of course the results of the interrogations—to roll up the ALQ network in this country and possibly in others as well. In Yemen and overseas."

"More excellent news," she said.

"But a warning," Abdulilah said, in his curiously dead English. "The terrorist acts recently committed in the Republic of Yemen represent a dangerous challenge for President Saleh. These groups intend to place us among the targeted areas under the pretext of fighting terror, which the whole world has agreed to fight. As is well-known, their ideals are alien to our Yemeni society. They contradict our deeply rooted and noble traditions and values."

"We completely understand," the DCM said.

"We are prepared to fight alongside other nations against lawlessness and terror. We will adopt a candid and frank discourse of wisdom and equilibrium in reacting to this phenomenon. The whole world needs to stand firm."

"Will we have access to Al-Nashiri again?" Aisha put in, getting impatient with the boilerplate, the posturing, the pretending.

The DCM blinked.

"Unfortunately, the international terrorist Abu-Hamid Al-Nashiri is dead," Abdulilah said. "Dying blindly in his wrong understanding of religion, in the absence of correct vision of the noble Islamic sharia based on dark and closed minds emanating from spitefulness. By his own hand, in his cell. Last night."

"That is . . . unfortunate. He could have told us so much." She looked past the two men, through the windshield, where Gamish stared steadily ahead, face stony.

So that was it. The Yemenis were on the side of the angels, had never dabbled in terror. And they'd all pretend that was how it was and look away and whistle if anyone said otherwise.

But the little man was still speaking. "However, I must convey a warning. We will accept outside support for our security apparatuses and further development of their technical capabilities. But it will not be overlooked again that foreign intelligence or police must not operate within the Arab Republic of Yemen. The security of our country must be based on our own sovereignty and our own police and independent judiciary."

"We hear you and fully agree," the DCM said, flicking a glance at Aisha. "Disciplinary measures are in hand against those who acted with an excess of zeal. Those lines will not be crossed again. We are merely guests in your land."

"That is most welcome to hear. I must further warn my friends, however," the minister went on. "President Saleh has worked very hard to foster a pluralistic, democratic society with full equality. But some have exploited these climates, the multiparty system, freedom of expression, to pursue evil goals which contradict peace and the supreme interest of the homeland. This is how the phenomenon of terrorism has been nurtured, and the president's reputation distorted. A firm hand must be shown. A policy of national consolidation has been decided on. This is the answer to terror, and we will expect your president's support in such actions, unpleasantly though they may be reported in the world press."

"And he will have it," the DCM said heartily. He held out a hand, and as the minister took it they turned as one to face a man crouching with a camera. At the instant the strobe flashed, Aisha lifted a fold of her head covering. Becoming a faceless one, whose dark eyes stared out at the camera, at the world, without expression, without comment, without opinion, forever a mystery and unknown.

14

Bagram Airfield, Afghanistan

D AN stepped off the helo into a once-familiar world of dust, jet exhaust, and windblown grit. The moon was an iridium sickle reaping a blue-black sky. Jagged mountains climbing like some fantasy-novel escarpment range on range against the stars.

He shielded his eyes, shivering, trying to get his bearings. The wind was freezing his eyelashes, and he'd been exposed to it for less than a minute. He had the three-color desert field jacket and gloves, but missed the enwrapping warmth of a Navy blue peacoat, or better yet, the long bridge coat. Those had kept him warm on the coldest winter mornings on Narragansett Bay, and much farther north.

But here, in a combat zone far from the sea, it was battle dress for everybody. Fortunately he'd kept his DCUs from Ashaara: desert tan boots, soft patrol cap, and the black-oxidized rank insignia. He'd debated bringing his nine-millimeter, but a pistol was more of an encumbrance than an advantage the way he usually had to travel, which was commercial as often as military.

This time, though, had been military transport all the way. The vast machine was grinding its gears from peacetime to wartime, and for most of his flights he hadn't even had to present orders, just sign the manifest and go. From Prince Georges County he'd endured four levels of outbriefing and inbriefing, DC to McDill. Then twenty-eight hours of travel, finishing with a harrowing helicopter flight from Tajikistan over the Pamirs in the dark. Some over Taliban-held territory, so when they weren't passing oxygen masks back and forth and fighting unconsciousness from hypoxia, the ramp and side doors had been open so the machine gunners could report launch signatures or fire back. They'd shared the canvas-and-aluminum buckets with ten others, mostly Special Forces, along with pallets of ammunition.

Someone bumped into him. "Damn, it's dark," said Monty Henrickson. Dan grunted. He'd asked for the little operations analyst, and TAG had released him, subject, of course, to his volunteering—you couldn't issue overseas orders to civilians as easily as you could to military. They'd dragooned the rest of TAG Bravo to pack enough gear to serve as Tomahawk targeters, if they could get upload capability. "Any idea where we're going, boss?"

"Uh, not really."

Blinding lights came on, illuminating the strip like a night game at Yankee Stadium. Dan shaded his gaze, blinking into dust and ominous moving shapes. "Over here. Over here. Everybody from that last chopper in from Dushanbe," a bullhorn announced as a fuel truck rumbled toward them.

They ended up with a sergeant who seemed to know who they were and where they were intended to be. He told them the base had only been secured for a few days. The Taliban and the Northern Alliance had been fighting over it for two years; at times the opposing forces had held opposite ends of the ten-thousand-foot main strip, exchanging fire over bomb-canted concrete slabs. The Alliance and the Tenth Mountain held it now, though the enemy was still active in the direction of Kabul.

"Tenth and Eighty-second Airborne," the noncom amended, as someone in Dan's group protested. "You-all want to stay inside the wire, okay? The Alliance commander's set up in the terminal, but I don't think even he's real clear on which Afghans are ours and which ones are still rooting for the bad guys."

"We've got two pallets of expensive gear," Dan told him. "I don't want to leave that unguarded."

"I'll stay with it, Commander," Monty said.

"You don't need to," said the sergeant. "Just tag it and come back in the morning. It's not goin' anywhere. See those strobes? That's the EOD guys. Unexploded ordnance. Stay clear of those, and watch for the yellow tapes."

"It's okay," Henrickson said. "I'll stay."

Dan didn't like leaving him out here alone, but someone had to watch the gray metal boxes. "I'll find out where we're supposed to be, where we can stow all this shit, and come back," he told the analyst. "Find someplace you can stay warm, at least. Here, take my jacket."

Without it the air was even more biting. Dan's hands were going numb; his knees were so cold he was stumbling. The sergeant led them along paths he could only now and then make out, past Humvees and Toyota gun trucks and shattered pieces of concrete with rusty rebar sticking out of them. He flailed at himself with both arms, trying to stimulate some circulation. Drumming gensets powered stand-mounted lights that illuminated mountains of supplies and troops furiously erecting tents on ground snorting front-end loaders had just backed away from after scraping it level. The wreckage of a MiG lay gutted like a dead carp in the lee of a bombed, abandoned hangar with stars shining through the roof. The dark air smelled of burning and dust, old shit and diesel exhaust. They threaded between unfamiliar hulks that he only at length identified as abandoned and wrecked tanks.

At last the sergeant swung open a flimsy, creaking gate of barbed wire coiled around two-by-fours and identified himself to a sentry. They emerged into an open space of shouting, running men and snapping, billowing canvas. Except for the lack of elephants, it looked as if a circus were setting up.

"This'll be the JOC. The Joint Operations Center," the sergeant said. Dan looked around. *Chaotic* was a gentle word for it. "They're not quite ready for prime time yet. Go find a bunk. Try over there by the red lights. Come back in the morning and we'll have things better organized."

Dan took the hint and dragged his duffel to a GP Medium, snagging a bunk walled in by palletloads of MREs in brown cardboard. There was a drop light, a heater but no fuel, and the inside of the tent was the same temperature as the outside. He was walking across the compound in search of a piss pit when a far-off thud caught his attention.

It was followed by two more, but he was sprinting, looking for a trench, hole, any sort of cover. The best he could do was a wall of sandbags around a wrecked revetment. He pasted himself against the cold, gritty sand leaking from shrapnel-punctured bags as the shells came down like broken-off chunks of the moon and lurched across the compound in flashes of yellow light and jolts like safes falling from the top of the Empire State. He wrapped his arms over his head, waiting for the next blast. Instead a distant clatter of small-arms fire grew. It crested, then tapered off.

It waxed again, until a series of deeper booms echoed off the hills. When they faded, the firing spluttered to an uncertain pause. The whistle of the wind was once again the loudest sound. Around him forms uncoiled from the ground like snakes suddenly given the gift of uprightness. "Just probing the east sector," somebody murmured, and the words threaded the dark with the swift wings of scuttlebutt.

THE next morning he snapped awake at 0500 and washed up from plastic bottles at a mountain of bottled water. The used paper towels went into a flaming drum. The wind was stiff with dust, and everyone in line was hacking and spitting. Some had cloths tied over their mouths, which might not be a bad idea. He was walking back toward where he'd left Henrickson when he smelled something good. He joined the line and got a tray for himself and one for Monty and carried them and precariously balanced fiberglass mugs of coffee back to the strip.

Henrickson was awake, sitting on the gear. With Dan's jacket on over his parka he looked like a kid in his father's clothing. "Thanks for watching it," Dan told him, feeling guilty all over again at leaving him there. But really, it hadn't been so great in the tent, either. "Get any sleep?"

"A little." Henrickson got half the coffee down in the first swallow. "Slept in the cab of one of those fuel trucks most of the night. Kept the heater running. It was nice and warm."

A C-130 trundled down out of the sky as they hailed a passing truck of Air Force construction troops and got the cases lifted into the bed.

The truck groaned past a tan-painted, aluminum-sheeting-roofed, bullet-pocked terminal building, through conex boxes and tents and windblown plastic and twisted, rusting trusses and wire and ancient garbage and discarded snowplow blades and more broken concrete. At the far end of a cracked apron dozens of wrecked aircraft lay canted two and three deep like plastic models stamped on and thrown aside by a violent and petulant child. A small team of troops in unfamiliar camo were slowly passing mine detectors across the ground, passersby skirting the yellow tape fluttering around them.

Sitting in the bed of the truck, Dan lifted his eyes to the walled horizon. The nearer mountains were pointed like young women's breasts and dotted with puffs of dry-looking brush. In the other direction they rose more steeply, furrowed, eroded, the morning light picking out the slanting striations of ancient sea bottoms. The farthest were gray as granite, snow-topped and precipitous and utterly remote. But the ruddy morning light on them was tremblingly delicate, and clouds streamed slowly through their lofty passes.

The view was so breathtaking he could almost forgive them for being so dangerous in the dark, in a heavily loaded, altitude-limited helicopter. Three Thunderbolts crouched on the canted, bomb-pocked slabs of the main strip, heat eddying behind running engines. By day the base looked even more makeshift, overgrown and wrecked and bombed, as if thirty years of war had washed back and forth over it, leaving fresh layers of junk and debris with each receding wave.

As of course it had. Only twentysome miles from Kabul, Bagram had been the staging point for the Russian troop insertion. Airborne and Spetsnaz had been based here, and close air support flown up to the last days of the occupation. Which had begun, Dan was uncomfortably aware, after the domestic communist government had tried to jail extremist mullahs, educate girls, and attempt to repeal some of the rawer practices of Afghani Islam. The country outside the capital had reacted violently, and the United States had funneled arms and funds to a growing insurgency, never considering the long-term consequences—as usual.

Now NATO was going to try, where the British and Soviets had failed.

Stepping, it appeared, in the very same bootprints. Hulks of tanks and personnel carriers still littered the base. They were gradually getting towed to a junkyard to one side of the runway to join the litter of burned-out fuselages, broken wings, and defective engines that seemed to grow up alongside any Russian airstrip.

He shook his head. Above his pay grade, as usual. This administration seemed assured they'd succeed where so many others had failed. Who was he to doubt?

"This's it, Commander. Want a hand getting your shit off the truck?"

"Yeah, yeah, thanks. Sorry to bother you."

"That's what we're here for, Navy."

The JOC had taken shape overnight out of GP tents and a section of hastily reroofed revetment-slash-hangar. Crews were still running cables even as headquarters staff ripped open boxes, snapped open folding tables, and began setting up computers and screens and cots for the watch sections. Dan stood back, letting the Army do its thing. Pondering, not for the first time, how organized human beings seemed to get at the prospect of destroying things. Something crunched under his boots. Looking down, he saw he was standing on a carpet of expended brass mixed with a box of nails that had broken open and been trodden into the dry dirt.

When he located what they said would be the targeting section, he and Henrickson moved in, taping up a ripped-off piece of cardboard box Magic Markered US NAVY TOMAHAWK CELL. This pulled in folks who'd been roaming the edges of the action, and by the time dark fell, Dan had a ATWCS version 3 crew set up with three chiefs and two lieutenants. He'd identified his intelligence flows and linked up with the briefing team, the S-3 and the S-2. He found a Navy Predator team and established a data link. Targeting from the drone to an in-flight Tomahawk, which was possible with the Block IIIs, would let them put a weapon on something as mobile as a vehicle convoy.

He also had his first assignment: to brief General E. H. Salter, USA, at 0800 the following day.

THE next morning Donnie Wenck arrived. Wenck was another TAG member Dan had worked with on previous missions, a Navy first-class OS whose aw-shucks demeanor and occasional spaciness disguised a mastery of arcane software fixes. Dan put him and Henrickson to work smoothing out the rough edges of uploading targeting information and at 0745 headed to the command tent, cargo pockets bulging with notes and printed-out references.

As it turned out, it wasn't a one on one, but a command brief, and the brigadier wasn't even there. It was good for an overview of the Joint Task Force setup, though. There were Spanish, Italians, Canadians, French,

Germans, and British, along with the occasional bewildered-looking Afghan, and what Dan suspected were Ukrainians too.

Two things swiftly became plain. The first was that the campaign was going astonishingly fast. The Air Force briefers glowed. Precision-guided munitions had stripped the regime of air defenses; B-52 strikes had decimated their ground forces, which had made the mistake of concentrating in trench lines in expectation of frontal attack. Alliance forces had taken nearly every major city and captured a third of the enemy's senior personnel. The second was that as far NATO was concerned, this was a Special Forces war. In fact, he got the impression that aside from air support, few regular forces other than the Tenth Mountain and Eighty-second Airborne had been committed.

When the chief of staff nodded, Dan stood for a three-minute overview of what his cell could offer in the way of planning and coordinating multiship Tomahawk strikes. Several officers had questions, all positive, which marked a change from the way the elder service had looked at the missile years before, when he'd first tried to sell it as a deep-strike platform.

The chief of staff said they'd be back to him with a follow-on target package soon. "Meanwhile, I have another question. We don't have a NAV-FOR LNO assigned. We were promised one, but he's not here yet. We're still not sure we're going to organize by functional component or by service, but we need capabilities and recommendations, and we need them now."

The LNO was a liaison officer, linking the supporting component—in this case, the Navy—to the task force commander. A sticky assignment, if you didn't have an exquisite sense of what was possible and what wasn't, as well as an extensive network of people you could call up and ask no-shit questions of. "Uh, yes, sir," Dan said, thinking fast about what he'd have to do to not fall on his face. C2 channels, staff coordination, getting some kind of written authority with Salter's name on it—that would do to start with. The Navy air side was the area he'd have to get smart on fast. The USN was providing most of the air support for operations in the south.

"You feel capable of taking that on? Remember this is a NATO operation. Look at STANAG 2101. There's a procedure and comms checklist."

"Yes, sir, I can handle that for you. Until you get someone senior."

WALKING back through the screams of descending aircraft, the higher-pitched whines of A-10s taking off, Dan tried to decide where he should be during the daily ops cycle to juggle both of his hats—heading up the targeting cell, versus fulfilling the traditional four duties of an LNO—monitoring, advising, assisting, and what was the fourth? Oh, yeah, coordinating. He had to call USEUCOM and let them know he was warming the chair until whoever they were going to send got here. He had to go back to the fusion cell, make sure the tie-in was there with targeting, and see if there was any other way TAG could help.

A huge earthmover beeped as it backed up. Halting to let it pass, he noticed a hollow rectangle of dirt being bermed up a few hundred yards to the side of the runway. Workers were stringing razor wire, guard towers were going up. The mover stopped, blasted black smoke from its stack, rattled forward again. He walked on.

"Call for you," said Henrickson when he came in. Dan looked at the note. *Tent 65, SOF Compound.*

When he lifted the flap, he halted. The long canvas tunnel held folding tables with at least a dozen laptops, all occupied, strung together with bright blue Ethernet cable. The cable led to a comm package, antenna pointed at the peak of the tent. Everyone was talking at once. Off to the side, a man at a screen made a come-here gesture. Another, next to him, was shaking the handset of a scrambled phone, frowning.

"Dan. We meet again. Let me send this and I'll be right with you."

"Tony," Dan said. Not without apprehension.

His path and Charles Anthony Provanzano's had crossed before. Most notably, in the Signal Mirror recon into Iraq, sent to find what they'd thought at the time was a quickie nuke mounted on an uprated SCUD. Just looking at him took Dan back to the Slammer. Provanzano, then a "civilian adviser" to CINCCENT, had visited the survivors at the Biocontainment Suite at Fort Detrick as Major Maureen Maddox had died slowly and horribly of a disease that wasn't supposed to exist anymore. Now he was wearing jeans, a button-down shirt, and a UNIVERSITY OF MARYLAND sweatshirt just faded and torn enough to suggest authenticity.

"Yeah," Provanzano said. "Salter happened to mention you were here."

"Does he know me?"

"Does he know you? Who do you think got you that medal?"

"Which medal?"

"The Congressional," Provanzano muttered in a tone that said, *I am exercising great patience; but I realize you are only a military man.* "Anyway, one thing led to another. And I thought maybe we could do business." Provanzano glanced at the other man, who was logging out of the phone. He locked it and put the key down his sweatshirt on a blue lanyard. "Dan, this is 'Beanie' Belote. Out of the bin Laden desk in DC, and the closest thing we've got to a Pashtun expert. Beanie, Dan Lenson, one of the sharper operators in the Navy."

Belote had massive arms and a bull neck. His black hair was rubberbanded back in a ponytail. He was in jeans and a black leather Harley-Davidson jacket. He and Dan exchanged wary nods. Dan turned back to Provanzano. "I'm not sure where you're going with that, Tony. And I've got a briefing to get ready. So—"

"I know about the briefing. Siddown." The Agency man pointed at a folding chair and lifted a plastic cup in a toast. "You don't drink, or I'd offer. But—do I understand right? You were actually in the Pentagon, when it was hit? Like to hear the story."

"It's not a *story*," Dan said. "Just a lot of innocent people, suddenly blown apart or burned to death. Not that complicated."

"I see . . . that anger's good. If it doesn't get in your way."

"It hasn't before."

"I see what you mean. You're a survivor. Dumb, but a survivor. I'll give you that."

Dan hesitated, then let himself down into the chair. "Yeah, just a dumb squid. What's on your mind, Tony?"

"Just thought we'd catch up. We kept tabs on TAG. The Shkval, getting your hands on it—that was a dirty, dirty op. And I hear you had something to do with taking down Al-Maahdi, or whatever he called himself."

"The guy behind the Cosmopolite bombing?" Belote said, looking interested for the first time.

"The same. Dan, you might be interested to know: his buddy, the little fat one, hasn't been seen since the Saudis took him into custody. We doubt he's going to be involved in any more bombings."

"Should I say thanks?"

"If you want to."

Belote said, "I don't know you, buddy, but there's no reason to take that tone. We're all on the same side, right?"

"Are we?"

Provanzano said, uncapping a small white tube, "Yeah, we are. And never more so than now. An attack on the continental United States. We have to work together on this one." He put the tube into a nostril and sniffed; then did the other one. When he saw Dan looking, he held it up. "Vicks. Helps, with all this dust in the air. Want a hit?"

"We might not have had to 'work together' if you and the FBI had shared files." Dan tried to keep the accusatory tone out of his voice, but wasn't succeeding. "The 'Bin Laden Desk' might have figured out something was funny. Arabs taking flying lessons, but not bothering to learn how to land."

Belote said, "Believe me, buddy, you don't have the faintest idea what you're talking about. We had a local team following bin Laden for three years. If during that time anyone had given us the green light—"

"Uh-huh." Dan removed his hands from the sides of the metal chair, which were unpleasantly sticky, as if someone who'd just eaten a Bit-

O-Honey had last grasped them. Wiped his palms on his uniform trou as the civilian went on.

"Point being, since 9/11 the rules have changed. The review committees, we can't do this, can't say that—ancient history. We need people in the field who know the field. We gutted our expertise during the de Bari years. Which reminds me, you hear the joke? Jimmy Carter, Dick Nixon, and Bob de Bari are on the *Titanic*—"

"I heard it," Dan said. "Look, you've got your responsibilities, I've got mine. And mine just got a lot heavier."

"They're the same responsibilities." Provanzano set the cup aside. Looked at the inhaler again, but didn't pick it up. Dan smelled scotch and eucalyptus oil.

"Since he's here"—Dan nodded at Belote—"I assume this is about bin Laden. Is it? About him? Which seems to me to be the highest-priority tasking for all of us."

"It'd be nice," Belote said. "See that box?"

A large, heavy-looking, drab plastic crate with locking latches sat in the corner of the tent. "What about it?"

"Want to know what's in it?"

Dan suppressed a sigh. "Okay."

"Dry ice. For shipping bin Laden's head back. That's our orders: Get the head."

Dan dredged for a response, but none came.

"But even when we do, that won't be the end. This'll be a long war. Now, I want to hear about this localization program. The one you got Al-Maahdi with."

"You mean CIRCE," Dan said.

"We've got something like it," Belote said. "But not as far along as yours, apparently. You started with what, a submarine program?"

"Antisubmarine," Dan said.

Provanzano called up a file on his notebook. Read off the screen, "'CIRCE: a Navy-developed stochastic modeling agent reasoning framework. Developed from an off-the-shelf circle-of-contacts product. Originally intended to integrate multiple near-chaotic inputs in a littoral environment to locate quiet submarines. Now a multiagent model that integrates comms, intel, social and spatial relations to predict both location and strategies of a unitary actor.' Accurate?"

"Close enough."

"Who's your contractor?"

Dan said reluctantly, "We brewed it up in-house. With a local company. You probably haven't heard of them. They're not Beltway players."

Belote dove for the plywood floor. Dan went down a fraction of a second behind him; Provanzano and the others in the tent dropped next. The *crack* was like the sky wrenching open. The tent rocked; dust sifted out of the fabric and made the air suddenly choking. A second explosion, even closer, jarred splintered wood into his cheek. He pressed himself into it, eyes closed. Waiting for the third and last detonation that would end them all.

Lying next to him, Provanzano just kept talking. Through the blasts, and the clatter of a machine gun from the perimeter. "Like I said: the gloves are off. We want bin Laden. We'll do anything necessary to get him. Any caveats?"

"No argument here."

"Good, because you're on board. With us. With CIRCE. To find him."

Dan considered it between explosions. He'd always steered clear of the intel side. Not even sure in his own mind why, but he'd avoided it. The table above them jumped, and a computer slammed down onto the deck and bounced. The lights went out to the shrill, insistent peeping of backup power supplies. The burnt-matches smell of explosives seeped through the canvas, and above him two rips magically appeared. "Getting serious," Belote said. Looking at him, Dan saw he was grinning.

"I've got two assignments already. Targeting and Navy liaison."

"By tomorrow, you'll be one of us orcs," Provenzano said.

"Not volunteering."

"Nobody asked you to."

"Put up or shut up, buddy boy," said the stocky agent. "You don't think we did our job, got the towers blown up? Okay, show us how it's done. Here's a clue. 'The sheikh speaks from the Place of Kings.' Chew on that for a while."

"Yeah," Provanzano said. "Raw intel. What do you make of it?"

"Not much," Dan said. The firing outside had stopped. He sat up warily, ready to dive again. Around the tent the others rose, dusting off uniforms and jeans, cursing as they examined their screens. "The sheikh—that's bin Laden?"

"Who can be sure? That's the richness of the puzzle, Dan. The frustrating richness of the puzzle. Thousands of pieces. Millions. The picture depends on how they're arranged. But there's never only one picture. That's the problem, you see."

Dan ran his hands over his face, feeling stubble and grit. "I don't know anything about intel."

"Hell, who does? Welcome to the Rabbit Hole," Provanzano said, and slapped him heartily on the back.

IV

Black Dust

15

Thirty-Six Miles
South of Kandahar

T EDDY lay shivering, wishing he'd brought more fleece-lined gear. During the night the ground sucked the heat right out. He'd eaten all the carbs he'd brought, fuel for the furnace, and was unashamedly cupped into the other guys in the hide—Tatie and Two Scoops and Knobby Swager, all Echo One—just like, he thought, faggots after a hot night's humping. But he was still shivering.

Long before dawn, and sleep wouldn't come, just jagged, uneasy dreams between midnight and two. Now it was past three by the tritium glow of his watch. Still no sign of light, but the sun couldn't be far away.

He unlocked his pelvis from Tatie's angular butt, half-rolled, and set an eye to the big scope. The lens was shielded so it wouldn't sparkle, even when the sun shone into it. The camo sheet draped over them was the same light tan as the dusty desert sand. He let a handful trickle through his fingers. The stuff was fine as powder, though there were bigger grains too, brown and white, even the occasional pebble. Beneath that skin of sand was more rock; after that, he suspected, rock all the way down, gradually disintegrating and then carried away by the endless wind.

They'd spent the last four days perched on a ridge that came up about fifteen feet out of the desert like the fin of a shark. "A sand shark, ha ha," Tatie had whispered before Teddy had shut him up with a glance. Didn't get them much elevation, but it was all there was. For many miles around the sand plain stretched to the horizon, interrupted only very seldom, here and there, by slight humps. *The lone and level sand stretched far away.* He frowned, trying to remember where he'd gotten that from. Every gust picked the powder up and blew it along the ground into their faces. They had goggles but the plastic lenses quickly fogged with millions of minuscule scratches. Meanwhile it was so friggin' cold they had to melt ice off the scope every morning, and everything metal was coated with a rime of frost.

The airstrip lay half a mile north, a good distance but there hadn't been any cover closer in. The plan was to insert a SEAL overwatch before the Marines arrived to make sure no bad guys used the area or left anything behind. Like mines. They could've planted them earlier, of course, but looking at how remote the place was, Teddy thought it unlikely. The briefer had said the strip had been built by a wealthy Arab, who'd used it for hunting trips. Teddy couldn't imagine what the fuck he'd hunted; in two days and two nights out here glassing by sun and starlight, they hadn't seen anything bigger than some kind of groundhog that only came out at night and once, far off, a line of small wolves trotting from nowhere to nowhere. The only human beings had been nomads trudging past miles away, images shimmering in the big scope. They scuffed along with blankets pulled over their faces, trailing a thin rime of dust, a ludicrously tiny and overburdened burro slogging along with them, occasionally getting flicked with a stick by one of the kids.

But there'd been more here than a deserted airstrip. Beside it was a walled compound with locked gates that hadn't been mentioned in the brief. They'd gone in over the wall the second night and reconned, walking single file on fresh blacktop. Offices, a repair shop, a big warehouse. No one around, the new buildings all empty. They broke into the warehouse. Not only was no one there, it looked as if no one ever had been, just a faint dusting of sand on new fresh concrete. A drug transshipment point? But he'd thought the Talibs had stamped out the trade, one reason why the Alliance had turned against them. Strange, and he'd squirted a full report back to Higher.

Lying in the hide made him remember Ashaara. Far away on the Red Sea, but not all that different, although it had been hot, not cold, and the air thicker than this thin, high brew. His collarbone twinged. It had snapped when he'd plowed into a vertical rock face, at the end of the HALO drop.

They'd buried the chutes, then humped to the site in the dark. He and Cooper and Kowacki and Donoghe had spent two days huddled in the foundations of a shattered, abandoned village. He still had a piece of broken porcelain he'd picked up there. Part of a bowl, with half a blue rabbit on it. They'd sweated absolutely motionless half-buried through the day and then the night again. Waiting was what SEALs did best. Absolutely motionless, blending with the sand, part of the wallpaper. The second night he'd crawled out to recon the firing point and barely made it back before sunrise. At which time some of the hostiles had come out to eyeball the meet site. They'd walked over them, right through the village. Looked right at him, once.

But hadn't seen them.

And then the Target of Interest, the terrorist leader they called the Maahdi, hadn't shown up where the source had said he would. Teddy and Coop'd had to crawl across nearly half a mile of open terrain. The drop had busted Teddy's rifle scope and he had to get in close, *close*, to get a decent shot.

Eight hundred yards, open sights, in a fishtailing wind, and he'd had his share of luck that day. The heavy, tapered, boat-tailed slug had plowed into the TI higher than he'd expected, skull instead of chest, and he'd watched the head blow apart into pink mist, not believing what he was seeing. But he'd take it, and he had loaded another round, to Cooper's calm chant: "Shot two, center hit, TI down. Call the cleanup crew."

THIS morning wouldn't be nearly as dramatic, but that was okay. No drama was fine by Teddy O these days. He turned his wrist outward. Coming up on H Hour.

Recon gave you time to think. He'd gone over all the contingency plans. Walked through everything in his head. If they saw a truck column coming to occupy the airstrip. If some wandering goatherd stumbled over their site. His SOP was to duct-tape them, morphine them silly, and leave them where somebody ought to stumble across them in a few days. Or not; goatfuckers had to take their chances, along with everybody else.

A finger scratched his back. He rolled over to where Two Scoops pointed. Pulled his goggles up and flicked the switch. The other SEAL made a serpentine movement with his hand.

In the green prickling seethe of amplified infrared a snake writhed slowly across the ground. Maybe ten yards off. Teddy eyed it. For a moment it appeared to want to come their way. Its head lifted, a wedged blur in the unfocused green. A shadow of flickering tongue. Then it altered its angle and slowly undulated away, leaving a rippled pattern like the passage of a rubber raft through calm water.

FOUR o'clock. He rooted through his pack and came up with two packets of Taster's Choice they'd broken out from the MREs, and found cream and sugar packs too. He tilted his head back and poured the bitter crystals into his mouth and followed it with the sugar, the powdered creamer, and a mouthful of water from his CamelBak. Pushed the gritty mass from side to side through his teeth by pushing alternately on his distended cheeks until it was half-dissolved. It wasn't Starbucks. More like bad rest-stop machine coffee. He followed up with two big Motrins, then one of the whey-protein bars Stroud had shoved in their pockets as they moved out.

It sounded disgusting and had a tree-hugger wrapping that put him off, but they weren't that bad.

He molded a Slim Jim around his gums to marinate and returned his attention to the scope. A slow scan revealed nothing changed. The black sky was still sequined with desert stars, but seeing the peaks vanishing-faint against it meant dawn was imminent. He shivered and pulled his jacket flaps up. He wasn't coming out here again without fleece.

He'd been surprised to get this mission. Force Recon must have had something else going, not to be prepping the way for their own jarheads. Sweeping farther east, he suspected, to start sealing the Pak border. But better sitting out here with your thumb up your ass than probing the same aperture back aboard *Kitty Hawk*.

You could get acquainted with your men, for one thing. Tatie, Two Scoops, Knobby. He'd heard stranger nicknames. Two Scoops had gotten his from a serious accident trying to crap into a Ziploc. His shaved head was bony and yellow. Teddy wondered what kind of hair the guy had that he thought shaving it off looked better. He was from El Centro and had a three-year-old son who lived with his grandmother. Swager, of course, was the skinny SEAL cub who believed the gun porn in the glossy magazines. The one who'd looked as if he was about to faint when they got the word to deploy. So far he'd held up, though. Tatie, squad leader for Echo One, had two years of prelaw at Idaho State but had either flamed out on the tests or lost his tuition money in a poker game, versions differed. Instead of the bar he'd found the SEALs. He had a country-boy affect and looked rawboned dumb, but Teddy suspected he was actually the smartest dude in the platoon. The kind of guy you knew he'd end up someplace significant, if he survived. Plus, he made a great hillbilly tuna, with the packets of mac and cheese.

Teddy's job was to get them through it. So far this hadn't been a demanding recon, but sometimes you turned a corner and suddenly there you were wading through lava up to your balls.

A green spheroid. A grenade. And Sumo Kaulukukui gives him that look. "War's a motherfucker, ain't it?"

"You fat bastard," Teddy subvocalized, almost saying it until subterranean discipline muted his larynx beneath the wind-fluttering cover. His fingers dug into the powdery, icy sand like the claws of a reptile. "Why'd you have to be so fucking noble? Why'd we have to be so fucking gung ho?"

Forget that. Forget it! This was another war. This time the fuckers had attacked New York, Washington. And the SEALs, the Marines, and the Air Force were bringing revenge. Land here and organize, then drive on Kandahar, capital of the Taliban. Bring America's regards to the too-tall, smiling asshole who'd planned and financed it.

Teddy tilted his wrist again. As if tied to the glowing numerals, a subtle whine drifted down from the constellations, a thin, dwindling song so vanishingly faint it could only be heard in the lulls of the wind. So distant, really, he couldn't tell precisely what it was. Probably a lingering Predator.

Scoops kicked as he came awake, almost getting Teddy in the balls. "Sorry," he whispered.

"Get rid of that when you wake up, Petty Officer."

"Rid of what, Chief?"

"That flinch. Get you killed, one of these days." Teddy debated telling him how it would have killed him if he'd woken like that with someone walking over a hide site looking for him, like in Ashaara, but didn't. The more the chief talked, the more they would too. No one was around for miles—no question of somebody sneaking up unobserved—but this wouldn't be the only recon they'd be on in this fight.

Although it was looking as if it might not take that long after all, the way the Northern Alliance was moving out. He'd expected it to take all winter to stage enough forces in for an offensive, that was how it had worked in Desert Storm, but this thing seemed to be running on a different schedule.

He low-crawled up out of the depression and peered out over the land. The engine sound from far above waned, as if the aircraft was climbing. He checked his watch again. Close enough. "Let's go. You two, north end of the field. Scoops and I'll take the south."

He threw off the cover and for the first time in two days rose to full height. His joints cracked, sending pings of pain along steel wires. He slung rifle and pack. Rolled up the cover. Kicked more sand over where they'd buried their shit. Then, when the others gave him the thumbs-up, started off across the desert, patting his chest to make sure he had the grenades.

Toward the airfield. They had to physically be there, marking both ends, before the helos would come in. Insertion was their most vulnerable moment. The jarheads would be coming in locked and loaded for a hot LZ.

It felt good moving out, planting one boot in front of the other after being cooped up so long. The bounce of the ruck, the swing of the weapon. He kept the NVGs powered up, kept his gaze moving. If there was another hide team out here . . . somebody not so well disposed toward U.S. Marines falling out of the sky . . . they'd be powering up their Stingers or Strelas right about now. He stopped and scanned the south end of the runway with the IR on his rifle, which had a different frequency response from that of the goggles. Nothing. He detoured around a hillock, then circled back and jogged up to check its top. It was unoccupied.

On across rock-littered sand . . . the asphalt of the strip glowed ahead, still warmer than its surroundings even after the frigid night past. Partially covered with blowing sand, it wavered in the green dim as if underwater.

He put his rifle to his face again and scanned for the other team. There they were, green blobs undulating slowly across the landscape.

"About here, Chief?"

"Looks good." He sank to a knee, breathing hard. His collarbone ached. He checked all around. Were they in someone's crosshairs? He pulled rocks together, piling a cairn like some biblical altar. Checked his watch one last time, then nodded to the second class. "Go ahead. Pop it."

Scoops stripped off the plastic wrapper and inserted the battery. He pushed the switch up and set the IR flare atop the cairn. They stepped back as it powered up with a drilling whine, and Teddy half turned away, not looking directly at it.

The first white flash of infrared outlined a vast circle around them. Teddy backed off, still not facing it so as not to fry his goggles. He searched the sky, but saw nothing. Lowered his gaze, to see a strobe from the far end of the strip echo his own.

He was lifting his wrist to check the time again when something black passed over, winking across the roadway of stars. The muffled whump of engine and rotors arrived at the same moment. It passed so swiftly he couldn't react, just stood holding his rifle and staring up openmouthed at the familiar nose-down, tail-up attitude like a curious wasp, twin comets of hot light coning out glowing-bright behind its engines.

"Cobras?" Knobby yelled.

Teddy pulled off his goggles. A vibrating grayness to the east. A mysterious glow that seemed to come up off the desert itself, as if the sand were radioactive. "Yeah," he yelled back to Knobby's outline, kneeling a few yards off, face lifted like his own. The blacker black of the strip stretching away before them. Another form raced across east to west, nose down as well but even lower, its wingbeats fluttering in Teddy's chest, hurtling into a turn that would boomerang it back on them within seconds.

"Cover," he screamed, before consciously registering they were rolling into a firing run. And lurched into a clumsy sprint for the hillock they'd just skirted. Behind him came the thuds of Knobby's boots digging into the friable soil as he too accelerated. Far out over the desert he caught another glimpse of occluding stars; too slow; *too slow*. He pumped his fists, sucking icy air, jamming his boots deep into Afghanistan. The roar swelled; twin elongated shapes swiftly grew as they rushed across the flat, level plain toward them.

He jammed every ounce of effort into speed, fighting the inertia of his body and the weight of his gear to push through the invisible wall of the sprint. A light began to flash from the lead machine. Just as they reached the lump in the ground, he reached back, collared the other SEAL, and dragged him down into the lee of the gritty ground.

The desert cracked open around them in a maelstrom of shattering noise, smoke, dust, and rocks that jarred his teeth and jabbed needles into his ears. A second or two of ringing silence; then a second, distant *tack-tack-tack*.

Then the end of the world all over again, mainly on the far side of the hillock but around them too, blasting to left and right and whining overhead. They crouched in its shadow as the roar grew, pressed down on them, then dwindled.

Teddy found himself lying on top of the second class. He slammed a hand down on his shoulder. "You okay? They're gonna be coming back," he screamed. The face that turned up to him was dazed. Teddy hauled him to his feet and pushed him toward the hillock. The only cover, but so small. If they used rockets instead of just the gatlings in the turret, they could blast it away. He slapped his load-bearing gear, located the angular hardness of the radio. "Marine Cobra, Marine Cobra, you're blue on blue, blue on blue. Cease fire, cease fire, don't you see our strobe? Cease fire, cease fire!"

A crackle, then an apologetic voice. Teddy gulped air. "You stupid fucking gyrene, what the fuck d'you think an IR strobe is for? Think we're fucking ALQ down here?"

"Sorry, man, nobody told us there were friendlies on the ground. Got a Predator report. Unidents, possible Talib patrol. Then saw the flashes and thought you were firing at us."

"Those were *strobes*. To mark the ends of the runway. Read your fuckin' op order! Call off your buddy, we're fucking SEALs down here. There's another team on the north end." He started to threaten the pilot, decided to leave it until later. File through channels, let the system discipline whoever'd screwed up. He left the radio on, listening to their chatter as they broke off and orbited to the west, accusing each other in turn. He kept a wary eye on them and stayed close to the hill, which was only about half the size it had started off as. Loose rocks lay blasted apart across the sand. A cloud of smoke and dust drifted downwind.

Then the slow, deep beats of heavy-lift birds penetrated the growing lavender light all along the horizon, and up out of the curve of the brightening desert pushed a throbbing avalanche of sound. Like a cloud of locusts they grew up into the sky, towered, and began to descend as the Cobras circled like sheepdogs at a radius of five miles.

Flares burst from the lead birds, then from them all, the whole first wave detonating in brilliant showering bursts of hot gold, pale green, tawny orange, all far brighter than they had any right to be. A whole Independence Day display over square miles of uninhabited desert. Teddy covered his face with one arm. Corkscrewing smoke-trails followed the golden comets as they plummeted. One huge bird nosed up, then with a remote clatter machine-gunned out dozens of smaller pyrotechnics that arched out to its flanks, peaked, then fell away, leaving smoke trails like the legs of an immense scorpion looming in the sky above Teddy and Knobby. Depleted canisters thunked around them, raising bursts of dust, rolling to smoking stops. Dust blasted up as the helos settled, rocking, and suddenly it was zero vis, like swimming in mud as grit blasted their faces and the world turned to sand. Teddy grabbed the second class and backpedaled; he didn't want to be the first shape some scared newbie, green-ass marine on his first combat insertion saw looming out of the murk. They squatted behind the hillock as the second wave rolled in. A squad trotted past in open order, cheeks blackened, bent under huge packs and antitank missiles. The squad leader wheeled, squinting; Teddy pointed to his shoulder, to the flag patch; gave him a salute. The marine nodded and waved his guys on.

Teddy sank cross-legged, feeling as if something had dissolved away inside. The first wave was lifting off. The second, coming in. More waves of tawny-tasting dust blew past, as if sandblasting him for a new paint job. Fuck, why were his knees shaking?

Knobby hit the ground next to him. Pulled off his cover and ran his hands though his hair, shaking out dust. "Man, that was close."

"No shit." That was why Teddy was shaking; only now was nearly getting blown away by a fucking trigger-happy pilot getting to him. But look at fucking Swager sitting there gibbering away as if four days in the hide had dammed up inside of him and now it all had to get out at once. Gesticulating like an Italian trying to sell you a lottery ticket.

The crunch of footsteps; yells on the wind; another squad trekked past, gear bouncing as they lurched in the loose footing. With them was a less heavily loaded pair in black trousers and gear vests and floppy purple bush hats. Teddy's gaze followed them, riveted by the hats; then sharpened as one turned toward him and pointed something. Teddy's rifle jerked up; then he got his thumb off the safety; only a camera.

"And who are you guys? Hey, you're not marines."

"Don't take pictures of us," Teddy said.

"Yeah, we're SEALs," Swager contributed. "Turn that camera off."

"Public affairs cleared us, man. We're embedded. The longest raid from the sea in history! We flew four hundred miles, refueled in the air. SEALs, huh? And you were already—"

Teddy said, "I told you, don't take pictures. There's nobody dead here. Nothing you want to see, you bloodsucking asshole."

"Hey, take it easy. I'm on your side. I'm—"

"Turn the *fucking camera off*!" Teddy grabbed it out of the man's hands, looked in vain over the silver surface for something resembling a switch, then lost it. The camera flew apart as it hit a rock. The reporter, cameraman, whatever he was, staggered back, started to yell. Then caught something in Teddy's face. Or maybe, spotted his hand reaching for his pistol. He scrambled to scoop up the camera, shook the sand off, and pelted after his squad, shouting for them to wait up.

"You weren't really gonna shoot him?" Swager said.

Teddy took a deep breath. "Course not. Fuck, no."

"Good. Okay." Swager's hand sought Teddy's shoulder. The dust-reddened eyes searched his. "We okay now, Chief? Everything under control?"

Teddy stared back blankly. Under control? He broke the other man's grip and elbow-butted him away. "Keep the fuckin' hands off, Swager. This ain't my first fucking rodeo, you know."

"Okay. Okay!" Swager backed away, hands up. Then turned as Tatie and Scoops emerged from the blowing dust, sand goggles pulled down.

"Everything cool here, war dogs?"

"Oh, yeah, Tatie. Everything's cool. Some asshole just got right up in the chief's face, that's all," Swager said, not looking at Teddy. Who just stood with his hands on his knees, bent over, trying to make them stop quivering.

16

Bagram Joint
Operations Center

T HE sides of the tents fluttered like sails on a slow passage. Bagram
had become an island, isolated and self-sufficient, and in the JOC
scores of flat-screen monitors pulsed to the steady thrum of generators.
From the airfield the howl of jets never stopped; only waned or grew
louder, day or night. Beyond the field was wire, berms, troops, and light
armor: the Eighty-second Airborne and Tenth Mountain. And beyond that,
half in ragtag camos and the rest still in *shalwar kameez* and *pakul* hats,
the hastily trained cadres of the new Afghanistan Military Force milled or
squatted in the velvety, tan dust. By day, tents and flags rippled in the
wind. By night, lights glared on concertina and machine-gun posts. Inside
the interconnected canvas tunnels the screens and power lights of dozens
of computers and transceivers glowed, and the nets whispered on. The
smells of dust and coffee and kerosene heaters, lived-in uniforms and jet
exhaust, were the smells of battle here.

Dan sat slumped, massaging his eye sockets. In front of him a network
shifted and danced. Constructed of points connected by lines of varying
colors and widths, it shimmered like a spiderweb in a breeze as data streamed
through the program. A boxed legend read CIRCE 4.2. DECEMBER 11, 2001. 1455 GMT.

His team had moved on from targeting, relieved by augmentees from
stateside, and relocated into a side tent running off the intel section of the
JOC—"behind the green door," as the saying went. The Fusion Cell had
activated days before. Fusion, as in merging all the in-theater intelligence
inputs, collating them with what streamed in from outside sources, and,
one hoped, producing actionable intelligence. Almost a hundred men and
women worked in the never-darkened warren, including dozens of civilians: FBI, CIA, DIA, and agencies that didn't officially exist. CIRCE had
been "fused" into something called the Joint Working Group, although the
lines between the various boxes were still in flux.

By dint of serious scrambling, Wenck and Henrickson had established broadband links back to TAG. CIRCE, or "she" as they occasionally referred to it, didn't actually reside in Bagram. Only its output, via satellite data link, was displayed before him. It was currently being modified for the project Provanzano had named Template. Template was the intel side of the search for bin Laden, Mullah Omar, Berader, Al-Zawahiri, and the other top-tier ALQ leadership. Once they got a fix, a special ops team called Hatchet would descend from the night sky. The Working Group had four subteams, of which Dan's was last. He didn't think that meant they were lowest priority, but being Navy in a mainly Army environment was seldom an advantage.

The Special Forces had a separate operations center, with its own compound and guard force. Dan had been over several times, for morning and evening briefs. They covered not only the latest enemy dispositions, but the operations of all Coalition special forces in-country, concentrating on the ongoing search for HVTs—High Value Targets. The most interesting had been a two-hour presentation by a former GRD colonel who'd lost an arm in Afghanistan, about mujahideen tactics, topography, caves and supply routes, Soviet mistakes and successes. Each time Dan had come away impressed with the special operating forces' cultural separation from Big Army. Hatchet, a SOF operation, was supposed to take marching orders from the Working Group, but it seemed as if most of its missions were self-generated.

"You okay, boss?"

Henrickson, in Levi's. A cotton plaid shirt buttoned to the neck and a down vest and waterproof insulated boots made him look like a down-sized duck hunter. He grabbed Dan's wrist as he pulled over one of the rickety Russian metal chairs they'd found in an abandoned revetment and wired back together. "You sleep at all? You ought to get out of here. Go on, man. Get your head down."

Dan grunted. He pawed through binders until he found his jacket. His gloves and a black wool watch cap were stuffed into the sleeves.

"Going to get some sleep?"

"Maybe."

"That Air Force imagery's still coming through without coordinates. Oh, and—forgot to tell you. The last watch, Donnie said there was somebody here asking all kinds of questions about CIRCE. About the algorithm for the reasoning framework, mainly. No-neck type. Ponytail. Looks like what's his name, the governor from Minnesota—"

"The who?"

"The guy, the *guy*—he was in the first *Predator* movie—"

"Jesse Ventura?" Shit; Henrickson meant Beanie Belote. "Good casting, Monty. What did Donnie tell them?"

"He said not much, but you know Donnie. Even if he did, no way they'd understand him. Unless they were down as far in the bits and bytes as he is. I had to loan him some of my socks. He didn't bring any."

"Just make sure he gets a shower once a week," Dan told Monty. "Okay, I'm going over to the JIF. Getting some funny reports out of the interrogators."

"Go to your tent. Get your head down. Anyway, we aren't on the access list over there."

"Supposed to be. See if we are now." He heaved up and out of the chair, then stood swaying like an old dog, forgetting what he'd planned to do next.

"Go on, get out of here," Monty said, and Dan lurched down the canvas tunnel into the main intel section. Turned left, through another fifty meters of field tables and the smells of fuel-fired heaters and canvas, pushed the flap aside, and stuck his head out.

Into night. He blinked, having thought it was still day. Running on Zulu time, he'd lost track. But the hazy sky was keyholed with stars. Bitter cold wind polished his teeth with talclike dust. Lights coruscated along the perimeter, reaching out hundreds of yards into the plain. Beyond them lay the mountains, a black invisibility that cut off the stars. He felt the grade rise under his boots, and a moment later was on asphalt.

Where was he going? Oh, yeah. The JIF.

The Russians had laid the field out north to south, with no crosswind strips. Engines howled as helos lowered themselves like spiders on silken threads. Lights glared as techs root-canaled an engine from an A-10. To the east, flat scrub was etched with half-erased defensive berms and eroded bomb dumps. The main road was a half mile west of the airstrip, with taxiways leading to aprons and revetments and huge hangars whose windows were broken, steel rusting, flaking concrete pockmarked with bullet craters. The Russian buildings hulked even from hundreds of yards away. The Coalition forces had set up within and among these hangars, with acres of GP tenting and stacks of containers and sandbags and Cyclone fencing and concertina everywhere. Every installation and nationality had fenced itself off from the rest.

Something huge descended from the night and floated above the strip. Rubber shrieked. He left the road and empty brass tinkled beneath his boots. He shivered and reoriented and headed for the salmon-tinted glows that made the Joint Interrogation Facility distinctive for hundreds of yards. He didn't like walking in the dark. The mine-clearance teams had been over the area, but there was always a chance they'd missed one. Halfway there he corrected course, and the massive walls towered above him like a socialist cathedral. Shouting rose above the drone of generators, the shriek and howl of engines from the strip.

A column of men swayed under brilliant light. Their heads were covered with what looked like grain bags. Their hands were locked behind them. Marines walked alongside, bayonets fixed. Dan approached by a graveled walkway lit with generator-driven floods. Two marines with riot guns checked his ID, then bumped it against an access list. "I should've just been added," Dan said.

"He's on it. Lenson, Daniel V. . . . No weapons inside the JIF, Commander. Check 'em at the booth."

"Not armed." He lifted his arms, watching as the new arrivals began filing through a gauntlet of men and concertina.

The senior guard grinned like a violin's fretboard. "Stand by a sec, Commander. You mind, sir? Just till we get the Bobs outa sight."

The column had halted inside the concertina, out of sight from the rest of the base, but in the glare Dan could see the process from where he stood. Large marines with black plastic trash bags cut into makeshift jerkins and pulled over their battle dress yanked the first man from the line and rodeo-wrestled him to the ground. The prisoner screamed as knives flashed. They sliced away clothes until he crouched naked in the shivering air.

Hauled upright, he was jerked to the next station, where a medical team waited, and the gauntlet sucked in its next subject. The marines stuffed each prisoner's stripped-off rags into steel barrels whose leaping flames added to the hellish feel. Farther along, still struggling, the captives were forcibly dressed in orange prison jumpsuits, then positioned before a vertical grid. A camera flashed. Then they were pushed into the cavernous maw of the hangar.

At first they all looked alike: slight, ragged men whose features when they emerged from the bags bore an identical expression of sheer terror. But as Dan watched, he began to see differences. All were bearded, except for those too young to grow them. But some were taller and lighter-skinned. None were exactly fat, but a few looked as if they'd grown up better nourished than the darker, squatter ones. He assumed he was seeing Arabs and Afghans, but reminded himself there were probably other nationalities and ethnicities as well. A few looked almost Asian.

The guard turned back to him and executed a crisp salute. Dan touched his watch cap in return. "Report to the check-in desk, Commander. Tell them who you want to see and what your business is. Have a nice day, sir."

. . .

YVONNA Jones-Potter was his contact at the JIF. The Marines ran the Joint Interrogation Facility, but they didn't interrogate. Jones-Potter's office was curtained off by blankets. A coffeemaker grumbled in the corner. Jones-Potter was small and fortyish. She wore jeans and a heavy wool Pendleton shirt and a brown T-shirt as a snood. Only the tan desert boots told him she was probably Army. A parka hung from a nail. She gave him a tenth of a second's glance from behind her field desk and asked what he wanted. Dan tried to ignore the screaming. As far as he could see, no one was being beaten, but the atmospherics were straight out of *Schindler's List.*

He opened with "Saw your new shipment come in. So, who are these guys?"

"You tell me. They dump 'em on us, but we don't have any idea who we're getting. They come off that plane for in-processing, they come in clean."

This seemed odd. "I mean, I know you don't have clear identifications. But where they were captured, what they were carrying—"

She pulled off the T-shirt, revealing short blond hair. "I mean *clean,* Commander. There's supposed to be a package with each man, his pocket litter, what he was carrying when he got picked up. If we get that at all, it comes in one duffel per shipment. We could find Osama's Day-Timer for the next year, and we wouldn't know which of these guys was his secretary."

Dan considered his next question. "Is that . . . Army SOP?"

"No, it's SPECOPS-to-JIF SOP. We're not even regular straightlegs to them. Most of us are reserves." Jones-Potter waved at the warren of makeshift offices behind her, heavy with plywood sheeting and hung blankets. "Forget I said that. All right?"

"Forgotten."

"How can I help? You're some kind of intel liaison, correct?"

"With the Joint Working Group."

"I'm not sure where you're taking us from."

"I'm sorry? I don't—"

She said patiently, "How are you getting our reports?"

"Oh. Off the Web, through CFLCC." He pronounced it *sea-flick,* the ground component commander back in Kuwait. "But we're only half a mile apart here, so instead of sending the request back up, I walked it over here. All right?" He waited, but aside from a wry face she didn't object. "We need to set up some kind of briefing for your people. How you link to the Working Group, how we link to Task Force Hatchet. Make the flow of information explicit, let you know what we need. Maybe even set up some of your interrogators to go out with the operators." She still didn't respond, so he went on, flipping open the folder he'd brought "We've been reading your reports. Especially from prisoners 343 and 347."

"The leprechaun twins."

"Excuse me?"

She sighed. "Some of the guards think they look like the Lucky Charms leprechaun. What's your question?"

"I'd like to see them. Ask some questions about a meet location that's come up. Also, if any of these new batch can tell us anything about OBL, any little detail, if they've ever laid eyes on him, we need you to shoot that to us direct. We can pass the word straight to a quick reaction force."

"There's a procedure for submitting our reports. They're not worth much until they're scrubbed down. Bumped against the standard protocols—"

"I understand that. What I'm saying is, it takes too fucking long! By the time we read your reports, they're cold. The big fish keep swimming off. To get them, we have to be able to react in minutes."

"Interrogation takes time, Commander. And we only have two Arabists. Very few Dari or Pashtun speakers. We've got some assistance from the Northern Alliance, but their English isn't that great."

The phone rang and she answered it with terse sentences. Something about mug shots. She hung up.

"That means I can't see them?" Dan asked.

Jones-Potter explained that since the Working Group had said those two detainees were of special interest, she was subjecting them to what she called "monstering." "That probably sounds worse than it is. Basically the echo—the interrogator—stays in the booth with them for as long as he, or she, can stay awake. A marathon session. Usually they break. If they don't, our chances go way down. Once they realize we've done all we're allowed to, to them, the fear factor goes away."

"Sleep deprivation?"

"It might look that way, but really, what's 'sleep deprivation'? Our interpretation of the Geneva guidelines: If the interrogator can stay up all night, so can the guy he's interrogating. We're not putting any strain on them beyond what our own troops are getting."

Dan was no military lawyer, but that sounded fair. "Okay. So I can see them? Are they in the—in the interrogation room now?"

"We call them booths. One of them is. Yes, you may observe, but please don't speak or interfere. Once you start a subject with one interrogator, there's an emotional link. Trust is built. Or fear. Or both—depends on the subject what approach we take. But the more faces, the less impact. Some of these guys, the hard core, they've gotten formal training on resisting interrogation. So you can watch, but don't speak. And I can let you talk to the interrogator, try to work out a balance between what you need right away and what he thinks he can get."

Dan agreed, since it seemed to be the only way he'd be getting in. Jones-Potter nodded and picked up the phone.

WHEN he looked down on the center of the hangar, he stopped dead. Generator-driven spotlights purred around an open central bay. At their focus, where a boxing ring might be in a large auditorium, sat four fifty-foot-long wire cages like oversize dog runs. At one end hung a huge American flag with several of the spots focused on it. At the other, an enormous banner depicted the outlines of the Twin Towers, the Pentagon, and the words 9/11: WE WILL NEVER FORGET. Within the wire men in saffron-colored jumpsuits sat or paced or reclined on blankets. Buckets in corners held brown liquid; a prisoner was squatting over one. Marines walked up and down between cages and looked down, carbines across their chests, from balconies. At one cage a man stood with his back to the gate; guards were shackling his wrists. At the far side of the hangar enormous rusting machines, stamping or welding equipment, had been shoved in a jumble back into the shadows. The whole setup reminded Dan of some gritty postapocalyptic film, maybe the Thunderdome in *Mad Max*. He could smell the shit and the generator exhaust from all the way up here.

The interrogation booths were a row of plywood-sided cubicles on the first floor. Following the sergeant Jones-Potter had detailed to escort him, Dan almost collided with a husky man in baggy carpenter jeans, a black Gore-Tex jacket, and a Cubs hat. His eyes were swollen almost shut, and he lurched clumsily to get around Dan. "Sir," the sergeant said, "this's the guy from the Working Group. Got questions about the Twins. CO sent him down to see you."

The interrogator introduced himself as Dix, no last name. They shook hands. Dan said, "We read your reports, 343 and 347, right? Tenth picked them up outside Kandahar? Made any more progress?"

"They have *cunyas*—ALQ aliases, like street names back in the 'hood."

"Arabs? Or Afghans?"

"These two, Afghans, but fairly high up. The one we're got in the booth now, he's something like a Taliban-ALQ liaison officer. Bin Laden doesn't speak Pashtun. Or else speaks it badly. When he has to sit down with the locals, work out a deal for protection or some place to stay, he needs a translator."

"I'd like to ask them some questions."

Dix was shaking his head before Dan finished speaking. His eyelids sagged closed, then jerked open again. "These guys've just cracked. The window's open, but it could slam shut. Tell me what you need. You can go back to the ICE and watch the interrogation on the screen. Or borrow a helmet and stand in the doorway, if you want, like you're one of the guards. But don't come in. What d'you want to know?"

Dan held up the folder. "In one of your reports, 347 mentioned a meeting at a place called Pajuar. It's not on our maps. It comes up one other time on the search engine, comm intercept a week ago. But still, no location. We need to know where it is, whether they've ever held a meeting there before, if he knows of another that's scheduled. Who was there before; if there was another, who'd attend."

Dix said he'd put the question, but it might take a while. Dan said that was fine. The echo went away and came back with two Cokes and took them into the booth. A moment later the guard opened the door. The sergeant escort handed Dan a helmet. He put it on, the Kevlar still warm, and stepped in.

The booth was claustrophobic, perhaps deliberately so. Six by eight, just enough room for a metal folding chair, a small table, another chair. The guard stood by the door, slung M4 pointed at the concrete floor. A TV camera was bolted above his head. Another man, Afghan by his dress, squatted on the floor. He wore a black balaclava, only his eyes showing. The walls were unpainted CDX with the manufacturer's stamp still on it. Stapled to it, incongruous on the bare plywood, was a tourist poster: a tropical beach, palms, an azure sky, a long stretch of pure white sand leading away, sucking you in, and green mountains in the distance. No windows or fans, but the top of the booth was open, screened by chicken wire. The lights glared down, casting everything into either brilliant relief or deep shadow.

On the chair a small, hunched prisoner sat with one leg tucked under the other, gripping one shin. He had a wild, dark beard, long hair with streaks of silver, and bruises on his wrists and under red-rimmed, weary eyes. He had a button nose and thick eyebrows and red-apple cheeks and maybe he did look like a leprechaun, if you had a good imagination or were really tired. Dan smelled his rank metallic sweat and the plywood and some volatile chemical like paint thinner. The interrogator put a Coke on the table. After a moment the prisoner cracked the pop top and drank, not taking his eyes from his captor.

Dix started with questions about a supply route, apparently what they'd been talking about before Dan arrived. The translation took a while; the squatting Afghan turned the Engish into what Dan assumed was Pashtun. Then the response came, and that took a while too, and then they had to wait for translation. Dix patiently noted the answer on a steno pad. It seemed like a very deliberate process. The prisoner swung his foot and glanced at Dan, then away.

"All right," Dix said. "Now, back to the meeting at Pajuar you told me about. First of all, where is Pajuar?"

The prisoner shook his head. He spoke briefly, not looking at the interrogator, but at the galvanized wire screen above them.

"He says, what is the use? He will answer no more questions."

Dix took his time. His gaze stayed on the Afghan, who seemed not to want to meet his eyes. "Remind him, the outcome is up to him. We can turn him over to the Northern Alliance. They have a prison in Kabul. Translate that."

The terp spoke for a while. When he stopped, Dix said, "It used to be a Talib prison. Maybe you remember it. Always used to be crowded. But it's funny, we keep sending people there, and they never say they have too many."

The prisoner didn't react. Dix reached into his folder. Took out photographs and put them on the table. "What're your kids going to do without you, Ahmed? You did want to see them again. Or you wouldn't be carrying their pictures. You have a choice. We can send you to Kabul. Or"—Dix looked at the poster, and Dan suddenly understood—"we can send you to Cuba. To Guantánamo. You won't see your family for a while. But eventually, after we sort out our friends from our enemies . . . it's your choice, Ahmed." Dix waited again for the translation, as the prisoner's eyes reluctantly fastened on the poster.

"Will he be able to walk on the beach in Guantánamo?"

Dix shrugged. "If he is our friend, why not?"

A hesitant question. "In Cuba. Will he be shackled and caged?"

"He doesn't bargain. This isn't a souk. He's either with us, or against us. This is what our president has said."

The prisoner lifted his head. He closed his eyes, then sighed. Spoke, a flood of resigned speech.

"He will tell you what he knows," the translator said. "More than that, he says, he cannot say."

Dix asked about Pajuar again, and this time the prisoner grew animated. He used his hands to show directions, glancing at the translator occasionally. Everyone else waited patiently. Finally the answer came through, but it sounded complicated. Dix noted it all down and asked how long it would take to walk there from various villages in the valley.

At the end of an hour the interrogator got up, stretched, rubbed his eyes. He looked at the prisoner, who hadn't changed position, but whose head was hanging down. He said something to the translator in Pashtun and jerked his head at Dan to step outside.

In the corridor, he tore off a page from his pad. "Going to be tough to get this down to a UTC coordinate. But this is the best I can give you. It's in the Shah-i-khot, that's pretty clear. What they call the Place of Kings. There are three villages in walking distance. He's described the trail from each village. There are halt points along the rat lines, for springs or cached supplies. What the mountain looks like to the east of it. Apparently there's a cave there, some kind of hideout. Hope it helps."

The Place of Kings. Dan had seen a reference to that before, an intel spot report from Yemen. And Provanzano too, had mentioned it. "I guess what I need to know is, can we trust what he says?"

"That's the five-dollar question, isn't it? I don't pick up any cuing that he's lying. If it helps, he swears it to Allah on his heart and limbs."

"Is that, like, a guarantee?"

"No. They all say stuff like that. Like a Mafia guy, swearing on his mother's grave."

"Uh-huh. Great. Thanks."

"Want us to follow up? More details on the location? Who's going to be there?"

"I already have an idea who'll be there. We just needed to know where 'there' was. But, yeah, if you come up with anything else, shoot it over. Anything that might lead us to the higher-ups. Here's my direct e-mail." Dan tore a scrap off the steno page and jotted it down.

The interrogator said he understood. He rubbed his eyes hard in the glaring light. "Okay, back to it. . . . Want a Coke? We keep feeding them Cokes. Figure, if they can't sleep when we give them a break, they'll be twice as fucked-up when we start the next session."

"This seems to go pretty slow."

Dix gave him a sharp glance. "It's a time-intensive process, good interrogation."

Dan took a deep breath. "Yeah. I see. I'll take one. And thanks. "

Standing once more on the balcony, drinking off the can in swift, too-sweet swigs, he pondered the chain link, the lights, the overflowing buckets, the casually leaning guards. The men in orange squatted or strolled under the blinding lights, between the hanging banners.

Seen close up, the enemy didn't look physically menacing. But men like these had blown up embassies, warships, flown airliners into buildings. For a moment he heard again the screams in the darkened, fuel-stinking corridors of the Pentagon. Blair had been through even worse. They had to be interrogated, to gather any intel they could yield. And screen out any innocent sheepherders. But after that, he couldn't think of anything better than a firing squad. He'd volunteer for it.

They said they wanted a new caliphate. Something like a new Ottoman Empire, based on sharia and Koranic justice. But by all accounts, Afghanistan under Omar had been no paradise. More like a totalitarian hell. Stonings. Executions. Noses, ears, hands, cut off. Schools closed. Women sold like cattle, beaten like slaves. But all that had been fine with the West. Until they'd attacked New York and Washington.

Maybe we needed a wake-up call, he thought. We let Hitler go too, and Pol Pot, and all the rest. Until it hits us, we don't react. Until it's too late, we don't care. We're focused on the next quarter's market results. The next election. Not what's coming ten years down the road.

Anyway, what business of it was his? Whatever he thought wasn't going to affect anything. Not one iota.

He finished the can, crumpled it, and tossed it into the darkness.

BACK at the JOC Dan passed the steno sheet Dix had given him to Henrickson to input into CIRCE. Then felt his way to a cot. He stared up at the slowly breathing roof of the tent. Tried to close his eyes, but the lids were on springs. Shouldn't have gone to the JIF. No, he'd had to. Part of his job. If only Provanzano or Belote had wormed an agent into bin Laden's inner circle. They could've stopped the whole plot. Now they were vacuuming up all this human debris, but did the bedraggled men wearing prison orange actually matter? Were they ALQ leaders? Or just hangers-on, pawns, or warm bodies turned in to settle clan vendettas: "Oh, him—he is a bad man. Yes, he is high Taliban, important Al Qaeda. Give me the thousand dollars reward."

Finally he got up. Henrickson gave him the eye but didn't say anything. Dan went to another terminal and read the latest reports, then searched again for Pajaur, Pajuar, Bajuar, Bajaur, and every other possible spelling. He got a couple more hits but nothing eye-opening. He went out into the main tent, woke a cartographer, and worked out a UTC coordinate from the directions the prisoner had given. Then went back to his own terminal and retrieved all the imagery he could find for that location. Nothing much was visible on the ground. A rocky valley. He zoomed in and out, squinting, searching for shadows or changes over time. Didn't see any.

He woke to Wenck standing over him. "Jay-wick meeting, Commander."

"Thanks, Donnie. You making out okay?"

"Yeah, okay. Boy, these guys are really interested in CIRCE."

"That so?"

"They wanna know all kinds of stuff. Keep asking for copies of the software. And I keep telling them, it doesn't reside here."

"Good on you, Donnie. Keep that up." Dan patted the kid's spindly shoulder. Then did a quick moist shave from bottled water, grimacing at his body odor as he stripped his shirt off.

"Oh, and, Commander—we're getting some high numbers on that meet site."

"High? How high?"

Donnie told him.

THE JWC meeting was in the bigger tent, five men and one woman around a field table. Army, OGA, spec ops, and Dan. Belote and Provanzano sat off to the side, not exactly part of the discussion, but also, Dan noted, not missing a word. Some wag had duct-taped a sheet of yellow paper to the back of his monitor. It read, *Many intelligence reports in war are contradictory. Even more are false. And most are uncertain. Clausewitz.*

An army colonel, the chairman, briefed first. After a quick overview of the last twenty-four hours, he said British communications intercepts indicated ALQ leadership were planning an emergency regrouping, or at least a meeting of the withdrawing high leaders, somewhere north of Kandahar. The location was not mentioned in the intercepts, but one of the speakers had mentioned "the woods." "The most likely meet place is the remote border region near Pakistan," he concluded. "That's the broad brush. The challenge is getting more specific, so we can get shooters or weapons there at the same time."

"I disagree," one of the analysts said. "Why meet on this side of the border? When the Pak side's safe? I think the meeting's in North Waziristan, the same sites we've seen before."

Belote said, "We need a firm location. We're throwing brains at this problem, but I'm not seeing results coming back."

The analyst shook his head. "We're on it. But these guys have pretty decent comm discipline. And we don't speak the language."

Dan sat back, listening to them wrangle. Once again, a split was growing between Defense Intelligence and the CIA. They started from the same facts, but interpreted them differently. One side wanted the meeting in Afghanistan; the other said it was going to be out of their reach, in Pakistan. Apparently bin Laden was as much at home on one side of the border as the other.

"Dan?" Belote said. "We've got a deadlock. What's your crystal ball coming up with?"

He sat for a moment, mustering his thoughts. He had nothing to prove.

But the numbers were getting convincing. "CIRCE's generating an eighty percent confidence level the meet'll be in Pajuar."

Heads came up; gazes sharpened. "Where's Pajuar?" a woman asked.

"We're pretty sure, based on JIF work as of this morning, that it's a valley to the north of the Shah-i-khot."

Dan keyed it in and turned his notebook so they could see the overhead. "Imagery as of two days ago. A steep valley. Wooded—so the phrase 'in the woods' could apply. Located at the intersection of trails from these three villages, so if someone approaches by one trail, there are two escape routes. Also, we're seeing a high degree of probability both OBL and Al-Zawahiri will attend."

The analysts looked skeptical. "This is based on what?" one said. "A computer program?"

"It does the same thing you guys do. Goes through tons of material and generates connections. Looks for patterns. Gradually outlines recurrent activities and infrastructure. It knits that into a web, then makes predictions based on probabilistic calculations."

"A computer can't do analysis," one of the analysts said. "You need to look inside your target's head. Live in his skin. All this thing is doing, it's re-creating the past."

"Not exactly." Dan understood where the analysts were coming from. All most people owned were their skills. No wonder they'd perceive his contribution as a threat. "I agree, it doesn't get into OBL's head, the way one of you could. It doesn't care *why* he does what he does. But does he repeat himself? Or does he do what you don't expect, because you don't expect it? At each decision point, the target has to make a decision. The program runs out the consequences, examines them from his point of view, and makes its predictions based on how he sees the world."

"But you can't know everything he knows."

"Of course not. This isn't a magic mirror from a fantasy novel. But when it gives us a probability that high, there may be something there. At least it's worth checking out."

"That's how you got Al-Maadi," Belote put in.

Dan turned to face him. "There were other inputs. HUMINT. Overhead imagery. But, yeah, that's what vectored us in on his hideout."

They discussed it, and the skepticism deepened. No one had ever heard of Pajuar. The interrogation report hadn't come through the proper channels, been scrubbed down and blessed by CFLCC. He found himself getting angry, starting to argue that if they waited, the opportunity would slip away. As so many others had. He started to quote Sun Tzu: *In war, the supreme consideration is speed*. But instead, closed his mouth. He pushed too hard. Had been told that over and over, during his career. Maybe this was one of those situations where stepping back, taking a deep breath, and admitting the other guy might be right was the better part of valor.

Tony Provanzano had been sitting off to the side, occasionally lifting the inhaler. Now he cleared his throat, and discussion stopped. "Can I put in a word?"

"Yes, sir. Go right ahead."

"We're not here to argue. Okay? Commander Lenson thinks it's worth following up. Your guys aren't convinced. So, here's what I suggest we do. Everyone go back to your terminals. If this place was ever a meet site, there's going to be some mention of it. Somewhere. Or it'll be in the document exploitation. Maybe under another name. We just need to drill down until we find it. Okay?"

The colonel pointed to a young analyst. "Mike, get the CTC in on it. I know we had a team in there two years ago. All right, everybody. Get out there and dig. We'll reconvene right after the morning brief."

Dan pushed back his chair. But as he headed for the exit, Belote took his arm. "Boss wants you."

"Before you leave. A little private conversation?" Tony Provanzano drawled.

THE OGAs had a separate berthing tent. Only the green wash of a dangling chemlight penetrated the darkness. "Sit on the bunk," Provanzano said. "Okay, first, what's this I hear about you pushing for privileged access to the JIF?"

Dan was astonished. Then realized, when you tried to short-circuit any bureaucratic process, especially when it had the letters *A*, *R*, *M*, and *Y* in it, the wires heated up fast, and sparks started to fly . "I was over this afternoon. Sat in on an interrogation. There was a report filed that—"

"I know what was filed, and that's the reason it's filed, so it gets confirmed and evaluated and cross-checked. What we don't need are Navy commanders playing interrogator. Then jumping to conclusions and putting their suspicions out as fact."

Dan was about to protest, then thought, to hell with it. As his eyes adapted to the darkness he made out the OGA agent half-reclining on the far end of the bunk. "Just trying to do my job."

"Your job's to run CIRCE for us. And to give us a window into it." A sniff; Dan caught again the sharp scent of eucalyptus and camphor.

"That's not my understanding of what the Working Group's been set up for."

"Then your understanding's wrong. Intelligence is a team sport, sport."

There wasn't much Dan could say to that, so he didn't say anything. Engines shrieked outside; tires squealed as another load of ammunition or fuel or human bodies touched down. He started to get up. "That all?"

"No. Sit down." Provanzano sniffed. "You're really seeing eighty percent?"

"I'm not saying he's absolutely going to be there. But right now, that's what the probabilities say."

"The fog of war."

"That, and these are cunning people. They've probably got several stories running, just to keep us scampering up and down these valleys."

"No, he's going to be there," Provanzano said.

Dan started to argue, then stopped. He was agreeing? "You have other sources."

"I agree, no intel picture's foolproof. But with the SIGINT, CIRCE, and your info from the JIF, it's the closest thing to a firm location we have."

Dan coughed into a fist. "So, what are we going to do about it? Set up a cordon, block the trails out, and put a Hatchet team down on him?"

A pause. Such a long one, Dan finally added, "I don't think I know where you're going here, Tony."

"Well, it's like this. OBL is what we call a locus. He attracts radicals. So? Let him do what he does best. Use him to vacuum up the malcontents and senior Taliban and other anti-US elements. Let them come to him, then take them out."

Dan couldn't believe what he was hearing. "You mean we *shouldn't* take him down?"

Provanzano gestured like Brando's Don Corleone. "Don't get excited! I'm just thinking out loud. We don't have to be as straight-line as the military. Sometimes the most direct path is not the one that gets you where you want to go. So we ask, is OBL actually the enemy's center of gravity here? Or is it the tribal militia leaders who ally with him? Of course we take him down eventually. But at the right time. Should we wait until we have more forces in-country? Cheese all the rats into one box, then pour concrete over 'em? The way we see it, this war's just getting started."

Osama bin Laden had been a CIA creation anyway, Dan remembered. He cleared his throat. "I'm not getting a good feeling, Tony. Is the Working Group going to take our localization up the chain? Because if you're not, I am."

A chuckle from the dark. "Just what I expected. Which is why you're getting passed over, right? Never going to pin on those captain's eagles."

He sat motionless in the dark, feeling cold.

The agent's voice went on, confiding, reassuring. A hand pressed Dan's knee. He looked down at it in the dark, oppressed by a nameless fear. "Don't worry. We don't work that way. What'd I just tell them in there? What're they doing, right now?"

"More research."

"Why?"

"To confirm the intelligence. Before we act?"

"Now you've got it. And if we get one more indicator, yeah, I'll take it up the chain. All the way. And we'll bust the Beard's bubble, for good."

Dan hoisted himself from the bunk. Hesitated, looking at the man smiling at him. Then lifted the flap and went out into the foreglow of dawn.

17

Leaders' Recon

TEDDY clung to the handholds as the six-wheeled Land Rover jolted and banged, raising a roil of powdery tan dust that pointed to them clear as an arrow for miles. The wind was icy cold, the clear sky darker than it ought to be. Far to the north contrails etched opal into that deep cobalt like scratches on a sapphire.

They were out on a leaders' recon, a hasty reconnaissance to get eyes on a village thirty miles to the east of Jaguar where the Alliance said there were a lot of Taliban, or anyway sympathizers. He suspected it was as much to let the locals get a look at them as to do a formal recon. The Aussies didn't drive on the roads, such as they were. Potholes and ruts, laid over some old-ass camel track; the going was only a little rougher completely off them. And you could hit a mine anywhere in Afghanistan; the Soviets had laid hundreds of thousands. He pulled his fleecy vest closer, grateful for the warmth. He'd ordered a dozen, on the Team credit card, and gotten them rushed in by the daily C-130 from Masirah.

He and Knobby Swager and Tatie were out with the SASRs. The bushies, as the marines called them. The Special Air Service Regiment had arrived a couple of days after the 15 MEU. They wore floppy bush hats, heavy beards, and strange, two-color camo patterns that Teddy thought made them look like toads. They were the most profane troops he'd ever served with, although at times it was difficult to tell exactly what they were saying. Still they seemed to be highly tactical, and almost every one he'd talked to claimed to be sniper-qualified. Two had even been in Desert Storm, though he and they had fought in different quarters of Iraq.

Echo was still out of Jaguar, still part of Task Force Cutlass. The weather was much colder than they'd expected. There'd been flurries of snow, though it didn't stick, evaporating in hours rather than melting. But although days had gone by, they hadn't seen action since Kandahar. The Special Forces were getting missions up north, but the SEALs were still just acclimating, training, at most doing these piddly patrols. The biggest thing that'd happened all week was when somebody had dropped an MRE heating tab into a plastic water bottle and popped it down the gas vent of the Porta Potti while Teddy was taking a crap. The explosion blew purple disinfectant all over him. The SEALs thought "smurfing" the chief a great prank. Every man denied knowing anything, but Teddy had his suspicions. The guilty party would pay.

"Let me see that," one of the Aussies said, a big sergeant with a heavy jaw and raccoon-ringed eyes. Teddy hesitated, then handed over his SOP-MOD M4. The guy looked it over critically, flicked a fingernail. "Same as ours. Colts."

"How about your sidearm, there?"

"Browning. Fourteen rounds of nine-mil."

Teddy nodded and returned his attention to the desert. The big, squared-off, desert-colored machine, open on top so there was no shade whatsoever, rolled as the ground dipped. Packs and comm gear and made-up tents were strapped all over it, as much, he figured, to protect them from RPGs as for stowage. They were much more heavily armed than the Marine Humvees, with a 7.62 on a flexible mount and a hulking forty-millimeter grenade launcher towering over what would have been a backseat had the vehicle had one. Instead a bench seat like one row of auditorium bleachers accommodated the gunner. Two more Rovers trailed them, antennas wobbling. The middle one carried the high-voltage VIPs, a marine colonel and two guys in civilian-style khakis and polo shirts and ball caps. One looked Italian, the other less categorizable; slicked-back black hair in a widow's peak, a beak of a nose; piercing blue eyes that examined Teddy for a fraction of a second, then moved on. His black cap had a logo of a snarling gray wolf. The interpreter—the "terp," Aimal—rode with them too, woolly, round cap and anxious, sharp-chinned face bobbing behind them.

TWO hours later the mountains seemed scarcely closer. The driver of the middle vehicle pulled up and waved them over. "Piss break," he called, and their own driver herringboned the Rover off to the right of the line of march. Teddy eyed the rock-strewn ground. He didn't see any bumps or depressions. He stepped down gingerly and followed the Aussie five yards off, where they stood side by side and unbuttoned.

When he looked around, the terp was standing by himself a little ways off, turned away from the Americans. Teddy waited until he was done—Moslems were funny that way—and strolled over, still keeping an eye on the soil. He held out a pack of Winstons. "You smoke, buddy?"

The Afghan eyed him sideways. He was young, probably about eighteen, and handsome, with long, black hair cascading from under the round, embroidered hat down over his white shirt and the field jacket someone had given him. Despite the freezing cold his brown feet were bare in flip-flops, and he was unarmed. Teddy caught a whiff of him; cold as it was, his body odor was like sticking your head into a urinal that hadn't been cleaned in years. "Yes. Thank you," he said.

"You the dude they call Animal?"

"Aimal. Some of them call me animal, yes."

"Aimal, what made you sign up with us? You're with Karzai's boys, right?"

"Hamid Karzai is my leader."

"You speak real good English, Aimal. Where'd you learn it?"

"From watching videos."

Videos? "And you're helping us out because . . . ?"

"I hate the Taliban as much as you. They attacked America, yes. But they forced their ways on us first."

"What'd they do? You're from around here, right?"

"I'm from Kandahar. My father owned a video store."

"That's cool. Okay, so you watched his videos."

"That's yes. I watched the movies at the counter. But the Taliban firebombed our store. My sisters had to leave school. There is nothing good left here. No Internet. If I translate for you, maybe I can go to America."

It sounded right, but in the field you trusted no one except your buddies; especially locals who showed up and wanted to be too friendly right away. "We'll be keeping an eye on you," Teddy told him. "You translate exactly what they say to us, hear me? Do that, and we'll be cool. I might even be able to help you get to the US. To Hollywood."

"Hollywood?" The one place, along with Disney World and New York, everyone had heard of. "You know Hollywood?"

"Grew up there, baby. Take care of us, and you'll be walking down Sunset Boulevard." Teddy kneaded Aimal's shoulder, digging his fingers in so the kid's eyes went wide. "But you jack us up, Aimal, set us up for an ambush, or we catch you stealing, and I'll kill you myself. With pleasure."

WHEN they stopped next, it was at a hamlet in the foothills. The fifty-foot-wide expanse of dirt and sewage that passed for a main drag was full of people and carts and vans and tables set up in the open, some with tarps stretched overhead.

"Bazaar day," the big Australian said. Teddy nodded, keeping outboard security with his weapon over his knee, a round in the chamber but the safety on. As they rolled in he eyeballed the crowd, taking recordings with his brain for the field intel report. The houses were mud brick. Grass grew out of their thatched tops, or maybe sod, and small bushes, like on a pioneer's hut back on the frontier. The stink hit in earnest as they slowed for a flock of muck-crusted, woolly sheep, tails and back legs smeared with shit. The kids were thin and too small, with black hair and dark eyes, most of them. But here and there pale jade eye too, and features that wouldn't have looked out of place back in California. When the Rovers braked, Teddy eased to the ground, scanning the field where the sheep were milling around, his carbine hanging muzzle down by its sling but still tactical, ready to swing up with one hand. From the stir of livestock a bearded man in *shalwar kameez* and sheepskin vest watched them, leaning on a staff. At second glance, Teddy saw why he leaned: He had only one leg.

Not speaking, the Aussies deployed out to surround the VIP vehicle. Teddy strolled a few yards away, sparing one glance at the mountains. Where the clouds moved, they were purple and nearly black, unimaginably huge, going up range after range in folds and peaks, like a whole continent tilted on its side and about to fall. He couldn't believe it wasn't already sliding, billions of tons of rock and ice coming down on them.

Her jerked his eyes away, to the kids. They'd stopped a few yards away, staring, then edging in. Cute from a distance, but as they got closer, he saw snotty noses, open sores, layers of dirt, scabby bare feet, rags stiff with dirt. They chattered and waved. When Aimal yelled, waving them away, they just pressed closer.

Few women on the street, all in burka, and as he watched, even these vanished into the huts. The adult males didn't approach, but they didn't look frightened, either. When Aimal called to one, he just raised a hand and walked away. Teddy strolled along the street, looking at what was for sale. Dangling carcasses of what seemed to be sheep, to judge by the severed heads artistically arranged in front of them. A blanket on the ground was covered with some sort of twisted, dusty roots. Another had three sheepskin coats laid out. Rugs, like those you saw all over the Mideast, but threadbare and dust-covered. Cheap plastic food bowls, tumblers, water jugs. Everything looked used, battered, and grimy.

One old man with a forked white beard to his waist huddled like a heap of propped-together sticks on a scrap of brick-patterned linoleum. Cast-metal pothooks and trivets and little flat brass pans and turned cups with a faint effort at enameled decoration lay on a gray blanket along with a long, nicked bayonet with a wooden handle and a hooked quillon. Their eyes met; the elder gestured silently to a bubbling pot of tea.

Teddy almost didn't accept, then said, *"Aiwa, shukran."* Not Pashto, but most people in this neck of the woods spoke at least a little Arabic.

The tarnished little brass cup was so hot it burned his fingers. *"Harr,"* he grunted. He blew on it, keeping his eyes going as he sipped. Christ on a pony, *strong* fucking tea. Guy must have boiled it for weeks. It tasted great. He found a familiar shape in his cargo pocket and bolted one of the big oval 800 Motrins they called SEAL candy and washed it down with the rest of the tea. He smacked his lips and handed the cup back. Hesitated, then offered the oldster a Motrin too. The old man backhanded it into his mouth without an instant's hesitation, grinning and jiggling where he sat as if Teddy'd told a dirty joke.

Teddy touched his cap and paced on, gaze dwelling on hands, faces, rusted Japanese pickups. He didn't expect trouble. From what the recon leader had said, this hadn't even been a planned stop. After a few firefights, a few ambushes, you learned to trust your radar.

By the time he circled back to the Rovers, four elders were talking to the VIPs, Aimal helping out with animated gestures. Teddy stood a few yards off, attention on the street, not the talk, but caught words here and there.

"No Taliban here, he says. They came and stayed for a time, then left."

"Is there a school? A clinic?"

"Years ago. Not now."

"A mosque?"

A wave toward a larger hut.

"The Talibs. How long ago did they leave?"

"A few weeks. Perhaps a week?"

"And where did they go?"

A gnarled hand waved vaguely at the mountains. "Out there, he says."

The big bushie shouldered up beside Teddy. "Got any Pashto?"

"Not a word."

"I can speak a little. But this is a waste of time. Get 'em inside their huts, put some bikkies on the table, we'll get useful intel. Nobody's going to say anything out here."

Teddy nodded toward the old man on the linoleum. "Try that good old boy with the teapot. He'll actually look at you."

The Australian squatted. He fingered the bayonet, turning it over. Then laid it down and in the same motion placed something else on the blanket, covering it with a fold of gray wool so deftly Teddy couldn't see it even though he'd been watching.

When the Aussie stood he tilted his head and winked. "Next village up the road. 'Toward the mountains,' he says. They left yesterday."

"The next village is where we're going," Teddy said. "Can you ask if there were any Arabs with them?"

"Already did. He saw foreigners, yeah. Six of 'em."

"'Foreigners.' Arabs? Al Qaeda?"

"Correct."

A good sign, that they thought of OBL's bunch as outsiders. Teddy checked his six. The other SASRs had the perimeter. They seemed like the sort of lads who'd stick to you in a firefight. He nodded to the old man and turned away and perambulated around the bazaar once more as the wind drove plastic scraps and dust and dead bushes across the road. The Rovers' engines had been running the whole time. When one of the drivers gunned his, Teddy and the sergeant strolled back.

BUT the next village wasn't a village. It was a mud-brick fort out of a sword-and-sandal epic. Each side was a three-meter-high wall that stretched perfectly straight for at least a hundred yards.

Teddy looked up from the Rover in awe. The thing looked as if it'd been drawn with a ruler. The gate was massive, with colossal oaken crossbeams that must have been dragged down out of the mountains, and thick iron hinges dimpled with the blows of blacksmiths' hammers. It could have been ten years old, or a thousand. The column sat parked in front of it for several minutes before anyone got out, and all that time Teddy's unease grew.

When the colonel dismounted, he took off his shooter's gloves and slapped the dust off his uniform with them. He was spare and balding and his face looked burned, as if he'd opened a pottery kiln without thinking ahead. His gear hung as if he'd lost twenty pounds since he'd strapped it on. "Tell 'em to open up," he told the terp. Aimal flinched as if something had stung him, but Teddy didn't see any wasps.

"This is fucked-up," Teddy muttered to the sergeant. Who shrugged, swung down, and began loosening up, stretching and doing a couple of quick squats. This looked like a good idea so Teddy did too. His joints creaked. He patted his knife and his pistol, then massaged some of the dust off his carbine with his sleeve. When he pulled the bolt back a couple of centimeters to check the chamber, he felt it grinding. Sand was never good, and that went double for a 5.56, with its small parts and tight tolerances. He got out the little squeeze bottle of CLP, squirted a stingy two drops into the gas ports, and wiped it down again. Oil and sand, not good either, but you had to have lubrication. Maybe he ought to go with that dry lube Swager was always raving about.

"What exactly we doing here, compadre?"

"Just paying a call, Obie. Just paying a call."

Teddy tried to shake off the willies and focus. Get tactical. But where was the buzz? He shifted and shook each arm out in turn, loosening up. The gate was grinding open, hinges grating as if they could use some CLP too. Aimal had convinced whoever was inside to open up. If he hadn't, Teddy figured they wouldn't be getting in, not without the kind of breaching charges they'd used on the raid the month before. Remembering that juiced him a bit. If armor was garaged here, they were butt-fucked, that was all. He drifted over to the colonel's vicinity, but didn't get too close. Asked the SASR lieutenant, "Hey, sir. Your guys got anything can take out light armor?"

"There's no armor here," the lieutenant said stiffly.

"Yes, sir. But you got any—"

"Let's move on in," said the colonel, and Teddy figured *fuck it* and oriented on his sergeant.

They went in smoothly, sweeping the inside of the gate, combat crouched, almost the same way the Teams did it, only with more talking, keeping each other informed. Which was okay in daylight, when somebody knew you were coming. The courtyard was huge, with a well near the center and the housing, all mud brick and those heavy beams, at the far end. Rusty bikes and a truck on blocks. A litter of oil cans and brake parts and tow straps. A lean-to over an old Land Cruiser, with the steel framework on top for cargo. It looked operational, and he wondered what kind of cargo they needed to carry.

"Clear."

"Clear."

He tail-end-Charlied into the housing area. Women with black cloth thrown over their faces squatted motionless, heads lowered. Kids stared with open mouths. An open hole for a latrine. Flies all over everything. An old man gesticulated, mumbling through a toothless mouth and wispy beard.

"Weapons," somebody yelled from the far side of the compound. Teddy's heart rate stepped up. He thumbed the safety off, keeping his muzzle clear of the man in front. The team leader spoke into a mike and kept going. Another room, jumbles of old furniture, old bedsteads, the musty stink of dust. Teddy sneaked out his canteen, swallowed hot mouthfuls that tasted of good American plastic. Better.

When they came back out into the courtyard, three used but functional AKs and an RPK were laid out on a madder-stained rug. Mustard-yellow sardine cans of ammo, with Cyrillic stenciling in black. A Tokarev pistol. A long, heavy, battered top-loader rifle that looked almost handmade, with a cloth belt of fat brass cartridges the size of small bananas. Beside them knelt a flex-cuffed young man in a beard and pillbox hat, head back and eyes closed as if enjoying the sun. Flies swarmed a bloodstained bandage that bulged at his shoulder. The Aussies were rummaging another room to the side of the lean-to, with much clattering and banging of thin metal. Aimal was murmuring steadily to the kneeling man, but he gave no sign of listening; seemed almost in a trance. Teddy thought: an all-day mission, twelve specfor trigger-pullers, and we get six small arms and one prisoner.

The colonel came striding through the gate, pistol held down by his thigh, the civilian to his right and the lieutenant on his left. He halted by the prisoner, looking at the weapons. Told the terp, "What he's doing here. How he got wounded. If he's seen any Arabs. The usual."

"He's not talking, sir. All he will say is 'Praise Allah.'"

"Good enough. Bag him and put him in the lead vehicle."

The Afghan opened his eyes. He lowered his head and spoke in what Teddy guessed was either Pashto or Dari.

"Where are you taking him? he asks," Aimal said.

"To interrogation," said the civilian. He smiled, dark eyes crinkled at the edges. The terp related this. Listened to a few sentences, bending, hands on knees, but not translating yet.

"What's he say?" the colonel prompted.

"Time."

"What?" said the colonel, leaning in.

The terp flinched again. "He said . . . he will remember my face. And they will find my family. Ah, and, I don't remember the word . . ." Aimal tapped his wrist.

"Watch," Teddy supplied.

"Yes. Watch. He says, 'You have the watch, the watches, but we have the time.' He means . . . it is a saying. Sooner or later, you will leave. And we—they—will be back."

An old man tottered out into the sunlight and slowly made his way toward them. He sank to his knees and clutched the hem of the civilian's vest, warbling what sounded like endearments in a low, supplicating voice. The civilian shook him off.

"What's he want?" the colonel snapped.

"He apologizes for the Russian weapons. But he wants to keep the oldest. His grandfather took it from the British when they invaded. It is a . . . keepsake, I think the word is."

"Who is this man? Ask him. Is he his son? A relative?"

The old man hesitated, glancing at the prisoner, who seemed uninterested in the whole process. The terp translated, "He is not family, but a guest. He asks us to let him go."

"Like hell we will. He's lucky we don't take his whole family. Ask him where the Taliban is."

The old man lifted his eyes. Looking at the top of the wall. No, Teddy realized; *beyond* it. "They're in the *tangai*," Aimal said. He pointed with his fist. "In the mountains."

"It's a weapon. Take it." The colonel holstered his pistol and spun around. Called back, "Load the prisoner. We'll do the interrogation back at Jaguar."

OUTSIDE, Teddy looked up at the sky again. So deep blue. The thin air, so cold. The endless ranges hovered in fold on fold of russet and violet stone. The Alliance was surging forward into a terrain wiped clean by the planes whose contrails combed the sky. But where were the prisoners? They came in trickles, where there should be thousands.

The enemy wasn't surrendering. He was withdrawing, into those high fastnesses where since Alexander the Afghans had held out against invader after invader. Or worse: sucked them into those steep passes, those roadless crags, and massacred them. Teddy kept looking up, letting the land seep into his soul. Thousands of square miles of rugged, nearly treeless rock that scuttlebutt said was full of caves. And on the other side, Pakistan, then the Kush . . . range after range, all the way to China.

The Aussies towed the prisoner past, his head wagging within the bag. Teddy saw how slight he was. Side by side with the Westerners, he looked like a fifteen-year-old. The troopers in their toad-colored uniforms were joking, reaching out when he stumbled, pushing him back upright just a little too roughly.

"Chief Oberg?"

As he turned, the big Aussie loomed from blowing dust. He held up a glove. "Just came over the blower. Sounds like the balloon's about to go up. They want us back just as quick as we can get there."

"About time we got our gun on," Teddy said.

"How fooking right. Load up, mates," the sergeant called, turning in a circle. Teddy looked for Swager and Tatie. When he had eyes on both, he swung up into the Rover too. Found himself next to the prisoner, whose covered head was slumped on his chest. His shirt had been cut off and a fresh bandage covered the wound. Teddy cleared his throat. Started to speak, but didn't.

For the whole ride back, for hours, they sat together, and shared not a word.

18

Bagram

FAR above the tormented earth, Dan circled over a possible landing strip north of Kandahar. Elevation and topo lines glowed into existence, crawling over the terrain. As he gradually descended, gray valleys bleached into green, yawning into 3-D vistas that erupted into tormented mountains. Minuscule callouts, when the operator put the pip over them, blew up into images annotated with line after line of data.

He straightened, rubbing cheeks gritty with beard-bristle and stiff as balsa from fatigue. He wasn't cruising high over rough terrain, freezing, on oxygen, wary every moment for a launch signature. He was in the Joint Operations Center, looking over the shoulders of a team of Army specialists at a large screen flanked by two smaller ones. The view was real time, from a Predator zoom telephoto linked to threat databases back at CENTCOM. He sucked a deep breath. "So, what's the conclusion? How much effective runway? We need someplace we can put down C-17s."

C-17s were the Air Force's most modern transport, replacing the C-130 turboprops for tactical lift. They were designed for unimproved, even improvised, runways. Which was what he was trying to do now, land them close to the battlefront to shorten supply lines that stretched back into Central Asia. A specialist moved a mouse, and the pip edged along a highway that paralleled a straight-line canal, climbing out of Kandahar toward a mountain lake.

Then zoomed down again, falling from thousands of feet. The trees leapt up like green detonations. Dan had to look away, close to nausea.

"Almost four thousand feet of runway, sir. And we think the load rating's adequate—the soil should take it. The problem's altitude. Five thousand feet, here. Five thousand, five hundred here. We can fly in, but the load capacity's going way down."

Dan rubbed his mouth. He was holding down at least three jobs now. The

ramp-up to a major effort, combined with what seemed to be a marked reluctance to send more officers to Bagram, had resulted in far too few staff.
He was attending all the briefings, and keeping Template—the fused intel
localization, including CIRCE—wired with the necessary intel inputs and
the outputs pipelined to the right people in the Fusion Cell, the Joint Working Group, and the operational staff. Then the J-4 had asked for help. Dan
had organized food and medical supplies during the famine and drought in
Ashaara; privately he considered he knew just enough to be dangerous, but
even that seemed to make him the local subject-matter expert.

Just now he was researching airfields, for both reasons, offensive and
humanitarian; exploring how to get troops and light armor to support an
assault, and how to get food and clothing to Afghans facing a bitter winter. Which so far had meant by airdrop, arranged with the Special Forces
teams in contact with the various tribes.

Unfortunately, there was only so much capacity, and in the past few
days Lieutenant General Randall Faulcon, USA, the Joint Special Operations commander, had been pushing to use most of those assets to carry a
major force down to the Gardez area, north of Kandahar and west of the
White Mountains. Lifted and supplied from there by helicopter, they'd surround Pajuar and pin down, attack, and kill Osama bin Laden and the
senior Al Qaeda and Taliban leadership.

Dan could see that as an endgame, but each passing day brought indi-
cations neither ALQ nor the Taliban were going to stay pinned. Both local
intelligence and SIGINT showed them withdrawing into the mountains,
rather than surrendering or fighting. The question being debated was
what to do about it. Special Forces and SEALs had conducted recons up
to the mountains, and in a few cases into them, descending on compounds
and caves where the enemy might be concentrating. The air strikes continued, but at the moment, the multinational effort seemed to be marking
time.

Sooner or later, they were going to have to move. Faulcon's idea for an
airborne encirclement seemed as good as any.

Dan pushed open the tent flap and strolled toward a ditch scooped from
the icy ground by a bulldozer, thinking as he unbuttoned his fly and gazed
at distant violet slopes about force availability. The Fifteenth and Twenty-
sixth Marine Expeditionary Units had leapfrogged up from Camp Jaguar
to the Kandahar airport, putting them a long stride closer to the White
Mountains. The Tenth Mountain and the Eighty-second Airborne were
mainly providing base security; they were available. And the 101st was on
alert to move to Afghanistan too.

But the more he saw of this country, the more daunting the logistics seemed. He was used to operating close to the sea, or at least with access to a port. But Afghanistan was landlocked. Worse, the roads were so bad you couldn't even truck fuel in to Bagram. It had to be "wet winged" out of transports into the swollen black rubber bladders that lined the airstrip. (He often wondered what would happen if one of the rockets that occasionally fell hit that tank farm.) The closest strategic airlift strips were in Kuwait and Turkey. From there everything had to be cross-loaded to smaller aircraft, which used up even more fuel and made it hard to schedule flow of assets into the theater. They could purify local water, but everything else—food, ammo, batteries, medical supplies—would have to go in by helicopter. And an attack into the high valleys could easily entail a six-hour hike from the helo LZs, either on foot or by donkey.

US forces would be restricted to the sort of logistics train that had supplied Lee and Grant during the Civil War. No, worse; there wasn't a single operating railroad in Afghanistan.

Dan was mulling this over walking back from the piss pit when a hulky figure in a fur vest intercepted him. Beanie Belote, pistol on his hip, in bandanna and black, Russian high boots, a *pakul* hat looking odd atop his braided pigtail. He hitched a bright green athletic bag higher on his shoulder. "Commander. What you working on? Right now?"

"Transport. Food relief. Keeping the magnifying glass on the HVTs."

"I'm going to Gardez. Tony thought you might want to come along?"

Why did Belote end all his sentences with an up inflection? "*Gardez?* Uh, I've got a lot to do right here. Sorry, but—"

"Down this morning, stay overnight, back tomorrow. You can get your eyeballs on these airstrips you're researching while you're down there?"

His initial reaction was too pat to voice without thought. So he reconsidered. Gardez was south of Kabul, west of the Shah-i-khot, Not too far north of Kandahar. Some sort of combined Agency/SOF operation was being run out of that city. If an operation was launched toward Pajuar, it would most likely stage out of Gardez. Not only would it give him a chance to see the ground, it was a chance to get out of the concertina-fenced Camp Bragg the airfield was becoming.

But why was the *CIA* asking him to go with them?

Belote took hesitation as assent. "Helo at sixteen hundred local," the agent said. "Don't wear uniform. Something scruffy—it'll fit in better? And dress warm?"

GARDEZ was a medium-size city surrounded by fields dry brown with the coming of winter. The helo landed in one of them and they drove in, in a civilian taxi, followed at a discreet distance by eight Northern Alliance soldiers in a jingly truck. Dan was in jeans, Chicago Bulls ball cap, and a gray Academy sweatshirt turned inside out to hide the trident and galley. He shivered in the cold. Belote had given him a short-barreled M4 and a pair of sunglasses someone had left in-country, but the prescription lenses distorted everything, and if he turned his head too quickly, he felt nauseated. Riding with the carbine by his feet on the floor of the taxi beside Belote's bag, he felt both freer and less safe than he had traveling behind armor in military convoys. Dull broom grass bristled along the dry, rocky side of the highway, and mountains floated far ahead. It looked like Arizona. They drove into a roundabout at the town center, then out toward the mountains again.

Orienting by the sun, Dan put the Shah-i-khot—or Shahi Kowt, as the Army was calling it—directly ahead in those eastern peaks. Strangely humped whaleback foothills, dun and tan like everything but the snow, rolled like swells from a far-off typhoon between plain and mountains. The peaks were invisible, shrouded in fog and trailing bridal veils of snow. On the other side of a loftier peak to the south would be small hamlets in valleys at eight-thousand-plus feet. One was Pajuar, the location of the planned ALQ meet.

But you couldn't just load troops into trucks and drive up. Working with maps, overhead imagery, and the Predators, he was beginning to grasp just how tormented this sub-Himalayan geography was. The mountains soared, buckled, and folded in violent ridges and deep valleys dotted with strataed caves. The hamlets were thinly linked by rocky trails mainly navigable by donkeys in summer and, in winter, only negotiated with difficulty by human beings acclimated to the altitude.

A vicious place to fight. It could conceal whole armies or suck other armies in. And now it was snowing up there, blinding both the drones and the air support so important to US forces.

All of which was, of course, why their enemy had retreated there. Sixteen thousand British troops had tried to fight their way through those mountains from Kabul back to India in the 1840s. One man had survived. Everyone knew about Alexander the Great, and the Soviet invasion, but those had only been two among hundreds of incursions, invasions, and civil wars—by Iranians, Mongols, Chinese, Macedonians. The country had never really been at peace since recorded history began. Each time, the natives had withdrawn to the mountains, harassing and ambushing and betraying the invader until he either surrendered or retreated. The only conquerer ever to subdue Afghanistan had been Genghis Khan.

"Doing okay?" Belote rumbled. Dan nodded. "Almost there. When we arrive? Don't take your time. Stay on my ass right out of the taxi."

They pulled off into a side street without warning. A man atop a wall cradling a Kalashnikov called to them. Belote reached forward to hand the driver a roll of bills. They piled out and he said, "Follow me. That on safe? Good. Try not to look so American, all right?"

Dan tried to slouch, to disguise his height, and they walked rapidly but not suspiciously so down an alley littered with garbage. Belote rapped at a back gate that looked like wood but sounded like steel. It opened immediately, pulled inward.

Four men looked up from bottles of lemon pop or mugs of tea, sitting under a leafless tree, around a rusting garden table. They were all in *shalwar kameez* and beards and parkas or heavy sheepskin coats. A brazier smoked, radiating heat.

Belote sighed, releasing some inner pressure, and parked the green bag by the brazier. He set his rifle in a wooden rack; hung a pistol from a whittled peg of raw wood; eyed Dan.

Dan set his M4 in the rack beside several Kalashnikovs and joined the men as they made room, bracing his back against the smoking brazier. The heat felt good, but the smoke made his eyes water. Two of the men were American, introduced by Belote without giving ranks. Dan made them as either CIA or Special Forces, part of the A teams that had worked with the local militia to such deadly effect thus far. The other two were Afghanis, one in his late forties or early fifties, the other perhaps twenty years younger. Dan figured them as local allies, tribal leaders. Pashtun, he assumed, which would make them of the same tribe as most of the Taliban. The older leaned forward to finger Belote's vest, which seemed to be of some sort of brown fur. Then patted his own, a red plaid, new-looking, down-filled Gander Mountain, looking satisfied.

One of the Americans started the questioning. "All right, Beanie, what's Faulcon got planned?"

"He's pushed for a major force package. Land them in C-7s. They'll surround, then attack."

Belote went on to say that the difficulty was that the SecDef and his assistant for Afghanistan, Roman Annunziata, were waffling. "Faulcon started small, a raid, but this Annunziata keeps asking what if this happens, what if that happens. They keep adding support units and increasing force size. Pretty soon it's going to be a major operation."

When the CIA agent translated this into Pashtun, the older Afghan looked worried. He spoke, and the translation came. "These troops. They will stay in Pajuar? On our lands?" Belote denied it, but disbelief and suspicion ignited in the older man's eyes.

After several more polite questions, the point the Afghans wanted to

make came through. The more troops, the more local leaders would resent their presence; perhaps even turn against them. What wasn't clear
was why. Dan shifted on his chair. "Okay if I ask a question here?" he finally put in.

The senior Army guy looked reluctant, but nodded. "You fought the Soviets?" Dan asked them.

The older Pashtun nodded and pulled up a sleeve. An anemic forearm
was seamed with scar tissue as if steel had been grapneled through the
live flesh. He spoke for a long while, waving his hands. Belote said laconically, "His war record. Your question is?"

"He seems uncomfortable about working with us. Because we're Christians? Americans? Or just outsiders?"

The younger man smiled, and Dan realized he understood English,
though he hadn't spoken yet at all.

The old man's words tumbled over one another. Addressing now not Belote but Dan, as if he'd decided he was the elder. Belote said, "He says, when
he was young, they had peace. But that was thirty years ago. First, the Russians came. They bombed mosques. Destroyed whole villages with tanks
and helicopters . . . wait a minute, he's going too fast . . . then they left and
the Arabs came. Bin Laden brought promises, but it is true, then turned
his hand to evil. He knows the Americans fear God. He knows they want
revenge for the attack on New York. But his land has been the toy of others for too many years. The Americans are welcome as guests. That is the
custom, he says. But a guest who stays too long is no longer a guest. This
is the same in every country. Why do people think Afghans are different?"

"Have you heard about a meeting of ALQ at Pajuar?" Dan asked them.
Belote looked startled, but translated.

"We have heard rumors of such a meeting,"said the younger Afghan,
speaking for the first time. Smiling. "Yes."

"Can your men help us in an assault? At least, provide guides?"

One of the Americans shook his head, warning Dan off. He made a fan-
ning gesture at his throat. The Afghans didn't meet Dan's eyes, but maybe
that didn't mean the same thing in this culture. "It might be possible," the
younger one said. He didn't sound enthusiastic. "But you know, it is snowing now. It would be very difficult."

Belote cleared his throat, and they all looked at him. He got up and retrieved the green bag. Set it on the table and nodded to the older Afghan.
The old man smiled and unzipped it. Dipped within and held up a few of
the shrink-wrapped packages. Each was an inch thick, a sheaf of green
and gray bills that looked brand-new.

Dan took the hint and kept quiet. The Afghans stacked the money, counting it aloud, then put it back into the bag and slid it under the table. They seemed friendlier now. The younger man said his men were assembling east of Gardez, ready for battle. "The Deobandis, you call them Taliban, we have no use for them. Bin Laden's Arabs give many oaths, but nothing happens. They live in luxury and treat us like dogs. America will feed our families and make us rich. So my men are eager to fight and die for America."

One of the Special Forces guys went into the house, and not long after a servant or employee brought out goat meat, rice, avocados, and boiled eggs on trays, and they ate with the Afghans, talking until long after dusk fell.

After the Pashtuns left, taking the gym bag, the Americans sat in the dark drinking beer and talking over the possibilities. Dan didn't say much, but made it his business to listen. So far, or so these operators seemed to think, a few OGA teams and Special Forces had managed to liberate every city in the country in only two months and were closing in on the last resisters in the last redoubts. More cash, weapons, and ammunition for the friendly Afghans, and they could wrap up bin Laden and start setting up for elections.

At last the Army guys stood. They said good night and left through the metal door. Dan hesitated, wondering if he and Belote were going with them. Apparently not; the OGA man went inside. Dan looked at the brazier again, then followed.

The house was bare, as if all the furnishings had been cleared out. "So, what did you think?" the Agency guy asked Dan. "They're changing, all right. Some of the background stuff I read, it said years ago they wouldn't eat with infidels. They threw the food away after you touched it. These guys, they dug right in."

"Those were Pashtuns, right?"

"Correct."

"And the Taliban are Pashtun too. So why are these suddenly so eager to play on our team?"

Belote grinned. "You kidding? You saw why. We pay 'em. Just like the Brits used to."

"That's it? It's that simple?"

"It's how things work here. Always have. The highest bidder. They make a big deal out of what they call *nanawatai*. One reason OBL ended up here: Pashtuns protect their guests. Even enemies, if they ask the tribe for sanctuary. But it gets harder when your guests start trying to take over. Like these Arabs did. Then the Taliban outlawed planting opium poppies. They made themselves real popular with a lot of local landowners, with that one."

Dan thought of asking what would happen if somebody else paid them more, but didn't. Then of asking what happened when you stopped paying, but that was so obvious he didn't bother. More and more of the links CIRCE was uncovering between bin Laden and ALQ subsidiaries in Yemen, Sudan, Britain, Saudi Arabia, Pakistan, Indonesia, and other countries was financial. Wealthy donors. False-front charities. Al Qaeda had trickled cash down into the cracked soil of countries without hope or education, other than madrassas taught by obscurantist fanatics. When the only job a young man could get was carrying an AK for Allah, too many saw no reason to refuse.

Bin Laden had lived in the White Mountains for years. He was a Robin Hood, a William Tell, a Francis Marion of the mountains. He had money, charisma, and a message that resonated across all Islam. Yet the Pashtuns were ready to sell him out.

The old man was right. "A guest who stays too long is no longer a guest."

Which meant, they had to get bin Laden soon. Or they too would no longer be guests, but invaders.

He spent the night on a cot in the basement with a kerosene heater that stank and smoked and was probably a bigger threat to his life than anyone in Gardez. But he still kept the M4 within arm's reach.

BACK at Bagram the next day, the planes were circling. C-130s, C-17s, coming in one after the other in a line that receded to the horizon. More of the big transports than Dan had ever seen before, and the helo had to touch down far west of the strip to stay clear of the landing pattern. He kept his eyes peeled, watching for the lance of smoke that would indicate a man-portable missile or rocket-propelled grenade, but none came from the folds of desiccated earth or carefully diced-up fields. When the ship settled, he scrambled down and jogged toward the compound. About half a mile, and he covered it in good time, and since he hadn't gotten to run for a while, it felt good. Lines of troops were trudging off toward blocks of tents that had sprung up while he'd been gone. Halfway there he remembered he still had the M4 Belote had loaned him, but its weight slung on his back felt good too and he thought, maybe I'll just keep it. Until somebody asks for it back, anyway. He looked at his watch and picked up the pace. Almost time for the daily video-teleconference.

The JOC was buzzing like a hornets' nest snapped with a towel. Every shift was up and on duty. Every terminal was two and three deep in off-watch operators and kibitzers. As he jogged toward the Fusion Cell a hand snagged his sleeve. "Your sweatshirt's on inside out," a Marine light colonel said. Sad, dark eyes, arms swelling under rolled-up sleeves. Dan groped for a name, then did it the easy way; dropped his eyes to the tag.

"Pete! Pete Friedebacher." They shook hands. "You made O-5. Congratulations. When did that happen?"

"Not long after Ashaara."

Friedebacher had led the Quick Reaction Team, the USMC/SEAL outfit that had tamped down the Maahdist insurgency in the Red Sea. Dan had worked with him to locate the hostages, with the idea that if they did, they'd find Al-Maahdi there as well. "Heard you and Monty were here. Stuffed back in the SCIF. What's going on? Got bin Laden nailed?"

"Just what you heard, Pete. Just what you heard."

"Working with the OGA?"

"And the Land Information Warfare Activity, and the intel cell down at Task Force Cutlass. Trying to sew it all together and Frankenstein something that walks like an intel picture."

"Wait a minute. And your output goes to Hatchet, and they go out and get him. Right? Shit, where do I sign up? They've got me reading books and boiling down operational lessons."

Dan asked what books, and Friedebacher told him two volumes the Army had had translated. One was by a Russian general, about tactical lessons from Afghanistan, and the other was interviews with mujahideen commanders, how they'd viewed the same battles the Russians described. He was supposed to meet with the guys who were drawing up concepts of operations and advise them how the Taliban might react.

"That sounds worthwhile," Dan said.

"Sure, but what'm I going to say, I read my way through the war? You find Osama, the way you found Al-Maahdi, I want in. Deal?"

Dan shook his hand again and said he'd like to talk, but had to get to the VTC.

The screens were set up at the end of the tent, walled off by canvas drapes that isolated a dozen folding metal chairs. He showed his ID to a sergeant and got the last seat. The others gathered were generals and colonels.

The image came up on the big-screen projector, centerpieced with the visages of the CENTCOM commander, General Steven Prospero Leache, US Army, and of Roman Annunziata, the bearded, somewhat effeminate-sounding assistant SecDef for counterterror. Dan knew Leache, a lame-duck CINC who'd narrowly survived sexual-harassment charges. He didn't know Annunziata. If the election had gone the other way, Blair might have been in his seat. The new assistant SecDef had worked on Star Wars and for think tanks. His thin face was bearded; with those full lips he might have passed for an Arab himself. Smaller subscreens surrounding the duo were of Faulcon, the SOF commander, and the other high-level players. Each of the stars had a camera and a monitor, and every one had an American flag prominently positioned just behind him.

Annunziata kicked off by asking for a round-robin. A two-star out of Oman summarized the day's activity across Afghanistan. Operations around Kondoz were complete; the area was pacified. Marines from Kandahar Airport and special ops forces from Task Force Cutlass, along with Australians and Germans, were conducting sweeps east and north of that city. Heavy bombing was continuing. An Air Force general spent a long time recounting each strike, so that finally Annunziata broke in, smiling, to ask him to cut it short. Faulcon introduced a Special Forces colonel, who spoke about tribal militias and their recruitment by his A teams. He seemed more optimistic than Dan, having just had tea with two of those leaders, thought was warranted.

Leache said, "Right now, we're focusing south of Gardez, the Shah-i-khot valleys. I want to put the Tenth Mountain and all the SOF we can muster in there. I expect that to happen as soon as possible, a big push. What are our limiters?"

Annunziata jumped in. "I want to keep the number of US troops to a bare minimum. I've made that point before. A light footprint. That's how we've gotten so far."

A colonel beside Dan leaned over. Sotto voce, he muttered, "He's the one who wanted more artillery support yesterday. Then he complains we've got too many troops in-country, like he's saving them for something else."

Dan had thought about this for some time now, and the meeting with the Pashtuns, the video-teleconferences, the arguments were coalescing into something he recognized. One of his papers for his postgraduate degree had examined the response of Hitler and the German High Command to the Stalingrad crisis. Washington 2001 wasn't Berlin in 1942, nor was Afghanistan Stalingrad. But there was the same mission creep. At first the target had been bin Laden. Then it had become regime change, ousting Omar. Now the Taliban themselves were the targets, and Afghanistan was going to have a democratic government. Each time the scope widened, the number of their enemies increased geometrically. One more step, and all Islam would fill the target window—which, from the news reports from home, would be all too welcome to some.

A split was developing within the military too. A crisis required three perceptions: high threat, time constraints, and a looming change in the military balance. In this case, the Special Operations Forces and the SecDef were on one side—light, highly kinetic operations that depended on local allies supported by overwhelming airpower. On the other side was Big Army, which dreaded being fed piecemeal into demanding terrain where the sensors and weapons they'd spent billions on could be frustrated by an agile fourteen-year-old with an AK.

If they went in too light, soldiers would die. If too heavy, they risked repeating the Soviet experience. Either way, if they failed, heads would roll and budgets would be reshuffled.

But that wasn't Dan's problem. As far as he was concerned, all they had to do was get the man behind 9/11. The one who'd nearly killed him at the Pentagon, and Blair as well. Blair—God, he had to call her. They hadn't spoken for days.

The conference wrapped, with Annunziata asking Leache to stay on the VTC for a one-on-one.

"How's the localization holding?" Dan asked Donnie Wenck as soon as he got back to the Working Group spaces.

The analyst shrugged, not taking his eyes off the screen. The stick of a lollipop stuck out of one corner of his mouth. His hair was too long, getting rumpled. He was sitting cross-legged on the chair, knees sticking out, a blanket draped over him. "Getting a little fuzzy around the edges," he mumbled.

This wasn't good news. Dan coughed. The thin, dry air irritated his lungs. A hard-edged polygon signaled a firm location. When the edges began to bleed, or alternate locations metastasized at other nodes, the probabilities degenerated swiftly. They had to move now. The way they'd been set up in Ashaara, when Friedebacher had honchoed the Quick Reaction Team. Small, fast, violent, and agile. Bin Laden was always on the move. That mobility was his primary security tool; an extensive network of caches, supporters, vehicles, and safe houses had made it work despite several attempts to target missiles against him. He'd built those networks out of cash, terror, and loyalty to tribe, religion, and family. Now he'd be calling on them to ensure his survival and, if it came to that, his escape.

Their quarry had never been a passive target. He made mistakes, but emerged from each setback stronger. He'd be readapting, setting up his own chess moves to counter the American victories. With each day's hesitation, each hour, their chances were going to drop. "Can you tell which way they're tending?"

"Not yet."

"Where's Monty?"

"Crashed."

"Link with TAG holding up?"

The petty officer said it was, but it was obvious his mind wasn't on the responses. He kept toggling alternate routines, causing the lines and intersections to jiggle, quiver, and finally settle in slightly different patterns. Like a digital I Ching. The lines were the yarrow stalks, the polygrams like the eight trigrams, 4,096 answers. Dan had considerably more confidence in CIRCE, though.

"They going in?" Donnie muttered. "You go to the VTC? They let you in?"

"Yeah."

"This's our chance for payback. We gonna take it?"

Dan sat massaging stubbled cheeks. He didn't know how to answer. So he just watched the vibrating images on the screen.

ALL that afternoon he watched as one after the other forces moved out of billets and formed up for embarkation. The howl of jet engines was nonstop. But even as troops lined up on the aprons, he listened to heated exchanges on the command nets, read e-mail traffic that argued against committing troops. Even the State Department was weighing in. Their cable laid out all the arguments against a major assault in the Shah-i-khot. Drew parallels to the joint Army/SEAL mission into Kandahar at the beginning of the war, the one that had resulted in heavy losses. It concluded that by inserting a large force in difficult terrain and bad weather without heavier organic arms, especially mortars and artillery, the Army ran the risk of casualties so heavy they'd erode support for the whole mission in Afghanistan.

Finally Dan picked up the phone. Provanzano's number didn't answer. Go over his head? It didn't take long to make that decision. He walked down the SCIF and caught a figure he recognized. General E. H. Salter. The Army one-star who ran the JOC. Template reported their results to him for transmission to Faulcon. And if what Provanzano had said about Salter's remembering him from Desert Storm was correct, Dan might even have a little traction.

"General, excuse me. Dan Lenson. From the Fusion Cell. Trying to track what's going on. Can you—"

The operations center commander looked him up and down. "I know who you are, Commander. And I remember what you did in Iraq. And that you're my Navy liaison too."

"Yes, sir. I didn't mean—well, never mind."

"What's going on is that we're waiting on a decision to launch this operation. You're CIRCE, correct?"

"Correct, sir. Out of TAG."

"I don't know what that is. And I guess I don't need to, if it's Navy. Is the localization holding?"

"No, sir. It's been degenerating since midnight local. The longer we wait, I'm afraid, the worse it's going to get."

The general swore, then added wearily, "I've got your output on my screen. Keep it coming."

"Sir, if CENTCOM or the White House don't approve a ground force in the Shah-i-khot, we should at least do a strike."

"An air strike? The weather's not exactly cooperating."

"We have Tomahawk. I have a package laid on."

Salter frowned. "My understanding was, the mountains gave you problems with the weapon's flight profile."

"Uh, yes, sir, unfortunately that's correct. If they're down in one of those valleys. But we could use a Hellfire from one of the Predators. We have to hit this meeting."

"No more missile strikes. That's what the previous president did. Anything he did, they're not going to approve."

"Yes, sir, that came through loud and clear. But that clock's ticking. This meeting—if they're still having it—"

"My information is that it's been called off."

Dan closed his eyes. That was why the localization was degenerating. "Where did that intel come from, sir? Did it get routed to Fusion?"

"I'll have to defer to someone else on that," the JOC commander said. Salter looked as if he was about to throw something, but didn't. He grimaced up at the roof of the tent. From nowhere, Dan wondered if it was light outside or dark.

DAN was back in the Fusion area, scrolling through reports from the interrogation facility, when Friedebacher stopped at his terminal. "Stand down," he said.

"What's that, Pete?"

"They decided not to go. Canceled the mission."

He felt cold and enraged and resigned. Because he'd seen it all happen before, and from both sides—the operating-force side and the West Wing side. He was all for civilian control. But there was a barrier between civilian and military as invisible yet as definite as that between water and air. Different mind-sets, cultures, attitudes toward risk. At its worst, an arrogance that assumed a man in a chair thousands of miles away knew better than the one confronting the enemy. "You're shitting me. After we had the troops loaded? Advance units in the air?"

"That's the way it goes."

Dan jumped up, fists balled, and stalked out into the main area. Operators were shutting down their stations, getting up. A hum of angry voices. "What a balls-up," someone said with a Scottish accent. Dan rubbed his face. The choice had been between using native allies, corseted with Special Forces, or the Tenth and Eighty-second. He'd heard reasonable arguments on both sides. But what possible justification could there be for scrubbing the operation altogether? Unless somebody didn't really want bin Laden caught.

No; that was paranoia talking. Maybe the special operators had him already and were just keeping it under wraps. But no such word had percolated up to the Working Group. They'd had him located. But now every time he looked at the screen, the polygon was bigger, the edges fuzzier.

"He's not there anymore," Dan said. Accepting the inevitable, bitter as it was and disastrous as the downstream might be. "We missed our chance."

Friedebacher had followed him. Dan added, "They're not meeting there. Or finished early. Now they're breaking up, retreating up into the White Mountains. Or over the border, into Pakistan."

The marine shrugged. "Then we go into the mountains after 'em."

"It would have been a lot easier, at Pajuar."

"We'll get him," Friedebacher said. "Take it easy. No way we're letting this bastard get away. Payback."

"Payback," Dan echoed bitterly. Trying to keep his hands from shaking, trying not to relive the terror of darkened corridors and flame and the rubbery give of body parts underfoot. "If he gets time to dig in up there, we may not be able to pry him out. Not without huge casualties."

"We'll get him," Friedebacher repeated. But doubt now seemed to haunt his voice as well.

19

DAN got no sleep that night. All the reachback comms to the United States and CENTCOM and K2 and the Counterterrorism Center went down. Donnie Wenck went off to help the techs from the Eighty-sixth who were working on it. They got it up again after two frantic hours, but the backlog kept all three of them at the terminals streamlining inputs. There was muttering about hostile hacking, but Dan doubted Al Qaeda had expert programmers. He admitted to Monty he could be wrong, though.

When Template finally came back up, the picture kept shifting. Then a report from British signal intelligence reported an intercept for a source close to bin Laden, and suddenly CIRCE zoomed in, not only localizing but beginning to show a direction of motion. Doing what Dan always found so uncanny: predicting where the target would move, as if it knew his motives, fears, and yearnings better than did its human subject himself.

He stared at the screen, hearing the hinge of fate creak. When you ran CIRCE alone, the target individual was centered in a black screen, connected by lines of different hues to other individuals of interest. Each line vibrated at five cycles per second, tugging each node or point of intersection this way and that in a Brownian motion that made it seem almost alive. The subroutines confirmed it. The HVTs were moving north out of the Shah-i-khot, ascending into even more remote heights. Dan moved down the length of the tent asking for Predator imagery, hoping to get eyes on the mountain passes their quarry seemed headed toward. But weather had grounded all the drone flights. From the topo, it would be a hell of a place to fight. He went into the historical files then, looking for hide sites and locations the mujahideen had used during the Soviet War.

Wenck came back, grumbling about DISNs and PIX Firewalls, port switches and STEP sites. "Major problem?" Dan asked, but all he got back was something about the "tropo scatter."

Wenck grumbled, "Everybody likes to buy all this off-the-shelf shit and they expect it to interface, but it never does and nobody ever asks why. They just throw more money at the contractors and wonder why it doesn't work."

"I'll tell you what I wonder," Dan said.

"What, sir?"

"Why General Leache is in Florida and the land forces component commander and all his staff are in Kuwait. Why the forward ground commander, the Tenth Mountain Division commander, has his headquarters back at K2, and the spec ops CO's here in Bagram."

"It ain't like the Navy, sir."

"Better or worse?"

"You need me, Commander? If you don't, I'm gonna get some sleep."

As the tent walls breathed in and out with the wind, Dan contemplated the fact it worked at all. Both the comms and the command relationships were bewildering and time-wasting. Still, instant comms with home had its advantages. Since getting to Bagram, he'd done most of his work on-line, over a supersecure, dedicated digital system called Spartan Prime. Now he had a hard time believing he'd ever been able to accomplish anything with the Navy message system and secure STU-III calls. It all came in via super-high-frequency TACSAT, the military tactical satellites. Not only local intel, from the field and the JIF, but every day and nearly every hour he got synthesized information from analysts back at the Pentagon and CTC and even, occasionally, the FBI.

They had data services, collaborative-planning and mission-analysis tools, and all kinds of digitized command and control. But there were only still twenty-four numbers on a military clock. Beyond a certain point it was like trying to drink, not out of a fire hose, but out of Niagara Falls.

At 3:00 a.m. local he had his recommendations nailed down for the morning meeting, which he would present at, since both Provanzano and Belote were still out in the field. Sleep? He was dead on his feet, but the way his brain was buzzing, he'd just lie on his bunk and vibrate. He told Henrickson to hold the fort and went over to another tent to a guy who had a cell phone that would actually connect.

Outside, he blinked in the darkness, astonished there was still a universe outside the SCIF. As his eyes adapted, enormous, cold stars appeared. The Milky Way glowed like spilled bleach if you looked away from the runway lights. Some of those stars moved, planets that gradually grew brighter: more transports, lining up for approach. A streak of soundless light scratched the black, revealing brilliance beneath. He tensed, ready to drop: incoming mortar, rocket? Then realized it was only a shooting star.

"Halt. Halt!"

A brilliant light dazzled him. He stopped dead, realizing he'd taken a wrong turn, was in a part of the compound he didn't know. A huge oval the size of a kids' wading pool loomed, mounted on some large vehicle. A trooper had an M4 trained on him. "Restricted area, sir," he said.

"Got it. Sorry."

"HELLO?"

"Hey, hon. It's me. Finally got to a phone without a line in front of it."

"Dan? You okay? You sound hoarse again. Where are you?"

"At the main base over here. I guess it's the dry air, all this dust. . . . How you doing?"

"They're starting the physical therapy. The scar tissue . . . it really hurts."

Her voice dragged, a note he'd never before heard; resignation, weariness? It didn't sound like her. He thought savagely, things will never be the same for a lot of people. Because of the religious idiots we're here to kill. "Sure you're okay, honey?"

"Actually, I'm not. I saw it on the TV for the first time. Dad would turn it off. To not upset me. Or I would, because I was afraid I wouldn't be able to stand it. But this time I left it on. All those people. Waving their shirts in the air, for help. But nobody could help them. . . ."

"It's all right. It's all—"

"And then they just . . . stepped out. Or tried to climb down, as if it wasn't a thousand feet. So they lost their grip. Then fell . . ."

Her voice had gone ragged, edged with torn steel. He felt helpless, exiled to the edge of the world when he should have been there helping her heal.

Her voice came stronger, infused with conscious will. "How about you? You're the one out there." She snorted. "I'm just sitting at home."

"We're making progress. The push is on. I'm hoping we'll have some good news in a few days."

"About *him*? That'd be nice to hear."

"How's Checkie? And Queekie?"

"I wish they wouldn't *hover*, but . . . I guess that's what parents have to do."

"The hip? Is it healing? I hear bad things about broken hips."

"Well, it's going to take time, Dan. And it does hurt. Sometimes a lot. But I can hobble around the house now. With a walker. I'm going in for some more work on my face next week. . . . You're not going into combat? Are you?"

"No, they've got the Eighty-second Airborne between me and whoever's out there. And lots of concertina. Mainly I'm trying to set up to get food and water up to some of the villages. Humanitarian assistance. Just like in an office, only in a tent."

They caught up on acquaintances, then ran out of things to say. He wanted to ask what she was picking up from her circle of contacts, but long indoctrination about phone security kept him from asking. "Uh, what's the *Post* saying? Are they following us out here?"

"They say Kabul just fell. Sounds like it's going faster than anyone expected. All the Taliban are surrendering."

"Kabul? We took Kabul last month. You mean Kandahar?"

"I guess so. Aren't a lot of them coming over to the ANA? Or are they just pretending to? Some of what I'm reading about this Karzai . . . he accepts a surrender, then the same guys who were fighting us turn around and suddenly they're our friends. Exactly the same people."

Dan said, "Maybe we can do it the smart way this time. In quick, get bin Laden, set up a government, get out. Like we did in Haiti."

"The longer we stay, the harder it's going to be to leave."

Dan said he'd gotten the same vibe from the local militia leaders. "But we have to have them on our side. These mountains . . . if ALQ digs in and fights up there, it's going to cost. But this could be the end. The next couple of weeks. If we can pin him down and get a bomb on him or push a shooter in close enough. Maybe his own people will turn him in."

"It'd be better to have a body."

Objective as the old Blair. "Uh, right. They've already got a box of dry . . . never mind. You're right, we need a body. So, got any plans?"

"Just talking things over with Dad. We'll discuss it when you get home."

A voice behind him. "Almost done, buddy? Other guys want to use that phone."

"Wrapping up," Dan said to the trooper. To Blair; "Gotta go, gotta get back on the stick. Can you pass to Nan I'm okay? I'll try to call her too, but connections are real limited."

They exchanged kissy noises, and that was his big call home.

THE morning brief. Mostly Army, majors and light colonels plus reps from the Special Forces, Marines, a civilian liaison to the humanitarian aid groups Dan was working with. The battle captain sat reticent, ready to yield to the ops cell commander. Salter sat flanked by his personal staff, listening as slide after slide flicked by. Dan attended with half an ear: friendly forces, enemy forces, current operations, tactical sustainablility. The Alliance continued to roll forward against a regime that, widely resented if not hated, had collapsed like a shack pushed over by an Abrams tank. Every major city had fallen. A quarter of the enemy's leaders were in custody or confirmed dead. Thirty ALQ training camps and weapons-testing sites had been secured, with between five and ten thousand enemy KIA and over five thousand POWs, and intel teams were vacuuming up documents, laptops, files, and weapons.

Finally it was the Fusion Cell's turn. Dan stood and triggered the first slide, conscious as he did so his news would not be as well received. "The Tora Bora valley. Based on the latest cross-pollination of all our sources, Template estimates a plus-ninety-percent probability OBL and his top associates, including Al-Zawahiri and possibly Omar as well, are headed there."

Salter turned his head. "J-2 agrees with that?"

The intel officer nodded, without enthusiasm. "Yes, sir. All source reporting corroborates that destination. Course, that's no guarantee—"

"I understand that."

Dan cleared his throat, taking back the floor before the OIC and the J-2 started bickering. "Now, is everybody here clear what the Tora Bora valley is?"

Some faces showed understanding, along with a reluctance to accept what he was saying. Others looked blank. "Tora Bora—literally, 'black dust'—isn't a single place. It's a district or region in the White Mountains about thirty miles east of Jalalabad. A network of caves, interlocked defense points, and weapons and ammo stores the mujahideen developed during the Soviet War. Thirty-six square miles of canyonlike valleys, sharp ridgelines, and jagged peaks."

He gave them overhead imagery taken in clear weather. The tent was silent as they studied it. It was a cliché to say a place looked like the surface of the moon, but this looked worse. "How high are these peaks?" someone asked.

"The area varies up and down two to three thousand feet, with an average of about fourteen thousand," the J-2 said.

"Thanks," Dan told him. "Bin Laden goes back a long time in this part of Afghanistan. He built there in the eighties, when he was supplying the resistance. He graded out a rough road most of the way up from Jalalabad with construction equipment from his dad's company. He used Saudi funding and ours to turn a natural fortress into a real stronghold. He extended the natural caves and dug new ones. Then dug connecting tunnels so fighters could move between positions without exposing themselves from the air. We really have no firm data on what we're going to find under the ground. One source says it's almost like the Maginot Line—a multistory bunker complex with its own ventilation system, armories, bakery, mosque, and hydroelectric power, and thousands of ALQ fighters who want nothing more than to go to Paradise fighting us.

"Bottom line, if you had the world to pick from for a place to make a last stand, Tora Bora would probably be it."

"It's also gonna be mined," one of the Army officers put in. "Which means no ground vehicles, until they're cleared. And we're going to lose line-of-sight comms—any of those ridges will isolate a squad."

"But we know where he is," the J-3 said, flushing. "So we could at least start bombing."

"Yes, sir," Dan told him. "We could start that."

"We can definitely supply you with bombs," an Air Force officer put in.

The OIC weighed in on this, that the center of gravity of the bombing effort should be moved north. Dan had expected that. You could move a bomber's target in hours. Getting any sort of infantry force up there would take considerably longer and entail a lot more risk.

The real discussion opened when a colonel who identified himself as representing General Faulcon, the JSOC commander, said, "Let me make a point. The Soviets pushed a whole motorized battalion into this area. They got their heads handed to them. Bombing will only buy you so much, especially against a cave system—or this bunker, if it exists. Even when we put in teams with laser designators, laser beams travel in straight lines. Basically, we'd need to pour in hundreds if not thousands of tons of ordnance. From the air, since we can't move heavy artillery in there, even if we had any in-country."

"We can do that," the Air Force officer repeated.

The J-3, who was Army, turned to face him. "We have to have boots on the ground. You can't drop a bomb into a cave."

"You can take a lot of casualties, clearing caves," someone else murmured.

Salter put in, "Bill? You had a recommendation?"

The SOF officer said the deciding factors were probably acclimatization and logistics. "Let's face reality. I've watched our infantry. They jump out of the chopper and keel over from the altitude. We can only insert with Chinooks; every other helicopter we have is altitude-limited. We're just not ready to fight at fourteen thousand feet in the winter."

Therefore, he went on, the Afghan allies should carry the brunt of the attack, supported by A-Teams and perhaps the Rangers. The Soviets had failed in a conventional assault, with forces far heavier than what the Coalition had in-country. He wound up, "We can kill people. That's not at issue. But the Russians killed a million Afghans, and there were always more. Isn't it smarter to get them to fight on our side?"

"If they want to die, I can accommodate 'em," a marine growled.

The OIC gave him a gimlet eye and the shaven-headed SOF officer went on, "Bin Laden wants to suck us in and clobber us. Like Aidid did to Task Force Ranger. It would take us months to build up a conventional force that might have a chance. And the SecDef's right about one thing. It would unite the Pashtuns against foreign invaders and make this a second jihad.

"Let's not do what he wants. Extend the war into years, in an area where the US has no vital interest."

Dan interpreted this as *no oil*, although he was sorry the moment after he thought it. He couldn't give way to cynicism.

General Salter said, "Okay, I'm hearing all this. Everybody's got great points. I'm leaning to the light footprint. Our Afghans, backed up by our Special Forces. And maybe the Rangers for stop groups, or on call for a QRF.

"But the final decision's going to come from the national level. My question, again: Can we trust the ANF? We didn't train these guys. We bought them off the shelf. We have no idea if—let's say they actually capture him. Will they turn him over? Or run him across the border themselves?"

"We have confidence in our allies," the shaven-headed officer said. "And we'll be beside them. The Alliance has momentum. They've taken every city in the country, with minimal help from us. Jesus Christ, what more have they got to do?"

The general said deliberately, "That's true, Colonel, but this time we're asking them to actually incur major casualties. And on the other side of these mountains, we're expecting the Frontier Corps—the Pakistanis—to cut off his escape, if he tries to get out? It doesn't sound airtight. And if it works, how does it look? Like the US Army subcontracted its war. You're saying, this is the best we can do?"

The Green Beret said, "No, sir. I'm saying, it's the *only* thing we can do."

Dan had again the familiar experience of standing at a screen with a pointer while the people who were supposed to be listening argued with one another. What was the right strategy? No one would know until the test of combat. Or maybe, with this terrain, this history, and this enemy, there *was* no right tactic. Short of feeding troops into a bleeding contest, and hoping you ran out of enemies before you ran out of friendlies.

In the breathing flutter of dust-filled air he sensed a disturbance in the Force, a shunting of destiny from one track to another. As one might have felt, on a pleasant day in September, watching the great silver airliners over Maryland and Pennsylvania and New York tilt their wings and slowly slide onto a new course.

He raised his voice. "Anyway, that's where he is. Template will continue to track and put out additional info on the command link. Any further questions?"

They didn't even look up, so he quietly resumed his seat.

20

Tora Bora

T HEY inserted from black MH-6 "Little Bird" helicopters on an uphill-slanted field swept with wind and dust and blowing thatch. All of Echo, plus a unit of British SBS and the Alliance interpreter, Aimal. Teddy unbuckled from the side of the bird and jumped down, staggering as he hit. Screaming through ravines at a hundred-plus knots, hanging off the bench seat looking down . . . almost *too much*, man. He wobbled a few yards and took a knee, staring up. Scraggly and bare as it was, the two-acre field was the only halfway flat terrain in sight. All around incredibly steep slopes angled upward, dotted with gray-green puffs of small evergreens. The incline they were on ended at an enormous . . . rockfall? Moraine? Above it the mountain just went up and up, vertical rock until the snow line. Fourteen thousand feet, the briefing'd said.

"Let's do this, do this. Stop fucking around," Moogie muttered as he trudged by, bent under ruck and gear and rifle wrapped with tape to break up the outline, goggles pulled down against the debris the choppers' blades were flinging as they pulled collective again, lurched, then plucked themselves up into the air. Dollhard trotted past, short legs flicking the ground like a goat's, with the radioman/grenadier, Ozzie Cannon, right behind him. To everyone's astonishment, Echo's tubby and truculent OIC had survived Kandahar. One of the rounds from the burning garage had struck his armor so hard in the solar plexus he'd been paralyzed. Even the corpsman had thought he was dead, though puzzled by finding an immense bruise rather than a wound. But Dollhard had rolled off the evac helo under his own power, refused further evacuation, and been back on duty within twenty-four hours.

Oberg stared up at boulders as far as the eye could see, from the size of refrigerators up to shipping containers, tumbled where they must have fallen off the mountain; yet each was rounded, worn as if it had spent time in a stream. They were gray-green, roan, purple, stained with lichen the color of dead cheeks. Here and there a stunted bush poked up, or less often, one of the pines or hemlocks.

"Could be a Q behind any one of those rocks," Dollhard said. "So, it's daylight. Get used to it, operators. Chief, move 'em out."

Teddy got Echo advancing by bounding overwatches up along what looked like goat trails. They ran on either side of an ice-bordered stream- let that splashed perfectly clear over a bed of rounded pebbles glowing ruby and garnet, opal and jade, as if a genie had paved it with jewels. Dry, dead-looking bushes overhung the stream here and there, but aside from that and the few low trees, there was little vegetation. Just bare, striated rocks. The goat-path petered out amid them. He scrambled from one boul- der to the next like an ant climbing a pile of number two crush and run, sometimes in shadow, sometimes in sunlight. He wheezed the cold and exceedingly thin air in and out. A sudden bruising fall that knocked the wind out of him taught him the lichen patches were slippery. And, once again, that it was nearly impossible to break a fucking MX-300R.

From the far side of a low ridge between them and what seemed to be the main action came the thumps of bombs and the distant crackle of small arms. Teddy looked back. He couldn't see them all at once amid the rocks, but waited till he'd sighted each. Echo One to the left of the gully: the new OIC first, then Tatie Wasiakowski, Oz, Smeg, Bucky, Two Scoops, and Mud Cat. To the right, Echo Two: Teddy and Verstegen leading, then Vaseline, Harley, Moogie, Tore, Dipper—also called Doc, the corpsman— and Knobby Swager.

Dollhard's briefing had laid it out. The hard-core ALQ had taken refuge in a thirty-cave system called Tora Bora." Sixty miles west of the Khyber Pass, it had been a redoubt all through the Soviet War. The Sovs had sent in armored columns, but bogged down and retreated. JSOC South— Cutlass's boss—had it that not only the core leadership but bin Laden himself was here. Not enough US forces in theater to attack, but some- one had to. The weather would only get worse; both air support and aerial recon would degrade fast. The Alliance was pushing down from the north. Three separate militias, each led by a different warlord. Spe- cial Forces attachments were coordinating the air strikes that covered the advance. Meanwhile, on the far side, the Pakistani army was sealing the border. "It's not going to be easy, taking down these caves," the OIC had warned. "But it's got to be done. Osama's in a shoebox; now we stomp on it."

Teddy caught himself from falling between two rocks, scrambled across a slanting, slick boulder, and rested against a larger one. The valley was gradually being revealed as they climbed. Far down it rose an immense bare earthen hump; to the right climbed the sheer escarpment of the mountain; far above contrails carved the sky. Smoke plumed, and the air shook. He raised the rifle and through the scope made out tanks atop the bare hill. Small figures advanced like wary fleas, with many stops and side dashes. Too far to tell if they were uniformed, but he didn't get the impression of regular troops. The complex would be to his right, bored into the mountain. The shock waves of another stick rippled across the valley like a handful of pennies tossed into a pond of dust and smoke.

"We could get him, huh?" Knobby Swager said, pulling a sleeve across a bright red face. He was wearing loose Levi's with some kind of padding beneath, maybe long underwear, and a skateboard helmet spray-painted tan and black. "Think they'll give us the twenty-five mil, we bring his head back on a stick?"

Teddy looked at him, then back through the scope. If only. Everybody kept saying this wasn't about one man. It was about networks, funding sources, terror cells. But maybe this could be it. He didn't give a shit about the reward. Give it to the fucking Afghans. Anyway, how could you win a war on terror? That was like winning a war against war.

A detonation deeper than any before shook the mountains, booming and reverberating away. Teddy found himself crouching, hands over ears. A mushroom cloud of smoke and fire built from the valley, toppled, and began drifting downwind.

"Holy *fuck*, Chief."

"Air Force is getting serious."

It was about time. For just a second Teddy imagined Echo Platoon leading the bearded madman back, hands zip-tied behind him. The tall, Lincoln-gangly leader with the sad smile and flea-bitten beard.

He wiped his face, slung his rifle, and reached for another rock. Bring him back, hell. For what? A trial? They should flay him and keep him alive in a saline bath with feeding tubes and a ventilator. We have the technology, he thought. If you really wanted to stop getting 911 calls from all over the world, that was how. Make an example they'd talk about for a thousand years.

But he didn't see the will for that level of lesson-teaching.

With a roar that scraped the inside of his eardrums, an Apache hurtled through the pass, canted as if it could only fit through sideways. So low Teddy could see the pilot peering down, and he signaled Scoops, who carried it, to lay out the identification panel. He turned again, sweeping his gaze up and down the rockfall. Pressed his mike for Dollhard. "Echo One, Two. Any word what's on the other side of this hill?"

"No real-time eyes, Chief."

"We want to go charging over that crest, sir?"

"Send a man up from each squad to check it out. Keep 'em a hundred yards apart. Everybody else, hold up abreast of that big black mother with the cunt-shaped crease."

Teddy clicked off and climbed the last yards to the black rock and got his canteen out. Two swallows. The CamelBak was his reserve. He field-stripped a protein bar and crammed the whole thing into his mouth to leave his hands free and pointed the rifle around the boulder. If somebody was hiding above them, this could be an unhealthy place to park. He looked down again as another B-52 strike rippled across the valley. Bursts of smoke and flame the color of the setting sun filled it with a seething veil opaque as a bowl of milk. Seconds later the rumble came, like a glacier collapsing into the sea. There were supposed to be monkeys, tigers, wild boars, in these mountains. He felt sorry for them.

"Hey, hey, take that, Osama."

"Payback's a motherfucker."

Teddy depressed his send button. "Clear the channel, frogmen. Crawl into those scopes. I want eyes on every place that can hold a shooter."

Word came back: The saddle beyond looked clear, though there could be dozens of snipers among the rock tumbles that were if anything even worse than on this side. Dollhard pulled the rest of the platoon to the top, then swung left and pushed out a stop line that peaked below the crest and descended two hundred meters on either side. He told Teddy and Verstegen to hold that line. "I'm going out a little toward the valley for a better look."

Teddy said, "Sir, we should be down there on the sharp end, busting the caves. Punching tickets at close range."

"Appreciate the input, Chief. But since our orders say to stay where we are, I'm gonna confuse everybody and follow 'em," Dollhard said.

"What about those guys down where those tanks are, L-T? Whoever's down there's trying a frontal assault on a well-defended position. They're gonna take major casualties. Even if we just move down and lay some flanking fire, we'll help them out."

The lieutenant scratched his beard, which was getting seriously woolly, but finally shook his head. He said the air would collapse the caves and the Afghans would do the mopping up. He climbed down into the rocks and vanished toward the firing. Teddy perched beside the assistant platoon leader on the black boulder, which was gradually heating in the pale sun.

They had no warning, none at all. Perhaps afterward he might have connected the high, thin scraping of engines against the sky; a distant glitter. Perhaps. But probably not.

The bomb went off no more than a hundred yards away. It was at least a thousand-pounder. All he saw was a white flash a hundred feet across, succeeded instantly by a globe of glaring orange fire. The shock wave rocked the ground and jarred his teeth and sucked all the air out of his lungs. His left arm flew out as he went over backward and caught the rock at an awkward angle. Something tore inside his shoulder. The whole valley below vanished in flying rock and dirt. His head rang like Quasimodo's bells as he cowered, brain blank. Then, realizing he was still alive, he pushed his head up into the smoke that blew back over them.

The bomb had hit downslope. *Dollhard.* "Lieutenant!" he shouted into the murk. No response, though he might not have heard it even if he was there. Teddy's head keened with sirens like a Friday night in South Central. *"Lieutenant!"* He keyed the Motorola. No response there either, except cursing and questions from the rest of the team. He transmitted, "Echo Two, Two, all hands, get your panels out and on the ground. Visual ID panels out, clearly visible from the sky. And take cover, in between these rocks."

Verstegen, face smeared with dirt and snot, blood dripping from under his bush hat. "Where's the L-T?"

"Down there."

"Fuck. Fuck. Mortar?"

"No mortar, sir. That was a bomb. Laser-guided? Maybe even a JDAM." He looked up at the sky, which suddenly felt dense as depleted uranium. Bright and hard with contrails. Filled with smart bombs that sometimes weren't so smart. He rubbed his shoulder, then checked his watch, filing facts for the report they'd have to write. He keyed the Motorola. "Ozzie, Ozzie, copy? Get on the air channel—"

"Already there, Chief—"

Verstegen had his sleeve. "Should we fall back, Chief? Get off the bull's-eye?"

"No, sir. We're where they want us. But we need to get the word out to Poker. Blue on blue on our position. Get our coordinates to the controllers in the valley. Or we'll get more heavies called down on us if the bad guys start coming this way."

When he felt sure the jaygee and Ozzie had it under control, Teddy checked his rifle, rolled over the edge of the boulder, and started crawling toward where Dollhard had disappeared.

He found him, eventually. There wasn't much to bring back; the bomb had blasted huge rocks into fragments, and the lieutenant had been deep within the lethal radius. The remains smoldered at the edge of a still-smoking crater. Teddy gathered what he could and dragged it back and turned it over to the corpsman. Dollhard had used up all his luck surviving Kandahar. Now Teddy would have to nursemaid Verstegen again, and since their set-to during the BMP action, they'd avoided each other. Once the corpsman was busy with the body bag, Teddy reluctantly ape-swung his way up the rockslide to the jaygee.

A long silence on the tactical circuit. Until maybe half an hour later someone said, "Chief? Lieutenant? Hey, you guys know there's a village back here?"

"Harley, that you?"

"It's me, Knobby. On the right flank. Anybody there?"

Teddy waited for Verstegen to answer, but the jaygee just sat looking down into the valley and rubbing his nose. "No shit, a village?" he said back.

"Well, not really. Just three or four huts. Three hundred meters behind us, up against the cliff."

"Not on the map."

"Better take a man and check it out," Verstegen muttered, proving at least he'd been listening.

Why me? Teddy thought, but nodded and hoisted himself on his rifle. Looked around. High noon. The air was almost warm. The air activity seemed to be slacking off. Tatie ought to be able to handle it. He hesitated a moment more, then started off.

THE village was four huts built cheek to butt cheek beneath an overhanging bluff. A dangerous-as-hell place to locate. The cliff looked as if it could come down any minute, especially considering how the ground was shaking. But maybe this was where the water was; anyway, Allah's problem, not his. As he and Knobby puffed toward it, hauling themselves over the rocks by handholds, he didn't see so much as a goat. His shoulder was starting to fucking hurt now. He bolted more Motrin and chased it with CamelBak water. The wind sang in the ravines until you could swear someone was playing a flute. A weird, unearthly melody. From moment to moment you almost heard the music whole; then it faded into the rush of the breeze, the harsh pant of your own breath.

He rounded the first hut and saw them on the far side, squatting on the bare, cold-rimed earth, watching the battle. Old men, women, kids, in ragged sheepskin and colorful dirty wool coats and the floppy flat hats, huddled in family groups with goats folded on their laps like pets. Oohing and aahing at each explosion as if the circus had come to town. Then an old man saw them and exclaimed. Suddenly thirty pairs of eyes fastened on them. Teddy let his M4 drop on the tac sling. Raised both gloves, wiggling extended fingers. "American," he told them. *"Salaam aleikum."*

The group stirred. Women reached for their childrens' hands and with the same motion shrouded their faces. Teddy wondered if he should search the huts. No; if they had hostile intent, they'd be down in the valley fighting. The kids bolted up and ran for them, shouting madly. In a moment they were surrounded, boys and girls leaping and grinning up through missing teeth. Swager accessed some Mentos, but those didn't go far. Teddy lifted his gloves again; he didn't have anything for them.

Someone was tugging at his CamelBak. Teddy turned, keeping his muzzle pointed low.

A boy, but with lipstick and eye shadow and dark hair to his shoulders. Too young to have a beard. Twelve? Thirteen? He stroked Teddy's hand, cooing something that sounded like an invitation. "What do *you* want, dude?" Teddy asked. Then figured it out as the kid tugged him toward one of the huts. Another made-up lad had cornered Swager, who was stammering, going red in the face underneath the dirt and goggles as the boy stroked his cheeks like a Sunset Strip hooker. The kids were shouting laughter, rolling in the dirt and holding their stomachs.

"Let's get out of here," Teddy said, starting to laugh. At himself. Big tough SEALs. Then he remembered Dollhard. Spattered on the rocks by US Air Force high explosive, like what was left after you gutted a deer. *The meanest bastards in the valley.* The world seemed to split in two, and which was real and which was mad? He gripped his jaw, digging dirty-gloved fingers into his gums to anchor himself in the pain. Then spat in the dirt and patted his assailant's shoulder instead of driving a fist into it. "You're gonna have to find another friend, Linda."

"Linda," the guy said, delighted. He pointed to himself. "Pretty?"

"Yeah, very pretty boy. But you don't want a bastard like me, I'll break your heart. . . . Knobby! Untangle yourself. Let's get back to business." He started to shoo the rest of them into their huts, then figured, let 'em watch. They didn't seem hostile. Just simple mountain people, despite the pimped-out boys. Maybe now these kids would have a chance to go to school. He backed out, keeping the smile going, and waved one last time before he turned away.

MIDAFTERNOON. He was halfway back to the position when the pop of rifles got louder. The tactical channel lit up as Echo started taking fire. "See him, there, the red boulder above Big Goober, dude in the sheepskin." "Diaperhead, my two o'clock." "Whack-a-mole, three o'clock high, two hundred meters, commencing fire." The stutter of full-auto Classic

Kalashnikovs was overlaid by the higher-pitched cracks of 5.56 going out single-shot.

"They're working around our right flank," he told Swager's whitening face, streaked with dust and sweat. And here it came: the combat buzz chilling him down, raising his hackles, the jab in his shoulder every time he lifted his arm gone now. He couldn't help grinning. "Trying to get out. We're gonna get above 'em and see they make their appointments with Allah. Hoo-yah?"

"Yah, Chief."

Teddy ditched his pack below a pyramid-shaped rock where he hoped he could find it again. He and Swager leapfrogged as fast as they could directly up the mountain. As they took turns scrambling and covering, the firing grew off to their left, reverberating off a thousand rock facets until it was impossible to tell where any given shot came from. They climbed and climbed and finally he couldn't anymore, he was done. He spotted an elevated, flattish boulder with another propped against it that ought to give decent cover from prone and put Swager twenty yards farther up the rockslide. He still hadn't eyeballed enemy, but the fire kept getting louder. He wedged his pistol into a handy crack, checked that his muzzle was clear, and eased his head up.

Smoke was boiling up out of the valley and blowing over their position, smelling of explosive and dirt and juniper. Like being underwater in bad viz. He scrutinized a tumble a hundred yards off with his Steiners. Then realized he didn't need them when a heavy bullet cracked two yards away, peppering his cheek with hot needles of splintered silica. "Son of a bitch," he hissed.

He spotted the shooter a second later as he sprinted from one rock to the next. Still above him, though he'd climbed his heart out. A dark face, a long sniper-type rifle. Teddy set his sights at the top of the rock, then figured a guy who could shoot that well wouldn't profile himself. He found a cutout at the side, lined up on that. Eighty yards and uphill, no hold over, point of impact at the crosshairs. The instant he glimpsed cloth he squeezed one off. The M4 bucked into his shoulder and something rolled out from behind the rock. It thrashed, then went still.

"Want me to spot for you, Chief?"

"Yeah, do that, Knobby. But if they get closer than fifty yards, help me out, okay?"

"Roger that, Chief."

Teddy caught motion farther back, on the flank. Someone's camo'd shoulder; must be one of Vaseline's guys in Echo Two. A pointed barrel, a burst of pale granite-smoke as M4 bullets chewed rock. He had a better angle. And there it was, a head bobbing up as the enemy stuck his AK out and unloaded a burst, then ducked back. Teddy lined up and held two minutes of angle over. He took the pressure out of the first stage and broke it the second the flat wool cap eased up again.

"Pink mist. *Nice* shot, Chief!"

"He was asking for it."

"Look to the right. Closer in. Hundred and fifty meters? Moving and shooting."

Teddy looked, but didn't see anyone though he could heard them yelling to each other in high-pitched yodels. No bone mikes on the other side. He glassed the rockfall. He'd fired two shots from the same position. A good spot, but he needed to move. Out of habit, he scouted for the empty brass, but it was gone down between the rocks. "Moving left," he yelled, and low-crawled ten yards before edging around a boulder and glassing again. His mouth was terribly dry but his CamelBak was almost empty.

The MX came alive. Verstegen was calling in air support to their right front. Pull back, he said. Teddy doubted this would do much good, but he and Swager took turns putting out bursts as the other scrambled to the rear, firing and falling back, until they were halfway to the village. At which point the lieutenant (jg) came back on and said, sorry, Air Force says no joy, get back on the line where you were.

Choking back a wiseass reply, Teddy climbed again, but Verstegen halted them before they were all the way up and moved them even farther up the gradient. What was he doing? Deliberately keeping Teddy out here on the flank, so could make all the tactical decisions himself? So what. Make my day, punk.

Teddy tilted his head neck-cricking back and looked up the mountain. It got real sheer up there, where all these rocks had let go. Almost a straight drop, but lots more mountain still above that.

"Our guys down in the valley are pulling back," someone said on the circuit.

"What the fuck? They got 'em on the run."

"Way it is, webfoot. They're taking a break. Having some of that nice hot goat stew."

Renewed firing, this time from the left flank. A probe? This might not be such a bad position. No one could get past above them, and the SBS was strung out down the slope below. Not the best use for either unit, but at least they could serve as a backstop while the Aghans did whatever Aghans did down below. Meanwhile, every few minutes another detonation went off in the valley as the air strikes continued. On the other hand, this'd make a great ambush site. The saddle, almost a ravine. The terrain would funnel anyone trying to retreat from the valley into it. Teddy glassed and caught movement again. Put his scope on it, but didn't see it repeated. Maybe just a tuft of grass.

Or Joe Talib in a sheepskin coat slow-snake-sliding between and under the rocks, taking his time. "I'm gonna snail-crawl a few yards upslope," he told Swager. "Get right up against that bluff."

"Roger-dat, Chief."

Curled against the icy-cold living rock of the mountain, high as he could get without going sticky-footed up vertical stone like a gecko, he glassed again. Wondering why if they were trying to punch through here, they didn't just attack, throw mortars or grenades and try to bust through. They'd take casualties, but thin on the ground as Echo was, they might get lucky. Once through they'd have an open field between them and the goal posts in Pakistan.

But nothing happened for the next hour, except that the shadow of the mountains deepened the gloom. Maybe they were waiting for dark. The buzz ebbed. He ripped open plastic and filled the hollow feeling with Menu 15: meat enchiladas and a chocolate chip cookie made of Martex. Bombs lit the dusk, boiling the milky fog below. Something caught fire and exploded in fountaining pyrotechnics of white flame that arched like comets, trailing colored smoke. "Just like the Fourth in Seattle," somebody said.

"Looks like we're gonna be here through the night," Verstegen said over the channel. "But stay alert. They may try to infiltrate through us in the dark."

Maybe he wasn't totally hopeless. "Pair up, if you're not buddied up already," Teddy added. "Share your water, but ration yourself. Work it out, who stays awake and who gets his head down. The one who's sleeping, turn your MX off. Practice battery conservation."

"Chief, can you come in? I'm still up here at the peak. By the big rock."

Teddy said he could. He took his time, though, not wanting to slip and twist an ankle or hurt his shoulder any more than he had to. It had settled to a dull ache, but something was torn. Even eating Motrin didn't help. It was an awkward time of day, too dark to see well, too light to use the NVGs yet. At last he found Verstegen and slumped beside him.

"Water up, Chief." A half case in bottles. Teddy grabbed two and made short work of one. Refilled his CamelBak and stuffed two in his cargo pockets for Knobby. Verstegen said, "They're going to try to come through us tonight."

"I would if I were them."

"I was thinking. Ambush?"

"Sounds like a plan. Classic L-shaped ambush. How do you suck 'em in?"

"Fire from the left flank, hold fire on the right. Swing the right flank back. Put the claymores out with trip wires and the Mark 46 behind them, in front of the village, and somebody sniper qual'd up by the bluff."

"Me?"

"You and Swager?"

"Okay."

They called O'Brien and Wasiakowski in and went over the drill if things went to shit, the fallback plan if they got overrun. Teddy asked if they had enough ammo and they said they did, hadn't expended more than twenty rounds a man so far.

Meanwhile it had gotten quite dark except for flames down in the valley and the stars and the planetlike lights that moved between them. When it was settled, Teddy and Vaseline went along the line making sure everybody had the word and was properly concealed and sighted. Teddy crossed the ravine, alert in case anybody was trying to infiltrate, and supervised setting the claymores. Had a couple of words with the gunner and moved him five meters to the left. Then climbed up to the bluff again, back to Swager. Put him in the picture too.

When everything seemed to be ready, he told Knobby to flake out, get a few winks. And sat motionless, head turtled, as the dark got darker and the shooting below died. Even the air strikes tapered off, though now and then he still heard engines. He pulled his NVGs up out of his blouse, fitted them carefully, and clicked them on.

At first he thought they were stars. Then realized they weren't. Or not all of them. The ones above truly were. Shining unblinking, the way they never did back home. They were that high, the air was that thin.

But the other lights lay below, and twinkled, wavering, tiny and far off but hundreds of them. He stared, only gradually realizing what they were.

"Echo One, Echo Two. I'm seeing campfires in the IR spectrum. Lots of campfires."

"Copy. Got 'em here too."

"See them up above us, sir? They're not all staying down in the valley. How about you let me do a little hunting?"

"Negative. Appreciate your aggressiveness, but stay put. Let them come to us."

"'Let them come to us,'" Teddy muttered through numb lips. "Fucking oblivious." Despite the fleece he was beginning to shake. The middle of December. Colder every day. The Afghans kept advancing, then backing down. Now they were taking dinner breaks. Probably shouting back and forth to their buddies in the Taliban. Were they going to push this into deep winter? What the hell was the Team doing here, anyway? You didn't need fucking Tier One operators for this. This was Tenth Mountain territory. Which, last he'd heard, were sitting on their cans in camp. While they were trying to corner O-sama with ragtag mountain men and a few spec-for commandos.

Beside him Swager stirred. Murmured, "Chief."

"What you need, Knobby?"

"Just wondered. This's my first time in combat."

"Well, no sweat, son, there's a first rodeo for all of us. What's on your mind?"

"Well, I don't know quite how to . . . like, when you shot those guys . . . what'd you feel?"

"What'd I *feel*?" What kind of question was that? "I felt the fucking butt-plate kicking my shoulder. That's what I felt." Swager didn't respond and Teddy added, "That answer your fucking question?"

"I guess so, Chief. I guess so."

"These are the *enemy*, Swager. Give 'em the chance, they'd butt-fuck you and then shoot you in the head. Hesitation, I guarantee you, will kill you in combat. You want to play head games, you'll have a fucking long time to do it. After you hang up your fins. Until then, you're a killer. Just like the rest of us."

The kid fell silent. After a while he started snoring. Teddy settled, trying and failing to get comfortable on the hard rock, wrapping his arms around himself against the creeping cold.

THEY came around three in the morning. Teddy blinked awake the moment Swager patted his head. Curled around his weapon, poncho pulled close, shivering. Only the edge of sleep, anyway. The cold kept him shaking, and his shoulder wouldn't let him stay in one position long before a thick needle started probing, right at the joint. His collarbone had started up again too.

Meaning all in all he was almost awake anyway, so he just opened his eyes, quietly pushed the poncho off, and reached up to turn on the AN/PVS-9s. A faint whine, and the night dissolved into a boil of pea soup as they powered up.

"There they are," Swager muttered, taking hold of Teddy's vision tube and turning it to point off to their left.

Teddy clicked the MX-300 on and quietly passed the word on the intersquad. When everyone rogered, he slid the sling up on his left shoulder and cinched it tight above the biceps. Adjusted his bone phone, which was pressing painfully into his skull after lying so long against the rock.

He was looking down. Had the high ground. Shapes oozed amid shadows. Each rock glowed a different intensity of green. But they were all dimmer than the outlines that wound slowly between them, in single file, climbing up out of the valley, each man with a hand on the shoulder of the one ahead.

He picked out a space between darker shapes where the pale shapes would have to pass. Powered the reflex sight and pushed his goggles up. He reacquired, estimated range, and without looking dialed it in. "Two fifty," he whispered to Swager.

"Want me shooting too?"

"No. Pull security for me. Keep a three-sixty, in case anybody back in that village decides to join the fun."

Swager clapped his shoulder and Teddy lined up on the column. Remembered voices whispered within his skull. He tracked the shapes. Could see vests swinging, the straight lines of slung weapons. One staggered under something heavy. Mortar baseplate? Gaps opened as the line straggled. His thumb caressed the safety. Left it on.

Two hundred meters.

The closer they got, the deeper they'd be in the kill zone.

Verstegen knew that. Had to know. But sometimes it was hard to wait.

After a while Teddy made out the rattle of stone against stone and metal against metal, then a little after that the harsh breathing of exhausted men. By then he'd made out the hotter shape of a small burro or donkey, heavily laden as well, sharp squares of ammo boxes perched high. He was dialed down to a hundred meters. The only other sounds were his own breathing and Swager's behind him and the wind and the high buzz of a drone lost somewhere over the mountain. He kept looking for a silhouette taller than the rest, but the only possibility was halfway down the line, and would Osama bin Laden really be leading a donkey? He didn't think so.

Less than a hundred. How close was Vogey going to let them get? Teddy couldn't see the end of the column. Then he could, far down the draw. The OIC was sucking them as deep into the zone as he could, get them all at once. Brass fucking balls.

"Stand by" came over the net. Wasiakowski, not Verstegen. But that was all right. "Commence fire."

It was over in seconds. The gunflashes, the screaming, the hasty scattering as men dove for cover and tried to get weapons into action. But the firepower from above was too heavy to face. Teddy, from the opposite flank and above, had shot after clear shot as they tried to find shelter. He traversed from left to right, closest first because they were the biggest threat if they saw his muzzle flashes. He kept clicking his sights up until he got to the end, then worked his way back again. It wasn't a fight, it was a massacre. Like a well-planned ambush ought to be. A few men at the head of the column tried to break out. They got a few dozen yards farther up the draw before the claymores went off and hundreds of steel balls clack-rippled away among the rocks. Then the 249 started up in bursts and the last men standing crumpled and fell. Somewhere in there someone shot the donkey. It was plunging and crying like a woman, and Teddy decided to put it out of its misery, but somebody else had the same idea before he got to it.

The crack of 5.56s died down. The 249 gave one more burst and then fell mute too.

"Cease fire," Verstegen transmitted, when they'd all stopped anyway.

They stayed in position for an hour. The excitement faded and he was shivering and freezing again. Teddy kept an eye downslope for a second wave. He kept looking behind and above him too. Then light started to filter down and Verstegen asked for reports along the line, anybody hurt, how many rounds expended and remaining. He ordered Obie to check out the kill zone on his side of the Clown Face Rock.

Teddy told Swager to stay above and behind him and moseyed in, safety off, putting one boot carefully in front of the other, not taking his eyes off the crumpled bundles between the tumbled rocks as he neared them.

Only a few of the infiltrators had made it up to where he and Swager had been posted. The MG and claymores had torn up those who had. He found one still alive, but the way his chest looked, it wasn't worth wasting a pressure bandage. Teddy could see the man's heart beating. He looked up without expression. Then the pulsing in the middle of the blood stopped and he closed his eyes. "Enjoy Hell, asshole," Teddy told him. Swager managed a laugh. Maybe the kid would harden up, after all.

Verstegen, on the tac net again: "Any prisoners, wounded, up where you are, Chief?"

"None here, sir."

"Got a hard count?"

"Tough to say, they're mixed all in among these rocks."

"Rough count."

"Thirteen, fourteen . . . fifteen. Might be crawlers, though."

Swager asked him, "What's disposition on these dudes, Chief? You heard anything?"

"The dog meat, you mean? Leave 'em for the villagers," Teddy told him.

He stood among the bodies as the gray light kept growing. More baggy *shalwar kameez*, shaggy, stinking sheepskin coats, flat wool caps, old Soviet gas-mask bags, worn-out AKs. They didn't look as if they'd ever had much to eat, and even less in the recent past. They were all small and all had beards. Except the boys. One lay on his back, smooth-faced, arms flung wide, eyes and mouth open.

But no tall, bearded, hound-dog-eyed Arab. None in black capes or black turbans either. These weren't Al Qaeda. Not the fabled Fifty-Fifth Brigade, Bin Laden's bodyguard, the shock troops of the jihad. Bad guys, but not the ones they wanted. He glanced back down at the valley, into the mist or smoke that hazed the ground down there. The boiling kettle the men they'd killed had been trying to escape. He took off his cap and scratched his head all over. Call in resupply ... they'd gone in light ... ammo, batteries, water, chow. Search the night's crop for maps, documents, anything intel could use. But the valley kept drawing his eyes.

Was he really down there? Bin Laden? Maybe he was. Maybe he wasn't.

But if the guy thought he was coming through here, he had another thing coming.

21

Joint Special Operations Center, Bagram

THE moving party had arrived. Five men, all laconically silent as they helped Dan and Henrickson and Wenck pack up. Everything resided either in their notebooks, the main server, or back at TAG. CIRCE herself was at TAG; the combined outputs resided remotely, accessed only by those with clearances and need to know via the SIPRNET—the Secret Internet Protocol Router Network. So all they really had to move was their computers and any personal snivel gear—tissue boxes, M&M's, and clean socks. No one told them why; it had just come down. Within two hours they were set up again and operating out of the JSOC. Still at Bagram, still in a tent, but in a smaller, even more elaborately fenced compound-within-a-compound. "Should've had you plugged in here from the get-go," Provanzano said, looking at their setup with fingers stuffed in the back pockets of his jeans. He kept sniffling, like a toddler with a cold.

"Need to take it easy on that inhaler," Dan said.

"Only thing lets me get any sleep. Okay, you went to Gardez with Beanie. And you're reading the command net. So you know what we've got written for bin Laden's last act."

"I know we're depending on the Afghan allies."

"Almost correct. Once one of the A-Teams can get us a GPS fix on that bunker, we blow it down on top of him. We're not gonna tunnel-rat around. Just blow it and bury him. Which is why you're officially with us now. Can you do that?"

"I can't give you an unqualified yes."

"Or a no? I see. Well, we fought off Big Army. With some help from upstairs. It's up to us to deliver. Get in and get this mopped up before winter closes us down." Provanzano peered at a map Wenck had taped to an equipment rack. "What else've they got you doing? I think we can throttle back on Template. Since we know where he is."

"We do?"

"The intercepted call."

"They're not sure that's him."

"We played it to a guy who knows him." The CIA man winked and started to leave, then turned back. "Tell me when you're ready. Actually I don't know if we'll call on you, we have plenty of Air Force, but it's better to have it and not need it, than need it and not have it. Any questions, ask Commander Laughland." Provanzano waved forward a compact guy who'd just come in. He wore the black SEAL insignia on his BDU.

Dan mustered his strength, but Laughland's grip wasn't as daunting as it could have been. "Dan Lenson."

"Denny Laughland. Heard about you, sir. You've worked with us before. "

"Yeah?" Dan was always astonished at how small a town the Navy was.

"Obie Oberg told me about hijacking the Iranian sub. How you got them out of it when he figured you were toast. Good job." This seemed to dispose of the courtesies, because Laughland went straight into asking what Dan could do for an assault in terms of missile support.

"Can't answer that yet, Denny. We need to get intimate with the topography. Especially those mountains to the south."

Laughland nodded and checked his watch. "We do a roundup at 2000. Let's see where we are by then."

Dan got more coffee at the mess in the back of the JSOC, abandoning his fantasy of a nooner. He and Henrickson and Wenck worked the mission profile all afternoon. Tora Bora was actually at the foot of a mountain range. They needed specifics—exact location of the caves, depth, structure, geologics. But the databases were bare. Special Forces had tried to penetrate the valley, get ground-truth intel, but hadn't made it in far. Plus, both altitude and terrain worked against a missile that had never been designed for mountain warfare.

Still, they worked the problem, and eventually Wenck found a pass to the south they might squeeze the missile through at the very end of its range, if they let it loiter en route to burn off its fuel load. Scrutinizing the topos, Laughland found several more passes, though most had approaches that rose too abruptly for the Block IIIs. And even if the bunker was deep in the valley, Henrickson found a way to combine a wide sweep north to shed altitude with the pop-up/terminal dive maneuver to get the missile down there. Exposing the airframe to fire, true, but the numbers showed a 90 percent–plus probability of survival. Dan multiplied this by the probable losses going through the passes. The results looked expensive, but war was never cheap.

By midafternoon he was confident about taking out a bunker of any reasonable size and construction. After all, the Tomahawk warhead had been designed to drive almost four hundred kilos of PBXN and a hardened detonator through the armor of a Kynda-class cruiser. Henrickson set up a five-missile mission from *Bremerton*, on station with the *Kitty Hawk* battle group. Striking one after the other, they calculated three surviving missiles should blast through forty feet of concrete or granite.

Meanwhile, though, those passes nagged. If there were routes through the Spin Ghahr, not only could missiles travel north, escaping AQT could go south. The Pakistani army was supposed to be in blocking positions. But were they up in the passes, the natural bottlenecks? Or down in the valleys?

Not in his in-box, but Dan couldn't let it go. When he had the mission as close to finished as possible without final coordinates, he left the sub on one-hour standby to terminal programming and went to find Provanzano.

First stop: mess line. The CIA man wasn't there, but Dan got a tray. He'd discovered years ago at sea that, to some extent, calories compensated for lack of sleep. Men stood nodding off, gazes distant. He ate at a folding table with three he didn't know. "Your guys doing all right?" one asked another. "Or are you still trying to kick-start 'em?"

"They're moving. Only trouble is, they all went home for dinner last night."

"They come back this morning?"

"Most of 'em."

Dan assumed this meant Afghans, but didn't ask. He leaned over his MRE and shut his eyes for a moment.

Someone shook him awake. He discovered his face pressing into the table. "No rest, buddy," one of the specfors said. "Last inning. Full-court press. Finish this up and go home."

When he got back, the CIA man was sitting with Henrickson, looking at the screen. "There's over thirty passes, just on the topo," the CIA man was saying. Dan looked down at the top of his head, suppressing a sudden urge to pull him over backward. This was *his* chair.

Damn. He had to get some sleep soon. "Tony. I help you?"

"We were looking at escape routes. Looks like you were, too." Provanzano rubbed a receding hairline with small white pimples breaking out on it. "In case he doesn't just sit still and wait for us to come to him."

Dan remembered the discussion at the JOC. "I thought that was his strategy. Sucker us in and clobber us."

"Maybe so, but there's also a strain of thought we're finding in some of the recovered documentation that says, when you're threatened by overwhelming force, retreat. Classic guerrilla tactics. Live to fight another day. They've got a safe haven twenty miles away. I know what the Army thinks, but we might need to do something more."

"At least, kick it up the chain," Dan said.

"Exactly." Provanzano stood. "Let's go see Faulcon."

Dan took a moment to react. "General Faulcon?" The commander of all Special Forces in Afghanistan.

"Why the hell not? He's a real approachable guy." Provanzano sniffed and strolled away. After a moment, Dan followed.

THE general was so gaunt his face looked vacuum-sealed. They said he had only one good eye, but Dan couldn't tell which one. Both were cold as a cryogenic experiment. His office was a corner of the TOC walled off with vertical dividers. A map of the Tora Bora valley was overlaid with grease-penciled Mylar, with numerous erasure smears. Remaining were curved arrows showing three axes of advance into the valley, the inward-toothed embrace Dan knew now meant "isolate," and the pronged arrows and bar that meant "clear" in NATO tactical shorthand. Each was lettered with the name of an Afghan warlord and the designation of his accompanying A-Team.

Faulcon's glance said he and Provanzano had a working relationship. "This is the guy I told you about," Provanzano provided by way of introduction. The general nodded in Dan's direction, then seemed to recall something. He frowned, then stood.

Faulcon saluted. Dan nodded, feeling awkward as always, then decided, to hell with it. And saluted back, even though the Navy didn't salute indoors. What could they do? Take away his birthday? Although Nick Niles probably would, if he could figure out how.

"The Medal winner," Faulcon said, sticking out bony fingers. "I'm honored."

"Thank you, sir." Dan endured a grip that felt as if it could fracture phalanges. "It should've gone to a National Guard doctor, and some marines. But I wear it in their honor."

Faulcon motioned to chairs. "What's on your mind, Tony?"

Halfway through the explanation Faulcon swiveled to a terminal and began bringing up screens. He studied one as Provanzano finished, then rotated the monitor toward them. Pricks of white dotted a black featurelessness. "IR," he said. As if every word cost him a dollar.

Dan leaned to see, but got no wiser. "Uh, what are those, General?"

"Campfires. Reaching up toward those passes."

"We haven't seen that imagery yet," Provanzano said. "But it only backs us up. What's our level of confidence in the Pak army?"

Faulcon considered. "Low."

"What if he doesn't want to stay and face the music?"

"I'm aware that's a possibility."

"Of course you are. Come on, Randy. I can give you two Twelve teams. You can draw assets from Ka-Bar and Cutlass. SAS, SBS, SEALs. Spot them in the most likely passes."

The general thought. "The passes are in Pakistani territory."

"So what?"

"No penetration. Even in hot pursuit. We need their cooperation."

Dan said, "There are, what, customs agents in these passes? Pakistani border guards? I don't think so. Who's going to see our troops?"

Faulcon's shoulders moved fractionally. "Pakistani special operations."

"In the *passes*?" Provanzano shook his head like a wet Labrador. "They're not going up there. Not those boys. If anybody's going to block them, it's got to be us."

"I proposed that yesterday. And was turned down."

"Sometimes you have to disobey a stupid order," Dan said.

Both men glanced at him, Faulcon with evaluating eyes, Provanzano with a smirk. The general leaned to a phone console. "Sergeant? I need the JAG in here."

The legal officer looked as lean and fit as any of the other officers in the headquarters. A little older, that was all; Harrison Ford–ish; slightly graying. Provanzano went over it again with him.

"You want to be very wary about irritating the Pakistanis," the adviser said. "We're going to be dependent on them, if he does escape."

"Let's see. We're going to neglect an opportunity to catch him, so we have a better chance later on?" Provanzano chuckled. He seemed to be ribbing the general, as an equal, perhaps even a superior.

"The ambassador to Pakistan has threatened to resign if we do any cross-border incursions. Musharraf has promised to render OBL to us."

Provanzano: "Again: Does he have the capability to do that? In a part of the mountains he doesn't even govern?"

"What about hot pursuit?" Dan asked. "Isn't that legal doctrine?"

The JAG said, "That generally pertains to the law of the sea."

"What's the difference?"

"Well, in general terms, any objection to hot pursuit at sea will be much weaker, since you're not actually infringing on the sovereign territory of another state."

Dan wished he'd known this when he'd been skipper of USS *Horn*, sweating their trespass into Egyptian territorial waters. But the JAG was still talking. "It's not a generally recognized doctrine when you're incursing across a land border. Which is why we couldn't use it in Cambodia. For example. Now, we just got UN Resolution 1373. That speaks to the issue of state sovereignty. A government has an obligation not to allow its territory to be used by terrorists. That's what we'd use to request him back. From Pakistan."

"Request him *back*?" Provanzano said.

"Extradite him."

"We don't want to extradite this guy," Dan said, suddenly disgusted. "Get real."

"The alternative's to let Pakistan try him in their courts."

"That can't be the only alternative," Dan said. "Not to get personal here, but he killed three thousand US citizens. You don't let a guy like that . . . you don't *extradite* him."

"Hear, hear," said Provanzano, clapping theatrically. "On the other hand, we're building this whole antiterror coalition around getting him. If we do nail him, how do we retain that momentum?"

Dan stared, not sure anyone could actually mean what the agent had just intimated. "You're saying we—what? Let him go?"

Provanzano chuckled. "Down, boy! Just thinking out loud. Best case: We locate his bunker tomorrow and either you or the Air Force turn it into dust and hamburger. All we're discussing is the goal-line play, if we don't."

Faulcon cleared his throat and the others fell silent. Not looking at the JAG, he said, "So these would be black missions. Never acknowledged. Never admitted."

The legal officer looked at the tent overhead. "If there's a clash with Pakistani special forces?"

"Our men lost their way. We apologize."

Provanzano said, "We execute the stop plan with SEALs and SBS teams, cross-border if necessary. We don't tell the SecDef or Pakistan. No one knows they're there. If they get him in Pakistani territory?"

The JAG said carefully, "It would be better if the body was found on this side of the border."

"Thanks for coming by, Tony. Nice meeting you, Dan." Faulcon nodded curtly, turning back to his screen. "The J-3, please," he said into the intercom; then, to them, "That'll be all."

"THAT went as well as we could have expected," the CIA man said as they walked back toward the intel tent.

Dan didn't answer. He was still trying to figure out what the agent had meant about bin Laden's capture harming the coalition. Wasn't that what going into Afghanistan was all about?

"You look pensive."

"Just tired."

"You must be used to missing sleep. At sea, and so forth."

"Yeah, well, it doesn't get easier."

"I'm sure. Which brings up something I wanted to sort of confab about."

"What's that?"

"In private."

Private turned out to be a sharp right turn toward the airstrip. Dan snugged up his field jacket against a chill wind, even though it was a sunny afternoon. He followed past rows of smaller tents and newly arrived containers being unloaded by a working party. A man in a black motorcycle jacket sauntered some distance behind them. Belote? Following them? Provanzano hiked without speaking for some minutes. A transport came in, hovered, touched down. The howl and roar swelled and faded.

They walked across empty ground, dried grass crunching under their boots. Dan wondered about mines. He was about to say something when they came to an abandoned revetment, or maybe an antiair position. A U-shaped earthen berm covered with more dried grass and stunted bushes. Provanzano sighed. He perched his ass on the slope of the middle berm, the bottom of the U. Reached behind a bush and came out with a bottle. "Want a drink? Just joking. I know you're not the type."

"Not for quite a while." Dan looked around, wondering where Belote had gone. He couldn't see him anymore.

"I admire that. It does help lubricate the occasion, though. Sure?"

"What did you want, Tony?"

But he wasn't going to be rushed. He screwed off the cap and took a swig, gazing off toward the mountains, over which heavy clouds hovered as if caught by hooks. Cutty Sark. Despite himself, Dan remembered the burn. The first swallow.

"Beautiful country, isn't it?"

"Haven't seen much of it."

"This part of the world is where empires go to die. I don't want us to be the next one."

"I doubt anybody does."

"You'd be wrong. We're gonna get seduced in here, just like *he* wants. It may go okay for a while, but then it's going to turn ugly. We can blow shit to pieces, but we can't fix this country. Or even hold it. Like I said: where empires go to die."

Dan stood hugging himself. "Get him, and get out."

"I hope we can. But he's not the only bad guy out here."

Dan started to speak; Provanzano waved him into quiet. "We're tasked to go after threats to the United States wherever they exist. And since 9/11, all of a sudden, our funding in that area's unlimited.

"Now, you've been passed over for captain. But we have quite a few former Navy people in our organization. You could be filling a seat with a lot more responsibility than the typical captain gets. A *lot* more. Let's get specific. I'm referring to a program like CIRCE, but more ambitious. I'm going DCI special compartmented now, okay? Our goal is to monitor every communication within the continental United States."

"Within the country? I don't think that's legal," Dan said.

"You don't think we do domestic surveillance?"

"I didn't say you didn't do it. I said I didn't think it was constitutional."

"What did you just say to Faulcon?"

"What?"

Provanzano repeated, "What did you just say? About how bin Laden killed three thousand Americans. Zircon Prime will prevent another 9/11. Use technology to spot terrorists inside the country, before they strike. And that's only the beginning. Big changes coming down the pike, my friend. *Big.* We'll get you Navy orders until your official Navy retirement date. Then transition you to FS status."

"But I don't want to work for you," Dan said. "I don't want to be part of expanding domestic surveillance. Or of anything else you do, actually."

Provanzano took another swig, frowning. An executive-style jet whistled overhead, touched down with a squeal of tires. "I'd hoped you'd grown beyond that attitude, Dan. Every institution has the imperative to grow itself. There isn't one that doesn't. The army. The navy. The church."

"The post office."

The bottle paused halfway to Provanzano's lips. "You fucking with me, Commander?"

"Just pointing out not every human institution is corrupt."

"*Corrupt* is a harsh word."

"Give me another, I'll use it."

"Okay, I'll give you another. *Realpolitik.* We need to be smart across the spectrum. The wave of the future will be asymmetrical threat. We want to *be* that threat. For Al Qaeda. And others who want to bring us down. That line's got to be drawn."

"Absolutely. But spying on your own citizens? There are certain things that aren't right."

"Even if it means more Americans will die?"

"Yes," Dan said. "Even then. A lot of us have died for our liberty before."

"Liberty. You think Americans still care about *liberty*? I think they'd much rather have security. Don't you?"

"I don't think they do."

"Then you're a dinosaur. This isn't 1776. Or even 1940. Protecting America isn't just about ships with guns on them. Or maybe the Navy thinks it's purer than the rest of us?"

Dan considered this. He'd asked himself this question over the years, in many different ways. "I think in some ways, yes. You learn at sea that falsehood kills. That means truth is absolute. Not relative. Duty's absolute. Honor's absolute too. Don't smile. Yeah, I used the H-word."

"Couldn't help it. Sorry. What else?"

"And you learn . . . you're all in the same boat. You take care of your shipmates. And they take care of you."

Dan paused, reaching for something bigger. Wiser. Something he was still trying to put into words. But maybe that was the problem. No matter how hard you tried, the things that really mattered wouldn't go into words.

The CIA officer leaned back on the embankment. He'd found a scrap of jagged steel, a piece of shrapnel, perhaps, and was tossing it in a palm. "Well, that might be true at sea. But in politics? Just not realistic. Hey, ask your wife! Let me quote Horace Walpole: 'No great country was ever saved by good men, because good men will not go to the lengths that may be necessary.'"

"I understand that," Dan said. "And I didn't mean we don't need intelligence. Just like we need armed force. But you can't trade freedom for security. Or actually, the illusion of security."

"They'll be happy to make the trade," Provanzano said. "And they'll thank us for it."

Dan cleared his throat and turned away; licked dry lips, trying to lubricate them. He kept thinking about all those years at sea. The dreams that hadn't come true. He'd always thought his duty wasn't to make war, but to prevent it. Now they faced an enemy that could never be vanquished. A war that would last forever and change America into something it had never been. That those who founded it had meant it *not* to be. He was overcome abruptly with such weariness he almost collapsed into the dead grass.

Maybe Provanzano was right. Maybe he was a dinosaur. But "the lengths that may be necessary" . . . he could only come up with a German phrase he'd heard somewhere once: *Ohne mich.*

"Without me," he said.

The CIA man waited, eyebrows raised. "So what'll you do, then? When you get out?"

"I don't know." Dan shivered. He hugged himself against a chill that penetrated flesh, bone, into the heart. So the world wasn't what he'd hoped it was. Maybe it wasn't possible, to always make the right choice.

But sometimes it was possible to avoid the wrong one. He cleared his throat again and spat into the dust. "See you around the compound."

"Oh, you will," the civilian said, smiling to himself. Reaching again for the bottle. "You will."

22

Tora Bora

INSTEAD of holding their position they were relieved before dawn by solid-looking troops in Flecktarn and field caps and here and there a maroon beret. The KSK, German Special Forces. Verstegen and Teddy held a short confab with their cadre, then pulled out. They trudged back toward the extract point, slipping and staggering, clumsy with fatigue and lack of sleep. The SBS, which had held their left flank during the night, was headed down into the cauldron. They'd help the Green Berets stiffen the Alliance forces, who seemed disinclined to press the attack. Echo was being pulled back. Verstegen seemed disinclined to talk. He didn't meet Teddy's eyes.

"You okay, sir?"

"Sure. Sure, Chief."

Dollhard's death still eating at him. Well, he'd get over it. "Back to Camp Jaguar, L-T?" Teddy asked him.

"Not at the moment. Hold at the LZ on one-hour notice. They're flying in resupply. Find out what the guys need and I'll have Wasiakowski radio it in."

Actually Teddy's job, but Verstegen seemed to be leaning on the Echo One squad leader. Okay by him; he'd rather be tactical than get tied down in loggies. They hit the stream again. It felt good going downhill. He stepped off the trail and as each man went past asked how he was doing, what he needed. He caught each man's smell as he went by. An empty canteen bobbed with a hollow *pook*. There was a run on batteries and 5.56 ammo, but not one man had used a grenade.

The sun was coming over the ridges when they got to the LZ. He put three guys out on security. Everyone else dropped his gear. Men leaned back to shrug off rucks, then collapsed. They broke out smokes or chews and started PMSing weapons. Teddy got out another MRE and wolfed through a package of sticky-sweet pineapple, suddenly ravenous. As soon as he was done, the helo arrived with thermos containers of hot hash and eggs. He ate two platefuls and had a truly wonderful, blazing-hot cup of coffee. He loosened his belt and lay back on his ruck, ankles crossed, watching the sun creep across the rocks. Musing on how torn up his boots looked. Making sure his rifle was still handy, of course. The jagged, nearly vertical peaks towered up all around them, and the scrub pines would be perfect cover for a sniper.

At 1035 word came on the command channel. Return to Jaguar. The men stirred and bitched, but without venom. Teddy figured they'd be back soon enough; judging by the pace of things in the valley, this wasn't going to be over soon. He sent two men to check out a rise that had begun to worry him, but they waved back an all-clear when they reached the top and squatted in the brush, disappearing as soon as they lowered themselves below the horizon line.

The flight back. He sat twisted on the nylon seat looking out the tail ramp. A frigid wind blasted through the gunners' doors, down the two lines of SEALs, out the back. A real freeze locker. But it wasn't hard to fall into a doze. Then suddenly Mud Cat was shaking him and the bird was pitching up and the frame jolted and bounced. He lurched to his feet, every muscle protesting, and filed out.

Verstegen went off to report. Teddy sent everybody back to berthing but told them to consider themselves on strip alert.

When he checked in with the master chief, Stroud squinted up, startled. "The fuck you doing here?"

"Relieved by the KSK."

"I was listening to command net last night. Somebody fucked up royal. You?"

Teddy told him he had no idea, likely one of the air controllers down in the valley.

"Okay, get me what you need and I'll have it out by the strip."

"By the airstrip. We going out again?"

"Chief?" Doc Dipper, at the door. "They want you over in the head shed."

THE comm suite was putting out continuous noise, the wind was buffeting the tent, the intel pukes were running back and forth with maps. Dust milled under swaying overhead lights, and despite a roaring heater, the air was so cold their breaths puffed frost. Lieutenant-Commander Laughland had circles under his eyes that hadn't been there back in the States. He introduced an Army helo pilot from the 160th SOAR. Dusty Palladino was short and shaved bald. He had warrant bars pinned to a three-color BDU, a festive red scarf looped around his neck, and a Glock in a black nylon thigh holster. He said he was sorry about Lieutenant Dollhard.

"He was a solid operator," Laughland said.

"None better, sir," Teddy said, remembering how he'd overhanded a grenade square through the doors of the burning garage. "Sorry about the remains. We brought in all there was."

"We'll need statements. We'll try for a Silver Star. Can I get those ASAP? Handwritten's fine."

Teddy doubted it'd go through for a Star, getting blown up by a friendly, but didn't say so. Why hadn't they put Dollhard in when it might have meant something to him? But all he said was "Hooyah, sir. On your desk today."

"What's the procedure, Commander?" Verstegen asked. "Do we get another replacement OIC?"

Laughland looked harrassed. "We'll get somebody slotted in. But right now, we have a time-urgent mission. You'll OIC Echo for the time being. With Chief Oberg's expert advice."

"Aye, sir."

"Higher suspects the Tora Bora valley's leaking. The Afghans aren't just lagging on the assault; some are actually letting escapees through. Whether for cash, Islamic sympathy, the weather, you name it. There aren't enough eyes to cover all the ways out."

Someone asked about the Pakistanis who were supposed to be sealing the other side of the range. "They haven't even started moving out yet," Laughland said. "Shitty, but there it is. ETA's the fifteenth now, and nobody's guaranteeing they'll be there then."

Some cursed; others looked bewildered. "Can't we get some conventional dudes in there?" Teddy asked. "The Marines. Or the Tenth Mountain?"

"Negative, denied. There's a force cap in-country. But we're scrambling the whole JSOF. We can do this, Chief. Unless you don't think your guys are up to it."

"Aye aye, sir."

Laughland called one of the intel guys over. Not SEALs, but they worked hand in hand, and Teddy had never felt inclined to pull the saltier-than-thou act with them. They could fuck you any number of ways.

"We had a firm intercept," the briefer started, setting up a notebook and bringing up a screen. "He's in Tora Bora, all right. But if we can't keep him pinned, the CIA thinks he's going to try to slip out. Either to the south, or more likely, to the east."

"Across the White Mountains," Teddy said.

"The Safed Koh—the border with Pakistan," the intel guy agreed, zooming back to show it, then pushing in again. "We're putting Rangers on the direct route. But there's a back way. It's difficult. Easy to get lost. But the local tribes know it. If BL pays the Ghilzai enough, or promises them guns, they might guide him. The trail leads south, over this mountain. Then down again. It comes out here, in this part of Pakistan that juts toward the west.

"It's called Parachinar—or sometimes, the Kurram Valley. Once he gets to the Tribal Areas, we lose him. Even the Pak army stays out of there." The briefer traced a dotted line and toggled back and forth between topo and imagery. "That route starts here. Only twentysome miles to the border, depending on which ravine he goes up, but they'd be twenty very hard miles. No roads. Damn near not even any goat trails. But smugglers use the routes. The CIA mule-packed weapons in over them, during the Soviet War. And we're seeing activity. Here. And here." Teddy peered; the tiny figures were dwarfed by snow and rock. "We think they're either deserters from the fighting, or advance parties for a larger movement, possibly by a VIP. And the Brits picked up SIGINT. In Arabic. Bin Laden knows the area. He fought his first battle against the Soviets at Jaji." The intel guy put his finger on a map. "In Afghanistan—but on the route to the Parachinar."

"I want Echo to cover that route," Laughland said.

Teddy peered at the figures, blown up to the limits of magnification. The shots had obviously been taken in IR, by either a Spectre or one of the specially configured P-3s the Navy was operating.

"Elevation?" said Palladino.

"Highest point, around fifteen thousand feet, MSL."

"This is behind Tora Bora?" Verstegen asked. Teddy frowned. Had he been listening?

"Roger, behind and above. Down here's where you were this morning. See? The trail runs up the mountain, heading south. Then into this high pass, between these ridges. The crest of the mountains is the Pak-Afghan border."

Laughland said, "I want you to insert via two of Dusty's E Chinooks on offset LZs and block the route."

"Can we *cross* the border? Once we're boots on the ground?" Teddy asked. Thinking, a black op. Direct action. At night. Excellent.

Laughland said, "Maybe I didn't explain myself adequately. You'll *be* across the border. You'll touch down in Pakistani territory. And you're a stop group. The mountains funnel anyone trying to get over right into your position. You stop, meaning *stop*, everyone trying to get down past you. Clear?"

"Clear now, sir."

"But especially, watch for and take down HVTs. One in particular. We clear which one?"

"Yes, sir," Teddy and Verstegen chorused. Palladino rubbed his scalp, turned half away, coughed into his fist.

"That's the primary mission. We're not looking for recon or intel."

Teddy asked the obvious question. "Kill or capture, sir?"

"Bin Laden won't be alone. They've already sent the women and kids out. Anybody you see up there will be either hard-core Taliban or Brigade Fifty-Five. Black turbans. Black capes. Chechens, most of them. If you encounter bin Laden, we need to confirm the kill. If you can't manage the body, bring in the head. If you run into him on the wrong side of the border, get him to the right side before you report in. He goes down in Afghanistan, *not* Pakistan."

"Clear," Verstegen said again.

"Nothing against you, sir," Teddy said to the pilot, "but did anybody look at a HALO insertion? A helo makes a hell of a lot of noise, even at night. And everybody knows, ever since Mogadishu, shoot one down and the wheels come off our bus."

Laughland said, "Chutes are too vulnerable to updrafts in the mountains. We can't get you there by vehicle, and it'd take days to get up there on foot."

"I've flown three missions into these mountains, and in from K2 eight or ten times," Palladino put in. "The fucking weather changes by the hour, and the ravines and valleys channel it. You can have thirty knots of wind at the valley mouth, and it's sixty by the time you get down into it. Snow. Dust obscuration. Zero viz. Downdrafts, on granite cliff faces. We have FLIR and multimode radar, and even for us, it's going to be edge of the seat."

"Your kind of mission, Chief Oberg," Verstegen said.

Teddy gave him a side glance. "As long as you don't put us down right on the trail."

Laughland said, "You're going to have to leave exactly where to Dusty. He'll make a decision on the inbound. We're going to string Echo out along these three passes. Find OPs overlooking the trails. But the weather's getting worse. Like he says, it's not going to be easy getting you up there."

"And I may not be able to pull you back out," the pilot added. "Our motto is 'plus or minus thirty seconds,' but at some point we have to consider crew safety, operational risk assessment. If the weather gets much worse, we might have to ground."

This sounded better all the time. "We'll manage," Teddy told him. "Go in heavy with MREs and ammo and wad ourselves in with extra blankets. Don't worry about us."

The lieutenant commander pinched his nose. Said carefully, "Laying it on the line: if you get pinned down, we may not be able to reinforce you. Or pull you out."

"Yeah, who's gonna be our QRF?"

"That's what I'm telling you. We're putting everybody out there to cut these guys off. There's not going to be a quick reaction force. Oh, we'll get somebody out there eventually, if you get your balls in a crack. Maybe the Rangers, out of Bagram. We can get you elint support—that's a Navy asset. Call sign Whale Watcher. But exactly who, right now, would go in after you . . . ?" Laughland shrugged.

"No problem," Teddy repeated. "But how about extract? The warrant here, Dusty, he says he might not be able to come back. What happens then? We exfil on our own?"

"Again, we'll deal with that later. Once more: if you're not comfortable with it, just say no."

"We'll deal with it," Verstegen said.

"All right, get your people together and brief out. You'll launch at"— Laughland checked his watch—"twenty-one hundred local; seventeen hundred Zulu. Dusty?"

"Check. Seventeen Zulu. Oh, and one thing. Do not bust out my windows. If you bust out my windows, you're not flying with me again, and I will personally fuck you up. Copy?"

Teddy grinned. "We won't, Dusty."

Laughland said, "Gonna be cold up there. You'll be at fourteen, fifteen thousand plus. Make sure—well, I don't need to tell you. You know the drill."

"No sir, you don't," Teddy said. All three officers looked at him, then away.

HE had four hours before they loaded out. Not long enough to do a timeline, and really, no need to. Starting this early, they'd be in position before daylight, even with other stops en route. From there on, they'd just have to get resourceful. Adapt. Cope. All those good SEAL attitudes.

Unless things didn't go as planned. Like for Lieutenant Dollhard.

He shook his head and went back to the hootches and passed the word. The squad leaders got Echo together, and he and Verstegen laid it out. Everybody was on board, though he caught thoughtful looks when they heard no QRF had been identified.

When they broke, Teddy went to his own tent and dragged his duffel out and laid out every piece of warm gear he owned. He pulled hard plastic weapons cases from under the bunk and lined them up and snapped them open. The M4 had worked okay last night, but three hundred yards had been a long shot for a 5.56. Up in the mountains, he might have to shoot across ravines. He gave the bolt another spritz of CLP and fitted the part back into its recess in the carrying case. Snapped it closed, and slid it back.

He snapped the upper and lower together on the SR-25, a heavier rifle but with better performance at long range. He ran a patch down the bore. It came out waxy from the white Teflon grease he coated the barrel with for storage. He racked the rear sight all the way down and locked the night scope and the laser on. Then thumbed open earth-colored cardboard boxes and loaded all five magazines with M118 heavy-bullet sniper rounds. He stuffed the suppressor and cleaning kit in his ruck with five more boxes of cartridges. Slid his thin-blade knife out of its sheath and wiped the dust off. He stripped the cartridges out of his pistol mags, checked the action, and reloaded the magazines. He put fresh batteries in the rifle scope, in his NVGs, and in his MX-300.

He hefted the ruck, grown shockingly heavy, and grimaced at a hot ice-pick in the crook of his shoulder. His collarbone hurt, and his hip ached where he'd fallen on the MX. Every fucking mission he seemed to pick up more fucking twinges.

When he had his gear squared away, he went to the next tent and collared the comm petty officer. He got extra satcom packages and the primary and backup and extraction freqs. He grabbed Knobby as the petty officer went by and told him he'd be carrying Teddy's spotting scope.

He went to the mess tent for rib-eye steak and mashed potatoes, bug juice, and ice cream. Then went back to his hootch to try to sleep. He was almost there when he remembered: the after-action report, Lieutenant Dollhard's write-up. He groaned, got up, found some paper.

At 1500 Zulu he was back at the strip. The guys were bucket-brigading two Hummers' worth of gear and MREs into the helos. Stroud stood with his clipboard, micromanaging everything and generally being a prick. Teddy looked around but didn't see the commander, so he handed the master chief Dollhard's write-up and asked him to give it to Laughland.

Echo reboarded in whirling dust so thick he couldn't see fifty yards. Cold as hell, but it would be much colder up high. Teddy kept flexing his shoulder. He'd thought about getting it looked at, but didn't want to risk a medical hold. As long as he kept eating Motrin, it was bearable. Once they got in the mountains, he could pack it with snow. They were inside this time, not straphanging off the outside with tailbones perched on six inches of aluminum. He squirmed around, elbowing himself some space, then plugged into the comm system and signed in with the crew chief and copilot. He leaned, looking along the line of huddled bulks. Blankets, parkas, watch caps, balaclavas, gloves, goggles.

Swager, boyish looks overlaid by black camo paint and fatigue. "Hey, Chief. Guess what?"

"What, Knobby?"

"Today's my birthday. Forgot till now. Can you feature that?"

"Fucking way to spend your birthday, Knobby. On mission. Don't get much better than that, does it? . . . Hey, operators. Today's Swager's fucking birthday."

Catcalls and hoots. A grenade came arching and hit Swager's chest. Teddy grabbed it and made sure the pin was still taped. "Goddamnit! Settle down! Smeg, what the fuck are you doin' up there?" The SEAL, hammering out plastic with the butt of his M4, froze. "Leave that fuckin' alone! We're going high and cold. Besides, you screw with Dusty's windows, he's gonna beat my ass. He's a mean little motherfucker and I believe he just might."

More catcalls, obscene invitations to both Obie and the pilot. Teddy grinned. "You silly fuckers," he whispered. The clamor of the rotors changed, from the flat *whick-whick* of zero pitch to a deep *whum* as Palladino poured on power. The deck lurched, and Teddy grew heavy as his sins. Then they were airborne, and the outlines of warehouses and tents swam past the open rear ramp. Past the squatting door gunner, straddling his weapon like a barstool cowboy on a mechanical bull. Teddy's heart thumped, shaking his chest. His collarbone, hip, shoulder, didn't hurt anymore. The fizz seethed in his blood.

Out of nowhere he remembered popping bad guys the night before. One ten-ring after another. Like falling plates at a pistol range. Payback was hell, all right. For the towers. The Pentagon. The bombed embassies. You'd never get them all, but sometimes you just had to thin out the cockroaches in the kitchen.

He wouldn't be able to do this forever. But it was way better than making movie deals, than hitting the rocks in his 4Runner. Better than fucking starlets until they cried and tried to get to the phone by the bed. If he bought it, he'd die with the best toys in the world in his hands.

The aircraft banked. He caught another shadow behind them, then another and another against the stars: attack helos, escorting them. He took deep, slow breaths, slumped against vibrating aluminum, swallowing to clear his ears. Smiling under his pulled-up scarf as the lightless wind roared in.

23

In the White Mountains

T HE Chinooks flew black. The only illumination was a faint radiance from up in the cockpit. Teddy saw now why Palladino hadn't wanted them to kick out the windows for better visibility. There wasn't any. Even with NVGs, the world outside was oblivion past the crouching tail ramp gunner. No stars. Overcast. No moon. The only light the comet of heat from an Apache riding herd. The freezing cold penetrated the icy aluminum. All the interior heaters were off; they diverted power from the engines. Maneuver buffet and updrafts threw them around until Teddy had to grope for the restraints with one hand, gripping his rifle drowning-tight with the other.

A perfect night for someone to slip away from a vengeful enemy who thought he had you surrounded.

The big Chinook could've carried all of Echo, if they weren't limited in lift by the altitude. But for that reason, as well as that they were being inserted at different points, Echo Two was in this bird while Verstegen honchoed One in the other. Palladino had wanted to land twice, at different offset HLZs, but Teddy had convinced him to do it in one touchdown, with the squad pushing both up and down the trail. Since they had two OPs to cover, they'd decided at the rock drill back at Jaguar that O'Brien would take the first stop group, composed of the best shooters—Harley, Moogie, and Tore. Teddy would lead the backstoppers, with Doc and Mud Cat and Swager, a few hundred meters down the trail.

Unfortunately, the mission had come down so fast they didn't have much beyond that single drill to run on. Usually, you preplanned code words and phrases the platoon would need during the op. Some identified specific geographic locations along the route to and from the objective. Others, locations or objects near or at the objective, rally points, or along the emergency evac routes. There might be different words for individual HVTs, types of enemy forces, weapons, equipment, or obstacles. Since the bad guys could be monitoring your freqs, experienced platoons changed codes for each op. At least they had a platoon standard terminology they could fall back on, and the usual hand and arm signals. An adhocracy, as Tatie called it.

But that was how SEALs trained. Take what you got and deal with it.

"End Zone in sight," Palladino said over the IC. "Not exactly landing point size four, but I can hold the rear wheels there until you're off."

Teddy had the helo's IC jacked into one ear and his 300 in the other. "LZ in sight," he passed to the others, then clicked back to the pilot. "You're shitting me, right?"

"Done it before. Uphill a quarter of a click and you're at the crest of the ridge."

"The trail runs along the ridge?"

"Ask the goats where the fucking trail goes. I'm just looking at what they gave me at the two shop. When you unass, make sure your guys don't get turned around and head toward the front of the bird. I'm gonna be hanging my dick out over a ravine, pressing my rear wheels into the slope. *Capisce*?"

Teddy wasn't sure he liked this. "You sure this is an achievable, Dusty?"

"Only Z up here. Rest of it's either straight up or down, or too narrow to go in on. Plus I want to be where I can't get hit by these downdrafts. They come over the ridgeline and curl down. We get caught in one of those, it's trouble. We got major power constraints, and that's a two-thousand-foot drop."

"Can you do a pass first? See if there's anybody down there? This is an active ratline, right?"

"I got FLIR on it. No movement on the ridge." FLIR was the Chinook's forward-looking infrared night vision, sharper and longer-ranged than the goggles. "A low pass'll just wake 'em up. Trust the intel, Chief."

"Trust the . . . fuck that! I want *eyes*. I don't want to insert if there's any-body—"

"In and out, Oberg. It is what it is: in and out."

Teddy finally rogered. Blind wasn't how he liked to go in. But this was a hasty mission. He splayed five fingers; six sets of NVGs looked back like the glowing orbs of lorises from the jungle night. And time crawled by.

"One minute."

He gave his guys one finger. Sixty seconds to being on the ground, in Pakistan, where they weren't supposed to be. Nobody said anything. Or maybe it was just inaudible over the engines, spooled up to max power to keep them aloft in this insubstantial air.

"Thirty seconds."

He flashed back to the Fenteni assault, where Sumo had gotten zipped. The guys crammed into the narrow box of a SH-60. Everybody coated in a buttery film of sweat like so many hotcakes.

Pineapple-flavored chewing gum.

They got us stone, babe.

Cold sweat broke all over Teddy's body. He couldn't do this. Not again. He let the terror build, then grabbed it. Turned it a hundred and eighty and there it was. The Buzz, bigger than he'd ever felt it. Blazing down every nerve, sheathing every bone with invincibility, every muscle with ten times his normal strength. Just like Superman.

"Concentrate and live," Teddy said into the 300. "Fuck up and die. Hooyah!"

"Hooyah!" It went down the interior of the helo.

The fuselage canted in a tight turn. Bodies leaned on bodies. Floated, grew heavy, then light. The turbines roared. Something rattled past along the outside, as if they were in a submarine and someone were dragging chains over the hull. Stones, whipped up by the rotorwash. The rear gunner, leaning out over the ramp, peering down into what still seemed like complete darkness. "Fifteen feet. Ten. Clear back here. Five—"

The whole aircraft jarred, the rear wheels slamming into granite in the dark. "Go," Palladino said, but Teddy'd already ripped the headset off, tripped the restraints, and jumped to his feet.

The ramp went the rest of the way down, and he ran toward howling darkness and a sudden chaos of wind. Grit and driven snow bit his face. He slammed into the rear gunner, caromed off someone else. They knotted, then broke free.

He dropped two feet, stumbling under a hundred and forty pounds of ruck and weapons as they plunged into knee-deep snow that prostrated the shadow ahead of him full length on the ground. For a confused frozen instant that seemed infinitely long, he wondered how he could see.

Agonizing light flared in his goggles. He doubled over, screaming, and snatched them off, squinting as the moisture on the surface of his eyeballs froze.

A magnesium-bright flare burned like a midnight sun directly above, driven sideways by the howling wind even as it hovered. As it declined, it outlined everything on the slanted mountainside with unendurable clarity. The chopper, cemented onto the slope by the downward thrust of blurring rotors. Its blunt cockpit, the insectile refueling probe extending over an abyss that plunged into darkness without end. In its anal maw Teddy caught the startled, uptilted face of the rear gunner, the glare glinting off his faceplate like a single bright eye. The outlines of two SEALs, one gripping a handhold above the ramp, the other folded over his midriff. And farther in, behind him, the backturned goggled visages of the side mini-gunners. The very scuffs on the aluminum flooring glittered, so harsh and intense was the light.

So much—he had time for the one thought, as he jerked himself up and goose-stepped forward through the snow—so much for the advantages of night-vision technology.

The aircraft tilted forward at the same moment as the clatter of Kalash-nikovs erupted above them. As the flare traced an arcing afterimage that burned green across the black sky, the aircrew snapped into their weapons. The port minigun searched, steadied. It fired one short, droning burst. No tracers; tracers pointed both ways.

The engines labored harder, rotors pulling air. Grabbing the wind, torqu-ing it beneath milling blades inches from slanting stone. The forward half of the craft swung as if on a string hung from infinite space. A gap appeared beneath the rear wheels.

A second shadow appeared under the laboring, slowly rising Chinook. The two angled away from each other. Teddy stared, stumbling backward, unable to make out what was going on.

The flare guttered and went out, a cherry-red spark falling away into the howling darkness below, as a blazing *thing* howled past trailing a bil-lowing white cloud. It flew over his head and disappeared into the Chi-nook's right turbine exhaust.

The world came apart into orange flame. Teddy was deep in the snow, hands over his head, as debris came hissing and whacking down all around. The flames penetrated the white with harsh, flickering yellow.

Concentrate and live. Fuck up and die.

He forced thought through noise and flame like molasses through a pinhole. Either a MANPAD or an RPG. And by the way it had homed into the engine, a man-carried portable antiaircraft missile.

Why hadn't anyone figured that the enemy would leave their own OPs to guard the escape route their HVTs planned to use? And that the opera-tors guarding that route, in a world where everyone knew Americans dropped from the sky in helicopters, would have Stingers?

"Ambush front!" he screamed.

He exploded out of the snow and, with one backward glance, saw a second flaming meteor pass just over the rotor hub of the flaming, falling helicopter.

Tearing his gaze away as Chisel 03 spun away into the darkness, shed-ding parts and great gouts of tangerine flame, he charged up the mountain, screaming and shooting. From the snow around him burst other shapes like whales surging from the deep. They shook snow from their weapons and oriented on the threat. Teddy noted muzzle flashes ahead and from the right flank, both at higher elevation than the ground Echo Two occupied. They were square in the kill zone. Their only defense was ferocious attack. "Kill the motherfuckers!" he shouted. He hasty-slinged and dropped to a solid kneeling position and fired out a magazine, the heavy rifle bucking into his shoulder with each squeeze of the trigger, aiming below the gunflashes.

"Magazine," he shouted, and rose and charged uphill again over snow covering loose scree as Moogie, at his right hand, went to full auto. Another flare ignited above them. He'd never felt so naked. *Kill zone. Exit the kill zone.* Rifle grenades whonked out, flashing along the ridge. His thighs burned. He fired again, on the run, powering up the last few yards to stumble over the lip of a rise. A windy darkness opened around him. A crest. His boots caught on something, and he tumbled into a shallow trench.

A form rose up, shaggy and dark, and embraced him with a hoarse shout. The flare wavered and dropped, the last glint dying red as hot embers. In total darkness once more he lost thought in the mindless immediacy of hand-to-hand, face-to-face, breath-to-breath. A struggle too close for any weapons but hands and knife. The other was strong and he fought but not for long. Not with a steel edge slashed across windpipe and jugular.

When his enemy groaned and slumped and his final breath rattled, Teddy rolled away, wiping the thin-bladed Glock on his thigh. His belly and upper legs were warm with the other man's blood. It felt good. He groped for his rifle and couldn't find it. Then remembered, and pulled up his NVGs.

His weapon blurred into shape and presence two yards beyond his enemy's outflung arm. Past it another SEAL swayed locked with a second fighter. As Teddy scrambled for the rifle, a hand rose and dropped and they split apart. One fell; the second staggered on for two steps before also drooping, as if melting into the snow.

A respite while he lay full length, gripping the weapon and freezing his lungs with each labored breath. His legs burned. His head swam. He gagged and a little vomit came up. He spat it out and crammed snow into his mouth and sat up warily, rifle mounted, taking stock past the lit circle of the scope.

Occasional bursts of fire stitched the dark. Whoever had fired the missile had pulled back, slightly upslope still, and to the right. They'd overrun an advanced fighting position, that was all. He tried to remember the terrain. The pass was flanked by ridges that were the top of the mountain proper. Both ridges were narrow and steep, stony blades jutting out of the snow. The bigger was to the west. That was where they'd planned to set up the OP.

Teddy burst up and sprinted, then sank beside one of the men who'd fallen. A partially unwrapped turban. A dark cape, spread over the snow.

The next sprawled form was the squad leader, O'Brien. But he didn't respond to a shake. When Teddy rolled him over, he saw the muj Vaseline had killed had managed to nearly saw the SEAL's head off. Teddy eased him back down. Then changed his mind, rolled him up on his side in front of him, and braced the SR on the dead man's ribs. He put his eye to the scope.

Green flashes outlined moving forms amid the blowing snow. He aimed carefully and fired. One dropped and stopped moving.

Whoever else was out there stopped firing. In the lull he hit the tac circuit. Moogie, Mud Cat, and Doc answered up. Doc said he didn't think Harley and Tore had made it out of the chopper. Teddy remembered the swaying forms, outlined by light. Swager didn't respond. Not him too? Teddy thought. Shit; down three shooters before they'd even set foot on the mountain. They put together a count and got eight on the opposing team.

"We really stuck our head in the fucking hornets' nest," Moogie said gloomily.

A spark in the dark, and a bullet snapped close to his head. A deeper boom than the AKs made arrived an instant later. Fuck, did one of the mujs have night vision? If so, this'd be a different ball game. Whoever was up there, they were a different story from the ragged Taliban they'd rolled up in the valley. Black turbans. Capes. The Fifty-Five Brigade? *No plan survives contact with the enemy.* As the muj fired again, another man rolled in beside Teddy. He had his pistol half drawn when Swager yelled into his ear, "Radio's fucked. I can hear you, but I can't transmit."

"Yo, just follow me." Teddy went back to the circuit. "Anybody see movement?"

"Nothing here."

"No movement."

"Obie, d'you see Vaseline?"

"He's down hard, Doc. Got his head cut half off. All hands: These guys are pure shooters. May be the double-nickel brigade. They had to be right at minimum range on the Strelas, or whatever they hit the bird with. Where's my electron fucker? Moogie?"

"I think I'm off to your right."

"See if you can get Verstegen, or the other bird. Or Boss Man, if you can."

Boss Man was the code name for the AWACS, the big eye in the sky that saw all and knew all. Or was supposed to, anyway.

"It's not going so good. I'm not getting a lot of cunt juice out of these batteries."

"Keep trying. If One can fall back toward us, we'll box these guys in, both ends of the pass. I'm gonna move up to you. Me and Swager and Mud Cat will cover. Cat, got the pig? Didn't leave it on the bird?"

"She ain't no pig. Gentle Lady's layin' here with me, Obie."

"Good. When we lay down cover, everybody else fire a 203, then fade back behind us and push hard over to the left. Maybe a hundred meters, there's a ridge. Get up there and dig in, then maybe we can get gunship support."

Disengaging under fire was an immediate action drill they'd all practiced hundreds of times. Except maybe Swager. Teddy slapped the new guy and they burst up together, or rather, staggered. The deceptively smooth snow disguised uneven rock and they fell again and again. He saw the others ahead and angled to the side. Another flash, another bullet, even closer. They had to get the play under way before the shooters above tried to flank them. He hoped they didn't have mortars. But tough to imagine anybody lugging mortars up here. He dropped and rolled and yelled, "Cat. Locked and loaded?"

"Right here, Chief."

"Any joy on One?"

"Haven't got 'em yet. Still trying."

Screaming figures appeared out of the flying snow. Black shapes flickered above them like accompanying demons, and Teddy blinked before realizing: the capes, whipping in the wind. For thirty seconds the SEAL line was a blaze of burst fire. All four attackers sank into the snow. Teddy slapped in another magazine and looked to reacquire, but there were no more targets. Just motionless, prone blobs and the green-black seethe of night vision.

Now whoever had C2 up there knew exactly where they were. If the sniper with the night scope hadn't already ratted them out. What he probably didn't know, though, was just how few men they were faced with.

And that they were SEALs, of course.

"One grenade each, out in front. Then we cut a chogie. Three-second rushes—I think they've got a sniper with green-eyes. One, two—*three.*"

As soon as the dark split with grenade flashes, they got up and rushed. Teddy slogged uphill by feel, by memory. Had to be a ridge up here. It overlooked the pass, maybe fifty feet higher. They rushed and dropped, rushed and dropped. He kept waiting for a bullet in the back from the guy with the larger-caliber rifle, but none came, and they wheezed up a slight slope and down another one.

"Was that it, Chief?"

Teddy went a few yards farther and almost walked off the ridge. He backpedaled hastily from a bottomless precipice. This had to be the far side from where Chisel 03 had gone down. The whole pass was only about two hundred meters wide, but it felt like a mile in the dark. Like Bitch Ridge at La Posta, the mountain training facility they ran up to sometimes from San Diego.

He was jogging back toward them when another boom echoed, followed by the unmistakable *whack* of a heavy bullet hitting flesh.

"Doc's down, Obie."

"Fuck. *Fuck*." Not their corpsman. Teddy crawled over and cradled his head as they searched for the wound. They found the entry under his left arm, but no exit. Dipper died without a word, bleeding out internally. Teddy laid him down, raging. For no reason he turned his wrist to expose the tritium numerals of his watch: 0250. A long time to dawn. "Line to the front, and I want your eyes out there crawling around."

"What do I do, Chief—"

"Get your claymore out. Low-crawl it out there. And make fucking sure it's aimed the right way. Now, now, *now!*" Something moved in the dark and the men on both sides of him fired. "Moogie, you *got* to have contact."

"I'm on the right freq, Chief. Wait a—wait a second." Moogie spoke at length in a muffled voice, then called, "One didn't make it in, Chief. They're orbiting, waiting for word on what to do."

"Oh, you are fucking kidding me," Teddy muttered, rolling over to where the radioman had the notebook-size radio set up, the spidery antenna rigged out. "What are you—you're on satcom. Okay. Who you got?"

It was the pilot of the other Chinook, who'd waved off when he saw the flares and missile-engine signatures. Moogie passed along that he didn't think dropping more men in what was obviously a heavily defended landing zone was a good idea.

Teddy reached for the handset. The pilot didn't seem to know Chisel 03 was down, but he didn't see why he had to be the one to give him the bad news. "This is Echo Two. I can't honestly disagree with you, dude, but we are looking to seriously get our asses kicked here. I have two KIA already."

"Roger that. Do you need the QRF?"

"No, I don't need the fucking QRF. What I need's the rest of my team.

These guys are Fifty-Five Brigade. Osama's personal bodyguard. If they're here, there's a reason."

The pilot said he'd pass the word, but he was coming up on bingo fuel. Teddy cursed and passed the handset back. "See if you can get a gunship. We could use some support."

"I've got Whale Watcher."

The electronic intelligence bird. "Great, but he's a nonshooter. Get a Spectre. Call Boss Man if you have to, but get us some fucking firepower."

Okay, Teddy, think. He had four shooters left: himself, Moogie, Knobby, and Mud Cat with the machine gun. They'd started with about eight hostiles. Couldn't be more than four or five left, after that badly advised banzai charge. But one had night vision and an accurate rifle on an overlook. Like being up in a tower. Even worse, that particular Q knew how to shoot.

But the bad guys they'd landed on top of had made one mistake. They'd pulled off to the best tactical position: the high ground, to the right. Unfortunately for them, that left Echo One right smack in the middle of the pass anyone trying to escape from Tora Bora had to thread to go south.

But he couldn't just sit tight. If bin Laden was really on his way and heard gunfire, he'd back off and take another ratline. Maybe one that the intel guys didn't know about.

He couldn't sit tight. He couldn't wait.

They had to kill all the men trying to kill them. Take the pass and hold it. That was the mission now.

Before the thought was fully formed, he was passing orders over the squad net. The responses came back clipped as he belly-squirmed through the snow. Along the lip of the ridge, the stone crumbling away under the cover. The howling emptiness to his left pulled at him like gravity itself. The lower boss or hump would give him cover for the first few yards. After that, he'd be in the open. He started to slip and clawed frantically at loose scree and snow, pushing it desperately into the void, but kept sliding, gathering speed. He jammed the butt of the SR into a crack and only just managed not to follow the rattling rock off over the edge. Crawled carefully uphill again, until he regained solid ground.

"Okay, *now*," he told them.

A crashing fusillade burst out. Tracers and flares, to burn out the retinas of anyone glued to a sniperscope. In the sudden glare Teddy caught an erect form ahead and above. In one swift movement he lined up and fired. It half turned and dropped from sight, and he rolled instantly to the right.

A bullet ripped through the space he'd just evacuated, followed by the *crack-boom* of the heavy rifle. Then all was dark again, until a burst crackled from the far right. Mud Cat, working his way around with his beloved Gentle Lady to take them from that flank. Teddy lay rigid, unable to cram enough oxygen into his lungs, his overspeeding heart shaking his whole upper body. So the one he'd shot hadn't been the sniper.

Another *crack-boom*, and a cry from the right flank. The rattle cut off in midburst. Fuck, they couldn't have gotten Mud Cat, could they? He had to zip this guy. Now. He rolled again, panted, and crawled a few yards forward, pushing up the snow to shield his own heat. Blew the flash hider of his rifle free of snow, checked the seating of the magazine. Then, slowly, pushed the muzzle up over the little heap of snow.

With a crashing blow and a burst of white light, a sledgehammer caught him squarely between the eyes.

HE came back from somewhere very black to find himself lying in the snow. He was turned on his right side, and the world was turned funny too. He blinked and pushed a glove gingerly toward his face. A moment later, he was sorry. Something pulpy bulged in the center of his forehead. He couldn't make his fingers press hard enough to feel exactly what it was. They were numb, anyhow. His skull was split open. His brain was oozing out. But surely that couldn't be, or he wouldn't be lying here wondering about it. Would he?

Then his NVGs fell apart under his fingers and something warm ran down from under them. He felt it again, still not quite able to assemble himself into anything he understood.

"Chief Obie. You okay?"

Swager, bending over him. Teddy grappled, trying to pull him down. Get him out of the line of fire. But Swager was dragging him instead, back behind a rock. His hand groped again, and Teddy sensed rather than saw him recoil. "Jeez. You are some fucked up, Chief."

"Shut the fuck . . . up."

"Good, it talks. Looks like you caught a ricochet, right in the AN/PVSs. They're a wreck. All you got left's the straps."

Teddy shook Swager's hands off and tried to sit up. Vertigo. Nausea. He leaned to the side and coughed. Waited, but nothing came up. ". . . head."

"Got a hell of a gouge there. Lucky it didn't take one of your eyes out."

Teddy lay panting, ears ringing, passing from thankfulness to respect to rage. A hell of a shot. If it'd been three inches higher, it would have split his face instead of the rock. Even as it was, the ricochet would have killed him if it hadn't impacted the night-vision goggles.

Whoever he was, this guy was damned good. Chechen? Arab? From the sound, he was shooting a full-power thirty caliber. Probably a Dragunov.

Semiautomatic, and not that different from his SR, except the cartridge was the Russian rimmed round. Effective range, upward of six hundred meters in skilled hands. And he had a night scope on it. Most likely the PSO-1. The PSO-1 had a night reticle, but it was too dark up here for that to do much good.

It also had a special countersniper feature: an infrared charging screen a shooter could use for passive detection of infrared sources.

That is, it wouldn't illuminate, like the SEALs' AN/PVSs, or like Obie's own rifle scope. But it would pick up radiation sources.

Such as the AN/PVSs themselves.

The sniper hadn't been aiming at them.

He'd been aiming at their night-vision equipment.

"One, this is Obie. Turn your illuminators off. This sniper's got a passive scope."

He could hear the slurring in his own speech. He sounded drunk. Felt toasted, too. If only the brunette could've been here with him. The cop. Salena. Funny, he hadn't thought about her in weeks. He lay with blood running down his chin, the savor slick on his tongue. Listening to the wind and the dark. The absolutely utter dark, now that they'd lost their night vision.

Bells tolled in his ears. He was thinking way too slow. Confusion, headache, dizziness, slurred speech. All symptoms of concussion. But he was still here. Still in condition to kick some ass.

The Mission comes first.

No matter what faces you, go over it, under it, around it. The only thing that can stop you is yourself.

He rose slowly out of the snow to a crouch. Then to his knees. Finally, to his feet, swaying in the buffeting wind. His forehead was numb already, passing from pain to freezing in seconds. He tensed, expecting a bullet, but none came.

They couldn't see him anymore.

Nor could he see them.

Blind men, grappling in the dark.

The net said in his ear, "Chief."

"Talk."

"They've got a radio active."

"Say again?"

"Moogie's losing battery power fast, but Whale Watcher says somebody's transmitting UHF off to the west of us. About a hundred meters. They don't have a translator for whatever he's speaking, but they're picking up the transmission. Sounds like . . . sounds like a cheap walkie-talkie."

Teddy rogered, looking over his shoulder as if he could pick them up. Their mama in the sky, the EP-3E elint bird. Crew of twenty-four, and more electronic analysis equipment than anything else the Navy flew. It would be thousands of feet up and dozens of miles away. Out of visual range, even if heavy cloud and snowstorm hadn't already cut them off from visual surveillance.

But now he understood the setup. Somebody above them, on the ridge to the left of the pass. Spotting for the sniper.

Or was the transmission from the sniper, rogering for the information?

No way to tell. He had the fuzzy sense he should be able to triangulate where the shots had come from, but couldn't force the tasking though his mind. It got lost in there and sort of stopped.

Anyway, there was only one way to break a combination like that.

He staggered through the snow, boots dragging, freezing air sawing in and out. A splitting headache, blinding flashes as if reality were coming apart, seams ripping, letting something searing hot beneath leak through. Then a hand grabbed him. "Obie. Where you going?"

". . . to get up there."

"You're fucked up, Chief. Got half your face hanging off. Want us to, just—"

"Maneuver and lay fire," Teddy slurred. "Doesn't matter at what. Just work your way up the pass, lay some fire down." He hit the intrasquad but couldn't get a response. Actually, the thing sounded dead. But it'd been working a minute ago. Either his batteries were butt-fucked or the bullet hitting his NVGs had put it into an intermittent fail mode. "You got comms? Oh, I forget, your radio's fucked—"

"I took Doc's."

"Uh-huh. Okay. So how we doing?"

"Moogie took a bullet through both legs. Mud Cat's with him."

So the Cat wasn't hit. "Is he stable? Can the Cat move him?"

"They say affirmative. But not far."

Okay, he'd be taken care of, anyway. They'd lost their corpsman, but every SEAL was trained in battlefield trauma management. "Tell them to work their way up, take it slow, and lay down some suppression. I'm going up left field. But for Christ's sake, don't turn their illuminators on. They can use 'em passive mode, but don't go to active. You support 'em. Copy?"

"Copy, but where you going?"

"Up that ridge."

Teddy shook himself free and staggered into the dark. About thirty yards, dragging through the snow, before he felt the ground lift under his boots. Lift, and grate, and shift under the creaking snow; the loose, shallowly concave deposit of scree or talus you found at the base of a weathered cliff. Just feeling that told him that even though they hadn't brought rock gear or belays, the cliff could probably be climbed. He put his hands out and his gloves met near-vertical stone.

Travel light and mooch, a Team saying. Probably not much to mooch at the top, but he wouldn't get there toting this weight. He unsnapped the ruck and swung it down to lean against the cliff. Eighty pounds lighter, he slung the SR and checked everything else was secure and wouldn't rattle; pistol holster snapped, knife and light handy. He got his boots locked into the first set of footholds and a found a cup for his right hand. He levered up and pain tore through his shoulder as his searching left hand found a nice big fracture in the rock.

The face wasn't quite vertical. He found a ledge and edged upward along it until he ran out of footing, then groped across the rock. Nothing. Smooth face. He retreated, still searching, and found a handhold and then another crack. He got up another couple of yards before one of the fissures crumbled under his weight, leaving him dangling by his left hand. He grunted. Something was tearing in his shoulder every time he put weight on it.

Off to his right in the dark firing broke out. He figured it for the rest of the team, probing the enemy, but couldn't be sure. Then heard the distinctive *poppoppop* of Mud Cat's 249 and knew. Still working their way forward. With any luck, distracting whoever was up top here from looking down.

The invisible ground fell away to his left into what felt like a gully leading upward. Yeah; that had been on the topo. He worked over into this and friction-climbed upward, belly to flat, jagged rock, alert for ice or the slippery lichen he'd noticed the day before. But there didn't seem to be any, just rock and a dusting of snow like powdered sugar.

He braced a foot and reached, got an outcrop. Pushed upward along a bald plane of cold rock. He had himself pulled halfway up when the outcrop shifted like a loose tooth and came free in his hand. He let go quickly and it rattled away into the dark, but he'd lost his momentum, jiggled his climbing rhythm.

Wait a minute.

The smoothness against his belly wasn't rock.

It was ice. Snow-powdered, smooth, frictionless ice.

He started to slide backward, pivoting to the left. His arms flung outward, scrabbling for purchase. The rifle sling slipped down his right arm. But just then his left Suzy finger snagged in a crack and brought him to a halt, though enormous pain shot through the damaged shoulder. He lay rigid, gasping, listening to the clatter and jingle of his departing rifle growing fainter and fainter.

No more SR-25. Leaving him with a pistol and a knife. Not a great recipe for facing heavily armed men in the dark. Especially if whoever was at the top had heard the rifle going down the slope.

For a second he wondered if it might not be smart to slide back down the gully. Pick his way back down from cup to crack. Gather whoever was left and retreat. Find the trail bin Laden would be taking down to the valley, and backpedal down it himself. Find the Pak army and turn himself in. "We got lost in the snow," he muttered. Surely no one could blame him for getting lost.

Instead he searched his gear pockets, wedged his remaining 7.62 mags into cracks, and started climbing again. This time, angling to the right of the gully, where the snow and ice might not have built up so thick.

And it turned out it hadn't.

He kept working his way up. It was a little easier without the weight of rifle and ammo, though he felt naked without it. Then he came to a sheer face. There were cracks for handholds, but they were too narrow for footholds. He could find nowhere to put his boots that didn't place them either square on slick ice or kicking close-grained vertical rock. He tackled it grimly and failed time after time, until he could feel his fingers bleeding inside the gloves. He grappled with the rock like an exhausted, nearly defeated wrestler, grunting, growling deep in his throat. But at last he put together just the right combination of leverage and pulled himself up with sheer body strength alone.

He came to a halt then, wavering, almost toppling backward. The searing fire was streaming from the cracks in the darkness. The pain was hot spikes being driven into the joint of his shoulder. He couldn't climb any more.

Down? Going down was ten times harder than coming up. He'd never make it. Just didn't have it. So that just wasn't really an option.

He reached up one last time.

His outstretched hand waved, groped in darkness. He lowered it to a gritty lip of loose, friable rock the size of clenched fists.

So, he was at the top.

He had his hand to his face before he remembered: no NVGs. And even if he had them, he couldn't illuminate. He clung like a spider to crumbling rock, rigid, muscles shaking, the ax embedded between his eyes, the void at his back. He searched from left to right, carefully, slowly, by sectors. Nothing but the dark, and the sigh of the wind, and the grate of snow crystals over snow.

The rocks shifted under his weight as he got an elbow over, and slowly, slowly fulcrumed himself up onto the slanted, narrow col. The horizontal wind told him he was at the top. Blowing directly into his face, it tanged of earth and burnt explosive. Straight from the valley of fire. To the right, another cliff face overlooked the pass. To the left, the ridgeline led west. The map lit in his mind and he saw its narrow pointed arrow of kinked topo lines. He sniffed and listened, turning his head from side to side. If the guy they'd picked up a transmission from was still up here, he couldn't be far.

Teddy waited. He hadn't heard any firing for a while. But he didn't want to move until—

Four rapid pops from an M4. Distant and trivial-sounding, but distinct. And a glimmer, just a glimmer, through the blowing snow, the falling, twisting white veils. A flare?

He saw the silhouette no more than ten yards off. Cupped by the col, it was sitting in the half shelter of a rigged tent.

Teddy was sliding his pistol out of the holster when something ripped through his side and a heavy impact flung him half-turned into the ground. But he'd sagged backward at the hit, trained to reflex through hours of hand-to-hand. His attacker kept going, expecting resistance, and toppled over him, shouting. He twisted as he fell, stabbing down into Teddy's leg, but he'd cleared the SIG, and as the muj got to hands and knees Teddy fired two rounds into his face at close range, the powder-flash illuminating dark eyes and heavy black beard with ruddy light once, then again.

Leaning back in the snow, he brought the handgun around stiff-armed and fired five more rounds through the flapping fabric of the tent, spacing them from left to right in the dying light of the declining flare. He instantly rolled left, ignoring something flappy and loose in his side. Came up and fired three more rounds, aiming down. The illumination glimmered out. He grabbed for his SureFire. The thing was so bright it blinded and disoriented. Once he hit the button, it would wipe out his night vision and make him a target for anybody within fifty yards. He aligned it with the pistol, aiming at where the shelter had been. Went to his combat-shooting crouch and hit the button.

The world burst into a searing glow reflected by falling snow all around. From it a dying man with a white beard and heavy black brows looked into his eyes. Teddy held his gaze for a fraction of a second that stretched out as if they were exchanging life stories. His seamed leathery face looked as if it had seen sorrow and loss. Slowly, he turned a hand toward Teddy and opened his fingers.

A small green spheroid rolled into the snow.

A green spheroid.

A grenade.

Without his thought the pistol blazed until it clicked empty. But the muj had already fallen forward, over the grenade. A second ticked by. Then another.

It didn't go off.

Teddy stood shaking, realizing only then he should've hit the deck. He clicked the light off and sank to his knees. Hellish pain throbbed in his head and shoulder. When he fingered his side he felt warm, slick blood. Knife, or bayonet—the guy had ripped through uniform and gear into his flesh.

Somebody calling, down in the pass? Was that a voice? He made sure the old muj under the tarp was dead. Checked the grenade, unfolding the body gingerly and rolling it aside. He looked at it in the glow of the thumb-shielded Surefire. The pin was still in. He clicked the light off again and crept to the edge and peered down. Not much to see, just darkness and snow. Then the call came again. "Obie. Y' up there?"

Moogie. "Up here," Teddy howled. Without night vision, no one was going to hit him based on sound.

"All secure down here. Got the last one." A pause, then the radioman added, "Mud Cat took a bullet, too."

Teddy didn't answer. Eventually Knobby Swager's high voice added the information that the Louisianan had been shot in the hand. "We got a tourniquet on it, though. Two more mujs down here, both dead," Swager yelled.

"Too fucking loud. Keep it down, I can hear you." Teddy lay feeling warmth spreading from his side and leg. Getting drowsy. He grabbed a handful of snow and rubbed it into his face and shouted down, "Bring me a dressing. Use the eastern slope. Less gradient."

Swager rogered and Teddy put his head down and just breathed for a while. His leg was going numb. Thermal undies, black fleece, and still going hypothermic. But they had the pass. Not in great shape, but they held the position. And he didn't feel that bad. In fact, he felt almost comfortable, lying here in the soft snow. The wind felt warmer too.

A stir, scraping, from down the bank. His SIG jumped into his hand. But it was only Swager, cursing as he negotiated the last few steep yards, thrashing and falling. The baby SEAL collapsed beside Teddy. "Jesus. How'd you get up here, Chief?"

"Took the shortcut."

"You okay?" Hands grabbed him, landing first, Teddy hoped by accident, on his ass. He pushed them off. "Sorry."

"I need a Kerlix."

"You hit too?"

"Knife wounds. Not too bad, but I'm leaking hydraulic fluid."

"Funny, Chief." Swager pulled Teddy's coat up and the cold bit his chest and stomach. He closed his eyes, breathing short and hard as Swager worked on his wounds. Then opened them again and stared into the dark. Taking inventory.

Two unwounded shooters left. Two wounded but still able to defend themselves, at least. O'Brien and the Doc dead. No air support. Getting low on ammo. Also, he'd managed to lose his rifle. So far Swager hadn't noticed. For some reason, having the newbie pick up on that worried him more than the prospect of bleeding to death.

"Okay, you're patched." Swager tugged the jacket down. "Doesn't look too hairy, Chief."

Teddy closed his eyes again, then gathered his strength. He rolled over onto hands and knees, getting ready to struggle to his feet. A crackle in his ears; his MX, fading as the cold ate the batteries, but back on. "Obie. You there?"

He hit the transmit button. "Yeah. That you, Cat?"

"Take a gander out to your front," the faint voice murmured. "I think there's somebody headed our way."

24

TEDDY lay full length, listening past his own harsh, wheezing breath. The snow-laden wind howled through these lonely crags like the souls of those who'd just died here. Then, beneath that, came a low bumping detonation, stripped of all higher frequencies by distance. A JDAM or iron bomb going off miles away, down in the valley of the black dust. Where the vise was closing on the architect of horror. The sad-smiling beanpole who'd sent thousands to their deaths, who would cost his own people and religion many more thousands; whose vision had changed the world. Just as other evil madmen had redirected history.

But maybe he wasn't down there.

Maybe he was trying to escape.

A muffled jingle reached his ears. He crouched like a cat, gloves splayed in the snow. Every sense tuned to where the smoky wind crept over the mountains and speeded up, funneled by the pass.

A jingle?

What the hell would *jingle*? Santa Claus? His fucking reindeer?

He shook his head violently. Concussion or not, he had to focus. Something was bearing down on them. And he had wounded guys who were not going to last much longer, and maybe he wouldn't either. But that didn't matter. He was the chief. He was supposed to get his team back in one piece.

A hand on his shoulder, a hiss in his ear. "Hear that?"

"Yeah. I hear it." He tried his MX, but dropped it, cursing; it had gone out again. An intermittent failure was more frustrating than a full-blown fuckup. "Who've you got, Knobby? Is Moogie still on satcom? We need more shooters. Got to get the word out we got wounded here. We need extract."

"Wait one . . . he's trying, but he doesn't have anybody. His batteries are dead, he says."

"Fucking great. How's his legs?"

"He's losing blood. Mud Cat's stable. They can man the pig, base of fire, but they can't move without help."

Two shooters, two KIA, two immobile wounded. Great. He squeezed his eyes closed, fighting the desire to drift off. He could lie here and bleed and just freeze.

Or he could follow through, like a fucking Tier One operator. Get his guys off the mountain before they bled out and froze. But he couldn't help feeling events were rolling over him. The fucking altitude. The fucking cold. A fucking SA-7 gunner who'd gotten lucky enough to have a fucking Chinook plunk down right in his sights. And a fucking retirement-age career sniper, who'd nearly on his own fucked up what remained of the squad pretty goddamn thoroughly before Teddy had put him down. No question, they were not in the best of fighting shape here. Without dependable radio contact, they couldn't coordinate fire support, even when daylight came. Might not even be able to coordinate extraction. No, that would happen no matter what. The rest of Echo would be back for them. They still had ID panels and flares. No man left behind. But it might be days before a helo could exfil them, if this storm got worse.

And meanwhile something out in the storm was moving steadily closer. "Tough fucking titty! Tell them I want that pig up. As close under the east-side ridge as he can get. I want their back right up against that elevation, so no one can work around behind them. Copy?"

"Got it, Chief—"

"And keep it down, the wind's our way but they're listening too." He paused. "Knobby—you didn't think to get their NVGs? Doc and Vaseline?"

"Uh, no, Chief. Sorry."

"How about your claymore? Did you police that up, or leave it—"

"Uh, sorry. I can go back—"

"No. Forget it." The last thing Teddy wanted now, with whatever it was out there coming closer every minute, was to split up the few shooters he had left. Be nice to have a claymore, though.

Nice to have a lot of things he didn't have anymore. Like his SR-25. Lying somewhere at the bottom of the cliff. If it hadn't just kept on going, slid all the way down the fucking mountain into Pakistan. Seemed like something happened every mission. In Ashaara the fucking scope, busted to shit on the HALO landing. This time, his rifle.

His rifle.

Wait a minute. He *had* a rifle.

It just wasn't *his*.

"Okay. *Okay*," he muttered, and turned in the snow to backtrack along the col in the dark. Too weak to stand. On all fours, like a dog. He caught the crack of flapping canvas yards off and homed in on that until he collided with the collapsed tent.

The old sniper was still sitting like a Buddha statue. Already, in the few minutes since Teddy had shot him, his body had frozen solid, as hard to the touch as the sharded rock it sat on. Teddy reached for his SureFire, then reconsidered. This was an old mujahideen route. Whoever was coming would be watching the ridge, alert for the faintest glimmer, the slightest sign of an ambush. He slid the flash back into its pouch. He just hoped they didn't have some kind of recognition signal worked out.

Could he hooker them in close enough to take them? Maybe. The ridge was a good shooting position. Mainly it depended on how many were out there.

He didn't even want to think about what would happen afterward. So he didn't.

His searching, outstretched fingers hit something hard.

He pulled the long, icy-cold length of Russian wood and steel toward him and checked it by feel. Magazine inserted. Scope attached. A thin wire led to the old man. Teddy patted the rigid corpse down and found a heavy object under its coat. The battery that charged the light-sensitive plate. He found another magazine in a bandolier, but it was empty. He broke the one out of the rifle and fingered icy cartridges with wooden fingers. Two? Three? No more than three. He felt around the corpse, under the tent, but came up with nothing more. He unplugged the battery and thrust it inside his own jacket and zipped the fleece closed on it.

As he crawled back, voices blew toward him on the wind. He had to stop and pant, face down in the snow. He fingered his side. The dressing was hard, the blood either dried or, more likely, frozen. His leg, where the muj had stabbed him on the way down, was numb, a dead log he dragged as he crawled. Again he felt the siren call of unconsciousness. Defeat.

Fuck that! He forced himself up and alligator-elbowed the last few yards to collapse beside Swager again. He groped for the second class's ear, but was silenced by Swager's mitten on his mouth.

Something being pushed into his hands. It whined. His lifeless fingers finally recognized the NVGs. He made sure the illuminator switch was off, passive mode only, and raised them to his face.

Shifting veils of green against black. The blinking red dot that meant the power was getting low. Then, off to the left, the searching beam of an infrared illuminator. It looked just like one of their own. Scavenged and sold, or looted and passed from hand to hand. He studied it as it shifted here and there. Still some distance away, but nearing. He shut the goggles off and handed them back.

"Okay, Knobby, listen up. You're going to take Mud Cat and Moogie back to Denver." The primary-extract LZ, fifteen hundred feet down the mountain and offset to the west of the trail down from the pass.

"What? Hell, no, Chief—"

Teddy reached out and got him by the throat. "What was that?"

"I mean—wait a fucking—*wait.*" Swager broke his hold; Teddy must be getting weaker than he'd thought. The petty officer coughed. "The extract LZ. You want me to—"

"Now you're hearing me. We don't have enough shooters left to hold this pass. Two or three hostiles coming through? Maybe. But any more, we're just gonna get rolled up. You take the wounded back to Denver. I'll stay here. If an HVT shows, I'll zip him. If it's just your rank and file, I'll let them traipse on past, let the Paks dustpan and foxtail 'em up. Copy?"

"I'll come back, Chief. Get them down to the LZ, then come back for you."

Teddy wavered, then gave in. Swager wasn't going to get two wounded men fifteen hundred feet down the mountain, then trek back up, until after dawn. And this would all be over before then. One way or the other. At dawn there'd be Coalition eyes on the pass anyway, Predators or air. As long as he bottlenecked it during the storm, they'd have accomplished the mission. "Okay, you do that. But your first priority's getting Moogie and Cat down to where we can call in the CSAR."

Swager hesitated, then rogered up. He gripped Teddy's shoulder, which didn't seem to hurt as much as a few hours earlier. Started to leave, but Teddy pulled him back. "Leave me the PVSs."

"Oh, yeah. Sorry."

Teddy felt the goggles thrust into his hands. Then the second class was gone, a fading shuffle of boots and sliding rock going down the slope.

HE lay for a good long time, every sense strained toward the pass. Wondering if he'd imagined the illuminator beam. He didn't think so. Maybe whoever was coming up the pass had turned back. The storm was getting worse. Every few minutes he had to squirm out from under a fresh fall of snow. If only he had his ruck. His poncho was in his ruck. But he didn't.

Oh, well. What the fuck, over.

At last he set the goggles to his head and turned them on again, keeping numb fingers well clear of the illuminator button. Shading them from the blowing snow, he peered into the night.

Shifting ghosts in black jade distance. He fumbled at it and the tubes flashed but didn't clear. Good as he was going to get, apparently. They were dying too. Everything was going hypothermic in the altitude and cold. He coughed and lightning shot through his head. He squeezed his eyes shut, then forced them open and peered again.

Four men in line abreast waded toward him through the snow. He couldn't make out more, not with passive alone, just the white, spotty infrared of heat. He almost hit the illuminator but remembered in time. If they had IR, it would be just like shining a spotlight. Their heads seemed misshapen, but not the way helmets would look. They were well spaced out, maybe five yards between each man.

He shifted the field of view left, knowing what he'd probably see, and there they were: two men separated from the main body. More, only barely visible, off to the right. Flank security, patrolling fifty or sixty yards uphill as the party came up the draw. The four in front were walking point. He studied them for a few seconds, then passed the goggles back to Swager. "See 'em?"

"We can hammer 'em, Chief. Get 'em between us and hammer 'em."

Then Teddy remembered. Swager wasn't there. But hadn't he answered?

He whispered, "We won't get 'em all. And they'll roll up Moogie and Mud Cat. Just stand the fuck fast. This isn't the main body."

Now he could hear the crunch of boots and low voices. The jingle came again, cutting through the snow-laden air with a spooky clarity. It *did* sound like sleigh bells. They couldn't have a sleigh. Could they? He shook his head again, wishing he could think. But everything was going fuzzy, soft, warm. Then rolling over, going to sleep . . . he bit his lip savagely, dug his fingers into the clotted flap between his eyes. He gagged on a near-scream, but the mists cleared a little.

When he looked up again, the snow was coming down so hard he had to continually blink it off his lashes. Damn. The wind was freezing his eyeballs. Let 'em go by, he decided. He could get one, maybe a couple, but those he missed would wheel and come up the pass and get Moogie and Mud Cat. "Then we'll have two more KIA," he whispered.

No, now he remembered. Swager was moving them out. They should be below the pass by now. Headed for the exfil point. Well, then, they'd come up here and roll him up. He was outnumbered and immobile and almost out of ammo. So he'd let them pass. The Paks could deal with them. Demonstrate their committment.

The decision made, he felt relieved. "Just watch 'em go by," he whispered. He started to tell Sumo to pass that over the net, to hold fire. But Sumo wasn't there either. He pulled the rifle up closer, felt to the end of the long, spindly barrel and dug around to get any snow or dirt out of it. Then pushed up snow in front of his position and settled the lower handguard. He pulled the battery wires out of his jacket and started connecting them to the terminals on the scope. This simple operation proved extraordinarily difficult. He kept losing the wires or forgetting what he was doing. Finally he got one looped where it seemed to be supposed to go and started to tighten the nut down. He turned it and turned it, wondering why it didn't tighten. Then felt nothing between his fingers.

He'd been turning it the wrong way, it had come off, and was now lost somewhere. "Fuck," he whispered through lips he couldn't feel anymore, with a tongue that didn't want to move.

Beside him he felt a familiar reassuring presence. Turned his head, and there he was, almost invisible in the dark, but he could just see his outline. Bulky, but not fat. Not fat at all. The big Hawaiian a mass of supple muscle. "Sumo. Where the *fuck* you been?"

"Right here now, haole."

"About fucking time. Gimme a hand with this. Can you—"

He wasn't sure who actually did it, him or his teammate, but they got the wire connected and bent to the scope. It hummed as it powered up. The field of view came on. It was much narrower than that of the goggles. The image was dimmer and spherically distorted. "Don't jiggle it or it'll come loose," Kaulukukui breathed into his ear.

"Spot me in, Main Meal. Talk me in."

"Thought you weren't gonna shoot."

"I'm not. Just do what I fucking tell you, all right?"

Teddy crawled into the scope, setting the butt into his shoulder and fitting his right hand around the pistol grip. The rifle felt too long and too heavy, and the angles on it were all wrong. But he'd fired Dragunovs in training, and they were accurate as long as you knew what you were doing and didn't push the range. A range finder was on the reticle, but he ignored it and just tried to figure out what he was seeing. The snow was coming harder. Every time a gust whipped it up, he couldn't see anything at all, just distorted milling fireflies, like dark green paint mixed with chrome sparkles being stirred around and around. "Got the four guys in front? And the flank guards?"

"Yeah. I saw 'em," said Sumo. "We gonna take 'em?"

"No. Just foot soldiers. Anybody behind 'em? Anybody back there?"

"I don't think so. I don't see any . . . wait." The space of a breath. The space of another. Then the big, soft hand tightened on his shoulder. Squeezed once. Again. And a third time.

Three targets. Teddy searched behind the point, but didn't see anything. He swung the scope left and the humming died and the picture faded. He jiggled the rifle. The scope buzzed, powering back up, and the mountainside came on in green and black but fizzy like licorice-and-pickle soda. He eased slowly left again and lowered the barrel.

There they were. Shifting ghosts, three of them. He blinked snow from his eyepiece and cheeks and crawled in deep, and there they were. Lit, not steadily, by their own heat—the scope wasn't sensitive enough for that— but only fitfully now and then by what looked like illumination from the goggles of the others. Three centaurs, horses' bodies and men's upper torsos, wavery as if sealed far away under murky green glass.

"Turbans," Kaulukukui whispered. "Capes. Shorty AKs. His bodyguard."

"Check. On the lead?"

"Check."

"See these guys behind them?"

"Roger. On horses."

Teddy didn't answer, scoping them. He didn't think he was imagining it, but the one in the middle, though slumped as if tired or wounded, sat taller in the saddle. Then the snow blew in, but he didn't think he was wrong. The middle horse was bigger, yes, but its rider was still taller than the others. He couldn't tell anything more, though. If he hadn't dropped the fucking SR . . . the night sight on it imaged clear as crystal, laser-ranged instantly out to a thousand yards.

But he didn't, and the scope he did have was shorting out and cutting off, and he was close to losing consciousness. He could let them go by, the way he'd let the first four pass. Trade their lives for his own.

Only . . . the mission wasn't to lie here and let the bad guys walk past.

It didn't matter what happened to him. If it was just him, he'd make the shot. Take out as many as he could before they knocked him down. It would be fun. A buzz. The way he wanted to go out.

Trouble was, he wasn't alone up here. Somehow it was different when you were the one telling them to lay down their lives.

He'd seen guys die before. Good guys. Like Sumo.

Wait a minute.

He turned his head, then put out his hand. No one lay to his left. He stared, blinking snow out of his eyes. Trying to force something jagged inside his head that somehow, no matter which way he turned it, would not fit through the hole. The snow was velvet soft and cunt warm under his belly. The pain was gone. He felt as if someone had jammed a syrette of morphine into him.

He was back at the Polo Lounge with Loki and Hanneline and Salena Frank and Sumo too. And a red-haired older woman he didn't know, and he didn't think how strange it was they were all there together, Sumo in the tentlike sweat gear he always wore working out. Then Teddy recognized the woman. His grandmother, so beautiful, such fine bones, and they were talking about how the movie would be made at last. Better than any other war movie ever made. Production values out of this world, and he felt good, really good, and Sumo was grinning too. "Your mother will be proud of you," Hanneline said, and she looked so pleased, and reached out to put her hand on his.

Only her fingers were cold as liquid nitrogen, and she shook him until he cried out, and his side hurt like Christ's on the cross and he was lying full length in the snow freezing and hammering his side with his fist and his face was frozen to a rifle butt with blood. ". . . the fuck," he muttered. "What do we do? Fuck if I know." He wanted to tell whoever was hitting him to fuck off. Instead he blinked and tore his cheek off the stock with a pain that felt as if his skin was flaying off. He got his eye back to the scope.

And there they were, there *he* was, filling the objective, nodding forward on the horse that looked dead on its feet, snow up to its withers, shoving its way uphill as one of the bodyguards flailed at it with a stick.

The man who'd killed so many. Who'd kill so many more.

Unless he, Teddy Harlett Oberg, nailed him. Right here. Right now.

He got the range off the reticle, corrected for the horse, corrected for the target's height. Held off for wind. Flicked off the safety, remembering it was on the right side like on an AK. Took a deep breath and let it out. Another, and let it out. Took up the slack in the first stage of the trigger.

A burst of snow wiped out the image, leaving him with only a seething speckle like boiling green oatmeal. He grunted, maintaining pressure on the trigger, not breathing. Then the snow parted and there were the three figures again, the central one haloed for an instant with an unearthly radiance as the beams of his guardians swept back and forth across him. Silhouetting him for his hunter. Teddy exhaled a little more and the crosshairs rose to quarter the chest region. The last ounce came out of the trigger. And the rifle, held perfectly still with his cheekbone welded to the stock and hand welded to the pistol grip and left arm thrust out supporting the fore end, went

click.

He lay rigid, following the sway of the upper torso with the crosshairs in case the round was a hangfire. Then cursed and worked the bolt. The dud ejected and buried itself in the snow. Then the wind came and snow whipped up all around him in a furious microburst. Fuck, *fuck.* Green frothed opaque between him and the target as he searched desperately to reacquire. Bad ammo. No telling how old, or how many times it'd been frozen and scorched, soaked and dried out. Too much gun oil killed primers. But the rounds that had killed Doc and wounded Moogie hadn't been duds. And Teddy had two left.

He lined up and waited. When the shadows swam up again, he exhaled, and slowly, so slowly, squeezed the trigger again.

Click.

"Son of a *bitch*," he muttered, counting it off, waiting out the hangfire. *One thousand.* A solid wedge of pain was forcing itself between the lobes of his brain like a white-hot hatchet head. *Two thousand.* One more fucking round. The last. Could it be the rifle? Broken firing pin? Lubricant, congealed in the utter cold? If so, he couldn't do anything about it. All his gear was in his ruck. *Three thousand.* He ejected and fed once more and steadied down, his whole being concentrated in the green. He breathed in. The snow veils wavered and fluttered. He breathed out. Nothing. He breathed in. Couldn't see. Then he could. He breathed out. His finger tightened. Then he couldn't.

Then the bowed figure loomed silhouetted in tinted light, bent over the pommel, and he corrected the slightest bit to shade left for the wind just as the veil closed again, the snow seethed, blotting out sight.

The rifle slammed into his shoulder. The scope flickered, but stayed on. As the boom rolled back from the crags, he caught a distorted glimpse of the riders to either side spurring to close up, gesticulating savagely. Heard high, peremptory shouts. Answering cries echoed from the flankers. The scope came back down from the recoil and he searched for the man he'd fired at. Wanting to see him sliding down, wilting. Dying in the snow. But couldn't see anything. Just seethe, and darkness.

And that was it. No surprise left now. Close enough to hear where he'd fired from, if they hadn't actually seen the muzzle flash. Any minute, they'd be up here. And there they were. The gritty grind of feet on loose rock, scrambling up the scree. Harsh calls back and forth. The hoarse cries of angry, frightened men.

Teddy Oberg laid the rifle aside and reached for his pistol. But instead of the SIG's grip, his numbed, unfeeling fingers stuck something hard and irregular. A mass of frozen blood attached to his side. Frozen solid, over the weapon. His hand instantly diverted and slid his thin-blade out.

Never jam on you, or run out of ammo. A voice in his ear. Calm. Determined. Sumo's? Or from farther back, the long chain of warriors who'd trained him and formed him? He couldn't remember. But it didn't matter.

He'd lost his way. But he'd found the trail again.

He rolled on his side and tried to sit up, but couldn't. So he just lay there, looking into the dark, waiting for them to come for him, out of the snow.

The Afterimage

Tora Bora

DAN was bent, panting, trying to force oxygen into his blood to go on, when he caught sight of the cluster-bomb module. The size of a Pepsi can, the hue of a ripe banana, it was caught between the rock he was standing on and the next one, wedged at an awkward cant that must have convinced the fuze it hadn't quite hit the ground. Slowly, he shifted his weight off the rock and stepped to the next one. Bent again, trying to catch his breath.

The air was much thinner than at Bagram, and bitter cold. He had to stop and wheeze each time he climbed even a small hill. Their wizened, tiny guide, an old man with a stained beard and skin like weathered fiberglass, stopped each time to squat and wait. As they trudged on again, the elder skipped from rock to rock like a goat, the torn blanket over his shoulders flapping, pointing and chattering each time he noticed an abandoned rifle, unexploded munition, abandoned pack.

Dan and Laughland and Belote were here for a Sensitive Site Exploration, joining the intel people picking over the ground for documents. Meanwhile the local boys wandered amid the goats and submunitions, picking up shrapnel and shell casings to sell for scrap. Dan rested again, hands on knees, looking up at the mountains and trying to imagine getting up such a grade with pack and rifle. Only a little more slope, and you'd need climbing gear to scale these traverses. The ground was rubble, shattered quartz-glittering rock punctuated with scrawny bushes tall as a woman, the lower branches nibbled to rattling sticks by goats.

One of the attacking warlords had turned or been bought off. Just as the militias started to push forward at last, he'd announced a cease-fire for negotiations. That night, as far as anyone could judge, hundreds of AQTs had drained out of the valley like dirty water through a suddenly unplugged drain. East into Pakistan. South into the Parachinar. Scuttle-butt had it a SEAL team had been caught in that movement, taking heavy casualties. JSOC was considering strikes farther south at Zhawar Kili, another stronghold where the faithful had gathered. But Big Army was folding its tents all over the country. As far as Faulcon was concerned, this war was over.

The lower half of a disarticulated corpse lay in the shelter of a rock. Starting to rot, by the old-garbage smell. Someone had gotten its boots and pants, leaving the pale, rain-washed, callused soles of its feet turned to the sky.

The old man cheeped from the mouth of a cave. Belote stood with him, looking sour. He had a scarf wrapped around his head under the *pakul* hat, a field jacket over his fur vest. An unlit cigarette dangled from his lip.

"What's he yelling about?" Dan asked, bending again to wheeze. No question, his lungs weren't what they'd been. The ground was littered with empty Kalashnikov cases, as if someone had fought from this position for a long time.

"He says this was *his* cave. The Sheik's. His nephew saw him here. Short life to him, he says. Everyone hated him for bringing the Americans and their bombs."

True? Or what he thought they wanted to hear? A week ago their guide could've been piloting Arabs through the passes, singing a different tune. Dan looked around for wires or strings. The old man handed him a rock. Dan weighed it blankly.

"For mines," Belote supplied. "Toss it in."

After four stones had thudded uneventfully onto the cave floor, Dan bent and crab-walked in. Rough rock arched overhead. The cavern, or tunnel, curved downward into darkness. He got his flash out and shone it ahead.

At the very end lay a closet-size grotto with a worn sleeping bag, empty potato-chip bags, a ragged, dirty towel, dead flashlight batteries, and a clay lamp that, when he bent closer, still smelled of some kind of sweet oil. He almost picked it up, but didn't like the way the sand had been smoothed over around it. Bin Laden's? Doubtful. Yet he lingered, looking around the cavern, trying for some sense of the man who *might* have slept here. Fanatical, ascetic, evil; yet he still had to admire his determination. If only those who said they desired peace were willing to give up as much to achieve it.

When he backed out into the light again, breathing hard, the old man had found a ragged, damp book. Belote flipped through it, then handed it to Dan. The text was in Arabic, partly handwritten, held together by brass brads. Dan turned the pages. He couldn't read it, but the diagrams were perfectly clear. How to destroy bridges, power lines, dams, aircraft. How to rig a car as a suicide bomb. A hand-careful schematic in colored pencil showed how to build a suicide vest. Other movements had produced similar documents. Anarchists. Communists. The IRA. The Red Brigades. The art of destruction and terror, to be inflicted on the innocent.

It had never worked for long, no matter how charismatic. The lust to destroy was inherent in man. But so was the will to fight back, to protect the fragile structure of give-and-take that, however imperfect, men settled for. And called peace.

He handed it back to Belote and lifted his face again to sheer rock and blue-black sky.

Their quarry had escaped. But he could not feel justified in saying anyone was at fault. Where empires go to die, Provanzano had called Afghanistan. The most remote battlefield on earth. Too high, too cold, too rugged, too far from the wellsprings of US power. And most of all, too vast. Its valleys and mountains had swallowed army after army; never defeated; simply outlasted by those patient enough to hide. Here bin Laden's supporters and friends had hidden and fed him, then spirited him away to some new bolt-hole.

But we'll get him, Dan thought. No question of that.

It was just a matter of time.

Prince Georges County, Maryland

Blair's father held the car door, courtly as ever. Her mother had a headache and had stayed home. It was Blair's first time out of the house, except for visits to doctors. She'd avoided all her old friends. Avoided even church, though her mother had tried to persuade her to go.

She didn't want to face anybody she knew. *Face* them. Yes, exactly. She understood bitterly now just what that meant.

"Coming, kiddo?" Checkie said. Still holding the door.

"Maybe I shouldn't—"

"You need to walk, honey."

She took a deep breath. Then another, glancing past him toward the bright lights, the high rose walls, the gay logos atop the buildings, each designed to be recognizable from miles distant. "That's okay, Dad. Why don't you go ahead? Here's what I need: Chanel Teint Innocence fluid number forty-five Rose. Or Cream Compact number forty-five Rose. Either Laura Mercier Secret Camouflage SC-2, or LM Silk Crème Foundation—"

His raised hand halted her. "Whoa! Hold on! I'll get the wrong size, or something. Like when I used to send your mom to the hardware store. But, hey, I'll go in with you. Come on, kiddo."

She started to say again that she didn't want to. Then bit down on the whining and seized the side of the door. Hauled herself up. The cold air was scented with the snow melting in piles in the corners of the lot. The cars all had American flags magnetized on their sides, or zip-tied to the aerials. She turned her head away as people streamed past. Older couples. Young mothers with strollers. Two teenaged girls, laughing, wearing what looked like secondhand bridal dresses.

"They're not looking at you, honey," Checkie said. "Nobody is. See? Nobody here knows you, anyway."

Standing on trembling legs, she touched the corner of her right eye with the tip of one finger. Drew it back and down, tracing the numbness. Like touching dead flesh. Dead, but still warm. Oh, the doctors were happy. They said the grafts had taken. But her face didn't feel the way it used to, and she certainly didn't look like the self she remembered. The autografts flamed and itched. She had to rub cream in twice a day to keep them from contracting. Her ear was . . . just . . . *ugly.* She was growing her hair longer, to cover it; but she could feel it, a nerveless, reddened nubbin, folded and warped. A small but hideous deformity. They said her hip was healing too, but it hurt like sin whenever she put the slightest weight on it.

"You can do this," her dad murmured. "Come on. Where's my brave soldier?"

She took a deep breath and forced herself into motion. Her hip stabbed at each step. Too late, she realized she'd forgotten the arm crutch. Checkie was striding ahead, though, over the wet-gleaming asphalt, as if daring her to race.

The air inside was stuffy-warm with central heating. She sank to a bench, dizzy, overwhelmed, and asked her father to go back for the crutch. As she waited, head down, white dunes seemed to roll beneath the floor. Colors swam, voices echoed from the immense atrium arched overhead like a glass basilica. Stores climbed like cliff dwellings toward the distant white radiance of skylights.

She sat feeling washed-out, watching shoppers stroll. There certainly seemed to be a great many obese folks at this mall. Or maybe she shouldn't point fingers; she'd gained ten pounds lying in bed. At least the cutting was over. Although the therapy, as her mother had warned, was even more painful. Still, she was going a little longer between the oxycodone tablets every day.

"Got to be strong," her dad said, handing her the crutch. "Easy enough to be weak. I know you went through a lot. But you can't crawl into a hole.

Can't just stay home. We'd like you to, but I know you. You'd be miserable. Take it out on your mom and me."

She smiled, though it hurt. "I don't plan to do any crawling, thank you."

"That's good to hear. But what about it?" he said, not looking at her. "What *are* you going to do? Going to get back in the ring?"

"Politically, you mean?"

He nodded, still looking away, as if it didn't matter. "It'd be easy in District Five. This guy's voting for everything the administration wants. In eleven months, they'll be looking to expand their majority in the House and get control of the Senate. They'll use the war to do that."

"Not everything's politics, Checkie. There are real enemies out there."

He wheeled on her, frowning. "Then say that! Show 'em you're a fighter. You look like one, now."

He looked frightened then, as if he might have said the wrong thing, but she only chuckled. "Yeah. One who's been pounding the canvas with her face."

He shrugged. "As long as you get back up again."

"Now you sound like Dan." She felt her strength returning and lurched to her feet. Fitted the padded aluminum tube to her arm. Hating it. Hating the weakness, the pain, but, yes, feeling stronger every day. It was worth thinking about. Maybe she could even do some good. Put some steel into a party that all too often seemed to lack it. Find some payback, though it seemed that was happening without her help. If the news coverage of the great battle in the faraway mountains was any guide.

"Feeling better now?" her father said, taking her good arm.

She shook his grip off, setting her teeth, ignoring the pain. And, taking one slow step after another, set her course.

New York City

Walking the street in hijab, Aisha felt the stares from the passersby. Some, openly hostile. Well, who could blame them? The great towers had been cast down, a proud city wounded. But the moment she stepped from the gray concrete sidewalk onto the green, she smiled to herself.

Even as a child she'd suddenly felt happy, just stepping onto that then-bright grass color. Like making it home playing tag. Loiterers had jeered at her mother, who'd held her and her sisters' hands tightly. A few even shambled drunkenly after them. But when they got to the green paint, they always stopped. As if sin itself halted here, unable to cross onto that holy color. (Though it might also have been thanks to the burly young men who'd guard stood outside the mosque.) This whole neighborhood had been crack city back then. It seemed to be doing better these days.

"Mommy, why is the sidewalk here green?" Bright chocolate eyes sought hers. Tashaara danced as they walked, skirts whirling. Aisha started to tell her to smooth them down, to be modest, but stopped herself. Let the child enjoy her innocence. How she'd grown, just in the year Aisha had been in Yemen! Nothing like the emaciated, dying infant she'd illegally rescued from a land descending into chaos. Behind the two of them hobbled her mother, using a cane, and two of Aisha's sisters.

She squeezed her child's hand. Someday she'd tell her about that. But not for many years. "It means we're where we belong, honey. Where we'll always be safe."

Inside, her mother was greeted with hugs by the women from the clinic, where she'd worked for many years. Everyone wanted to shake Aisha's hand and ask where she'd been. When they got free at last, she helped her mother up the painted steel stairs, smelling the familiar smells, to the second-floor mezzanine.

She fell in prostration before Allah with the other women, the worn, wooly-smelling carpets soft beneath her, mother on one side, daughter on the other. It was the same. But she slowly realized it was also different. No one gossiped. She caught side glances. Then she looked down, to where the men sat cross-legged on carpet, to where the imam was beginning to speak.

She stiffened. Two strangers stood against the wall, sides to her as she looked down from above. One was white and the other black, but both men wore identical dark suits and ties. They stood with relaxed insolence, arms crossed, listening as the imam, somewhat hesitantly, began to speak about what jihad really meant. How it did not mean a literal holy war, or at any rate, not primarily that. How it came from the Arabic word for "striving," or "effort." Other words derived from the root meant "to labor" and "to become tired, from work." The men listened intently, one writing occasionally in a notebook. She wondered for a moment what the FBI was doing here, then understood.

She wasn't home now just because she wanted to be. It was the letter she'd written to the director, detailing her suspicions about the Yemenis and the reliability of information yielded by enhanced interrogation. Maybe not a wise career move. But she'd had to speak the truth, even against her best interests. That too was in the Quran.

The deputy director himself had sat her down to explain why she was being pulled off counterterrorism. "This is to protect you," he'd said, so earnestly she knew he was lying. "Protect you from targeting by ALQ. And your family's in New York too, aren't they? Your daughter." But the grapevine worked both ways. One of the other female agents had told her the real reason.

It had made her bitter. And why not? When all she'd done was her best.

Below her the imam was reaching the end of the sermon. Saying to them all, the listening men, the women, even the agents, that what jihad really meant was each soul's struggle with evil. The labor of perfecting self in the face not only of one's own laziness and sinful desires, but of outside rejection and misunderstanding—something their community had been familiar with from their very founding. But others—the Irish, the Germans, Jews, Italians, Japanese—had faced and overcome the same persecution. "It will take time to convince America we are as much Americans as those who came before. Who were persecuted and suspected because of their faiths too, each in their turn."

No bitterness, she thought, quieting her fidgeting daughter with a gentle hand. That did not belong here. All things were connected, and all directed by a wise Creator. As she murmured the words of the concluding *du'a*, asking for forgiveness and divine guidance, peace floated back into her heart. He was with her and in her.

With her, Allah.

Always and everywhere, and forever.

Amin.

Landstuhl Regional Medical Center
Ramstein Air Base, Germany

The man in the darkened room breathed slowly. An external fixator covered his face like a crouching stainless spider. Tubes hung from him, and shining metal rods extended through purpled, puffy skin, screwed into holes tapped into bone and skull. The machines had been rolled back a few hours before, to another bed in another room. He murmured and twitched.

Then his eyes opened.

Teddy Oberg stared up for a while, not really thinking. Then a cold terror shook itself awake and crawled along his bones like hungry worms.

It was coming back. Not where he was, or how he'd gotten there. These things he did not know. But he remembered the mountain. The cold. An old man frozen rigid where he sat. He scratched the sheets with nails that seemed excessively long. The bed seemed to be tilted to port, as if he were on a listing ship. A ship? He listened, tried to sense motion, but couldn't. Still felt that queer leftward cant in the surface he lay on, though. A hard object was nestled into his right hand. The button. He recognized that, somehow. Press the button if it starts to hurt. It wasn't hurting now, though. Maybe he'd pressed it already?

He cleared his throat. Rolled his head.

A silent figure sat in shadow by his bedside. He tensed, squinting, trying to make out who it could be. But he couldn't distinguish features. Maybe just the silhouette of a piece of equipment.

Then a man sniffed, and Teddy caught through the hospital smell something strange yet familiar; a minty tang with a whiff of acetone.

"Who the hell," Teddy suggested.

"Back with us?" The voice was low, confiding. When Teddy only grunted, it went on, "Chief Petty Officer Theodore Harlett Oberg? US Navy?"

"Uh . . . yeah."

"You're in a Level Four treatment facility in Germany. Landstuhl, if you know where that is. You damn near died. But you'll be headed home soon. Back to the States. To Bethesda, probably. Any questions for me?"

". . . d' I get here?"

"I don't have all the details. But one of your men brought you down from the mountains. You ordered him to get your wounded down to the LZ. He did that. Then went back up after you. Found you freezing to death. Got a line on you and lowered you down the ridge. Got you down and medevaced you out."

Teddy lay contemplating this. Fucking hard to believe. Skinny, limp-dicked Swager had come back up, in the dark, and found him? Manhandled him single-handed all the way down that bitch of a mountain, fifteen hundred fucking feet to the extract LZ?

Eventually he found he could manage that. He'd underestimated the newbie, the guy they'd called the Baby SEAL. He was a Team guy, after all.

What he couldn't understand was Sumo being there too. It hadn't been a hallucination. You couldn't hallucinate a three-hundred-pound Hawaiian. "Sumo?" he croaked, then immediately thought, that was a mistake.

"Sorry, what?"

"Nothing. Nothing . . .'n' who're you?"

"Just a guy with a couple of questions. About the mission. If you got the time."

"I don't discuss missions."

"You'll discuss this one," the man said. "In the Safed Koh, over the Pak border, to get bin Laden. The back way, the Ghilzai route to the Parachinar.

Where you lost Dusty Palladino and most of Echo Two. We on the same page now, Chief?"

". . . Guess so."

"Actually I really only have one question. And since you were the only dude on the scene, you're the only one can answer it. Here it is. Did you get him?"

Teddy closed his eyes. Tried to replay it, and only got part. He heard another sniff and smelled menthol and eucalyptus. "My guys. Moogie. Mud Cat. They make it?"

"Some of 'em. Not all. But you already know that."

"Who? Which—"

"I'm not privy to that level of detail. We can have someone get you that info, though. But my question. Did you nail him?"

Teddy thought for a while. Trying to be exact. But the endless wind, the snow-smoke, the sparkling green murk, seemed to have blown across his memory too. Finally he said, "Don't know."

"You *don't know*."

"I . . . might have. Last round. Too dark. Scope was . . . fucked."

"Well, if you don't know, I do," the shadow said. A faint sound, as if he were spitting out a bit of tobacco, though the guy didn't seem to be smoking. "You missed."

". . . How?"

"Intercepted radio transmission. Well into the Parachinar, into the Tribal Territories."

"So it was—?"

"It was him, all right. Confirmed by one of his aides we captured."

". . . See if he's . . ."

"We checked. Sent in two operators. Found your overwatch point. Where you ambushed him. Nothing else, though. Hell of a mission, from what I hear. You can be proud of yourself, and your team. Just shitty luck there at the end."

Teddy lay drifting, contemplating it. He wanted to squeeze the button now, but forced himself not to.

"I'll get back on my feet," he said. "Build myself up. Then go after him again."

"That's a great attitude. I like that. But unfortunately, there are certain things you won't find so easy anymore. Accepting that, they tell me, is the first step back."

"What . . . talking about?"

For answer the shadowman leaned over him. Took Teddy's hand and guided it down his side. He tried to resist, but didn't have the strength. His fingers slid down his leg. Then met cold steel, tubes, wires. The pain flared. He caught his lip in his teeth.

"Tissue damage. Frostbite," the man said. "They can't tell me if you'll keep the leg or not." He set Teddy's hand back on his chest. Patted it, then stood. "We'll carry on. Don't worry about that. This war's in good hands. But if you got anything else you always wanted to do, start thinking about that.

"So, I'll leave you to it. But I will say this. You're a hell of an operator."

The shadow touched its forehead. When Teddy grasped it was a salute, he lifted his left hand and wiggled the fingers, like a toddler saying good-bye.

And with his right, pressed the button.

WHEN he opened his eyes again, the chair was empty. Maybe it'd been empty all along? Like with Sumo, he'd imagined the guy? His head swam. His mouth was puckered dry. What had they been talking about. Oh, yeah. Fuck yeah. That he'd missed, there at the end. Fuck.

He felt for his leg again, hoping like hell it had been a bad dream.

Nope.

He lay there in the dark, feeling by turns bitter and relieved. Then angry. But pretty soon, instead of himself, he started thinking about the guys he'd lost.

He probably wouldn't be able to make the funerals. Like a chief should. But he could meet the families, at least. Tell them just how brave their sons and fathers and husbands had been. When it counted.

Maybe he could do something else, too.

If you got anything else you always wanted to do, start thinking about that.

Was there? Maybe a stocky, cocky brunette in the San Diego Sheriff's Department? Yeah. Maybe. But something else too. Something much more important.

He couldn't bring them back. Dusty and Moogie and Harley, Doc and Vaseline. The L-T, Dollard, blown into bits so small they hadn't even looked human. And so many others. So very many others.

But he could stay on mission.

He stretched out an arm and dropped the button over the side of the bed. It hit the floor with the crack of breaking thermoplastic. He took a few breaths, pumping himself up. Doubled his fists. Then pushed himself to a sitting position.

Rested for a few minutes, panting as if in high, thin air. Then fought like hell and finally got his foot on the floor. He rested again, pulse pounding, almost fainting from the pain, but enduring it. Forcing himself to take it.